MORE THAN JUST....
A PRETTY WOMAN

A Novel
By L. Jaiy Hart

For Maureen

My Darling Mum, One of my soulmates,
My dearest friend.
From one hopeless romantic to another.

For the RiverHart Horses

All Thirty-Five of them.
One day I will tell our story.

© Lindsay Hart. All rights reserved. No part of this book or any work under the 'More Than Just' name may be copied or shared without permission.

Dedication – To Love

For all hearts. For the wounded. For the world.
This book is dedicated to all the souls....
Who are suffering in pain,
Displacement, devastation, and unimaginable grief.

It is for the children and the family's enduring horror.
It is for all those trapped in wars not of their making.
Those wars on the inside as well as the outside.
It is for those bearing witness.
It is for the medics, surgeons and volunteers, whose courage and work are vital and heroic.
It is for those who cannot look away.

This is not a political statement.
It is a human one.
A sacred one.
From a heart that has known grief
And returned from its darkness
Changed
Deepened
More devoted

I am not a protestor.
I do not carry signs or chant in crowds.
I carry sorrow in silence.
I sit with grief.
I pray.
I feel the weight of what I see and what I cannot change.
But I can write.
And I can give.

This story has lived with me for fifteen years.
It has carried me through some of the darkest nights of my life.
Now I release it into the world with the hope
That it may carry light into someone else's.

If joy is found in these pages,
May it lead to healing.
If profit is made,
May it be shared.
To feed the hungry
To hold the broken-hearted,
To support those who will
Rebuild what was destroyed.

Because after the bombs,
There must be bread.
After the silence,
There must be hope.
After the trauma,
There must be truth, tending and tenderness.

As women we often carry the quiet torch of romance and longing.
We hold the thread of the soul's yearning…
The belief in a soulmate, in enduring love.
And as we hold our children's hearts,
We pray for a future where peace may last,
Flowing freely across the lands.
Where kind men rise with courage,
To overcome ruthless regimes.

Where perhaps for the first time
We can unite in the sacred hope
That Mankind can become….
Kind-Man.

This book is not the answer.
But perhaps it can be a beginning of one.

We are 'More than just'... A legacy of pain
We must become the Evolution of Love.

With love and in memory.
Lindsay Yasmin Ahmed Hart. 12-06-2025

More than Just....
A Pretty Woman

Chapter 1

As the gleaming white Aston Martin wound its way through the late afternoon sun-drenched hills outside LA, its sleek curves gleamed against the rugged backdrop. The engine's purr hinted at the raw power beneath the bonnet, with each turn, the car seemed to dance on the asphalt, a graceful beast relishing its freedom. Far off in the distance, the iconic Hollywood sign emerged, a silent sentinel overseeing the approach to Los Angeles.

Tanned long fingers gripped the leather steering wheel as Gabriel relished the feel of the formidable machines power. Glancing in the rear-view mirror he glimpsed his own reflection, his skin was deeply tanned the creases around his eyes were etched by his appetite for fun and laughter, it was however wisdom's lessons along with one or two scars that had carved elegant lines in an incredibly handsome face. The dark blue lenses on his aviator sunglasses hiding his mesmerising ice blue eyes, the sort of eyes that could make a model of a man. Though Gabriel had certainly had his fair share of female adoration over the years he was far from a model with absolutely no interest in vanity in either sex, social media held no interest to him, the idea of a personal brand being a total anathema in his opinion, he had learnt long ago the dangers of an over inflated ego.

Gabriel's stunning good looks stemmed from his mixed parentage, his mother a strong and beautiful Scottish woman had fallen in love with his father who was Canadian born. His father was the son of an immigrant who had fled Cuba escaping a harsh life in search of a dream, making his way north he had ended up in Canada where he met and married Gabriel's grandmother a wealthy Canadian heiress whose parents had died when she was twenty one leaving her incredibly rich, easy prey for an enigmatic stranger who could tango like a professional, but that was a story for another day. Gabriel had grown up in a variety of extraordinary places and had known an early life of privilege in the USA with a father who while charismatic and charming had a lethal temper inherited from his own deeply flawed Papa. Gabriel had always known that there was a very dark side to wealth that could be manipulative and cruel.

Glancing at his sleeping passenger he noted the time. They had been travelling a while, and both needed to stretch their legs and quench their thirsts. Gabriel wryly acknowledged to himself that his thirst was for something entirely different than tea, he checked the time, tea would have to do for now. Searching the satnav he located a nearby restaurant, changing course he accelerated towards their new destination.

Gabriel's powerful car now headed in the direction of a humble roadside diner; he slowed the car as it neared its approach. The small restaurant itself was unremarkable, weathered by time, its once vibrant paintwork now faded and peeling, a testament to the countless years it had stood there. A place where dreamers and drifters collided on their journeys.

Inside, Rosie, the waitress, meticulously wiped down the tables, lost in memories, echoes from a past filled with the monotony of her routine. The clatter of dishes and the hum of the old jukebox were Rosie's only companions as the diner was empty. As she glanced out the window, something unusual caught her eye, a sleek white car pulling up to the parking lot. She squinted, straining to see through the sun's glare bouncing off the windshield. The driver's door opened, and a man stepped out, immediately commanding her attention.

Gabriel emerged with a grace that spoke of a life well-lived. His silvery grey hair gleamed in the daylight, contrasting with his deeply tanned skin, which bore the marks of countless sunrises and sunsets. He was tall, well over 6 foot with, strong broad shoulders, dressed in an effortless blend of casual though expensive looking clothes, a loose-fitting white linen shirt and soft beige chino trousers, complemented by dark sunglasses and well-worn leather loafers. The sleeves of his linen shirt rolled to the elbow revealing deeply tanned strong arms, his appearance just like his car was one of defined elegance belying the power within the bodywork. He moved with the ease of someone who had long made peace with the world and himself.

Rosie's breath caught in her throat. The man before her exuded a magnetism that was both undeniable and disarming. "Oh, be still my beating heart." She murmured to herself, momentarily forgetting her surroundings. Then, snapping back to reality, she called out. "Taylor! Taylor, we have got customers. Look alive!" Under her breath, she added. "Classy ones, too."

Gabriel walked around the car, opening the passenger door he acknowledged his companion with a warm, affectionate smile, he extended his hand to assist his fellow traveller. Slowly, an older gentleman stepped out, his movements stiff from the long drive. Babaji, dressed in simple yet elegant traditional attire, accepted Gabriel's hand, once standing beside the car he affectionately reached up to pat Gabriel's face smiling warmly.
Babaji's green turban was a vibrant splash of colour, contrasting with his long white beard and the rich, dark pools of his eyes, which sparkled with a wisdom that seemed to see beyond the ordinary. Nestled in the folds of the turban was a sparkling brooch in an unusual shape which held in place a real, delicate soft pink rose. The addition of the flower and the jewels hinted at the charisma of the elderly man who was the focus of Gabriel's concern and attention.

Gabriel retrieved a small leather case and a walking stick from the car which he handed to the older man, then gently taking Babaji's elbow, he guided him towards the diner. The two men were a picture of contrasting yet harmonious styles, one, the epitome of modern elegance, while the other, a symbol of timeless tradition. As they entered the diner, Rosie hurried over, trying to mask her curiosity with a professional smile. "Good afternoon, gentlemen. Can I show you to a table?"

"Thank you." Gabriel replied, his voice smooth and calm. He had removed his sunglasses revealing eyes that made Rosie's step falter as his piercing gaze settled on her a gentle smile softening their impact. "One by the window, please." Rosie led them to a table close to the door, aware the elder man seemed weary, the booth was one that offered a view of the dusty road and the fading afternoon light. Once her new customers were sitting comfortably, Rosie politely handed them both the menus, though Babaji seemed lost in thought, gazing out the window.

"Our specials today are..." She began, but Gabriel's gentle voice interrupted.

"Thank you. Rosie." Gabriel said, glancing at her name tag. "We won't be needing menus. Could you bring us two glasses of water and a pot of boiling water, please?" Rosie hesitated, she could not help the feeling of disappointment cross her face, her new customers were not intending to stay.

"Just water? You aren't going to eat something?" Gabriel smiled, a mischievous glint in his eye.

"Just water. Do charge us for coffee, though." A little taken aback Rosie questioned Gabriel's decision.

"Why don't I just bring you coffee?" Gabriel's smile widened, firmly he replied.

"Just the water will be fine, thank you." For a moment the disappointment she felt could have turned into frustration, a nagging thought crept into Rosie's mind. They did not like the cafe and worse still did not want any to eat there. The light in Rosie's eyes seemed to dim fractionally as uncomfortably she nervously smoothed the wrinkles in her crumpled apron, her self-conscious action betrayed the nerves fluttering in her stomach, as the warm smile slipped momentarily, her inner critic making her achingly aware of the dinners aging decor.

Gabriel correctly read the older woman's body language. Her self-soothing as she fidgeted with her uniform, her shoulders slumped slightly, doubt clouding her soft, pretty face. He reached forward to reassure her and gently brushed her arm with his wide palm, sending a frisson of sensation through the older woman's body. The warmth of his touch brought Rosie's attention immediately back to Gabriel's face, his touch had been fleeting, had she imagined it, yet her skin still tingled. Looking into his steely blue eyes her breath caught in her chest, Gabriel's gaze softened into a look which could have melted ice. He had not meant to reject or offend her in any way, and his touch was a silent reassurance of his intention. Momentarily Rosie seemed caught off guard. The combination of Gabriel's warm charm, undeniable charisma, and obvious sex appeal, contrasted yet oddly complemented by Babaji's serene presence, shrugging her shoulders she nodded, an uncomfortable smile played on her soft lips.

"Okay." A little bemused she stepped away from the table, unable to gather her thoughts, the men's presence was undoubtedly unnerving. There was something about these men that not only made her stomach flutter but also, she felt intensely curious as everything about them begged questions, Rosie was fascinated by her most unusual guests. They embodied wealth, calmness, and elegance, yet they seemed a most unlikely pair, together they carried an air of mystery that intrigued her making her feel like she was in the presence of someone special, they may even have been famous. As Rosie turned to leave, she caught herself staring at Gabriel again. His gentle warmth affected her in a way she had not felt in years. A blush crept up her cheeks, she quickly looked away, embarrassed by her own reaction. Looking up once more she glanced at Babaji, his kind eyes met hers with a smile that melted her heart. It was a smile that seemed to silently say, 'thank you.'

If Gabriel's eyes were the blue of the sky, then the older man's eyes were shinning pools of something unfathomable, deep, dark like the ocean, it was like falling through time looking into the richness of a soul exposed with no ego. Her step faltered making Rosie snap back into reality shaking her head she retreated to the kitchen, her mind whirling with thoughts and feelings she hadn't entertained in decades. "Oh, my." She whispered to herself, feeling oddly like a schoolgirl with a crush. Gabriel smiled to himself as he watched the lovely lady in front of him really 'see' Babaji for the first time. It never ceased to amaze him the effect the elderly man had on people; he was magnetic, gentle, even serene. It was like watching the moon in action, people gravitated towards him like spring tides. Gabriel knew that feeling all too well, he had never loved a man the way he loved this man, it was an honour and a privilege to call him brother. Smiling indulgently Gabriel's mind wondered as he placed the small leather case on the table. He opened it with care, revealing a beautifully crafted Chinese teapot with a delicate wicker handle and two small China bowls. He spread out an intricately embroidered mat, and with deliberate, practiced movements, he began selecting the tea. When Rosie returned, she carried a tray with the requested items, two glasses of water and a pot of boiling water, all presented in her best China. She had also added a plate of her homemade cookies, a small gesture of hospitality that she could not resist offering.

Placing the tray on the booth table Rosie was surprised as Gabriel started to prepare the tea putting the one, he had selected in the pot, Rosie found herself at a loss for words. She watched in silent fascination, feeling as if she were witnessing something almost sacred. Finally finding her voice she practically blurted out.

"Oh, I'm sorry Sir." Her cheeks flushed bright red, a hint of regret in her voice. "But you can't drink that in here."

Gabriel looked up at her with a warm, ridiculously innocent smile. "Really, Rosie? My dear friend and I share a passion for special tea. We wanted to sit here in your peaceful establishment, enjoying the view, while we take time to sip our tea. Surely there is no one here we could offend." He gestured around the noticeably empty diner. "As I said, I am willing to pay you for coffee. And the cookies, they look delicious. That is okay, isn't it?" Gabriel's voice was as smooth as silk his words more of a caress than a question. His tone held a resonance that spoke to something lost inside, it was not just the way he spoke to her, it was much more than that, it was his whole demeanour. Gabriel's impeccable manners made Rosie feel special, as if she were the only person in the world at that moment. She nodded, a sense of relief eased her previous disappointment, they wanted to stay a while, a soft smile warmed her expression lingering on her lips, she hesitated only momentarily, her eyes meeting Gabriel's once again, he was asking her permission. This beautiful man was asking her if she would allow him to break the rules in her own cafe, the nerve of the man.

The irony of the moment was not lost on Rosie, Gabriel was probably the most handsome man she had ever seen, not to mention obviously powerful, rich, sophisticated and undeniably intelligent, a man who could literally buy and sell her business in a heartbeat was asking little old Rosie for permission. Gabriel's eyes danced with humour, his wide smile betrayed the knowledge that he knew exactly how to get what he wanted from a woman, Rosie was no exception. 'What the hell' she thought, this was the most exciting exchange with a man Rosie had had all year, she grinned back at Gabriel her eyes sparkled indulgently.

"Oh, I suppose it won't hurt. Go ahead, okay." Rosie nodded, her words a mere whisper she felt weak at the knees, as she turned away, she touched her cheek, feeling the warmth there, chiding herself for acting like a teenager. She retreated to the kitchen, slightly dazed, her thoughts scattered and her heart unexpectedly light. Gabriel continued preparing the tea, while Rosie, still feeling the impact of the encounter, peered through the serving hatch, watching the two men. Mesmerized by the calm; almost ritualistic way Gabriel served the tea. Taylor, the younger waitress came to stand beside Rosie.

"What are they doing?" Taylor quietly asked, her curiosity piqued.

"Nothing." Rosie replied quietly, her eyes still on the two men. "Nothing that we need to worry about." She smiled, feeling a rare sense of peace. "So, for now, I'm just going to stand here and enjoy the view." Taylor frowned.

"Yeah, but Hank will go nuts if he comes in. You know Hank, you know what he thinks about freeloaders." Rosie shook her head, her smile unwavering.

"There is nothing freeloading about those men. You just hush up and go finish those dishes for me. You can let me worry about Hank." As Rosie continued to watch the men, who had yet to exchange a single word, she felt a deep sense of nostalgia wash over her. She sighed softly, her thoughts drifting to memories of a man she had loved and lost long ago. A gentle smile played on her lips as the warm glow of the setting sun filled the diner, painting the sky outside with shades of pink and gold. As the two men relaxed quietly in the booth their silence was companionable, their presence bringing with it a sense of peace that settled inside the unlikely haven, the late afternoon sun cast long shadows across the worn wooden floor. Through the large front window, they appeared as calm figures against the warm, fading light. Gabriel's white linen shirt seemed to glow softly, while Babaji's green turban added an exotic vibrant contrast to the otherwise muted interior of the small restaurant. Outside, the world moved on, indifferent to the quiet moment unfolding within.

A little while later the powerful sports car was back on the road but not before Gabriel had left a handsome tip for Rosie. Attentively he guided his old friend back to the car, soon they were on their way, once again Gabriel taking pleasure in navigating the picturesque roads they glided effortlessly through the winding routes, heading towards the city of dreams. The journey ahead led them into the vast expanse of Los Angeles, where the skyline rose like a glittering jewel in the distance, towering above the sprawling cityscape. Inside the diner Rosie had watched as her elegant guests had left, knowing that it was unlikely she would ever see them again, their exchange would stay with her, the moments so brief yet memorable.

Sighing, a feeling of warmth and serenity settled in Rosie's chest the spell only broken as she cleared the booth, somehow wiping away the physical evidence of the encounter. Hank arrived grumbling about something, his usual crumpled appearance as familiar as an old pair of slippers. They had been friends for years and business partners since his brother Ted had passed leaving his share in the dinner to his beloved Rosie. Hank was no Gabriel, but he was a hardworking, honest man. Gabriel on the other hand was now a memory that would warm Rosie's heart whenever she remembered his beautiful face, but it was the older man whose enigmatic eyes that had stirred Rosie's soul, they would remain in her dreams for years to come.

As the car approached downtown, the energy of the city began to pulse more intensely. The streets became busier, the buildings taller, and the vibe more electric. Palm trees lined the avenues, and the famous Hollywood landmarks came into view, signalling their approach to the heart of LA. The Strip emerged, a riot of neon lights, billboards, and flashing signs that lit up the late afternoon sky. People from all walks of life crowded the sidewalks, tourists with cameras, aspiring actors chasing dreams, and street performers showcasing their talents. The air buzzed with the promise of excitement, each corner teeming with stories waiting to unfold. Gabriel would be back later but for now he turned the car towards the more salubrious part of the city heading for the Regent Hotel his next stop.

Chapter 2

Away from the main thoroughfare, in a narrow side alley just off the Strip, a different story was taking shape. The alley was dimly lit, the noise from the street muffled as though entering another world. Here, two unsavoury characters, Magpie and Stretch, stood in the shadows, their presence both threatening and purposeful. Magpie, the older of the two was broad shouldered with lean hips, his face hard and sharp-featured, his dark hooded eyes gave nothing away, while Stretch the taller of the two seemed wirier, he leaned casually against the brick wall, the picture of streetwise confidence. In front of them, two young men, Hugo and Mac, shifted nervously. Their clothes and demeanour marked them as students, the fear in their eyes suggested they were far from their comfort zone. Hugo's hands trembled slightly as he handed a photo to Magpie, his voice barely steady as he tried to explain its significance. Magpie took the photo without a word, studying it with an intensity that made the youngsters even more anxious. His posture changed subtly as he processed the information, standing taller and more imposing.

Mac, pale and sweating, kept glancing over his shoulder, the sense of danger in the alley amplifying his nerves. He fumbled inside his jacket, eventually pulling out an envelope, which he handed over to Magpie. He accepted it with a slow, deliberate movement, his cold eyes fixed on the two young men. The students exchanged worried glances; their earlier confidence now eroded by the grim reality of their situation. Magpie finally looked up, locking his gaze with Hugo his tone icy and threatening.

"Just remember, that's the down payment." Hugo's voice by contrast seemed oddly high pitched and young, instantly blurting out.

"You'll get the rest when we get the shot." His tone filled with a bravado that was total fiction. His shaking hands revealing his real nerves he looked away from Magpie unable to meet the man's intimidating cruel stare. Mac nodded his agreement a little too eagerly, trying to muster a semblance of control. He blurted out.

"The money's no problem, boss." Mac, realising he sounded ridiculous, forced a weak smile.

With the exchange complete Magpie stood to his full height glaring at the youths in a menacing fashion, their presence, no longer required, they were beginning to irritate Magpie. Taking their cue to leave Hugo and Mac quickly turned and hurried out of the alley, their footsteps echoing on the pavement as they made their escape. Fear quickened their pace as by the time they reached a shiny new black pickup parked nearby they were practically running, jumping in the truck they burst out laughing their relief palpable. Pushing one another they began to jostle, the play-fight an obvious release of tension. Hugo was in the driver's seat, turning the key urgently the engine roared to life, the truck came bursting out of the alleyway as if chased by the devil as they sped off, eager to put distance between themselves and the evidence of their new contract.

Magpie and Stretch watched as the boys drove away; both of their expressions unreadable. Magpie reached into his pocket, pulling out a phone. He dialled quickly, speaking in a low, indistinct voice, his words inaudible, the seriousness in his tone unmistakable. The earlier façade of arrogant nonchalance had vanished, replaced by a hardened focus on the details of the task that lay ahead. The two men exchanged a cynical look, a silent understanding passing between them. Magpie gave a curt nod, without another word, they strode purposefully out of the alleyway heading down the Strip. The lively energy of the street seemed to fade around them as they moved with intent, their expressions cold and determined. They entered a nearby pawn shop, the door closing behind them with a soft jingle, leaving the alley and its shadows behind. The bustling energy of the Strip resumed its dominance, unaware of the shady dealings that had just transpired in its quieter corners, the dark heart of Los Angeles, where the line between dreams and nightmares was often indistinguishable.

....

A distance away on the other side of the city, a quite different scene is unfolding. Harsh fluorescent lights flickered slightly, casting an unforgiving glare over the shabby public bathroom in the LA police department. The walls, a dull blue grey, stained with years of constant use, their colour as uninspiring as the setting itself. The faint, sharp smell of disinfectant hung in the air, a lingering reminder of the room's utilitarian purpose. At the far end of the bathroom, young woman stands with her back to the room, intently focused on the mirror in front of her. Her figure is stunning, clad only in lacy black lingerie that wraps her feminine curves in delicate silk. Her short white peroxide-blonde wig a sharp, carefully styled bob, which she adjusts slightly, ensuring it sits exactly right. Standing on her tiptoes, she leans in closer to the mirror, her bright sapphire blue eyes scrutinizing her reflection with meticulous care, she carefully removes a stray hair from her dramatic eyelashes which frame the sultry dramatic eye make-up that a professional would be proud of. Pulling out a tube of bright red lipstick from her cosmetics bag she confidently applies it, the bold colour sliding smoothly over her wide, inviting smile. The lipstick, the final addition to her transformation, grinning at herself, the satisfaction is evident in her eyes. This is Maddison, Maddy as she is known to those familiar with her. The mirror reflects her now fully transformed persona, one of a woman who knew exactly what she wanted and how to get it.

Checking the time on her phone Maddy starts to get dressed; pulling on a tiny lilac snakeskin skirt that barely reaches mid-thigh, followed by a tight white boob tube that hugs her torso. Over this, she dons a three-quarter length dark red jacket, the sleeves rolled up to the elbows. The jacket's black collar frames her face, adding a touch of sharpness to her otherwise playful ensemble. She finishes her look with thigh-high black stiletto boots that click sharply on the tile floor as she moves. The finale touches to her daring outfit, large silver hoop earrings that dangle from her ears, and a series of bangles that clink softly against each other with each movement. A black hat, worn at a cocky angle, completes the outfit, giving her a striking, dangerous allure. Next to her, on the grimy tiled floor, lies a pile of discarded clothes, a sharp contrast to her outfit, an expensive looking holdall beside them. A variety of colourful office files lay scattered haphazardly around, mingling with the crumpled clothes and the expensive trainers she has just taken off, remnants of her previous, less provocative identity.

The sound of a toilet flushing echoes through the room, a moment later, a stall door creaks opens, an elegant older woman, Sylvia, steps out, moving with a grace that contrasts sharply with the dingy surroundings. The sight of Maddy makes Sylvia pause her expression a mix of indulgence and mock disapproval. With a slight shake of her head, she walks to the sink, washing then drying her hands with practiced ease. As Sylvia heads toward the door, she passes close to Maddy, leaning in to whisper in her ear.

"There's going to be hell to pay." The words are spoken softly; however, the warning they carry is clear. Maddy seems unfazed. A wide grin covering her mouth she looks affectionately at Sylvia's departing back, her focus momentarily shifting from the mirror as she continues perfecting her look. Her hands move with practiced precision, each stroke of makeup carefully placed, each detail finetuned to create the perfectly painted disguise. Putting in her EarPods Maddy carefully selected a track then cranking the volume up she dances to music only she can hear, the music firing her confidence which she is going to need if she is to pull off her role convincingly. Swaying to a silent rhythm she closes her eyes as she begins to spin, the only sound in the bathroom is faint hum of the fluorescent lights, accompanied by clicks from her sharp heels and the occasional drip from a leaky faucet. The atmosphere feels electric almost tangible there is danger in the air, as Maddy completes her transformation, she is more than ready to dazzle unsuspecting victims.

....

In a completely different area of the city unaware of Maddy's transformation the driver of a black two-door sports coupe sits idling off a quiet boulevard, the cars sleek, understated lines blending into the shadows of the side street. Inside, Amelia's reflection stares back from the rearview mirror. Dark sunglasses conceal striking hazel eyes, her thick chestnut coloured hair is carefully, pulled back off her elegant olive complexion revealing small diamond stud earrings that add a touch of class to her sharp, professional businesslike appearance. Dressed in a dark, expensive trouser suit with a fitted white shirt open at the collar, Amelia looks every bit the epitome of understated style. With a sigh, she removes her sunglasses, rubbing her eyes with her neatly manicured fingertips the deep ruby red nails the only obvious nod to glamour in her outfit. Despite her polished exterior, the fatigue is evident, yet it does little to diminish her beauty. Her skin is flawless, her makeup pristine even as she fights the weariness creeping in. Reaching into her jacket, she pulls out a lip balm which she smooths over her lips, she pinches her cheeks the simple act bringing a touch of colour back to her face.

Her phone beeps, pulling her attention away. She checks the message, a tut of annoyance escapes her lips as she quickly hammers out a reply, her irritation plain. Just as she finishes, another sound fills the car, her second phone vibrating in the console. This time, she checks the message, a smile spreads across her face. With a quick turn of the key, the car roars to life, the powerful engine revving as she accelerates out onto the main road.

As she speeds away, strains of classical music float through the open driver's window, immediately drowned out by the sudden wail of a police siren. Blue lights flash from the grille, revealing that Amelia's sleek car is, in fact, an unmarked police vehicle. Driving with precision and skill, Amelia navigates the streets of LA at breakneck speed, the music within the car shifting to the powerful swell of opera. Her destination soon comes into view: a seedy motel in downtown LA, its parking lot crawling with police cars and officers. As she pulls up, two plainclothes detectives, Bill and Sam, step forward to greet her. "Hi, Bill." Amelia says as she jumps out of the car. "How many did you arrest?"

"Six, including Vinnie Boss. Connors in the car." Bill replied. "Well done, guys." Amelia replies with a satisfied smile, nodding at the detectives before heading toward the black-and-white squad car. She opens the door and slides into the backseat, where a small, wiry man with a hat sits, handcuffed and looking both uncomfortable and irritated. Amelia smiles coolly at him.

"So, Connor, my friend, what an interesting week you are having. Guess what? Things are about to get a whole lot more interesting, too." Her expression hardens as she leans in closer. "No, seriously! You are in this up to your eyeballs. You better start giving me something, or you, my little friend, are going to get to know Hector's boys a whole lot better." Connor squirms in his cuffs, his eyes pleading as he stammers with a soft Irish accent.

"Look, I know you don't like these guys. If they even get a whiff of me talking to you. They're going to blow my head off. You know they are. I told the detective over there; I don't know nothing." Amelia's smile turns icy.

"Not to worry, Connor, my dear. If you say you don't know anything, then we will keep you safe at the station and charge you with murder." Connor's eyes widen in panic.

"What? You can't pin that on me! I wasn't even there last night. I didn't have anything to do with it, I swear." Amelias tone sharpens, her patience wearing thin.

"You can swear all you want. I never mentioned last night. One way or another, you are going to tell me who ordered that hit." Amelia opens the door to leave; she is halfway out of the squad car when Connor's desperate voice stops her.

"No, wait. No, not here. People are watching." He whispers, nodding towards a group of dubious looking locals loitering across the street. Among them are various gang members, eyeing the scene with suspicion. Amelia straightens up exiting the car she stands to her full height her expression unreadable as she calls out to the detectives.

"Take him downtown and book him with murder one." Slamming the car door on Connor's protests Amelia strides over to Sam. As she gets within earshot of the young detective Sam, she lowers her voice. "Take him to the station, Sam. Get him to give you something. He knows who gave the order. Put him in the cells, we have until Monday. By then, he will be wanting a hit so badly, Connor will be begging to tell us who killed Skinner." Checking her watch before turning on her heel she heads back to her car. Once back behind the wheel Amelia takes a deep breath the strain of the day showing in the furrows on her forehead. Switching on the engine of her powerful police car she heads off at speed a determined look upon her beautiful face. Amelia arrives back at the LA Police Vice Squad offices. She marches up the stairs into the department, several detectives stand huddled around a computer, laughing and chatting. The moment she enters, they spring into action, the room suddenly buzzing with activity. "Something up, guys? Anything I should know about.... Joe?" Amelia asks, her tone serious, she singles out one of the younger men. Joe, one of the detectives, squirms under her gaze.

"No, Ma'am. We were just checking the reports on the homicide from last night." Amelia raises her eyebrows regarding him with a doubtful stare.

"Really? Anything you would like to share with me?" Her voice carries a hint of warning sarcasm, the other detectives quickly disperse, leaving Joe to face her alone. Before Joe can respond, a chorus of wolf whistles erupts from the adjoining offices. Detectives leap up to get a better look at the drop-dead gorgeous young woman who has just strutted confidently up the stairs and into the department. Amelia remains unnervingly still, her back to the commotion, her focus entirely on Joe.

Joe groans under his breath. "Oh, crap." Nervously running a hand through his hair. He takes a deep breath, trying to compose himself before looking Amelia in the eye, though he quickly averts his gaze under her intense stare.

"It's Maddy, isn't it?" Amelia asks, her voice flat. Joe steps forward, grabbing Amelia's arms inappropriately before she can turn around.

"Auntie Mia, please wait. Remember, your birthday is tomorrow." Joe pleads, his voice low and urgent. Amelia smiles at him, patting his hand condescendingly until he releases her arm. She takes a moment to steady herself before turning around to face the source of the commotion, Maddy.

Chapter 3

The brazen young woman starts strutting confidently down the aisle between the desks like a catwalk, working the room with ease. She blows bubbles with her chewing gum, a disrespectful smile playing on her lips, swinging her hips provocatively she sashays down the department. Amelia visibly bristles, her expression hardening. Joe, sensing the tension, coughs loudly to snap his colleagues out of their collective daze. Suddenly, the room fills with a flurry of activity as everyone returns to their work. Maddy stops a couple of feet from Amelia, still smiling defiantly. Without a word, Amelia steps forward, grabbing her daughter by the elbow and pinching her hard.

"My office, now, Madison." Ameli's abruptly demands, her tone leaving no room for argument.

"Ouch, Mom!" she protests. Unceremoniously, Maddy finds herself briskly marched across the room by Amelia, struggling to keep up in her stiletto boots with her mother's pace. "You're really hurting me, Mom." Furious, Amelia does not respond until they reach her office. She slams the door behind them, revealing the name: DCI Amelia Cartwright, emblazoned in gold and black letters. Inside, Amelia finally releases Maddy, pacing the room as she tries to contain her anger.

"OK, young lady." She begins, her voice trembling with controlled fury. "You get one shot at this. What the hell do you think you are doing dressed like that?"

"Calm down, Mom." Maddy starts, but Amelia cuts her off sharply.

"How dare tell me to calm down! Who do you think you are? Waltzing into my office looking like a $20 whore? Tell me right now what you think are you playing at, Madison?"

"Hang on, Mom, this is what we agreed." Maddy protests indignantly, her voice wavers a little, she seems unnerved by her mom's fierce expression. Amelia narrows her eyes.

"What!" Amelia nearly chokes on the word as she stares at her defiant daughter. "I most certainly did not agree to this, Madison." Maddy takes a deep breath, trying to explain.

"Yes, you did. You said that Spencer and I could make a short film about your story. This, Mom.... Is your story." She twirls, showing off the outfit. The gesture only makes Amelia wince, her face pales, her expression tightening as if she is on the verge of losing control. Her posture stiffens, every muscle tense with barely contained anger. Maddy, has seriously misjudged her mom's response, now is not the time to back down, sensing the storm brewing, Maddy steps closer, her voice softening into a desperate plea, she continues to fight her case.

"Mom, you know how important this project is for my summer coursework. This is going to affect my overall grade." Maddy, her eyes wide and earnest looks imploringly at Amelia. "I need to do something special, something original. This is why I asked you in the first place. Even Professor Martin thinks the film is a great idea." Amelia's eyes narrow, her voice trembling with disbelief.

"Wait a minute? You are telling me you have already discussed this with your tutors? Maddy, you never said anything about this." The colour has begun to drain out of Amelia's strained face. "You told me you wanted to film the Strip, to capture what happens there, not this...." Amelia waves dismissively over Maddy's provocative outfit. "You absolutely cannot dress up like a hooker Maddy. You will get arrested, I am a cop. I cannot let you do this. I am sorry but the answer is no, absolutely, not."

"Mom, please, just hear me out." Maddy insists, her voice growing more insistent. "Spencer and I were talking about how to make this film have real impact. How to show what it was like on the Strip all those years ago." She pauses looking at her mom from under her lashes. "We wanted to show why you set up the shelter, and just how hard it was for you to fight for it. We realised this would be so much more powerful if I played Miss Mia rather than just filming the people there." Maddy watches her mom, who now looks pale and conflicted, she tries to gauge her reaction. "I want to tell your story, Mom." She pauses looking her mom directly in the eyes.

"This isn't just your story anymore though mom. It is still the same for these women, if not worse from what you tell me. I want people to know what life is really like for these women." She pauses, searching her mother's eyes, hoping to find a trace of understanding. Her tone softens, as she offers a small, tentative smile. "Mom, I really want people to see how important the charity is. I want to show why you set it up in the first place." She stands back straightening her shoulders. "Your story will inspire others; I can't just capture that with nameless faces."

Amelias face remains tense, her emotions barely contained beneath the surface as she raises a hand to stop Maddy from continuing. "Maddy, just stop right there. Let me get this straight, you are telling me that you want to go out on the Strip tonight, dressed like that, and pretend to be me as a Hooker? Am I understanding you correctly?" Maddy nods slowly, her determination clear despite her mother's obvious disapproval.

"Yes, Mom. I want to do this. To show people what these women go through and why your work at the shelter is so important." Amelia stands frozen, torn between her protective instincts and the realization of what her daughter is trying to achieve. The gravity of the situation bears down on her, Maddy has simply no idea just how difficult seeing her dressed like that is for Amelia. How could she it was decades ago, yet the pain, worse still the shame was still intense. Seeing Maddy parade through her office of all places was too much even for a professional like Amelia to contend with. For a moment, she feels caught between wanting to shield Maddy from the harsh realities of the world and understanding her desire to make a real difference, all the while having to face her own past. Looking at Maddy dressed as a hooker was like looking into a cracked mirror she had long ago hidden away. The memories of that period of her life were fraught with shards of emotional glass far too sharp and filled with shame to inspect too closely. Silently she acknowledged that Maddy was not to know how painful those memories still were. The conflicting emotions rising in her chest were becoming too much for Amelia to contain, she struggles to find the right words.

Joe now at his desk, pretends to focus on the paperwork in front of him, his attention keenly directed to the tense scene unfolding in Amelia's office. He watches as Amelia paces back and forth, her frustration mounting with each exchange. His eyes flicker back to his desk occasionally; it is clear his mind is much more occupied with the argument between the two women he cares about. Inside the office, Maddy's voice takes on a pleading tone as she continues to try to wear down Amelia.

"But Mom, can you not see, that is just what I will be doing. I am not doing anything real, just pretending. There is a real difference. You know that better than anyone." Amelia's face hardens; her voice laced with hurt.

"Cheap shot, Maddy!" She raises her voice wounded by her own daughter's insensitivity. "Do you have any idea just how dangerous it is on those streets?" Amelia glares at Maddison. "This is why I became a cop. This is not just a game you are playing here. There are real lowlifes out there that I deal with every day. I am not going to let you put yourself in danger for a film assignment." Maddy meets her mother's eyes, resentment simmering.

"Talk about double standards, Mom. How can you justify what you are saying. Somehow you think it is okay for you to go out there every day, risking your life as a cop. I do not get a say in the matter, I'm not allowed an opinion, am I?" Maddy is annoyed by the argument, feeling incensed by her mother's blatant hypocrisy she shouts back. "The minute I want to do something original, something a bit risky, you shut it down. Thats not fair. I didn't have to ask your permission. Spencer and I could have just done something else, something out of your jurisdiction. Then you would not have had any control over what I do." Amelia stares at her daughter's defiant expression, her expression a mix of disappointment, frustration, and something more perhaps. This is the first time Maddison has really stood up to her. Uncomfortably Amelia realises there was just a tiny bit of parental pride too. Unwilling to allow Maddy to see her beginning to sway she bites back.

"Emotional blackmail, Madison? You are getting good at that." Her words delivered in a cold, flat tone that makes Maddy look up at her mom, surprised by the harshness of her accusation.

"That's not fair, Mom." Maddy seems hurt by the sting in Amelia's words but realising her mom is being protective replies, her voice softening. "Can you not see how proud I am of everything you have achieved. I just want to tell your story." Her eyes brighten as she adds. "Anyway, I wouldn't be in any real danger because Joe will be there." Overhearing the mention of his name, Joe suddenly becomes very engrossed in his paperwork, but Amelia's sharp gaze locks onto him.

"What do you mean, Joe will be there?" Amelia's shoulders stiffen at the mention of the young detective's name. Maddy continues, oblivious to the tension she is causing

"Joe said he would put a wire on me, you know, so that he can listen in and keep an eye on me. I thought he told you. Amelia's expression shifts from confusion to irritation.

"No. He hasn't mentioned it." She walks to the office door, opening it she stares directly at Joe, raising her voice she calls across the department. "Detective St John! According to my daughter your undercover skills are required for this evening. Would you like to join us please!" At the mention of his surname Joe swallows hard, muttering under his breath. "Oh, shit." With a forced smile, he stands up, in a louder voice, says. "Right. I will be right there." As he walks across the office, a quiet chorus of 'busted' from his colleagues follows him. Joe ignores them, focusing instead on Amelia's cool, assassin-like smile. Once inside the office, Amelia quietly closes the door behind him. From outside, the detectives in the office cannot hear all the details, the odd word filters out, 'irresponsible' and 'dangerous' standing out in the otherwise muffled exchange. Sitting on the edge of her desk, Amelia looks down at her feet, clearly exhausted by the argument. Sensing her fatigue, Maddy and Joe jump to their feet, both aware of Amelia's resignation. Finally, it is Amelia's shoulders that sag, a little defeated by the boisterous energy of the youngsters, she sighs deeply, crossing her arms defensively. She looks at them both, slowly standing and moving behind her desk.

"I don't like this one bit, Maddy." Her voice heavy with resignation. "I hope you realize the position you have put me in. Joe, in future do not go making promises that I must back up." She studies them both for a long moment before continuing. "You can do this on one condition. Joe, you make sure that Maddy is wired properly. You watch her the whole time, Joe. Do you understand me?" Maddy lets out a squeal of delight, jumping up to kiss Joe on the cheek, making him blush. She then rushes around the desk to give her mother a huge hug which Amelia tolerates with a forced smile. Joe, still red-faced, quietly reassures Amelia.

"Don't worry, Auntie Mia, I'll take care of her." As Maddy and Joe are walking out of the office, arm in arm, grinning at one another, they pause when Amelia calls after them.

"Let me know when you're ready to go, and I'll meet you downstairs." They freeze at her words, the finality in Amelia's tone stopping them in their tracks. "What? You didn't think I would just let you go out there without seeing for myself what is going on?" Amelia's ice cool tone leaves no room for further argument. Maddy hesitates as if considering going back to argue, Joe sensibly catches her arm, gently leading her away from his boss's office.

"Leave it, Maddy." Joe warns. "You got what you wanted, don't push it." Maddy looks like she is about to argue, then sensing her victory changes her mind. She smiles up at Joe, linking arms with him as they head downstairs together. Sitting behind her desk Amelia's shoulders slump with fatigue as she gathers paperwork from the various meetings of the day. The quiet of her office a welcome relief, however her tiredness is palpable. Just then, Sylvia, the attractive older lady who had earlier made a brief appearance in the restroom, stepped into the doorway. Looking up Amelia forces a small smile, sighing deeply as Sylvia enters. Sylvia, with a gentle tone, asks. "I did the right thing messaging you, didn't I?" Amelia nods, though her weariness is evident.

"Yes, yes, of course you did, Sylvia. You know how Maddy is, she is so headstrong. She would have just batted those big blue eyes at Joe, and he would be putty in her hands. He cannot say no to her." Sylvia smirks ironically. "I can't imagine who she gets that from!" Amelia shakes her head defensively.

"Hold on a minute! I did not flirt my way to this position, Sylvia. I am not one of those women who can work men to get what they want. I never could." Sylvia laughs softly, a knowing look in her eyes.

"No, sugar, you're one of those women who works her ass off and scares the life out of any man who dares to get in her way." She pauses for effect starring at Amelia whose face registers her surprise. "You forget, Mia, I have been working here for what, 17, 18 years and I've seen the casualties. I have watched men fall at your feet, and you, you just step over the bodies without a second glance. Amelia looks mortified, her voice comes out as a whisper.

"That is an awful thing to say, Sylvia. You make me sound like a cold, heartless bitch." Sylvia interrupts gently.

"No, Amelia. Those are your words, not mine." She leans on Amelia's desk looking her friend in the eyes. "You my dear friend are one of the most stubborn, determined beautiful women I have ever had the pleasure of working with. Believe me, it has been a pleasure to watch you make your mark. Never have I met anyone who can keep people on their toes like you can, Mia. That office out there." Sylvia gestures toward the door. "That room is full of men who respect you, not just because of your looks, though I'm sure that doesn't hurt." She leans her hip on Amelia's desk looking sideways at her. "It is because you are the best boss they have ever had. Remember, they talk to me." Amelia, attempting to deflect the compliment, replies frostily.

"Remind me never to ask you for a reference. You are supposed to be my friend, not my shrink. You are the psychologist for that lot out there." Sylvia silently makes the decision that the conversation needs to be more private. Crossing the office, she closes the door behind her, turning back to Amelia she takes the chair opposite her friend, now seated behind her desk. Amelia stops shuffling paperwork, she is in no mood to dissect this latest development, her expression registering her fatigue as she looks at Sylvia who she had certainly not invited to share her thoughts.

"You are right Mia I am your friend. That is why I am going to say the one thing. I know you do not want to hear, but you need to." Amelia, sensing the seriousness in Sylvia's tone, shifts uncomfortably standing up, she glances around the office for an excuse to leave.

"Just the one Sylvia? Please do not hold back on my account." Amelia stares at her friend, her voice edged with sarcasm. Sylvia points back to the chair.

"Sit down and listen for a minute, Mia." Her tone is firm but kind as she stares at Amelia. "I know you are tired. You are angry and I know you are frustrated. But I care about you. It is time someone told you the truth." Sylvia takes a breath knowing that Amelia is going to resist her next sentence. "Mia honey, you have got to start living. Let yourself be happy, fall in love. You are lonely. I see it, Maddy sees it, everyone sees it. But you are so scared of letting yourself feel anything because you know what it means." Amelia immediately rolls her eyes, trying to shrug off Sylvia's words, Sylvia presses on. "Yes, Mia, you have simply got to learn to trust someone again. You are turning 40 tomorrow. It is time to enjoy life, to relax a little, even take a risk on someone." She smiles warmly her eyes filled with compassion and patience. "You have done an amazing job raising Maddy, but she is so grown up now, more than you realize. She is your finest achievement, your cheerleader and friend as much as she's your daughter. You can't keep using her as an excuse to hide from the possibility of a relationship." Sylvia pauses looking at Amelia's tight restrained appearance, smiling broadly her eyes sparkle mischievously.

"Amelia what you really need is passion and excitement in your life. In fact, what you need more than anything is hot spontaneous sex. Do something irresponsible for once live a little." Amelia flushes red as she registers the unfiltered, unashamed comments.

"Really! Don't sugarcoat it, Sylvia. I thought you were supposed to make me feel better, not drive me to drink." Slyvia smiles warmly.

"Mia, my dear. No-one can make you feel or do anything you don't want to. You are far too strong for that. You don't need me or anyone else to put you down, you do that far too well yourself." Sylvia frowns knowingly. "It's time to let go of the past, be proud of what you've done, and decide that you're going to be happy." Amelia, growing increasingly frustrated with Sylvia, spots Joe and Maddy returning to the department. She seizes the opportunity to escape the conversation.

"Oh, sure, it is that simple, isn't it? Tomorrow I'll wake up, snap my fingers, and just decide to be happy. Life's just sunshine and daisies" Intensely frustrated with the conversation Amelia slams the papers she has been sorting down on the desk a little too hard. "Then what? Prince Charming is going to just ride into my life and sweep me off my feet? Can we not forget, I messed up that way once already." Amelia's face is pink, flushed with emotion. Sylvia seems unaffected by Amelias' display of irritation, she chuckles softly.

"Why on earth are you waiting for Prince Charming! To make you happy? Don't you see by now. It's your job to make yourself happy, no one else's." By now Amelia has rounded the desk and is standing beside Sylvia, she is a little taken aback when Sylvia stands up pulling her into a spontaneous, affectionate hug. "I love you, Mia. But you are wound up so tight, you're going to snap if you don't find a way to let some of this go." She grins giving Amelia a suggestive wink. Amelia, stiffens at first, then gradually relaxes into the embrace, letting out a long, weary sigh. "Maybe you're right." She concedes softly, her expression remains conflicted as she pulls back. "But right now, I've got a daughter, dressed like a prostitute and a pile of paperwork to finish." Sylvia laughs at Amelia's comment she releases her from the hug, smiling with a mix of affection and concern. She looks her friend in the eyes, squeezing her arms reassuringly before she lets her go completely.

"And you will handle them both beautifully as always. Just remember, Mia, you deserve some of that care and attention too." Amelia watches as Sylvia heads for the door, her mind trying to digest everything that has been said by her friend. As Sylvia leaves, Amelia glances back at her desk, the weight of her responsibilities pressing down on her once more. Sylvia's words linger, forcing her to confront the truth she has been avoiding. Amelia turns to Sylvia with a tired smile on her face.

"They broke the Mold when they made you, Sylvia. What would I do without you to kick my butt?" Sylvia grins back.

"What, you mean I'm not just here to make you coffee? Want a cup before I take my sorry-self home for the night? Looks like you are in for a long one." Amelia nods, glancing down the office. Both women notice Maddy and Joe, have been joined by a tall, handsome young man with expensive camera equipment. Maddy is all smiles, her hands playfully resting on Spencer's chest, flirting shamelessly. He leans down, kissing the tip of her nose, while Joe, standing nearby looks away, clearly annoyed he looks uncomfortable. His whole stance changes, fists clenching as jealousy flickers across his face. Amelia sighs softly.

"Oh Lord. I think you might be right Sylvia!"

Chapter 4

The strip is at its vibrant, colourful, dangerous best. The soft pinks of the evening have given way to the night. In the dark, all the unsavoury elements of Hollywood's night scene are coming to life, plying their various trades up and down the street. In the front seat of a police surveillance car, Amelia and Joe sit side by side, both with wires in their ears, listening to the feed from Maddy, who is across the street, strutting along the sidewalk. Amelia glances at Joe, her voice tinged with concern.

"Joseph, how the hell did I let you persuade me this was a good idea?" Amelia is already regretting her decision. "Don't you dare tell Jack about this. You know how your dad is, he will be horrified. You know how he feels about Maddy." Joe nods, a small smile on his face.

"Yeah, I know. Dad's a big softy, but when it comes to her... No worries, I won't say a word. But Maddy, she's the one who can't keep her mouth shut." On the sidewalk, Maddy is pacing in front of a sleazy takeaway, one hand on her hip and the other adjusting her earpiece. She whispers playfully.

"I can hear you; you know. And for your information, Joe, I can keep a secret. Need I remind you about the fake tan incident?" Inside the car, Joe blushes deeply, quickly cutting her off.

"Yeah, okay, point made, Maddy." Joe sounds a little irritated by Maddy's teasing. Amelia, catching Joe's discomfort, grins at him. "This sounds like a story I'd like to hear." Joe shifts nervously.

"No, no, Maddy was just kidding, weren't you, Maddy?" He scowls out the window, trying to avoid Amelia's inquisitive gaze.

Maddy giggles through the earpiece, wiggling her hips as she continues to sashay up and down the sidewalk. "What's it worth, Joe?" Maddy quietly whispers with a grin. Amelia interrupts, her voice firm but amused.

"Okay, you two, you can carry this on later." Scanning the street her eyes search for Maddy's boyfriend. "Now, where's Loverboy Spencer? Oh, look, there he is. Joe, why don't you go and give him a ticket? He's parked illegally. You'd enjoy that, wouldn't you?" Joe laughs, Maddy scowls in response.

"Mom, stop it. Leave Spencer alone." Nearby, Spencer seems diligently focused on filming Maddy, completely oblivious to the conversation about him. Suddenly, a mean-looking young woman in a tiny miniskirt stomp's over to Maddy. She is wearing a low-cut top and platform shoes, her stature short but her attitude fierce.

"Move on Bitch, this is our turf." The young woman, Celeste, shouts at Maddy. Amelia's voice comes through the earpiece, calm and instructive.

"Maddy, that's Celeste. Tell her you work for me." Celeste points a finger aggressively at Maddy, her intent clear.

"I said... Move on Bitch!" Celeste snarls, going to push Maddy. Maddy is quicker. She grabs Celeste's hand, twisting it around in a way that leaves the young woman unable to move, a squeal of surprise not to mention pain escaping her sultry pout. In the surveillance car, Amelia tenses, about to jump out, Joe grabs her arm, pointing across the road.

"Look, Maddy's got this." Maddy, taking control of the situation with cool confidence, says with pure swagger.

"I'm working here tonight BITCH. You move on." Amelia's voice is exasperated in Maddy's ear.

"That's not what I said, Maddy." Celeste, more embarrassed than hurt, pulls away, her pride wounded. She struts off, hurling insults over her shoulder from a safe distance. Amelia relaxes back into her seat, a small smile tugging at her lips. Joe, watching both women, shakes his head in admiration.

"She's a chip off the old block." His accurate words make Amelia stiffen slightly, her smile fading just a touch.

"Less of the 'old,' Joe. But looking at her tonight, you're not wrong." On the strip, Maddy grins, hearing the exchange through her earpiece.

"I can still hear you, guys. Can we focus, please?" Maddy quips, her voice light, her attention now sharpened. Fuelled by a hit of dopamine that her mother's words spark her confidence rises as she resumes her role. Maddy stands a little taller strutting up and down at the edge of the sidewalk. Amelia's phone rings inside the surveillance car, she motions to Joe that she is stepping outside to take the call. Opening the door, she jumps out, leaving Joe alone with his thoughts. He fiddles with the radio, the song 'My World' by Calum Scott begins to play softly over the scene. Joe's eyes drift back to Maddy, who is sashaying up and down flirting outrageously, smiling at passing cars, touting for business. A complex mix of emotions washes over Joe's face as memories of their shared past flood his mind. He thinks back to their childhood, the countless moments they have spent together, the laughter, the arguments, the times when he quietly admired her from a distance. He is desperately in love with Maddy, she pretends she does not see it. She flaunts her friendships with other men in front of him, oblivious to the depth of his feelings. Joe's heart aches as he watches her, knowing she is not ready for a committed relationship with him, and perhaps, she never will be.

The montage of memories in his mind comes to an abrupt halt as Amelia gets back into the car. On the strip, Maddy continues to work the sidewalk, her attention suddenly drawn by the roar of a sports car pulling away from the lights a couple of hundred feet away. Intrigued, she steps out into the road to get a better look. Gabriels gleaming white Aston Martin screeches to a halt right in front of her. Maddy quickly snaps back into character, shaking her hair and sauntering around to the passenger window.

Inside the car, Gabriel sits with his mouth open, utterly shocked at the sight of Maddy. She misreads his stunned expression, thinking he is a potential client and an incredibly handsome one at that. With a confident smile, she opens the car door, sliding into the passenger seat. Gabriel is too startled to stop her. In the surveillance car, Joe suddenly sits up, panic flashing across his face.

"No! No, what is she doing?" Joe shouts, frantically looking at Amelia, who is just putting her phone away. Amelia's head snaps up, her eyes narrowing as she sees Maddy in the Aston Martin.

"Maddy, get out of the car! What the hell are you doing?" Inside Gabriel's car, Maddy, still chewing gum and maintaining her character, ignoring the voices in her ear, looks around the luxurious interior.

"Wow, mister, this is some kind of car. You look-in for a different kind of ride?" Gabriel, still reeling, stammers.

"What? No. No, I just, I lost my bearings for a minute when I saw you." Maddy, leaning in closer, purrs.

"Where are you going? Do you need some company?" She smiles suggestively, but Gabriel is clearly shaken.

"No, no, really, young lady." Gabriel insists, his voice firm. "I just need directions, that's all. Please, get out of my car." Maddy does not miss a beat, leaning back with a sly smile.

"No problem, honey. Just show me the money. I'll give you all the direction you need." Inside the surveillance car, Amelia's eyes widen in disbelief. She inhales deeply.

"No, it can't be." Muttering. "That son of a... Madison! GET OUT of that car this minute!" Her voice is sharp; there is a thread of panic woven through it. Joe looks at Amelia shocked by her urgent reaction and the fear in her voice.

"Do you know this guy?" Amelia nods her head frantically, her mind racing.

"YES! Maddy, did you hear me! I said Get out of the car. NOW!" Amelia does not wait for a response. She presses a switch on the dashboard, the unmarked car transforms as the siren blares and blue lights flash. She points frantically at the Aston Martin.

"JOE GO!... MOVE!" Joe's reaction is instant, he slams the car into gear, screeching across the traffic toward Gabriel's car. Almost before the car has stopped behind Gabriels, Amelia leaps out, charging over to the driver's side of the sports car, her gun already drawn. Inside Gabriel's car, the sound of the police siren immediately snaps him out of his daze. He looks in the rearview mirror, seeing the unmarked police car screeching to a halt behind him. The situation registers with him in an instant. He groans, covering his eyes with his hand. Amelia races around the car, her face set in a fierce scowl, pointing her gun through the now-open driver's window.

"Get out of the car, sir. NOW." She orders. Amelia's voice low and controlled. "You are under arrest." Gabriel, unable to suppress a small, incredulous smile, shakes his head slowly. He opens the door and steps out carefully, raising his hands in surrender. As he comes face to face with Amelia, their eyes lock, his filled with a mix of amusement and disbelief, hers blazing with anger. Gabriel lets out a quiet laugh, which only makes Amelia's temper flare more.

Maddy, meanwhile, jumps out of the car, clearly annoyed by the interruption. She stamps her foot then flounces over, her face a mixture of frustration and confusion. A short distance away, Spencer continues filming, completely unaware of the tension unfolding. Gabriel, standing calmly in front of Amelia, meets her furious gaze with a bemused smile.

"I think there's been a misunderstanding." Gabriel says lightly, but the humour in his voice only seems to fuel Amelia's anger. Amelia, her voice a dangerous whisper, retorts.

"You think!" Amelia can barely contain her anger as she gestures with her gun. "You have no idea what you've walked into." Gabriel, still holding his hands up, nods slightly, looking pointedly at her gun his expression more serious now.

"Perhaps not. But I would sure like to find out." Amelia does not lower her weapon, her eyes flicking to Maddy, who is standing close by, looking both annoyed and shocked by her mom's reaction.

"Maddy, go back to the car. NOW." Maddy opens her mouth to protest, something in her mother's tone makes her think twice. She huffs, turning on her heel and walking back toward the unmarked car, shooting Gabriel a glare as she passes. Gabriel looks at Amelia, his eyes softening.

"Hello, Mia. It is so good to see you again too." He stares at Amelia his gaze piercing and direct, Amelia is totally blindsided by the feelings that ricochet through her system. Maddy's mouth drops open in surprise, she spins around.

"What? Do you know this guy, Mom?" Gabriel, gapes stunned by Maddy's words, he repeats quietly.

"Mom...?" All of Amelia's senses are on high alert, she cannot afford to give anything away turning to Maddy, her expression hardening, a frisson of fear crosses her eyes, she can't look at Gabriel as she shifts uncomfortably.

"Maddy, get in the car with Joe. After a stunt like this, we are most definitely done here tonight." Maddy's eyes widen as she realizes the seriousness of her mother's tone.

"But Mom, we just got started!" Amelia's fury is barely contained. "Do as I say right now, Madison." Gabriel watches the exchange, utterly bewildered. He whispers again.

"Mom...." Amelia ignores Gabriel completely, her focus solely on Maddy. Maddy, sensing the intensity of the situation, does not argue further. She mutters all the way to the surveillance car, shooting her mother a sullen glare as she gets in. Joe stands by the car, looking at Amelia with concern. Amelia turns to him, her voice firm.

"Joseph, take her home. Now. Straight home. No detours." Joe nods, understanding the gravity of the situation.

"Yes, Ma'am." Gabriel, still bemused by the unfolding drama, quips.

"Yes, Ma'am? You're a cop now? The boss, Amelia?" Amelia turns her gaze on Gabriel, her scowl deepening.

"Surprised? Turn around." Gabriel does not move, still staring at Amelia as if trying to piece things together. Amelia realizes she is still holding her gun and quickly lowers it, holstering it with a sharp click. She steps forward, grabbing Gabriel by the arm, forcefully turning him around, pressing him against the gleaming white sports car. The unnecessary force of the movement surprises him, bringing them into sudden, intimate contact. The unexpected closeness makes Amelia's skin prickle, unsettling her even more. Gabriel, however, chuckles softly.

"Hey, gentle Mia. Can you at least tell me what I'm supposed to have done?" Annoyed by the familiar term of affection, Amelia responds curtly.

"Gabriel Sinclair, you are under arrest for soliciting a prostitute. Anything you say, can and will, be used… Against you in a court of law." Gabriel, still not entirely serious, shakes his head.

"What? Are you kidding me? Are you telling me your daughter is a prostitute?" He turns his head to try and look at Amelia. Amelia has her hand in the square of his back preventing him from turning around.

"Don't be absurd." Ignoring his protests, Amelia swiftly cuffs Gabriel's hands behind his back and begins frisking him for weapons. The action is routine for her, but the moment she touches him, a spark of electricity seems to pass between them. Gabriel's voice drops to a soft murmur.

"Well, that's one hell of a way to say hello. I always preferred champagne and strawberries myself; hey whatever works for you, Mia." Gabriel's direct mention of a memory from their first night together makes Amelia gasp. She snatches her hands away from him as if his skin has burnt her. The sudden rush of old memories, not to mention the physical closeness totally throws her normal ice cool composure, stepping back, she tries to regain her composure. Gabriel does not notice her reaction as he is still facing away, her mind races with the unexpected feelings that have surfaced. She snaps.

"Are you for real? You're still out here picking women up off the street? I thought you were different. Clearly, I was wrong." Gabriel turns around, his hands now cuffed, his expression is more serious. He steps closer, standing to his full height he squares his shoulders, his proximity making Amelia uncomfortable.

"No, Amelia, you are wrong. You know me better than that. You might not want to admit it, but we are not strangers." He pauses staring at her incredulously. "I almost crashed my car when I saw, Madison; did you say that's your daughter's name?" Amelia nods stiffly, the weight of his words pressing uncomfortably on her, suddenly his height and the breadth of his chest seem very close, she unconsciously takes a deep breath, trying to regain a semblance of order in her mind. Gabriel notices her body shift as he watches her reaction he continues.

"When I saw her, she nearly gave me a heart attack. She is the image of you the night we met." Aware that his presence is a shock for her, Gabriel leans back against the car, his gaze sweeping over Amelia. She straightens up, refusing to be intimidated, his words hit closer to home than she would like to admit. "I can't believe it has been 20 years, Mia. Seeing you here feels like it was just yesterday. You look amazing."

Amelia's breath catches as he speaks, the flood of feelings making it hard to maintain her composure. She shakes herself, grabbing Gabriel's arm again and pulling him towards the passenger side of the car. As she does, she notices that Joe and Maddy still have not moved, both gaping at her watching intently from the surveillance car. Impatiently, she waves at Joe to leave, at the same time pulling the earpiece from her own ear Amelia leaves it dangling around her neck resting on her chest. Realizing his mistake, Joe quickly starts the car, driving off he stops briefly to explain to Spencer what has happened before finally driving away. Amelia shoves Gabriel into the passenger seat, her movements brusque.

Gabriel is laughing softly to himself. "You know, I could call this police brutality if I wasn't enjoying it so much." Amelia slams the door, then pauses before walking around to open the driver's side, inhaling again she tries to catch her breath to steady herself. Inside the surveillance car, Joe and Maddy exchange glances, both bewildered by what they have overheard through their earpieces.

"What the hell's got into your mom?" Joe mutters. "I've never seen her like this." Maddy shakes her head, equally confused.

"No, I haven't either. I don't know who he is or what he did. I have never seen her this upset." Joe's expression shows his concern. "Come on, lets head home. Liv might remember who he is." Maddy suddenly sits up brightening.

"That's a great idea your mom's bound to know."

As Amelia stands next to Gabriel's car her face looks tense, flexing her shoulders she opens the driver's door, gripping the frame of the door tightly as the scent of expensive leather and aftershave hits her instantly filling her senses. Without thinking, she inhales deeply, momentarily thrown by the familiar smell, an echo from a long-buried memory. Gabriel's eyes are on her, he watches her every move, his gaze intense. The heat between them is palpable, Amelia's skin prickles she feels totally overwhelmed as once inside the car with the door now closed the atmosphere is private, intimate, charged, and dangerous. The car's luxurious interior blocking all the noise and interruptions from the street. Amelia and Gabriel find themselves alone for the first time in two decades.

Gabriel, clearly enjoying the situation, leans closer. "Well, this is an unexpected pleasure. Where are you taking me, Amelia?" Amelia turns in her seat, trying to mask her discomfort with forced politeness.

"The station." She says curtly. "Car keys, please?" Gabriel, a mischievous glint in his eye, replies.

"Sure, they're in my pocket." He nods towards his trouser pocket. Amelia sighs.

"Of course they are." Looking at him she realises as she has cuffed him, she has no other choice than to retrieve them herself. She reaches over, hesitating only momentarily as she must force her hand into his tight trouser pocket, she stretches her finger's acutely aware she is intimately searching inside Gabriel's pocket. Unable to find the keys easily, she has no choice but to dig deeper, her frustration mounting as Gabriel's grin widens. He leans forward slightly, trapping her hand between his thigh and groin as he whispers in a seductive gravelly voice.

"Other pocket." His warm breath sends a shiver down Amelia's spine. She pulls her hand free as if stung, trying to ignore the sudden sexual tension exploding between them. Amelia feels the taunt in Gabriels words, he is daring her to come closer, instinctively she takes the bait stepping into the trap, she leans across him to reach into his other trouser pocket. With Gabriel's hands cuffed behind him, his chest seems wider than Amelia remembered, it is forced forward, filling the space with so much of him, it brings them face-to-face and chest-to-chest. For a breathtaking moment, they are so close that the air between them evaporates leaving only static. Amelia's whole body feels charged. She stares at Gabriel.

They are so close their breathing begins to synchronise. Amelia's eyes flick to Gabriel's mouth, his lips velvety soft the memory of those lips now brought into sharp focus. Amelia subconsciously runs her tongue across her own mouth the action causing Gabriel to drop his gaze staring at her wet lips, his own breath hitches as he looks at her. Gabriel responds with unashamed arousal he groans softly; his voice filled with desire.

"My God, you're still as beautiful as I remember." Without thinking, he closes the small distance between them, kissing Amelia firmly on the mouth. Amelia's first instinct is to pull away, after a brief hesitation, she finds herself responding to the unexpected kiss, an intense wave of old feelings flooding back. The heated kiss is charged with the weight of unspoken words and unresolved emotions. Suddenly, Amelia's phone beeps loudly, snapping her back to reality. She jerks away from Gabriel, her heart pounding. In a flash of anger and confusion, she slaps him. The sting of the slap surprises them both, but it is Amelia who looks more affected. Gabriel shakes his head slightly, a rueful smile playing on his lips. Amelia presses the back of her hand to her mouth as if to somehow cover her own reaction.

"You'd strike a defenceless man?" Gabriel teases gently. Amelia glares at him, struggling to regain her composure.

"There is nothing defenceless about you, Gabriel. Now, where are the car keys?" Gabriel's smile widens in a breathtakingly sexy way.

"It's voice-activated, actually." Amelia scowls at him bemused and incredulous. Aroused in every way by the sudden erotic kiss she tries desperately to hold onto her power.

"What? Are you James Bond now?" She stares at the dashboard which looks more like an aircraft cockpit.

"Start!" Frustrated she shouts at the car. Nothing happens. Gabriel can barely contain his amusement. A deep chuckle rumbles in Gabriel's chest.

"You got to be polite. It's British." Amelia glares at him, exasperated. In the back of her mind memories of shared laughter and Gabriel's wicked sense of humour resonate unwelcome. Like a spectre hovering in her mind, the memories the sound awakens makes Amelia deeply uncomfortable, their shared sense of fun was the part of their relationship she had missed the most. Their laughter held such fondness without realising she winces at a pain in her chest his chuckle evokes.

"Seriously?" She stares at him trying desperately to bury the tide of feelings this man elicits from her. She then adds with forced politeness. "Start, please." Gabriel bursts out laughing, the sound deep, joyful and throaty, he is thoroughly enjoying her frustration. Amelia looks like she is about to explode she is beginning to lose her temper completely. Her voice drops, dangerously calm. "You know I carry a gun, Gabriel. It is loaded." Her voice is low the threat barely concealing her raw emotions.

"Okay, okay." Gabriel says, still chuckling he tries desperately to stop grinning at her sombre expression knowing he is deliberately creating friction, he cannot help his reaction to her. Especially hearing her use his name. "181099." The car roars to life, but Gabriel's next words hit Amelia like a punch.

"You do know what date that is?" Amelia stays silent, refusing to acknowledge him. "It's the day you were supposed to marry me." Gabriel says the sentence softly, but his words land exactly as he expects them too. Amelia turns in her seat to stare open mouthed at Gabriel, the impact of what he has just murmured in no way diminished by the gentleness of his tone. Her eyes flashing with deep, painful memories masked by a well-practiced defensive glare. She cannot speak, nothing could have prepared for his appearance, this encounter has overwhelmed her senses, she struggles to find a response finding it impossible to maintain eye contact with him, quickly she turns away, slamming the car into gear. The wheels screech as she speeds away, the car tearing down the road. It takes minutes before Amelia's grip on the wheel loosens enough for her to sit back in her seat. She is acutely aware that Gabriel's eyes are on her.

The power of the car is exceptional, handling like a racing car. Amelia has always loved the thrill of driving at speed she is an accomplished driver; Gabriel's car gives her the opportunity to channel her heightened reactions. Expertly she weaves through the traffic the rush of the acceleration mirroring her emotions and the adrenaline running through her veins. Amelia's phone buzzes, breaking the tension. She slows the car to read the message, her frown deepening as she checks the time. Without a word, she expertly makes a U-turn, heading back up the strip. Gabriel remains quiet, watching her closely as she seems lost in her own thoughts. It is, Gabriel who once again tries to break the tension.

"You know, you're still the most beautiful woman I've ever met." Amelia snorts aghast at the temerity of the man beside her, flashing him a quick, angry smile.

"Somehow, I doubt that." Gabriel tilts his head slightly, noticing her irritation.

"By the way, you do know I don't have my seatbelt on. Isn't that an offense?" Amelia had not even registered the noise that the seatbelt warning light flickering insistently on the dashboard was making. Her mind was trying desperately to keep hold of the reality that Gabriel had appeared once more into her life completely, as far as she was aware, out of the blue. Amelia shoots him a sharp look, her breath catching in her throat at the intensity of his stare.

"You always were a gambling man. You will have to take your chances with the airbag." Gabriel laughs once more a deep full sound that fills the car, clearly enjoying himself.

"I'm so glad you still have a sense of humour." He chuckles the sound rich and sexy, Amelia's face hardens, the echo of his laughter does strange things to her insides, she clenches her jaw, then bites her bottom lip a little too hard as Gabriel relaxes back, stretching out his legs. Her attention caught instantly by the movement, the sight of his strong muscular legs just inches from her own is deeply unsettling. Every move he makes seems to heighten her awareness, and he knows it. Trying to distract herself, Amelia switches on the stereo, only to have Prince's music blast out of the speakers. She quickly switches it off, glaring sideways at Gabriel when he laughs.

"Hey, forgive me." Gabriel says with a grin. "It is my first time driving in L.A. for a long time. I just wanted something to remind me of you." A deeply mischievous look in his eyes, they seem to dance with amusement annoying Amelia more.

"Why?" She snaps. Amelia's tone is incredulous, her voice sharp, and a little too high pitched she sounds almost desperate. Visibly shaking herself she snaps. "No, don't answer that. In fact, do not say another word, Gabriel." Gabriel, sensing her agitation, sits back in his seat, he unashamedly studies her silently, chiding himself, he has said too much, way too soon.

Amelia reaches for the stereo again moving the soundtrack to shuffle, this time, the song 'Lightning' by The Wanted starts to play. She turns it up trying to drown out the now loud insistent warning noise. She stares straight ahead the words of the song a perfect mirror for her frayed nerves, driving fast, trying to focus on the road and not on the man sitting beside her. The noise of the seat belt warning becomes too much for her anxiety to tolerate, not to mention the fact that she is in fact breaking the law. Spotting a lay-by, she pulls in sharply. Without a word she jumps out of the car briskly walking around to Gabriel's side of the car she pulls the handle. The door is locked. For a moment she places her hands palms down on the roof of the car and stares up at the night sky. Could this night get any worse.

What she has not realised, is that by resting her hands, on top the roof of the car, her jacket has parted, the tailored fabric lapels open revealing her delicate white silk blouse, Gabriel's expression is priceless. He gasps, given his place as a passenger his eyes are just inches away from her. Gabriel cannot help but stare. Amelia's breathing is heavy causing her chest to heave in agitation, the thin fabric inadvertently revealing a whisp of heavenly lace just below. Gabriel looks away, feeling like a teenager, caught peeking at a teacher. Shaking his head ruefully, he silently acknowledges that he is too old to feel like a kid again, the memories Amelia has stirred in his body are more powerful than he thought possible.

Completely unaware of the effect she is having on her passenger Amelia moves. Gabriel watches her from the passenger seat admiring the woman in front of him, a woman he had once known so intimately. This woman however was feisty and fierce, older, wiser and way more confident. Gabriel could feel his pulse respond, his body betraying just how instantly attracted to her he still was. He had to calm down or this was going to derail all his carefully laid plans, he slowly took a deep breath, this was not at all what he had expected. She was still as sexy as she ever been, only now he was in real trouble, as she was, after all, practically a stranger. Wryly a smile tugged at the corners of his charming mouth, not for long though. She was the reason he was here. Amelia was the one he had come in search of; he had been planning this for weeks. This most unexpected development was more than he could ever have expected.

Shaking herself Amelia clenched her fists feeling her nails bite into the palms of her hands, the sharp pain just enough to redirect her focus, steeling herself she walked back to the driver's door. Climbing in again wordlessly reaching across Gabriel for his belt. Once again close enough to kiss him, her eyes flash like fire silently warning him that any movement towards her would elicit a fierce response, she can feel the heat coming from his body, it makes her own achingly aware of him. Gabriel bites his lip, holding his breath as a wave of Amelia's warm sensual aroma invades his nostrils making his body respond to her closeness in a way he had long since forgotten. Once his belt is secured correctly in place, she silently sits back in her seat calmly putting on her own safety belt she deliberately presses the indicator, checking the mirrors she pulls out into the traffic, her countenance, collected and professional, a perfect veil for the turmoil currently wreaking havoc in her system. Gabriel slowly allows the air to leave his lungs as he adjusts himself in his seat, the handcuffs biting into the flesh of his wrists a welcome pain, enough of a distraction to ease his errant thoughts. As Amelia drives, she is acutely aware that Gabriel is still watching her, for once, he says nothing. He silently revels in her ability to handle his car, feeling the reaction in his body to her as the intoxicating energy created by their chemistry, the music, and the cars powerful speed, builds like static.

Amelia's mind reals at what has transpired in the past hour. Their brief reunion, fraught with old emotions and unresolved tension, had left her pulse racing, her mind vulnerable, and her body defiant. There was no way she could have prepared herself for seeing Gabriel again, nor could she have allowed for the possibility of the heady reaction she felt for him. For that meeting to have happened when Maddy was there watching, was Amelia's worst fear realised, the thought of Maddy was instantly sobering.

She had done everything possible to avoid something like this creating havoc in her carefully controlled life. Amelia's errant musings cause her slim, delicate fingers to grip the steering wheel tightly, her thoughts totally preoccupying her attention leaving Gabriel free to study her from the passenger seat. Amelia's nerves get the better of her as she absent-mindedly begins to chew her soft full lip her anxiety at Gabriel's proximity bubbling in her chest making her heartbeat faster. Glancing across at him Gabriel's expression was unreadable, his quiet observation of her somehow now seemed more unnerving for her than his cheeky flirting. Amelia immediately grasped onto that thought. Why, on earth would he flirt with her. It had been 20 years since she had left him, he had every right to demand to know why she had run. The cold stark memory sliced through her mind making her shudder imperceptibly. That was far too dangerous a place in her thoughts to visit now. Amelia's skin pricked as the hairs on her arms stood proud her body reacting with intensity as one of her darkest shadows threatened to step towards the light. She could not allow that to happen now. There was no way she was ready to tread near those memories or that time, memories that were loaded with emotions, feelings she had buried for two decades, and she was in no mood to dig them up tonight.

Finally, they had arrived. Amelia's relief was palpable as she pulled the car over outside a large, old building. A disturbance on the sidewalk catching both their attention. A young Latin American woman was in an intense argument with a nasty-looking, heavily tattooed white man. The car's sudden stop interrupted the argument, and the man's slimy smile redirected towards Gabriel's car breaks the flow of the exchange. A small, discreet sign on the wall reads 'The Cartwright-Sinclair Foundation.' Amelia unfastened her seatbelt, turning to Gabriel, she orders him.

"Stay here, Gabriel. I mean it, don't move." Gabriel nods silently, leaning back in his seat to get a better view of what is happening, his attention instantly focused on the sign. There it was, imprinted on a brass plate, the evidence that she had not forgotten him. Gabriel's gut twisted as he swallowed hard trying not to allow an old wave of intense sadness to envelop him. They had lost so many years. A bitter lump formed momentarily in his throat, almost taking his breath away, Gabriel softened his shoulders, closing his eyes he willed himself to release the inevitable emotions that he had known would arise the moment he saw her again.

Amelia was out of the car in a flash, momentarily forgetting her passenger, switching instantly into full police mode her focus now on the vulnerable woman in front of her. Without hesitation, she stepped between the arguing couple, trying to mediate. The man sensing an opportunity suddenly pushed the young woman, causing

Amelia to react with force, adrenaline coursing through her body as she pushed him hard against the brick wall, twisting his arm behind his back, her reflexes immediate and calculated. Gabriel watching from the car is unable to help, gasping as he watches Amelia from the sidelines, his awareness spikes at the potential danger not to mention his instinctive desire to protect her. Amelia's emotions were running high she was in fight and flight. This however came as second nature to Amelia it is what she had trained for, using the intense energy in her body she easily keeps the surprised man under control. Once he has calmed down and agreed to walk away Amelia releases him with a warning. Witnessing the scene Gabriel silently chides himself for not giving her enough credit for her knowledge or her professionalism. He expelled the breath he had been holding realising Amelia was more than capable of managing the situation. Taking control Amelia sends the young woman inside the building before turning her full attention to the arrogant young man who eyes her appreciatively. She spins him around, giving him a verbal lashing before sending him on his way. The man saunters off looking a little ruffled he shrugs nonchalantly with a cocky grin, disappearing around the corner.

Amelia looks back at Gabriel, mouthing the command. "Stay there." Nodding, Gabriel remains with his uncomfortable thoughts in the car. His body and his emotions all on high alert, he needed a moment alone to regain a level of control again. The realisation that he could not help is sobering. Seeing her like this he acknowledges the fact that everything about their meeting has left him in no doubt whatsoever of his feelings, seeing her in action has left him even more hot under the collar and deeply turned on. The shock of seeing her so unexpectedly, then having her so close to him has completely flawed him. Now to watch her in action, wow he had to calm down. Shaking his head he could still smell her perfume. The thought of her lips and her reaction to him was just as he remembered; that alone was enough to take any rational thought off the table. She aroused him more by just a look than any other woman he had ever met. Gabriels's brow furrowed in deep thought his mind racing as he had watched her control the situation. What had he expected? This evening had so far been a million miles away from the carefully planned rendezvous he had so painstakingly organised.

Right on que, Amelia reappeared at the door this time with an older woman. They exchanged a brief, affectionate kiss on the cheek, Amelia watched as the older woman locked the door, waving as she returned to the car. Amelia looking troubled as she opened the car door to get back in. Gabriel's voice is soft, his tone one of concern.

"Are you okay?" A tight smile crossed her mouth; her expression though was unreadable.

"Okay, Mr. Bond, let's go." Gabriel repeated the numbers without hesitation; the car starting smoothly. Amelia moved the car easily into the traffic driving on autopilot, Gabriel watching her closely, clearly wanted to say more, aware of the words about to burst from Gabriel's mouth she cuts him off before he can.

"Not a word, Gabriel. Do not say a word."

Chapter 5

The LA Police Station. Outside the police headquarters the Aston Martin screeches to a halt, drawing the attention of two young, uniformed officers who pause to admire the sleek impressive car. They exchange surprised glances when they see Amelia jump out of the driver's seat her face flushed, her body on full alert.

"Nice ride, Ma'am." One of the rookie officers' comments, clearly impressed. Seeing her strained expression the officers stand straighter suddenly aware they are in front of a senior officer, despite Amelia's obvious flustered appearance. Amelia nods, offering a tight smile as she rounds the car to open the now unlocked passenger door for Gabriel. Swinging both his legs out of the car, standing up in front of Amelia, towering over her he looks down into her confused eyes grinning. Flexing his shoulders Gabriel winks at the younger men, his arms still restrained by the police cuffs, his confinement making his arms ache. He steps away from the car so that Amelia can shut the door, the smile on his face making him look ridiculously handsome. Clearly Gabriel is enjoying this way more than Amelia, he is in a good mood, much to Amelia's annoyance, she slams the door. This does not look like a usual arrest, the younger officer's attention is not discreet as they watch one of their bosses, finding the interaction between Gabriel and Amelia a source of amusement. Amelia is instantly conscious of the unwanted attention.

"You know, Gabriel." Amelia says, her voice laced with frustration. "We take soliciting very seriously in this city." Gabriel laughs lightly. He softly responds looking at her his eyes sparkling mischievously.

"Yes, I completely agree but I did not do anything illegal, Amelia. By your own admission, your daughter is not a prostitute she was obviously acting tonight." He pauses leaning towards her, his voice is deep, rich, and husky. "So, would you mind telling me exactly why you brought me here? Not that I haven't enjoyed the ride." He pauses risking a comment designed to make her react Gabriel softly continues. "Being driven by you always was one of my greatest pleasures.... You are such a talented driver."

Amelia is painfully aware of the double meaning that Gabriel's taunting words are laced with. A very private erotic joke reminding her clearly of their lovemaking in cars. One of the officers' coughs making Amelia embarrassingly aware of the curiosity in the looks of the two young officers still lingering nearby, listening to every word. Clenching her jaw, she grabs hold of Gabriel's sleeve, impatiently turning him around, then silently marches him up the steps into the precinct, trying to maintain her composure.

As they pass through the precinct doors, the uncomfortable realization hits her; what is she doing with Gabriel? He is right. She has no legitimate reason for bringing him here, all she had wanted to do was get him as far away from Maddy as possible, but what now? Her usual cool composure slips, she finds herself looking for an escape, somewhere to collect her thoughts, better yet she needed somewhere to hide for a moment. In the bustling lobby of the police station, Amelia spots a young officer.

"Sergeant Porter, would you please take Mr. Sinclair here up to Interview Room One for me? Tell them I will be up in a couple of minutes." Without hesitation the officer reacts to her clipped command.

"Yes, Ma'am." The young woman replies, leading Gabriel towards the stairs. As soon as they are out of sight, Amelia makes a beeline for the downstairs bathroom, the same one Maddy was getting ready in earlier. She stands in front of the mirror, leaning heavily on the sink. The cool water she splashes on her face does little to calm her racing thoughts. Staring blindly at her reflection, she mutters.

"What the hell am I doing?" Suddenly, a flashback hits her. The scene shifts to twenty years earlier, in a luxurious bathroom and dressing room, the height of elegance and wealth. A younger Amelia stands before a grand mirror, her hair wet from a shower, a bathrobe wrapped around her. Hanging on the long mirror is an exquisite white Cinderella-style wedding dress, complete with shoes and a veil. A housekeeper flits in and out, fussing over the details, smiling warmly at Amelia, who looks oddly out of place and uncomfortable. "Do you know where Mr. Sinclair is?" Amelia asks the young woman, her quiet voice tinged with nervousness.

"Yes madam." She eagerly replies with a bright smile. "He is in the lobby. Do you want me to call him for you? You do know you really should not see him before the wedding. It is bad luck."

Amelia returns the smile, albeit shyly. "No, no, that is okay. I just wanted to get a little fresh air, thank you." As Amelia moves to leave, she passes by the dress, pausing to admire the delicate lace. The housekeeper, noticing her, says.

"It is such a beautiful dress, simply fit for a princess. You are going to look so beautiful." Amelias breath catches in her throat, instead of joy, a wave of sadness crosses her face. Her smile fades, and without another word, she rushes out of the bathroom. In the corridor outside, Amelia runs along the plush carpet, her bare feet making no sound. She reaches a landing at the top of a magnificent staircase suddenly she stops abruptly. Below her, in the grand lobby, a much younger Gabriel is having a heated discussion on the phone, dressed casually in sweatpants and a top. Below her in the lobby, Gabriel paces as he speaks on the phone.

"Henry, I know you have my best interests at heart, but this is my wedding day. I have already told you; I don't want a prenup." Amelia freezes at the mention of the contentious document. Gabriel pauses listening, he seems a little frustrated by the comments. "I trust Amelia completely. She is not going anywhere. In any case, where would she go? This is her life now. That is all ancient-history." He stops once more, then clearly irritated, continues.

"Henry, I do not need you or anyone else to tell me who she was. I know exactly who she was and what she used to do. She is not that person anymore. Do you really think I would be marrying her if she was… This is all she has ever wanted, this is Amelia's dream, her happy ever after. I can promise you; I am all Amelia wants. End of story." Gabriel sighs deeply, clearly exasperated. "Look, if it is going to make you feel better, I'll look at the papers. Send them over. There is plenty of time before the service starts. It isn't until three."

He hangs up, frustration etched on his face, completely unaware that Amelia has overheard every word. He walks to the front window, rubbing his face, running his hand through his hair, he sighs. Needing to clear his head, Gabriel pulls open the front door stepping outside for a run, breathing in the crisp autumn air he shakes himself as he sets off at a pace. At the top of the landing, Amelia sinks to the floor, the weight of Gabriel's words hitting her like a ton of bricks. Tears stream down her cheeks as she struggles to process what she has heard. Moments later, she wipes them away with the back of her hand and stands up. Determination replaces her earlier sadness as she heads back to the bedroom. In their elegant bedroom, Amelia frantically grabs a holdall from the closet then begins stuffing her belongings into it. She is clearly preparing to run away. Pausing only to grab a selection of sentimental items from the nightstand, including a bottle of Gabriel's cologne. She opens the bottle, inhaling deeply, and closes her eyes, a vision of Gabriel flashing in her mind. Shaking herself, she throws the cologne into the bag, the fear of being caught spurs her on as she doubles her pace. Amelia grabs a pen and paper from the nightstand and hurriedly scribbles a note.

Now dressed in jeans, a shirt, and a jacket, she moves to the closet, where she opens a small safe. She punches in the combination, opens the door, and pulls out a large wad of cash and her passport. She takes half, leaving the rest in the safe, there she places the note on top of it. Her gaze falls on the stunning solitaire diamond engagement ring on her left hand. With a pained expression, she pulls the ring off carefully placing it on top of the note. She stares at it for a moment a look of deep sadness mixed with regret clouds her young face before closing the safe door.

Back in the present day, Amelia stares blankly at her reflection in the police station bathroom mirror, an older wiser version of the stunning young woman she once was, the emotions of the flashback still fresh in her mind. She wipes away a tear and washes her hands, taking a deep breath to steady herself she chides herself, who was she trying to kid, right now wisdom was the last thing she was feeling, it was the old familiar regret, guilt and shame that was always lurking just below the surface. Just then, the bathroom door opens, and a young female officer, Stacey, walks in. The young officer smiles at her, the warm smile fading slightly as she sees Amelia's less than composed appearance.

"Are you ok Ma'am?" Making a valiant effort to pull herself together, Amelia straightens up, her voice firm the smile she gives is forced.

"Yes, yes, thanks, Stacey. I'm fine." Throwing her tissue in the bin, squaring her shoulders, Amelia straightens her jacket, standing to her full height she shakes herself as one would if you were about to face a worthy opponent. With her composure regained, she strides out of the bathroom, ready to face Gabriel, the man who remained the only one she has ever truly loved. Marching determinedly through the reception area of the police station lobby, Amelia's heels click sharply against the floor. Gripping the stairwell banister, taking the stairs two at a time she hurries up to the first floor, her mind racing as she heads straight for Interview Room One. Without acknowledging the detectives already assembled in the department, she crossed the room, closing the door behind her with a firm click. Inside the interview room, Amelia starts pacing, her frustration evident as she glares at Gabriel. Barely missing a beat, turning all her emotional intensity on him, in her best interrogation voice she demanded to know the truth.

"What are you doing here, Gabriel?" Gabriel, seated and calm, hesitates for a moment before calmly answering. His smile faint but noticeable he speaks softly his tone deceptively passive.

"I was going to ask you the same question, Amelia. Is there any chance you could take these cuffs off? I can assure you I'm not a flight risk." Amelia balks at his words, feeling heat rise to her face as her cheeks flush a soft pink, once again she felt her composure start to crumble. It was as if Gabriel could read her mind, he seemed to sense her turmoil. On autopilot she pulled the handcuff key from her pocket, crossing the interview room she walked behind him. As she leant down to unlock the cuffs, Gabriel half-turned in his chair, his chin brushing against her shoulder. Amelia inhaled sharply, caught off guard by his proximity. Gabriel's voice is soft, a whisper. "I'm here because you brought me here."

Pulling back instantly Amelia steps away from him, starring at his shoulders incredulously her mind spinning. Bewildered she blurts out. "No, Gabriel, that, is not what I meant. Why are you in L.A.?" Gabriel sighs, his tone shifting. Now was most definitely not the time for the truth.

"I'm here to see someone, Amelia." Pausing, his eyes study her, Gabriel wanted to gauge her reaction. Mischievously he quietly dropped another line perfectly timed to disturb the professional composure that she is desperately trying to hang on to.

"You know, I remember the last time you put me in handcuffs. I seem to recall we had an especially good night then…. What about you, Mia? Do you ever think about us? What could have been?"

Amelia's discomfort is glaringly evident. She almost chokes at his brazen reference to their past, intensely passionate relationship her already flushed cheeks go a deeper shade of red as she cannot help recalling that particularly erotic memory that Gabriel is so candidly referring too. He is acutely aware that all Amelia's senses like his own are on high alert, her pupils dilated, and her breathing is shallow all telltale signs that adrenaline is coursing through her system.

"You can hardly expect me not to remember that night Mia. You have had me restrained like this for the last 30 minutes. I am only human after all.... Seeing you like this.... Wow it feels like no time has passed. I don't think I have been this.... How can I put it, aroused in 20 years."

Amelia gawps at Gabriel. No one in her life spoke to her like this. In fact, she went out of her way to avoid intimacy wherever possible. Gabriel was breaking all her rules and making her whole body respond to him just by bringing up their shared history. A realisation came like lightning through her mind. She feared him. Not because he could do anything dangerous, it was far worse than that. Gabriel wielded a power no other man had. He had the power to make her feel feelings she had tried to avoid at any cost. Trying to deliberately avoid his gaze Amelia moves abruptly, walking across the room to the door, her mind made up, she must take back a level of control. She opens the door, announcing in a loud voice that echoes through the department.

"I am terribly sorry for the misunderstanding Mr. Sinclair, I apologise that I have inconvenienced you. It was my mistake. I thought you were someone else. You are free to leave." Standing by the doorway with her arms folded defensively Amelia waits for Gabriel to take his cue. Gabriel taking his time to stand, watches her with an unreadable expression. A resigned smile playing on his lips as he approached the door, where Amelia waits, now holding it open.

"As I said, I do apologise for the trouble I have caused you. I hope you have a pleasant evening. Enjoy the rest of your stay." Amelia's words are clipped, her voice strained. Gabriel stopping directly in front of her, lowers his head slightly to speak softly.

"What exactly are you apologizing for, Amelia?" Instead of answering him, desperate to put distance between them, she turns away quickly, only to find herself face-to-face with Jack, who had just appeared behind her. Catching her in a familiar embrace the moment allows Amelia's tension to ease visibly as she recognises his friendly face. His smile broadening as he looked over her shoulder at Gabriel.

"Well, if it isn't our old friend, Gabriel Sinclair.... Hello, Gabriel. What an unexpected pleasure. How have you been?" Jack's tone is warm and friendly as he reaches across Amelia to shake Gabriel's outstretched hand. Amelia looked at him incredulously as if he had completely lost the plot. While Jack simply ignored her obvious discomfort and instead continued.

"Hello Jack. You are looking well. Life must be good." Returning Jack's smile with genuine pleasure Gabriel looks pleasantly surprised by Jacks sudden appearance. Amelia instantly seizes the opportunity to end the exchange. Feigning an adoring look at Jack, she deliberately interrupts before Gabriel has the chance to answer. Smiling meaningfully at Jack her eyes widen as she stares at her friend.

"Jack, darling... Gabriel was just leaving. I have detained him long enough this evening." Looking at Jack imploringly Amelia's eyes search Jack's for understanding. However, Jack looked a little non plussed, releasing her he steps back, pausing for a moment he considers Amelia questioningly, as if trying to gauge her sudden shift in persona.

"So, I've heard... 'darling'. Joseph and Maddison came home. It seems, that they couldn't wait to grill Olivia." Pausing his eyes move from Amelia to Gabriel, adding in a steady tone. "Olivia wanted me to invite you both for dinner." Amelias' mouth instantly dropped open in shock. In a pitiful attempt to quell the scream threatening to erupt from her chest she shut her mouth with a snap, a small squeak escaping her panic-stricken face. Before she could stop herself, she demanded.

"What? How did Liv know I was with..." Reaching his hand forward towards Amelia Jack picks up the earpiece still hanging around her neck. He raised an eyebrow at her.

"Apparently, Joseph and Maddison said they overheard some of your conversation through this, I presume?" Amelia looks completely mortified at the thought of Maddy overhearing her conversation, she unconsciously grabs hold of the earpiece, trying to recall everything she might have said in front of Gabriel.

Whispering to herself. "Oh no, I forgot all about this." Frowning, a deep crease crosses her brow as she pulled at the earpiece, glancing at Gabriel she could see that he was still smiling broadly. Wordlessly, she glared menacingly at Jack. Then seizing on a thought, she snapped a little too sharply. "No. No, Jack. Gabriel can't. He's meeting someone. He wouldn't want to come for dinner anyway." Gabriel sensing her desire to escape, interrupted her with a smile.

"Actually, Amelia, I would love to. That is thoughtful of you, Jack. My meeting's tomorrow, so if that is alright with you... I wouldn't want to impose, though, at such short notice." Grinning Jack responded.

"Not at all, Gabriel. We would love you to come over, wouldn't we, Amelia? Besides, if I went home without you tonight, Olivia would not be a happy woman." Looking intrigued Gabriel plays along with Jack, all the while knowing full well that Amelia would try her level best to find an excuse to avoid prolonging the evening.

"Olivia's your wife?" Smiling warmly at the mention of his wife's name Jack replied.

"Olivia is my second wife. Amelia has known her for a long time, they were best friends, if you remember. You might recall her as Liv." Gabriel looked suitably surprised. Jack shrugged. "It's a long story. I'm sure you will hear all about it over dinner."

"Sounds fascinating." Gabriel replied. "Thank you for the invite, Jack." Taking Gabriel at his word Jack seemed to want to break the spell that Amelia seemed to have fallen under as she had become completely still. Clapping his hands together Jack seemed delighted with the new arrangements.

"Shall we go?" Jack wasn't waiting for an argument from Amelia he appeared determined to ignore her feelings by continuing with the plans for the evening. Amelia however was not at all sure what was happening around her, she felt like she was having an out of body experience, one in which she had lost complete control of the situation. Trying to save herself, Amelia desperately started to backpedal.

"Actually, Jack, you go on without me. I am on duty tonight. I have so much to finish off before I leave." Desperate to escape Amelia started to back away; however, Jack was having none of it.

"No need to rush off, Amelia. I was just catching up with Jerry." Turning to Gabriel Jack continues. "Jerry is Amelia's boss." Jack looks pointedly at Amelia. "Jerry says you aren't supposed to be here at all. Apparently, Amelia your leave started this morning. So, if you don't mind bringing Gabriel with you, I have got to pick up one or two things for Olivia on the way home for supper." As Jack speaks, he is already turning, heading toward the stairs, waving over his shoulder. Leaving Amelia, no option but to follow him with Gabriel. "Supper will be in half an hour, so get your skates on, Amelia." Amelia, calling after him, tries valiantly to stop his exit.

"But Jack..." Without hesitating Jack disappeared down the stairs, whistling merrily as he walked away, her protests apparently falling on deaf ears. Leaving Amelia all but stamping her foot in frustration. Turning on her heel, she glared accusingly at Gabriel, who frustratingly looked clearly amused by the entire situation although he couldn't quite look at her.

"I don't know what you're smiling about." She snapped. "You're the one in for a grilling tonight from Liv when she gets hold of you." With a triumphant smile, she turned her back on him then marching into her office, she shut the door firmly behind her. Gabriel sighed, the amusement fading as a weary expression crossed his face. He perched on a nearby desk, folding his arms as he watched Amelia through the glass. His attention drawn to the name on her door, DCI Amelia Cartwright. A curious expression on his face, intrigued by something, standing up, re-energized Gabriel looked for an officer.

"Excuse me, detective. Could you tell me where the restrooms are?" The detective nodded.

"On the ground floor, near the duty desk, sir." The officer grinned at Gabriel, all the detectives in the department had been watching the exchange with keen interest, it seemed that their boss had met her match in her recent arrest.

"Thanks." Gabriel replied. "Would you be kind enough to let your boss know where I am, so she doesn't have me arrested again?" The detective chuckled.

"Sure thing." In her office, Amelia was standing behind her desk, pretending to be busy, irritated by her own inability to shake her curiosity about where Gabriel is headed. As soon as he is out of sight, she opened the door calling to the young detective to come over.

"The gentleman's gone to use the restrooms." The detective pre-empts her question. "He said he would meet you downstairs. Is everything all right, boss? You don't seem yourself at all." Amelia forces a tight smile.

"Thanks, Tony. I'm fine, really. Just tired." Amelia's words sound vague as she looks towards the stairwell.

"You need to go home and get some rest." Tony smiled a look of concern in his eyes. "It's your big day tomorrow. You want to look your best." Amelia's smile became softer, more genuine, though tinged with weariness.

"I don't know what all the fuss is about. It's only a little award." Tony looked surprised by Amelia's dismissal of the commendation.

"Yeah, right. They don't go to this much trouble for a little award. Me and the boys will be there, cheering you on. We've all rented our tuxes. I've even got new shoes." Smiling Amelia felt instantly touched by the sentiment, she can't help but respond to the genuine support her officers have shown her.

"Save a dance for me, then." Finding some comfort in the light conversation with a member of her team Amelia was steeling herself for the evening ahead. As she lingered Tony continued unaware of his boss's confused emotions.

"You bet." He replied, enthusiastically. "I'm first on the list." The young officer grinned at Amelia.

"There's a list?" Amelia is the one to sound surprised, raising a questioning eyebrow.

"Sure is." His grin now spreading broadly across his face. "It's not every day you get to dance with the most beautiful lady in town, especially when she's the boss." Amelia laughs, enjoying the relief the banter offers her in the moment. She picks up her bag and keys from the desk, slinging the bag over her shoulder. As she heads downstairs, a chorus of "Goodnight" and "See you tomorrow, boss" echoes behind her.

Chapter 6

In the lobby of the police station, Gabriel leant casually against the front desk, chatting with the night sergeant, a middle-aged woman who seemed genuinely amused by his charm. They share a light-hearted joke, as they laugh, the sergeant shuffles her paperwork, suddenly becoming more professional when she spots Amelia stepping into the reception area. Amelia's expression is unreadable; her presence immediately changing the atmosphere. Gabriel notices and smiles at her, the easy grin still on his face.

"All set?" His question familiar, his tone light. "Hmm." Amelia's reply is noncommittal, her tone clipped. Outside the police station, they descend the front steps together. As they reach the sidewalk, Gabriel stops, turning towards her he gently catches hold of Amelia's arm, halting her in her tracks. "Mia." He begins softly. "I know you are not comfortable with this, but we do need to talk. Can we go somewhere after dinner?" Amelia sighs, turning to face him with a look of resignation.

"Really, Gabriel, after all this time, what could you and I possibly have to talk about? We talked our relationship to death back then. I don't see how talking about it now will change anything." Studying her intently, Gabriel's eyes search hers.

"Mia, you, and I are vastly different people now. I know we are both older and wiser. We've both lived full lives, haven't we? But there are things I need to know, things I want to say to you. You never gave me the chance, Mia. You just ran away." Once again flawed by his directness Amelia cannot help staring at him, caught off guard by the honest vulnerability in his voice. Her gaze drops to her hand still resting in Gabriels firm grip, all the strength seeming to leave her she tried hesitantly to pull her arm free. Gabriel sensing her conflicted feelings tightened his grip slightly.

"Let me go, Gabriel." Amelia's voice a mix of pleading and frustration. "And please, stop calling me Mia."

"Not a chance, Amelia." Gabriel responded, his tone firm but gentle. "You think I am just going to let you walk away again? Sorry, Mia. But no, it is not going to happen. If you prefer Amelia, I'm okay with that for now." Gabriel relaxed his grip on her arm. Feeling the release in the tension of his grip Amelia immediately pulls away. Without hesitation Gabriel reacts, suddenly pulling her closer, holding her tightly against him. The unexpected move taking her breath away. For a moment, they are locked in a tense, intimate embrace. In a low, almost hushed voice, Gabriel whispers in her ear.

"I still want you, Amelia, but I need some answers too." Starring at him wide eyed, Amelia is shocked by the intensity in his eyes. The world around them seeming to disappear, the spell broken when a young officer passing by quips.

"Get a room, Ma'am." Stepping backwards Gabriel looks at the officer, a wry smile tugging at his lips, while Amelia seems slightly dazed. Shaking her head as if trying to clear her thoughts she looks ruffled. Gabriel walks to the car and opens the door for her, a knowing smile lingers on his face.

"I think I'll drive this time." Gabriel's words, murmured under his breath are for her ears only; he is fully aware that he is causing emotions in Amelia she is desperately trying to keep a lid on. Nodding wordlessly, she is too shaken to argue. Amelia gratefully sinks into the soft leather seat, feeling the tension in her body start to dissipate. Gabriel climbs into the driver's seat, once again the air between them crackles with the intensity created by a myriad of unspoken emotions. Sylvia's words echo in Amelia's mind, making her wonder how she got here. Gabriel reaches across the space between them, gently he caresses her cheek, his thumb grazing her lips. His touch sends a shiver down her spine, when he reaches for her face taking it gently in his hands, Amelia does not pull away she turns towards him as Gabriel leans in looking deeply into her troubled eyes, she feels her resolve slipping.

"Seeing you like this today, I think I'm still in love you, Amelia." Gabriel speaks softly; his voice filled with raw emotion. "I think I always have been. You broke my heart.... It took time but I understand why you ran away. Believe it or not, I am glad you left when you did." Amelia gasps shocked by his honesty, as she opens her mouth to protest, Gabriel simply silences her with a kiss, passionate, sensual and deep, filled with years of pent-up emotion. She does not resist; she can't. The sadness, the pain, everything they have held back, erupts between them. For a moment, nothing else matters. Memories flood both their systems as forgotten emotions, passion, loss, and grief surface between them, the connection is undeniable. It has been pulling them towards this moment all evening. The tension between them a sweet pain.

A discreet tapping on the driver's window, pulls them back to reality. Gabriel breaks the kiss, Amelia, dazed and disoriented, sinks lower in her seat. A senior officer stands outside the car, wagging his finger at them, while several other colleagues on the sidewalk smile and laugh. Amelia's face flushes crimson wanting to disappear, Gabriel simply smiles nodding at the officer and starts the engine, the powerful car roaring to life. Amelia sits up, trying to regain her composure.

"I don't know what's got into me." Bemused Amelia mutters to herself. Gabriel glances at her, raising an eyebrow suggestively, which only makes her embarrassment deepen she looks away, a small grin tugging at her lips. The moment is disturbed when an alarm starts beeping loudly in the car. The mood shifts instantly as Gabriel's expression changes from playful to serious. Quickly switching emotional gears, his face is clouded with concern, as if doused with cold water. He places a reassuring hand on her arm.

"Amelia, would you mind taking your own car? I have got to go to the hotel urgently. Can I meet you at Jack's house?" Amelia, still trying to gather her composure, looks up, her focus now on

Gabriels's face, she scans his expression for signs of rejection, doubt instantly clouding her hazel eyes. Gabriel's face gives nothing away his expression intense, she nods silently. Opening the car door, she steps out onto the sidewalk, feeling like she is on autopilot. Amelia shuts the door behind her hesitating as Gabriel opens the window.

"Amelia, I need the address." Handing her his phone he waits for her to take it from him. "Can you give me Jack's number and address, just in case I get lost? I seem to get in trouble here when I ask for directions in this town."

Amelia, still a little dazed, takes his phone entering the details automatically, as she hands it back to him, she stares into his eyes searching for a sign of dismissal or worse still revenge. He gazes up at her without a trace of negativity in fact quite the opposite, Gabriel looks positively, devastatingly handsome wearing a soft smile that softens his chiselled features. Amelia feels utterly confused, her mind a whirlwind of emotions. Gabriel takes the phone but keeps hold of her hand, his gaze never leaving hers.

"Thank you." His tone is firm, his voice gentle and sincere he stares into her confused eyes trying to reassure her he adds before she can turn away. "Amelia, I do need to talk to you later. Don't you go disappearing on me. I know where to find you this time." Releasing her hand he gives her a sexy smile before setting off. Amelia watched his car disappear down the street, feeling a deep sense of loss. Standing starring after the car, time seems to stand still. Moments pass, Amelia stands completely stationary, a shiver passes down her spine as her awareness kicks in, she shakes herself realising that she is looking bereft in front of colleagues she respects, the sound of a siren jolting her back to reality. Suddenly the realization that she has left her bag in Gabriel's car surfaces; she looks at the dark night sky annoyed at her own confusion. Now she would have to find another way to get to Jack's house as her bag contained her car keys, phone, everything. Frustrated, she turns and huffs walking back towards the precinct. Suddenly another deeply disturbing thought occurred to her; she could run. A familiar sinking feeling entered her stomach reminding her of the night she had left. Swallowing hard the thought made Amelia shiver. All these thoughts were unwelcome, the passion, the intensity, the loss. Amelia did not feel remotely able to deal with any of it. Was this her punishment for what she had done? That upsetting thought sliced through her clouded mind, what if Gabriel went to Jack's house and Maddy was there. Suddenly an inexplicable feeling of pure panic gripped her stomach the thought of her daughter seeing Gabriel again without her being present making her feel instantly fearful. Was Gabriel testing her. Was he trying to see if she would run again or worse still, did he suspect something. That thought alone sent her entire system into a different gear. Amelia headed back to the precinct her footsteps far quicker than her heels allowed for as she practically sprinted up the steps.

In Gabriel's car, he glanced into the rearview mirror, watching Amelia grow smaller in the distance. Driving away, the song 'Remember the time' by Michael Jackson started playing softly on the stereo. The sight of Amelia in the mirror triggers a montage of memories from Gabriel's past that run through his mind as the distance between them increases. Gabriel clearly recalls the first time he met Amelia, the laughter they shared, their intense physical attraction to one another, the love they felt, and the pain of losing her. His mind takes him back to a memory indelibly imprinted in its recesses. The memory of twenty years earlier in the bedroom that is the same one as Amelia's flashback earlier. Gabriel, dressed in his wedding tails, storms into the luxurious room. His expression is a mix of anger and despair as he takes in the remnants of Amelia's hurried departure. He opens the safe and finds her engagement ring resting on top of a letter. Picking up the ring, he stares at it for a long moment before placing it back in the safe. Opening the letter, his eyes scan its contents, his expression hardening with each word. As he finishes, he crumples the letter in his fist and storms into the bathroom. Seeing her wedding dress hanging by the mirror, Gabriel's anger erupts. Grabbing a bottle of perfume from the counter and hurls it at the mirror. The glass shatters, shards flying everywhere, covering the dress in a spray of perfume and glass.

Gabriel stands there, shocked by his own reaction, breathing heavily, as the scent of the perfume fills the room, mingling with the broken fragments of their shattered future. He falls to his knees knowing in his heart that it is over. Just like the mirror that he has smashed beyond repair, she has broken his heart into a million pieces.

Gabriels fingers tense once more on the steering wheel as the police station disappears completely from view. Amelia is the reason he is back in LA. He had been planning this for months. But seeing her so unexpectedly this evening, well that had come completely unexpectedly. Never in a million years had he thought their first meeting would happen the way it had tonight. He smiled ruefully to himself. Under his breath he muttering to himself.

"What do they say about the best laid plans!" As Gabriel pulled up in front of his hotel, The Regent, the memories of that day still haunt the corners of his mind. If he is going to change this for them both then he knows there is no place for ghosts when he sees her again. Resolutely he gets out of the car handing the alarm key to the concierge momentarily while he dashes into the hotel. This would not take long then he would change and be on his way to Jacks for the impromptu dinner invite. Looking up at the night sky, smiling to himself, perhaps fate was on his side after all. There was no possible way he could ever have imagined that this evening would unfold the way it had. Now he just had to make sure Babaji was ok.

Chapter 7

Jack and Olivia's home is a very substantial large suburban house on the outskirts of L.A. It stands serene and welcoming, with a white picket fence and roses blooming around the door. The sound of children laughing fills the air as the couple's two children Georgia and Albert, aged 10 and 8, shoot hoops at the side of the house. A police squad car pulls up in front of the house, and Amelia steps out, waving to them she grins at site of her God children playing.

"Thanks for the lift, Dave. I'll see you tomorrow." Closing the car door behind her Amelia looked at the house relieved to see neither Gabriel's nor Joe's cars are parked in the vicinity of the house. She heads up the curved driveway, a wide smile spreading across her face as the children spot her rushing towards her, they nearly knock her over in their excitement.

"Aunty Mia, come and shoot some hoops!" The younger boy, Albert, 'Albee' to his friends, exclaims, beaming up at her. "I'm beating the pants off Georgia tonight." Georgia, the older of the two, rolls her eyes and nudges her little brother playfully.

"Only because I'm going easy on you, squirt. Mom said I had to. She says you are tired tonight." Albee pouts and protests.

"I'm not tired! Mom just wanted me out of the kitchen. We won the match today, so she's just fussing, Auntie Mia. Mom's busy making something fancy for supper, that's why she wanted me out of there." Amelia smiles indulgently at the children, ruffling Albee's hair affectionately.

"I thought you two would be getting ready for bed by now. I better go in and see if your mom needs any help. You guys keep playing. If there's time after supper, we can have a quick game, okay?" She winks at Georgia then heads in through the back door, leaving the children to their game. Inside the lovely kitchen diner, chaos reigns. Liv, Amelia's best friend in the world, is up to her elbows in flour. Surrounded by ingredients, her kitchen is transformed into a culinary battlefield. The aroma of delicious food fills the air, Amelia can't help smiling fondly at the sight of Liv, who has fully embraced her role as a classy Italian mamma, complete with an apron and a smudge of flour on her cheek.

"It looks like you've got half of L.A. coming to eat." Amelia teases Liv, laughing lightly. Caught by surprise Liv screeches in delight, spinning around, an excited smile on her face.

"Hey, babe!" Liv exclaims excitedly she beams at Amelia, her eyes full of unashamed curiosity. "So, how was it? Tell me. Tell me what happened."

"How was what, Liv?" Feigning nonchalance Amelia replies with a sigh. Wandering around the kitchen Amelia acts as if she doesn't know what her friend is talking about. Liv nearly hyperventilates pausing she looks at Amelia her eyes narrowing as she stares at her friend. Liv all but stamps her foot in frustration with Amelia.

"How was what? Are you kidding me, Mia? It's been, what, 20 years since you walked out on the love of your life? On your wedding day! And now he's here, in L.A., you arrest him? And you are asking me how's what?" Barely able to take a breath her words tumble out. Amelia holds her hands up defensively, avoiding Liv's gaze.

"There's really nothing to tell." She mutters.

"Bullshit!" Liv retorts. "Mia, this is me you are talking to. I know what's going on under that smart suit of yours." Amelia glances at her friend, a little flustered.

"Liv, watch your language. You know Jack doesn't like it."

"Stop avoiding the question, Mia." Liv insists. "How did he look? What did he say? Tell me everything. I want to know." Amelia looks at Liv's pouting face. Her best friend's eyes plead for information as she bats her eyelashes, Amelia smiles, she chooses to put her friend out of her misery, though she looks slightly sheepish.

"He looked really nice, Liv." She admits shrugging her slim shoulders, shaking her head. "But then, so he should. He has got the money to look after himself, hasn't he?"

"Look at me, Mia." Liv demands, stepping closer. "Stop avoiding me." Amelia meets her gaze, then quickly looks away. "Oh no, oooh no...." Liv says, her voice rising with excitement. "I know that weepy look. You kissed him already, didn't you?" Amelia's eyes widen in horror at how easily her friend can read her. Liv, elated, begins jumping up and down, dancing in a circle. She rushes over to Amelia, wrapping her in a floury hug, leaving handprints on Amelia's jacket. "Did I not teach you anything about men, Mia?" Liv's absolute delight is obvious, teasing Amelia she giggles like a schoolgirl.

"Stop it, Liv." Amelia protests, trying to sound stern but failing. "It wasn't like that. I don't know... One minute I am arresting him, and the next he is kissing me." Amelia slumps down onto a chair by the kitchen table, resting her head on her forearms. Liv shakes her head with a knowing smile. She heads to the refrigerator and pulls out a bottle of champagne, grabbing a glass from the cupboard.

"Do you want one?" Liv asks, popping the cork her absolute glee evident as she literally waltzes around the kitchen.

"You know I don't drink, Liv." Amelia replies, lifting her head she can't quite cope with Liv's exuberant delight.

"Yes, I know. I just thought tonight you might need one. You don't mind if I do, though." Liv pours herself a large glass, leaning back against the counter as she studies her friend.

"I can't believe you arrested him. Maddy said you had cuffed a guy she tried to pick up. I nearly choked when she told me his name was Gabriel. She said you seemed freaked out and that you knew him well." Liv pauses staring at Amelia questioningly. "What the hell was he doing picking up Maddy anyway? You know what they say, a leopard." Liv pauses, her glass in mid-air, her expression wry as she nods in Amelia's direction raising her eyebrows and her glass at the same time. "They never change's their spots."

Amelia bristles at Liv's insinuation. "It wasn't like that, Liv!" Amelia surprises herself at how defensive she feels about Gabriel, the thought making her frown. "Oh gosh, it is such a mess. He stopped the car because he was shocked when he saw Maddy dressed like me…. When I heard his voice, I just panicked." Amelia freezes, sitting bolt upright she stares at Liv.

"What did she say, Liv? What did Maddy say when she came here? Did she ask you who Gabriel was?" Suddenly the realisation makes her words tumble from her lips coming out fast as her mind goes into high alert. "I don't know how much she overheard. I just needed to get her away from him." Liv watches Amelia as she becomes agitated with concern, her voice calm.

"Mia, calm down. Of course she wanted to know who he is. Maddy's never seen you react like that with a guy." Sighing dramatically, she continues. "What do you think she is thinking? You do the math. She didn't ask me outright, but she is not stupid. She wanted to know why you were so mad at him." Liv stops talking letting her words sink in. When she sees Amelia's expression register the reality of what has happened earlier she carries on. "You can't blame her, Mia. Maddy has no idea who her father is. And you going nuts at someone from your past is bound to make her suspicious." Amelia goes pale.

"Liv, what did you tell her?" Her voice is low the tone flat. Liv turns back to her cooking with a casual shrug.

"Nothing, babe. I didn't tell her anything. I just covered for you. I said he might have been your pimp."

"What!" Amelia shouts, horrified. "Liv, you didn't!" Jumping to her feet she nearly knocks her chair over. Liv bursts into laughter, waving off Amelia's panic.

"Oh, calm down, Mia. Of course I didn't. I just made up some excuse about a lawyer who messed you about way back when. She was really upset that you sent her home with Joe, though." Amelia looks completely disoriented, shaking her head.

"I know. That's what I mean, Liv. I really panicked when I saw him and Maddy together. Oh, God, this is such a mess. What do I do?"

"About which bit?" Liv asks, she shrugs her shoulders, her voice softer now. "Don't worry about Maddy. She is just mad that you stopped her filming tonight. But the other stuff... that is up to you, babe." She raises her eyebrows looking quizzically at her friend. "He does have a right to know, though. You do realize that don't you? So does Maddy." Amelia is trembling now, her hands running through her hair in frustration.

"No. No, he doesn't, Liv. I did what I had to do. He mustn't ever know. Promise me, Liv." Liv looks torn, her expression troubled.

"Mia, I love you. You know that, right? I am always here for you, but I don't think this is right. Maddy's a big girl now. You know she deserves to know the truth." She crosses her arms her expression more serious. "He is here now Mia. You cannot ignore what has happened tonight and I don't think you should."

"It's too late..." Amelia whispers, her voice breaking. "She would never forgive me. Any more than he would. Don't you get it, Liv? I could lose everything. If Gabriel found out that Maddy is his, he would never understand why I left, or why I didn't come back. He would not forgive me. Not after all this time." Liv sighs deeply, her heart aching for her friend.

"Look, I'm sorry, babe, but you know how I feel about family. You and Maddy, well, you are my family. The truth has a funny way of coming out. Look at what happened tonight." Amelia's eyes flash with panic.

"Yes, just look. What were you thinking, asking us here for supper? Do you know how difficult tonight is going to be for me? Where are Maddy and Joe, anyway? They are not here, are they?" Liv glances away, looking a little guilty.

"Joe took Maddy home to change her clothes. You have got to give the guy a break, Mia. It's no wonder Gabriel nearly crashed the car. I nearly died when Maddy walked in here dressed like that. Do you realize how much she looks like you?" Amelia nods, the thought clearly disturbing her.

"I know. Yes, I know. Spooky, wasn't it? They aren't coming back, though. Joe and Maddy, they're not coming here tonight for supper, right?" At that precise moment Jack walks into the kitchen, a warm smile on his face.

"They've just pulled into the drive." He announces. "Is there a problem?" Jack walks over to Liv, looking at her fondly. He kisses her on the forehead, wiping away the smudge of flour from her cheek. Amelia watches the loving exchange, feeling a sharp pang of unease. "It seems, my darling." Jack says to Liv, "That you have outdone yourself this evening. Shall I help clear up?" Across the kitchen Amelia is beginning to panic as soon as Jack says the words, that Maddy has come back she is on her feet already rushing to the kitchen window, her anxiety skyrocketing as she looks outside. To her absolute horror, she sees the sleek Aston Martin pull up next to the house. Gabriel steps out of the car, she watches as Joe and Maddy, still standing in the driveway with the children, head over to greet him. Amelia shrinks back from the window, her stomach twisting in knots.

"Oh, Holy Shit!" Amelia's voice cracks, her hand flying to her mouth, she feels her head spin, feeling faint, she reaches out to steady herself. "I think I'm going to be sick. They are all here. I need to go." Jack, surprised by her unusual curse can't help but smile, sensing her distress he moves quickly to her side, catching her by the arm. He looks into her eyes with a calm, steady gaze, pulling her into a tight hug.

"Calm down, Amelia. Everything is going to be absolutely fine. I promise. Just relax." Though Jack's tone is soothing as he tries to give a sense of reassurance to Amelia's taught, over sensitised frame, his words have little effect on her.

"Relax?" Amelia nearly borderline hysterical laughs, she makes a funny noise that comes out more like a choked sound. "Are you nuts, Jack? My life is about to explode in front of my eyes, and you want me to relax?" Jack exchanges a look with Liv before gently steering Amelia towards the stairs.

"Olivia my darling, would you take Amelia upstairs to calm down and perhaps freshen up? I will get the kids to clean up in here while I make our guests comfortable." Liv nods, taking Amelia's hand, she guides Amelia gingerly towards the stairs, almost as if she is a hand grenade with the pin pulled out, they are both very aware that she may just explode at any moment. Jack, still holding her by the shoulders, gives her another reassuring squeeze.

"You can do this, Amelia. You know you can. You still love this man. We both know that." Jack feels Amelia's shoulders go tense, so he gently squeezes them again. "Maybe this is fate's way of giving you both another chance. You need to put things right. I saw the way he looked at you tonight. I don't think Gabriel got over you as easily as you think he did." Amelia looks at him, her heart pounding in her chest. She wants to believe him, it's just that the fear of what is coming overwhelms her. Jack gives her one last supportive nod, then gently nudges her towards the stairs.

"Now go and get ready." He says with a small smile. "I'll see to things down here." As Liv and Amelia head upstairs, Jack watches them go, a knowing smile tugging at his lips. He turns back to the kitchen, surveying the scene, then mutters to himself with a grin. "Let the games begin."

Chapter 8

Upstairs, Liv leads Amelia into her bedroom which is a bright and airy room with a huge window overlooking the front garden, it is decorated in a beautiful soft pastel colour palette with elegant chic furnishings. Amelia collapses onto the bed, burying her face in her hands.

"I can't do this, Liv." Amelia mumbles, her voice muffled by the bedspread. "I just can't." Liv sits down next to her, gently rubbing her back.

"Yes, you can, Mia. You are stronger than you think. You've faced worse than this, you always come out the other side. You will get through tonight too, perhaps this is an opportunity for a fresh start?" Amelia lifts her head, her eyes filling with tears.

"What if Maddy finds out? What if Gabriel realizes who she is? I have kept this secret for so long, Liv. I don't know how to deal with this." Liv sighs, brushing a strand of hair away from Amelia's face.

"I can't promise that it will be easy, but I do know one thing, you have been running from this for far too long. Maybe it's time to stop running." Amelia looks away, unable to meet Liv's eyes.

"What if I lose them both? What if they hate me?" The pain in her words is almost too much for Liv to bare. She instantly tries to take away the distress that in some small way she feels responsible for. Liv is beginning to feel increasingly uneasy about the dinner ahead. Her words come out a little more abruptly than she had intended.

"Maddy loves you, Mia. You are not going to lose anyone." Liv says firmly, then seeing the doubt in Amelia's eyes she softens. "Perhaps so does Gabriel, whether you want to admit it or not. You need to give them the chance to know the truth. Whatever happens, I will be here for you. We will get through this together." Amelia looks at Liv her face a tortured mix of fear, desire and doubt. Her heart still heavy with uncertainty. Liv stands up, heading over to the dressing table. "Come on." She says, trying to lighten the mood. "Let's freshen up. You need to feel good about yourself tonight. It will help." Amelia stands slowly, her mind still racing.

"I'm not sure there's enough makeup in the world that can help me feel better about this." Liv flashes her a supportive smile.

"Oh... you may be surprised. Now, let's see what we have..." Grateful to do something practical to help her friend Liv busies herself selecting various items and placing them on the dressing table in an attempt to distract Amelia. Downstairs, Jack is ushering the children inside, smiling he hugs them both. Joe and Maddy linger by the car, exchanging pleasantries with Gabriel. Jack steps outside to greet them.

"Welcome, Gabriel." Jack says warmly, extending his hand. "Glad you could join us, and your guest too. Babaji an absolute pleasure to meet you." Jack smiles genuinely at the older gentleman offering his hand to help him up the back steps inside. He looks beyond his guests acknowledging his family. "Maddy, Joe, come on inside. Olivia has gone to town with supper so I could use a hand to restore a little order." He smiles winking at Maddy affectionately. Gabriel shakes Jack's hand as he steps into the kitchen, smiling appreciatively.

"Thanks, Jack. I am really looking forward to it." Gabriel has changed his clothes he now wears smart black trousers and a beautiful slim fit navy shirt. As always, he exudes charisma his style is effortless, his aftershave expensive and sexy. Maddy can't help but stare at him, she watches him a little overwhelmed by the presence of such an enigmatic stranger. As they all head inside, Gabriel's gaze is drawn upward, up towards the bedroom windows, as if he sensed Amelia was upstairs, his eyes searching for a glimpse of her. All he had seen was the reflection of the evening light. In the main bedroom, Liv hovers nervously watching Amelia fix her makeup, her eyes soft with concern.

"Mia, no matter what happens tonight, remember, you have us. We are your family. You are not alone in this." Amelia gives her a shaky smile, grateful for the support.

"Thanks, Liv. I don't know what I would do without you." Liv grins, reaching for her friend's hand she squeezes it tightly.

"Hopefully you won't ever have to find out." Liv looks away sharply so that Mia can't see the tears that have formed in the corners of her eyes. "Now, come on. Before we go downstairs to face the music, put on your perfume you know Gabriel could never resist you in Channel." Taking a deep breath, Amelia smiles shakily.

"You go ahead I'll be down in a minute." Liv nods, a knowingly smile lingering on her lips, she hesitates by the bedroom door about to say something more, she frowns slightly then turns leaving Amelia to gather her thoughts. In the kitchen, the atmosphere is warm and lively as Jack, Joe, Maddy, and the two children, Georgia and Albee, bustle around. Gabriel is seated at the large round kitchen table, quietly observing the dynamic of the household. Beside him sits Babaji, who remains silent for now, his presence calm and composed. Best friends Amelia and Liv have yet to make their appearance. Gabriel turns to Jack, a sincere smile on his face.

"Thank you for the invitation tonight, Jack. It's such a pleasure to meet your lovely family. I must say, Madison, I prefer this outfit, though." Maddy, who now looks completely different, younger, and more innocent, blushes shyly, her long dark blonde hair flowing down her back. She is dressed in jeans, sneakers, and a casual shirt.

"Yeh, look, I'm really sorry about before." She says, laughing softly. "I had no idea you were a friend of Mom's and Pops'." Gabriel's freezes his eyes flash towards Jack; eyebrows raised in real surprise.

"Pops?" Jack, noticing Gabriel's reaction, chuckles.

"Yes, Madison has called me Pops since she was a little girl. She picked it up from Joseph. Madison idolized him when they were little." Gabriel looks at Jack with newfound understanding tinged with something more.

"Joseph's your son from your first marriage?" Gabriel is quietly fishing for information which Jack is instantly aware of. Jack nods, his expression softening.

"Yes, Charlotte was my first wife. Sadly, she passed away when Joseph was eight. Thankfully, Olivia, Amelia, and Maddy were all a great comfort and support to Joseph. Well, for both of us, to be honest." Jack looks at his son smiling a sad look in his eyes, the memory still holding power over his emotions. Gabriel's face reflects his empathy.

"I'm sorry to hear about your loss, Jack. You too, Joseph. I lost my mom when I was young. You have my sympathy." He turns to Joe with a kind smile. "Do you prefer to be called Joe or Joseph?"

"Joe, thanks." The younger man replies. "Actually, Liv made it much easier for me. My mom and Liv became very close when Amelia came back to LA." Joe pauses for a moment, uncertain if he has said too much, his eyes dart to his dad's face. Jack smiles reassuringly so Joe continues. "Before my mom died Liv was there for me. She kind of became my stepmom even before Dad realized he had fallen for her. Liv has always called me Joe. Dad prefers Joseph, though." Gabriel nods, smiling at the thought.

"My mom was the only person who ever called me Gabe. My dad hated it. It's funny, I would never have put your dad and Liv together. It just shows how wrong you can be about people." Jack smiles ruefully, his gaze distant as if recalling old memories.

"You and the rest of my family. I can't tell you how many jokes I have heard about sugar daddies. I will let Amelia tell you the full story, though, as she is the one who played Fairy Godmother. I couldn't see what was right in front of me. I was struggling with grief after losing Charlotte, not to mention that I was so much older than Olivia. I just never imagined she would be interested in me." He pauses, smiling privately at the memory. "It was the best decision I could have made as I've got two amazing children to show for it and Joseph has the brother and sister he always wanted."

Sensing the question in Gabriel's eyes he pointedly speaks to his son. "Joseph, would you and Maddy go and pick some wine from the garage, please?" Jack deftly changes the subject, turning his attention back to the present. "Georgia, Albert, go and wash up, please. Oh, and Albert, can you change that T-shirt? It is filthy." Without hesitation, the youngsters do as Jack asks, leaving the room in a flurry of activity. Gabriel watches their retreating backs with admiration.

"They are lovely children, Jack, all of them." You must be very proud of them Jack nods, clearly pleased by Gabriel's kind words.

"Thank you." Gabriel barely hesitates for a moment before asking the question that Jack can feel is burning in his brain.

"Can I ask you a question, though? I hope you are not offended." Jack looks up, waiting for the inevitable question, he smiles knowingly.

"Go ahead." Gabriel's expression turns serious as he carefully asks.

"Is Maddy your daughter?" He pauses waiting for Jack's reply, holding his breath. Jack stops what he is doing, his smile fading slightly as he meets Gabriel's gaze. After a moment, he shakes his head.

"No, Gabriel, she's not." Gabriel's eyes immediately show his relief, the tension in his body easing fractionally, his eyes narrow with a mix of hope and fear.

"Is she, my daughter?" Jack's face becomes unreadable, his expression guarded. He considers Gabriel's question for a moment.

"If you want the answer to that question, you will have to ask Amelia. Like I said to you on the phone, Amelia is not with anyone right now, but that has not always been the case. This is something between the two of you."

In Liv's bedroom, Amelia is finishing getting ready. Amelia adjusts her hair one last time, letting it fall naturally over her shoulders. Reaching for a bottle of perfume she sprays the familiar fragrance over her neck and wrists, holding her hand to her nose inhaling the fragrance she closes her eyes as if trying to calm her own nerves with the sweet scent. Liv who had been across the hall helping Albee find a clean t-shirt comes back into the room. She smiles warmly at her friend whose nerves still haunt her beautiful eyes.

"Ready?" She asks softly. Liv smooths down the fabric of her outfit. Both women are a bundle of nerves, though Liv hides it well behind her supportive smiles. Amelia exchanges a look with Liv, a mix of apprehension and determination in her eyes. As Amelia stands up, she pulls at her shirt nervously. Liv walks over and hugs her tightly silently offering a reassuring smile and squeezes her friend's hand. "Ready to face the music?" Liv's tone is light yet filled with understanding. Amelia takes a deep breath and nods.

"As ready as I'll ever be." Her nerves suddenly get the better of her and she dashes towards the ensuite.

"It's all going to work out Mia." Liv calls after her. "I am sure it is.... I'll go first you come in a minute." Liv hesitates in the bedroom doorway hovering like an anxious parent needing to know that Mia is ok. Her own nerves also creating havoc with her tummy which growls loudly. Catching sight of her own reflection in the mirror opposite, Liv couldn't quite look herself in the eye. Guilt. She silently reprimanded herself. It was not nerves it was guilt that was really causing her anxiety.

For the past three weeks Liv had known that Gabriel had been in contact with Jack. How could she have lied to Mia about this. Tugging at the blouse she has just changed into Liv silently acknowledged her part in the evening's events. Feeling totally disloyal to her best friend had been bad enough in private, but this, what had happened this evening went way beyond telling a 'little white lie' to protect Mia. Liv gripped the doorframe to steady herself. Should she tell her now before they went downstairs? Liv had been toying with that question from the moment Maddy and Joe had burst through the door earlier. The two youngsters had arrived desperate for information about the handsome stranger that

Mia had arrested. Finding out that Mia had arrested Gabriel had taken Liv completely by surprise. Liv had panicked and called Jack immediately as she was terrified that the truth would come out before she had had chance to come clean to Amelia.

Liv was beginning to feel sick herself. Why had she let Jack convince her that dinner was a good idea. When Jack had heard about Gabriel's arrest, he had instinctively decided that getting Mia and Gabriel together in the safety of their home was the best idea as it was neutral territory; that way, Jack had said, they could mitigate the fall out. Now Liv was not so sure. Seeing Amelia in such a state had completely rocked the certainty she had felt. Why hadn't they all stuck to the original plan. Liv began to fidget second guessing herself. What was she thinking, shaking herself she straightened her shoulders, looking at her own reflection, not quite able to look herself straight in the eyes she chided herself; this kind of thinking wasn't going to help anyone. It had been nearly a month since she had overheard Jack in his study talking to Gabriel, she had been so upset with him. They had had the worst row they had ever had, for the first time in their marriage Liv had made Jack sleep in the spare room for a couple of days.

That had been three weeks ago. Somehow, she had allowed Jack to persuade her that Gabriels's intentions were completely honourable, that he just wanted a second chance to make things right between Mia and him. Jack had sworn that he had not told Gabriel about Maddy. He had reassured her that Maddy was a private matter that only concerned Amelia and Gabriel. Liv had known that Jack was right, she trusted his judgement implicitly. Jack would never do anything to hurt Amelia. More importantly Jack treated Maddy like his own child which meant that Liv felt certain that whatever happened Jack had everyone's best interests at heart. Liv had always known that Jack had struggled with the idea of keeping Maddy a secret from Gabriel, he felt that a father had the right to know if he had a child.

When Amelia had run away all those years ago, he had gone back to see Jack at the hotel demanding to know if she had been there.

Jack clearly remembered that Gabriel had looked like a different man to the one who he remembered. Jack had decided there and then that if he did see Amelia again, he would protect her as he felt there was far more to the story than a lover's quarrel.

He had of course been right. It was however over a year after seeing Gabriel that he had bumped into Amelia, that was the first time he had met Maddy. Amelia had Maddy in a papous strapped to her chest, her hair wild and her face glowing, Jack would have recognised her anywhere. She had been rushing down the street to meet Liv at a coffee shop in the neighbourhood where he lived with his first wife Charlotte. Joe had been a little boy, his hand in Jack's, they were on their way to the park. Amelia had been absolutely thrilled to see Jack and meet Joe. Both Amelia and Liv had gone to the park taking Jack a coffee and it was during that afternoon when fate stepped in and changed all their lives. Jack's phone had rung and to his dismay it had been the hospital. Charlotte had had a seizure and had been rushed in. Amelia didn't hesitate in offering to look after Joe so that Jack could rush to his wife's side. The rest was history now but from that first meeting they had all become the closest of friends, like family to one another.

Jack would never have considered betraying Amelia's confiding in him, and he had always respected her decision not to tell Gabriel about Maddy saying that, only she knew what had happened between her and Gabriel. But Liv had always known that he had struggled with it. Then a few weeks ago when she had overheard him on the phone Jack had insisted that he had nothing to do with Gabriel's reappearance. He had reassured Liv that once Gabriel found out about Maddy from Amelia, it would then be up to Gabriel to do the right thing. No matter what had happened in the past he felt that Gabriel had a responsibility to step up if he wanted a relationship with Maddy; in Jacks' opinion Maddy was old enough to make her own decisions about Gabriel. He had just hoped and prayed that it wouldn't damage her relationship with her mother.

Liv was not a religious person but suddenly she found herself silently asking for forgiveness and praying that their interference in their beloved friends' lives wouldn't backfire on the happiness they all relied on within their special family. Jack was everyone's rock he had never once let her down. He was quite simply the most honest, truthful, kindest person that Liv had ever known which is why she had promised to keep the secret for a while.

    Last week though she had put her foot down and insisted it was time for them all to come clean to Amelia. Liv had been the one who had insisted that Gabriel had to come to LA before Mia's birthday. How could everything have, gone so wrong so quickly. There was no turning back now. The die was cast and one way or another the truth would come out. Taking a deep breath Liv headed downstairs. She quite simply had to make things right for her friend; but to be able to do that though she needed to make sure she would get chance to speak to Gabriel before he saw Mia again. In the upstairs landing she heard the kitchen door open making her stop once more in her tracks.

Chapter 9

The atmosphere in the kitchen, was light and jovial as Maddy and Joe returned with bottles of wine. The younger children now freshly washed were both excited to be part of the adult evening, Georgia and Albee burst through the kitchen door, their energy filling the room. Jack handed them plates, mats, and cutlery, and they eagerly set about laying the table for supper. Jack turning to Maddy with a smile asked.

"Maddy can you please go and ask the ladies to join us for dinner?" Grinning innocently, she jumped up immediately heading to the kitchen door, flinging it wide she yelled up the stairs.

"Mom, Liv!... Dinner's ready!" Jack raised an eyebrow at her, his voice teasing.

"Thank you, Madison. It is good to know the expensive education your mom's given you has paid off." Maddy blushed rushing over to Jack, kissing him on the cheek, she coyly added.

"Sorry, Pops." Gabriel chuckled, watching the exchange with amusement. Maddy's cheek turn a delicate shade of pink, but she laughs along. Jack shakes his head, still smiling.

"Are you going to Olivia's salon tomorrow with the ladies?" Maddy shrugged not wanting to commit.

"No, I don't want to spend all day getting ready. It will take me 20 minutes tomorrow evening. You know what they're like. Aunty Liv is all set on a full day of pampering for mom. I told her that I would meet them for lunch, though." Gabriel, intrigued, looks over at Jack.

"Does Olivia run a salon?" Jack's smile widened with pride.

"You could say that. When Amelia came back to L.A., she was determined that Olivia finish her beauty course. And she did, finished with honours, I am proud to say." Jack smiles recalling the memory. "Amelia helped her set up a small business, my wife Charlotte did the accounts for Olivia then the business just grew from there. Olivia St. John is now the leading eyebrow queen to all the Hollywood stars." Gabriel whistles, leaning back in his chair.

"Wow. That sounds like quite a story. I can't wait to hear the rest." Jack chuckled.

"Now, Gabriel, we have been neglecting our other guest. Would Babaji like anything particularly to eat or drink? Olivia's made plenty of food, I know you mentioned earlier that he is diabetic." Jack addresses his questions to the older man directly, Babaji, sitting quietly at the table, smiles graciously at Jack but remains silent. Gabriel responds on his behalf.

"That is kind of you Jack. Babaji ate at the hotel, he cannot miss meals due to his special diet. I had his medication in my car, which is why I had to go back. You will find that Babaji is an easy guest, he has simple requirements. He is fond of a good cup of tea if you have any." Babaji nods, his eyes twinkling with warmth. Jack raises his eyebrows at Maddy, who immediately gets up to boil the kettle. Whispering, she asks Gabriel.

"He's very quiet. Does he speak English?" Before Gabriel can answer, the kitchen door swings open, and Liv enters like a whirlwind, elegant, beautifully made up, she radiates graceful sophistication. She smiles warmly, moving straight to Gabriel and kissing him on both cheeks.

"Gabriel, what a pleasure to see you!" Pausing as her eyes acknowledge the stranger at the table. "And you brought a guest?" Liv's eyes land on Babaji, she looks momentarily taken aback. "How lovely." She says, regaining her composure. "Pleased to meet you, Mr....?"

"*Babaji.*" Gabriel says quietly. Liv offers her hand, Babaji stands slowly, nodding respectfully instead of shaking her hand. Liv pulls her hand back, smiling though slightly thrown by the unexpected guest.

"Lovely..." Liv is obviously unnerved by the appearance of a new guest but quickly covers her surprise with a bright smile.   "Right, I'm sure you're all starving. Mia's on her way down, so let's get supper served, shall we?" Gabriel smiles and asks.

"Would you mind if I just go and wash up before we eat?" Liv grabs the opportunity to speak to him.

"Sure." Liv replies moving towards the door she gestures through the kitchen door. "The bathroom's just down the hallway, the door nearest the front window." Under her breath as Gabriel passes her, she whispers, "Amelia is coming down now..." Surreptitiously she glances towards Maddy. Maddy is busy by the sink. Liv steps into the hallway behind Gabriel, in a hushed urgent voice she whispers. "Please be careful with her Gabriel she is more sensitive than she appears. Your being here has really upset her..." Liv freezes hearing movement on the landing. Gabriel hears it too walking past Liv.

"Thanks." Gabriel nods silently understanding Liv's concern. He walks down the hallway as Liv disappears back through the kitchen door, Gabriel heads towards the bathroom just as Amelia begins descending the stairs. Her hair now falls loosely around her shoulders, her makeup is flawless, the jacket she wore earlier removed. She looks more relaxed, though her eyes are still alert, filled with a mixture of emotions. Gabriel stops at the bottom of the stairs, watching her intently. As Amelia nears the last few steps, a soft wave of her perfume reaches him, triggering a flood of memories. Gabriel inhales deeply, his body reacting instantly to the familiar scent. Standing taller, his eyes meet hers.
"As I said before." Gabriel murmurs softly. "Beautiful." Amelia smiles self-consciously, brushing off the compliment, she is achingly aware Gabriel has changed and now looks even more dangerously attractive.

"Hardly, I just got off work." Gabriel's gaze remains steady; he can't look away from her.

"Well, you look beautiful to me, Amelia." His eyes soften with concern. As she reaches the bottom step, Gabriel gently takes her hand, his fingers brushing over her ringless, manicured fingers, his eyes linger as he inspects her dark red nail polish. Amelia frowns slightly, caught off guard by the intimate gesture. Gabriel looks up, his eyes locking with hers as he lifts her hand to his lips. Just before he kisses it, he turns it over, pressing his lips instead to the inside of her wrist, where the scent of her perfume lingers. Amelia's breath catches, her knees going weak as they stare at each other, the air between them charged with unspoken words. Just then, Maddy bursts through the kitchen door, looking surprised and a bit embarrassed to catch them in such an intimate moment.

"Oh, I'm sorry." Maddy says, her voice breaking the spell. "I was just coming to get you. Mom, supper is ready. Get a move on." Amelia freezes quickly pulling her hand away, stepping in front of Gabriel as she flashes Maddy a forced smile.

"Thank you, Maddy." Amelia blushes feeling very unsettled by Maddy's sudden appearance. Her daughter retreats to the kitchen leaving her embarrassed mom alone with Gabriel once more. Gabriel chuckles softly and excuses himself to the bathroom, leaving Amelia to collect herself. When Gabriel returns to the kitchen, everyone is seated around the table as Liv serves supper. The room is filled with the comforting aromas of home-cooked food. Gabriel takes his place between Babaji and a slightly flustered-looking Amelia. As Liv serves the food, Amelia turns to Gabriel, her voice low.

"You never mentioned you were bringing a friend." Mischief dances in Gabriel's eyes as he replies.

"No, I didn't, did I? May I introduce you to Babaji?" Amelia gives him a tight smile.

"Thanks, we've already been introduced." She glances at Babaji, who regards her with a calm, steady gaze. Amelia quickly looks away, clearly uncomfortable. There is a brief, awkward pause before Jack offers wine to everyone. Simultaneously, both Amelia and Gabriel cover their wine glasses in silent refusal, their eyes meeting for a fleeting moment. Gabriel smiles, but Amelia quickly looks away, her discomfort evident. In a bright, forced tone, Amelia asks.

"So, Gabriel, are you in town for business or pleasure?" Gabriel is just taking a sip of water and nearly chokes, grinning at Amelia as he remembers the last time she asked him that very same question. His voice softens as he looks directly into her eyes.

"Pleasure, this time, Amelia." Liv, trying to ease the tension, interjects with a warm smile.

"Gabriel, I hope you like lasagne?" She begins serving the food, but as Gabriel passes his plate, he politely declines the lasagne.

"Actually, Babaji has already eaten and I'm vegetarian, but the salad and bread look fantastic, thank you for going to all this effort." Liv looks momentarily crestfallen, her cheeks flushing with embarrassment.

"Oh, I didn't realise..." Amelia whose nerves are totally on edge immediately jumps to her friend's defence, her voice sharp and annoyed as she glares at Gabriel.

"Olivia is one of the best cooks in this town. It's the Italian blood in her. She can make a feast out of just about anything." An awkward silence follows as Amelia realises, she may have overreacted. Liv coughs politely.

"Erm... thanks Mia. It's not a problem." Liv quickly gestures to Joe to pass his plate and tries valiantly to fill the silence. Taking a deep breath Amelia tries again and asks more graciously.

"So, Gabriel where are you staying?" Gabriel still smiling takes the salad from Joe, also passing the bread to Maddy. He half turns to smile innocently at Amelia a provocative glint in his eyes he answers her without missing a beat.

"Where else Amelia. The Regent." Gabriel is fully aware that at the mention of the hotel Amelia's body unconsciously tenses, she is acting like a cat on hot bricks. Gabriel knows that he is stoking the fire but part of him is enjoying seeing her composure slip as she flushes red once more. He does however catch Liv's disapproving glance and silently decides to stop trying to provoke her.

"Of course." Amelia replies, her words clipped, her voice laced with irony. "It wouldn't be anywhere else would it. I presume you are in the penthouse?" Gabriel knows he must answer her, but he is mindful of Liv's warning. His smile doesn't waver his eyes keeping track of her every response, he answers her dig disguised as a question calmly keeping his tone deliberately light, he doesn't want to bait her but can't quite resist the urge to make her blush.

"I wouldn't want to disappoint now, would I. It does bring back such fond memories." Liv can't help the snort that unceremoniously escapes as she nearly inhales the mouthful of Champagne she is sipping. Amelia frowns immediately stiffening, acutely aware that the conversation is veering into dangerous territory. Glancing sideways at Maddy, she notes her daughter's wide-eyed expression. Maddy is deliberately starring at her salad, wisely trying her best to avoid giving her mother any eye contact, she feels her mother's gaze across the table. Maddy turns looking at Joe for help, she shifts uncomfortably in her seat. Gabriel sensing the tension he has created tactfully changes the subject.

"Liv the salad is fantastic. Did you grow the vegetables yourself?" With practised ease he directs the conversation towards more neutral territory. Liv beams at him, grateful for the change in topic.

"Actually, yes, I do. We have a small vegetable patch out back. Jack and the kids help me keep it going. We did have chickens but sadly the foxes kept using us like the local deli. The garden is my special place, one of my little joys." The two children giggle as Albie mutters to his sister.

"If Gigi hadn't kept leaving the chickens gate open then the fox wouldn't have got in." Liv stares at her children who have just dropped the unsuspecting elderly housekeeper in it. She can't help grinning as the children giggle innocently. The light banter seems to lift the atmosphere, the meal moves along accompanied with easier subjects, the adults all trying to help ease the obvious tension in the room, however the undercurrents of unresolved emotions still linger between Amelia and Gabriel. As the evening continues that balance subtly shifts once again as Gabriel addresses Jack unaware, he is yet again about to expose another touchy subject for Amelia.

"Jack you were telling me earlier about how you and Olivia got together. I gather it was something of a remarkable love story. You mentioned that Amelia had something to do with it. You didn't finish though. So, tell me, how did it all happen? Did Amelia wave her magic wand, so that you instantly fell in love?" Amelia coughs, covering her mouth with a napkin, she shares a quick, meaningful look with Liv. Her cheeks colour soft pink, Liv blushes starring wide eyed at Jack unable to look at Amelia she covers her mouth with her hand to cover the shock on her face at Jacks potential faux pa.

"Hardly, Gabriel." Amelia's response is a little snippy, her tone holds more than a hint of sarcasm. "That's not how it works in the real world, is it?" Gabriel's eyes search hers, challenging.

"Don't tell me you've stopped believing in fairy tales, Amelia. All the best stories have a happy ending. You taught me that." Amelia meets his gaze, her expression hardening.

"Yes, well, that kind of stuff should be reserved for kindergarten. The real world's not like that, is it? It's sharper at the edges. If you keep your head in the clouds dreaming, you'll fall, that's how you hurt yourself. Sometimes, it is too hard to get back up." The room falls silent, the weight of her words hanging heavily in the air. Gabriel studies her, a mix of concern and curiosity in his eyes.

"Amelia? Gabriels's smile is genuine as he looks at her face. "Where has the hopeless romantic gone? You sound almost cynical. I can't believe she isn't in there somewhere!" He pauses turning in his seat to study her. Amelia looks away she cannot withstand his gaze. "Perhaps the cop disguise is a little too tight for a dreamer." There is an uncomfortable pause. Maddy raises her eyebrows, casting a glance at Joe, who silences her with a look. Trying to ease the evident tension, Jack steps in, smiling reassuringly at Amelia.

"Don't let appearances fool you, Gabriel. If Amelia had not been able to dream big, then the charity, not to mention the shelter would never have been opened in the first place." Amelia's shoulders relax fractionally as she smiles at Jack's attempt to help her save face.

Seemingly delighted that Jack has brought up the Shelter Gabriel seizes the opportunity to steer the conversation to safer ground.

"I am glad you mentioned that, Jack. Amelia, how on earth have you managed to get where you are? Balancing such a demanding role in the police; running a charity, as well as being a single mom at the same time. You must be some kind of superwoman." Amelia's shoulders instantly stiffen again her hackles rising at the comment. Turning in her seat she looks at Gabriel, her voice sharp.

"Well, I didn't sleep my way to the top, if that's what you mean." The moment the harsh words leave her mouth, Amelia regrets them. Maddy's mouth drops open in shock. The room plunges into an awkward silence. Albee, oblivious to the tension, leans towards Liv, whispering.

"What does Aunt Mia mean? Is it like sleeping on my top bunk?" Liv pats his arm gently, her voice a little too eager to silence her youngest, she purses her lips to stop herself from laughing at the innocent comment. "Eat your supper, darling. It's nearly bedtime." Maddy tries to hide her face as she coughs into her napkin turning towards Joe her eyes plead for help as she tries to control the fit of giggles threatening to explode out of her chest, she has never seen her mom look so uncomfortable or so completely out of sorts. Amelia looks thoroughly embarrassed by her own unnecessary outburst, glancing sideways at Babaji she instantly regrets her stinging rebuke, his features are soft though he is watching her with an unreadable expression. His steady gaze only deepens her discomfort. Gabriel, however, remains completely at ease, as if unfazed by the tension in the room. Desperate to change the subject, Amelia turns her attention to Maddy, more than a little annoyed that her daughter is obviously enjoying her discomfort.

"Maddy, I thought you and Joe might have gone bowling tonight." Maddy face quickly changes, she frowns, clearly confused by her mother's out of character behaviour she is immediately irritated by her Amelia's attempt to patronise her.

"Mom, we're not twelve. I still have work to do. Joe said he would take me over to Spencer's to see if we have got anything we can use from tonight of the footage we shot. Auntie Liv, can I stay here tonight and interview you in the morning?" Liv is very aware that Amelia is becoming more, and more stressed, wanting to protect her she is eager to shift the conversation, smiling warmly.

"Fine with me, babe. You can sleep in with Georgia. Does anyone want more lasagne?" The question lingers in the air. Liv's smile is met with murmurs of appreciation and polite refusal. Amelia has barely touched her food, her thoughts clearly elsewhere. Georgia pipes up, her eyes full of affection as she looks at Maddy she is eager to talk about less serious conversation.

"Yey... Can I wake you up when I get up, Maddy?" Maddy smiles at her with equal affection.

"As long as it's not too early, pumpkin." Amelia's watches Maddy her mind still concerned with the earlier debacle she focusses her nerves on her daughter.

"I do not want you going out again filming tonight, Maddison; On the strip, do you hear me?" Amelia stares at Maddy, her eyes move to Joe who is sitting next to Maddy looking uncomfortable. "Joe, I am making you responsible for getting her back tonight without any more nonsense." At the mention of his name Joe sits a little straighter he nods wordlessly. He has never seen Amelia as on edge as she is tonight and he has no intention of upsetting her. Maddy huffs in frustration.

"Honestly, Mom, you make me sound like such a child." Sensing the mounting tension, Gabriel tactfully changes the subject. Looking at Maddy Gabriel surprises Amelia when he asks her daughter a direct question.

"Is it your major; film studies, right, Maddy?" Maddy smiles innocently, nodding at Gabriel more than grateful for the distraction.

"Yes, it is. That's what I was doing tonight. My boyfriend, Spencer, and I were shooting a short documentary based on Mom's life for our summer assignment. I wanted to show how hard it is for the girls out there on the streets. Mom's shelter has made such a difference to so many young women. She just gets all overprotective." Jack looks at Maddy with a mixture of sternness and affection.

"And rightly so. It's a good thing I didn't know what you were up to tonight. You too, Joseph. Your mom has every right to be overprotective where you are concerned, Madison." Maddy, looking contrite, lowers her eyes.

"Sorry, Pops." Jack softens, his voice gentle.

"I think it's your mom who deserves the apology, Maddy." Maddy looks embarrassed, mumbling an apology to Amelia, who nods in acceptance but remains visibly unsettled. It is Gabriel who rescues the conversation, feeling a little responsible for her uncomfortable moment he turns to Maddy with a warm smile.

"I know a little bit about the film industry Maddy. Babaji's nephew is a film producer in Bollywood. He has made several big-budget films, mainly Indian action movies. Many of them are quite well known over here. In fact, it is one of the reasons I came back to America. I'm here to see a producer for him, a special effects specialist." Gabriel's words land like a grenade in the room, triggering a range of reactions. Maddy sits up, her interest piqued as she looks from Gabriel to Babaji with newfound curiosity, she stares at Babaji with respect. Amelia, on the other hand, looks like she is about to explode, her frustration and anxiety barely contained. Liv, aware the situation is getting the better of Amelia, quickly stands up from the table, wanting to change the subject and diffuse the situation.

"Mia, would you give me a hand with the dessert, please?" Amelia, still reeling from the conversation, hesitates. Liv's tone becomes more insistent. "Mia! The dessert! Now, please!" Reluctantly, Amelia gets up from the table, carrying her plate of uneaten food and Gabriel's empty plate to the sink. Behind them, a more animated discussion about the film industry takes place, with Jack and Babaji smiling indulgently at the exchange. At the sink, Amelia and Liv stand shoulder to shoulder, working in silence for a moment. Liv glances at Amelia, hissing under her breath.

"Mia, stop it. You are making it obvious. If you don't want anyone to realize something is wrong, stop looking like hell just froze over." Amelia grips the counter, her knuckles white.

"I can't handle this, Liv. I feel like a wreck. Can you get rid of Joe and Maddy, please?" Liv, ever the problem-solver, pushes the cake she had made aside, turning to face the room with a feigned apology.

"Sorry, guys, the cake's still frozen. We will have to save it for Mia's birthday tomorrow. It is getting late. Joe, Maddy, if you are going to do some work, then you need to get going. And you, my two angels, it is bedtime. Upstairs please." Jack raises an eyebrow at Liv, clearly aware that the cake isn't frozen as it's homemade, he takes the hint. Joe, who has been watching the entire evening in silence, also gets the message. He stands up, pulling Maddy with him.

"Come on, Maddy, let's take these two up for Mom before we go." Maddy hesitates, wanting to continue her conversation with Gabriel. Joe gently but firmly pulls her to her feet as Maddy is oblivious to Liv's blatant excuse to get rid of them. He ushers her and the younger children out of the kitchen into the hallway. Just as the room begins to quiet down, Jack's phone rings. He steps out to answer it, leaving a brief pause in the conversation. When he returns, his expression is serious.

"I am sorry, everyone. That was the shelter. Carol called. They are having a few problems with Jesse's ex." Amelia's demeanour shifts immediately, her focus sharpening, relief floods her system, Amelia seizes the opportunity to escape.

"Yes, he was there earlier. I better go take care of it. Thanks, Jack." Jack stares at Amelia registering her desire to run. Pausing he considers his answer then smiling at her he shakes his head, his tone finale.

"You will do no such thing, Amelia. You stay right where you are." Jacks' expression is resolute as he fixes her with a look that silences any argument she may have raised. Seeing the expression on Jack's face Amelia thinks twice before opening her mouth to argue with him. This was not a battle she was going to win and besides she was too tired to even try. "I told Carol to ring the station. Bills on duty tonight. I am going to head over there now and check on things myself." Jack pauses considering something for a moment then turns to Gabriel making a statement that surprises Amelia though she is quick to hide her feelings.

"Gabriel if it's ok with you I will take Babaji back to the hotel now." Gabriel, who had been quietly listening, nods in understanding. Amelia turns her attention towards Jack giving him a strange look which he pointedly ignores.

"Thanks Jack, I appreciate that. If it is not too much trouble. We have had a long day, I know it has been a tiring one for him." Jack nods satisfied that events have fallen unexpectedly into place turning to Babaji with a respectful smile.

"Of course. It is no trouble at all. I need to check on one or two things at the hotel anyway for tomorrow evening. Shall we go, Babaji?" The older man stands slowly, bowing graciously to the ladies before turning to pat Gabriel affectionately on the arm smiling up at him there is a twinkle in the older man's eye. He turns to follow Jack out of the room but not before flashing Amelia an amused smile. Liv hurries after them, fussing over everyone as they say their goodbyes, leaving Gabriel and Amelia alone in the kitchen. Amelia is a little taken aback by the directness of the older man's gaze she looks at Gabriel, her expression guarded.

"He's not very talkative, your friend, is he?" Gabriel pauses, considering her words before replying softly.

"No, no he isn't." There is a long pause as they both stand there, the silence between them thick with tension simmering. Amelia turns away, breaking the moment by starting to clear the table. Gabriel watches her in silence then starts to help her, before he has even lifted a plate, Liv reappears in the kitchen.

"Guys please you two leave those." Liv insists, stepping in to take over. "I will clear up. You have both had a long day." Amelia looks at Liv, exhaustion creeping into her voice.

"Liv, if it's okay with you, I am going to call it a night. I am tired. Thank you, this was lovely as always." Liv stares wide eyed at her friend, concern etched on her face, but Amelia avoids her gaze, clearly wanting to escape the evening's emotional weight. Amelia turns to Gabriel, her voice more formal now. "I'll say goodnight, Gabriel. It was lovely to see you again." Gabriel stares at her, his expression unreadable.

"I've got your purse in my car." Gabriel's reply is a statement which he follows with a command that sets Amelia's nerves on edge. "I'll take you home." His words are polite but firm. Amelia shakes her head quickly, almost too quickly.

"It's okay, Gabriel. I can catch a cab home. Really, don't worry." Gabriel's eyes hold hers unflinchingly.

"I'm not in the least bit worried, Amelia, but I am taking you home." He turns back to Liv, smiling warmly. "Thank you, Olivia. It was so good to see you again. Thank you for welcoming us into your home, it really was delightful to meet your wonderful family." Liv opens her mouth to respond, but Amelia immediately interrupts.

"It's okay, Gabriel, really. A cab is fine." Gabriel's gaze doesn't waver.

"As I said, Amelia, I'm taking you home." Liv surreptitiously watches the exchange, understanding that there is so much more happening than is being said the undertones are so strong, the chemistry between Amelia and Gabriel is undeniable. She looks at Amelia concerned that this is moving too fast for her friend. Liv hesitates for a moment knowing that this is a life changing moment for Amelia. Following her husband's lead Liv brightens putting a disarmingly happy smile on her face then stepping aside she opens the door to the hallway to usher the couple out, allowing Gabriel to take charge. In a light voice she smiles.

"I'll pick you up tomorrow around ten, Mia." Liv's words are a gentle reminder that she is there for her friend, she nervously adds. "So that I can work my magic. Not that you need any magic, but it is always nice to feel like a princess on your birthday." Amelia forces a smile, nodding slightly she knows to refuse Gabriel again would appear petulant and childish.

"Thanks, Liv." At that moment, Maddy and Joe come down the stairs, entering the hallway. Joe opens the front door, and the cool night air sweeps into the house as they all step outside. Liv stands in the doorway, her gaze following them. Gabriel shakes Joe's hand, his tone polite.

"It was really nice to meet you both." Maddy, blushing shyly, steps forward and kisses Gabriel on the cheek. Amelia freezes at the sight, her breath catching in her throat. Maddy smiles, her voice tinged with excitement. "I would love to talk to you some more, Gabriel, about films. Are you coming tomorrow night?" Before Gabriel can answer, Amelia's eyes widen as she interrupts, her tone sharper than she intended.

"No, Maddy. Mr. Sinclair is a busy man. I am sure he has a lot more important things to do." Gabriel turns, a smile playing on his lips as he looks at Amelia, his voice calm.

"Actually, I am available tomorrow evening. Are you having a birthday party?" Maddy's face lights up with delight she catches Gabriel's arm playfully her innocent enthusiasm is evident.

"Mom's up for a special award tomorrow. We don't know the details yet. They are keeping it as a surprise. We are having a big, combined party for her. Jack has arranged it all. The party is at your hotel Gabriel, will you come... Please." Gabriel's smile widens as he looks at her excited face.

"Really? That sounds wonderful Maddy. I would love to." Turning to Amelia his eyes hold a challenge for her. "Maybe you can tell me all about it on the way to your house, Amelia. If I am invited, that is?" Maddy beams at him.

"Gabriel you are most definitely invited. I look forward to seeing you there, bring Babaji too." She smiles mischievously. Maddy senses that Gabriel may just be an ally, she is certain there is much more to this relationship between her mom and Gabriel. She makes the most of her mom's quietness, feeling empowered that Gabriel appears to be able to ruffle her mom's feathers. Gabriel nods, he too feels a much stronger bond with Maddy, a bond that he is determined to resolve but for the time being Gabriel is more than happy to have found common ground with Maddy. He glances back to Amelia, concerned that his thoughts somehow may betray him. He needn't have worried as Amelia seemed preoccupied by her own worries. She does however look far from pleased.

"Thanks once again, Olivia." Gabriel smiles warmly. He knows now is not the time to prolong the goodbyes. "Until tomorrow." His smile turns into a mischievous grin, mock bowing to Maddy he turns on his heel heading towards his car, leaving Amelia gaping after him. Looking a little defeated she quietly says her goodnights. She leans in to kiss her family, exchanging a significant look with Liv, who mouths.

"Call me." With a reluctant sigh, Amelia nods before turning to follow Gabriel across the driveway to his car. Always the gentleman, Gabriel opens the door for Amelia, waiting as she climbs into the passenger seat. Liv, Joe, and Maddy stand in the doorway watching them as Gabriel walks around to the driver's side and gets in. Liv disappears inside leaving the younger couple standing outside. Maddy grins at Joe, tugging on his arm she propels him towards his car.

"Well, that was interesting. Come on I want to google him, my phones dead can I borrow yours." Joe rolls his eyes. Maddy is up to her usual tricks.

Chapter 10

As they pull away from the house, it is Amelia who breaks the silence.

"You can drive me home, Gabriel, but that's it. I'm tired. I've got an early start tomorrow." She sighs looking out of the window into the darkness, her thoughts creating the anxiety that Gabriel can see in every aspect of her body language. Gabriel listens to her quietly, his patience unwavering. He nods respecting her request. Amelia gives him the address for the sat nav which then enables her to remain quiet as they drive the few kilometres to her home.

They ride in silence for the rest of the journey, the atmosphere in the car heavy with the weight of unspoken emotions. Amelia's nerves are so frayed that when Gabriel reaches over and turns on the stereo, she jumps misinterpreting his movement towards her. To ease the tension and relax her Gabriel deliberately selects one of his favourite artists filling the car with the soft, melodic strains of opera. 'Regresa a mí' by Il Divo begins to play, the hauntingly beautiful voices of the tenors echoing in the quiet car.

Amelia studies Gabriel as he drives, watching his hands as they rest on the steering wheel. Even his hands were sexy. This thought disturbs her, making her skin prickle. Everything about him is disturbing, Gabriels's skin has a deep tan, his are arms strong, his fingers long and certain as they wrap around the leather wheel. Amelia instinctively closes her eyes letting the music wash over her, for her own sanity she had to block her errant thoughts out of her mind. Taking a deep breath, she turns away from him, instead resting her cheek on the safety belt, for the briefest moment as she watches the world pass by, she feels emotionally drained she closes her eyes willing herself to relax.

Glancing across at her Gabriel is aware of every nuance in her reaction, his expression unreadable he knew she had been watching him. He could feel her eyes on him. Biting his lip, he had forced himself not to react. Maintaining his own sense of balance was imperative as too much was at stake to allow his desire for her to frighten her away at this crucial point. Focusing his own thoughts, Gabriel turned his attention to driving as he navigated the dark streets. Amelia murmured, her words were barely discernible as she began drifting to sleep, lulled by the movement of the luxury car, wrapped in its warmth and safety, lost in her private thoughts. The journey did not take long as the roads were practically empty, soon Gabriel turned into a quiet side street, lined with older homes, pulling up outside a pretty villa style home, a single-storey house nestled in a large spacious plot at the end of the road. The property was illuminated by soft, romantic lighting, revealing a charming garden that surrounded the quaint home. Gabriel raised an eyebrow, impressed. Reaching across to gently wake her, he moved the hair that had fallen across Amelia's soft skin, his touch as light as a feather on her cheek.

"It's beautiful." He words though softly spoken make Amelia jump. She wakes, immediately becoming guarded as she glances at him, her voice is husky, she is a little disorientated. Gabriel repeats himself. "Your house is lovely Amelia." Amelia sits up feeling suddenly self-conscious that she had fallen asleep so quickly. Her words tumble out of her mouth.

"It belongs to Jack. It was Charlotte's aunt's place. When Charlotte died, she left it to Jack. He didn't know what to do with it, so I offered to take it on, do it up, and rent it from him. Jack's never taken a penny off me in rent...." She pauses for a moment staring at her beloved home, feeling a little embarrassed that she has been babbling on sharing too much of herself so quickly, even so she can't seem to stop herself as she continues. "He put all the rental money I paid him into a fund for Maddy's college studies. He never told me until she was fifteen. He always said that no one else would have taken the place on as it was in such a mess, he said that I was doing him a favour." Gabriel nods, understanding.

"Jack's a good man." He looks at the house again, then back at Amelia. "Another one of your lost causes that needed saving?" Amelia bristles at his words, her defences rising.

"No, actually. I love this place. It is important to me. You wouldn't understand, Gabriel. It's not grand or impressive, but it is my home, it's a special place, I love it. Maddy's grown up here. It has looked after us. I am very grateful to it and Jack...." Pausing, she appears to make her mind up to end the evening. "Anyway, thanks for the ride." Reaching for her purse she gets ready to leave, but Gabriel gently places his hand on her arm, stopping her.

"It looks lovely, Amelia. I did not mean to offend you. I would really like to come in and see your home.... May I come in for coffee? We need to talk." Amelia hesitates. Her heart is conflicted. She is exhausted, emotionally and physically spent from the day's events, but something in Gabriel's tone makes her pause. She sighs, her shoulders slumping slightly as she meets his gaze. Her eyes, filled with sadness, search his face.

"No, I don't think that's a good idea, Gabriel." Her voice is tinged with resignation. Gabriel raises an eyebrow, deliberately turning off the car's engine he turns in his seat to look at her, a small smile playing on his lips.

"Just coffee." Gabriel's tone is light but insistent. Amelia sighs again, feeling conflicted, she chews her lip seemingly too tired to argue she stares at Gabriel he seems determined they should talk. Finally, she nods, giving in. They both get out of the car, Gabriel follows Amelia up the winding brick pathway, which is lined with overgrown plants and herbs spilling from its borders. The scent of lavender and rosemary fills the evening air as they approach the front door. Amelia unlocks the door and steps inside, flipping on the lights. The house is warm and inviting, a stark contrast to the darkness of the garden. The interior is simple yet cozy, decorated in soft pastel shades with patchwork cushions, an open fireplace and rustic touches fill her home, it speaks of a lived-in comfort. Gabriel looks around, taking in the homey atmosphere with a smile.

"It's charming, Amelia. Really." She hears his words shrugging. Smiling softly, her shoulders relax fractionally as her gaze takes in her much-loved home, her heart instantly feels eased by the familiar surroundings. Heading for the kitchen she puts space between them. Gabriel closes the front door following her he studies her in her home as she relaxes. Amelia busies herself in the kitchen, which is undeniably the heart of the home, turning on the lights under the cabinets, filling the room with a soft glow. A large tabby cat stirs on the window seat that overlooks the back garden she blinks yawning her sleep disturbed, stretching lazily she starts to purr as Amelia can't resist giving her face a soft loving stroke.

"Hello Vivienne. Have you had a good day sweetheart?" The cat sits up mewing softly at Amelia. Gabriel leans on the doorpost taking in the scene as Amelia relaxes into the gentle ambience of her delightful home. A soft smile lifts the corners of his mouth as his gaze follows her movements about the kitchen. Amelia starts making coffee, her graceful ease automatic, though she can't help but feel the acute awareness of Gabriel's presence or the undeniable chemistry between them. Her own nerves, that have simmered just below the surface all evening finally start to ease in the comfort and sanctuary of her surroundings. Gabriel notices the subtle change in her shoulders as she softens imperceptibly, he steps closer, his voice barely audible is just above a whisper.

"I knew she was in there somewhere." Instantly Amelia's brow furrows, and she turns slightly to look at him.

"Who?" Gabriel meets her gaze, his expression earnest. His tone is soft, like liquid silk.

"The real you, Amelia. The one you have locked away. She is here, everywhere. Romantic, soft, feminine. This is who you are, the one who believes in happy endings." Amelia bristles again, turning back to the coffee.

"Please do not start that again, Gabriel. It is just a house. I don't know where you are getting all that rubbish from. I've seen far too much real life to believe in fairy tales anymore. People let you down. Life can be hard and cruel." Gabriel watches her intently.

"Really? Are you telling me that's what you truly believe?" He pauses considering his next words carefully. "Amelia, I never met a more honest, truthful person than you. If this is what you are telling yourself then no wonder you are so stressed, you are lying to yourself. That is not who you are. It is just loneliness and disappointment talking."

Amelia's grip tightens on the counter, her knuckles white, how can he still know her so well. Amelia can feel heat building inside her body, confused if she feels anger or desire, she swallows. Gabriel's sensual tone is undoing all her attempts to resist him. She doesn't turn around, doesn't respond. The silence in the kitchen is only disturbed by Vivienne's purring as Gabriel has stepped over to the cat and is now running his fingers gently over her back. 'Traitor' Amelia sends the cat a sideways glance. She can't help remembering how it felt to have Gabriel run his fingers gently over her skin. The thought brings colour to her cheeks; her body instinctively shivers. The atmosphere in the kitchen is electric she can feel the energy between them heating up, chiding herself, she frowns, perhaps that was just her own thoughts, Amelia checks herself. Gabriels's presence is awakening responses in her body she had forgotten existed. If she was completely honest, they were desires she had buried just like the memories that had flooded her mind all evening making it impossible to walk away. Silently she grimaces as the realisation dawns, her first response should have been to walk away, in fact not only should she have walked away, but she should have run as fast as she could in the opposite direction. She was playing with fire; she was going to get burned one way or another. Gabriel steps closer to her making every fibre of her being react to his energy, his voice softer now, more seductive.

"You don't have to do this, Amelia. You don't have to push everyone away just because you are scared. I know you have been hurt, that doesn't mean you have to shut yourself off from the world." Amelia sighs deeply all the air leaving her lungs, her shoulders slumping.

"You don't know anything about the real me, Gabriel. Twenty years is a hell of a long time. You've no idea who I am now. In fact, you didn't really know me back then, either." She turns to face him finally; her eyes filled with a mixture of pain and defiance. He is so close. Too close. Her resistance fires her response making her lash out at him.

"You think you can just waltz back into my life and act like nothing's changed? Like we can just pick up where we left off? It is not that simple, Gabriel. Life isn't a fairy tale." Gabriel is unfazed by her emotional outburst, he takes another step closer, closing the distance between them.

"I am not saying it's simple, Amelia. I don't live in a fantasy. I am saying it's worth considering revisiting. We were something very special once, and I believe we can be again. I need you to believe it too." Amelia shakes her head, a tear slipping down her cheek.

"Why Gabriel? Why now? I don't understand?... I can't, Gabriel. I just... I can't." Gabriel reaches out, gently wiping the tear away with his thumb. His touch is tender, filled with all the feelings he has been holding back.

"Yes, you can, Mia. You just need to let yourself." She pulls away from him, turning back to the counter, her voice barely above a whisper.

"It's too late. Too much has happened. You wouldn't understand." Gabriel's heart aches at her words, he has waited too long for this there is no way he is walking away now, he simply refuses to give up them.

"Then make me understand. Talk to me, Amelia. Tell me what is going on inside that beautiful head of yours. We can figure this out together." Amelia remains silent, her hands trembling slightly as she pours the coffee. She knows she should push him away, tell him to leave, her heart won't let her, what if Gabriel rejects her when he knows the truth. Amelia's errant thoughts chase through her mind as she turns Gabriel can see the anxiety in her eyes. She doesn't respond instead, she simply hands him a cup of coffee, their fingers brushing as she does, Amelia refuses to look up into Gabriel's eyes. Gabriel takes the cup, his eyes never leaving her face.

"Thank you." His voice gentle, his words soft, full of meaning that goes beyond just the coffee. They stand there in the kitchen, the distance between them filled with a thousand unspoken words. Finally, Amelia speaks, her voice small and broken.

"You don't understand what it was like, Gabriel." Gabriel's eyes soften they are filled with regret he wants to make this easier for her so that she relaxes, he interrupts her.

"I never wanted to lose you, Amelia. You were my whole world. When you left that day... it broke me. I didn't know how to find you, how to make things right. You just disappeared. You were gone." Amelia's breath catches in her throat. She had not expected him to be so honest, so vulnerable. She looks at him, really looks at him, seeing the pain in his eyes that mirrors her own. She cannot bear the pain she caused him, unable to maintain his gaze she looks down.

"Gabriel I am sorry I can't do this tonight. It's just too sudden. I.... I'm sorry. I think you should go." Gabriel steps closer again, his voice is deep, his words filled with emotion.

"You didn't have to protect yourself from me then Amelia. You don't have to now. I loved you. I still love you." The words hang in the air between them, sincere and full of truth. Amelia feels like the ground beneath her is crumbling, the walls she has built around her heart starting to crack. She wants to believe him, wants to let herself fall into his arms forgetting the past twenty years. Biting her lip she silently acknowledges that she can't because she is still too afraid. Afraid of getting hurt again, of opening herself up to the possibility of losing him once more.

"I don't know if I can do this." Her words are whispered, tears filling her eyes. Putting his coffee down Gabriel gently takes her free hand in his, holding it as if she is the most fragile thing in the world.

"Yes, you can, Amelia. We can do this together. But you must trust me." Amelia stares at him, her heart pounding in her chest.

She knows she is standing on the edge of something huge, something lifechanging. She can either take the leap and trust him, or she can once more retreat, back into the safety of her solitude. She pulls her hand back, his touch is just too much, too overwhelming, turning away from him Amelia puts her coffee aside she stares unseeing out into the dark garden. After a long moment, she finally nods, the smallest of nods, but it is enough.

The coffee is forgotten. Amelia can feel Gabriel's eyes on her back, the intensity of his gaze, the heat in his desire literally makes her skin tingle sending shivers down her spine. She stands up straight, trying to muster the strength to resist the pull between them, it is no use. Gabriel steps closer, his voice low and intimate, as he runs his fingertips down her back. The touch is electric, she inhales deeply, unable to ignore the effect he has on her. Gabriel is so close now that Amelia can feel his warmth through her blouse. She trembles involuntarily, her body shivering in response to his words, sensations flood her chest as her nipples harden against the thin fabric of her blouse. Gabriel brushes her hair to one side, exposing the delicate curve of the side of her face, he leans in to gently kiss the secret space at the nape of her neck, his hands gliding down her arms in a tender caress, he rests his hands on her hips. Amelia's body instantly responds to his light touch an aching desire begins to pulse through her. Gabriel murmurs his voice deep and thick laden with a history of passion for her.

"You may be very different from the Amelia I fell in love with. You're older. We both are.... I know this much...." The timbre of his voice melts her resistance, like a velvet caress, Gabriel's words whisper across the soft skin of her neck. "When I touch you, you tremble. I can feel your pulse race. You can deny that you care... Your body tells me a different story. Right now, being this close to you, your perfume, the way you smell..." Gabriel leans in close, his nose glances across the skin of her neck, he inhales deeply, shuddering slightly Amelia realises he is barely able to contain his own response to her. Knowing the effect, she is having on him merely serves to fan the flames of her own irrational thirst for his touch. Amelia grabs the countertop for support, her eyes closing as she tries to steady herself. Her mind wanders as a thought lingers making her hesitate; if she was completely honest with herself, she had known that the moment Gabriel had touched her earlier in the evening, her resolve had begun to crumble, she wanted him. She knew that her body ached for his touch once more. Gently he turns her around, lifting her chin so that their eyes meet. The connection between them is undeniable, Amelia feels her defences weakening.

"No, Gabriel, I can't..." She begins to protest, her words faltering as she looks deeply into his eyes. The gentleness she sees there dissolves the last of her resistance. All the resistance, all the walls she's built around herself, seem to fade away in his presence. Gabriel never takes his eyes off her as he leans in, giving her the time to decide, the pressure of his hips against hers makes her swallow hard, her pelvis tilts instinctively towards his making her gasp. A low moan escapes Gabriels's mouth as the heat in his body increases. Amelia hesitates, her gaze shifting to his mouth. She catches her own bottom lip between her teeth, trying to hold back, suddenly the loneliness and longing she has felt for so long surge to the surface. Gabriel is her home, she knows it. So does he. There is a sweet relief in surrender. Amelia leans into that feeling finally allowing herself to drift, trusting the inner wisdom she allows herself to feel the tide of sensations sweep through her. In that moment her heart opens and is filled once more with the deep resonance of love.

Needing to steady herself she reaches out, her hands finding his strong muscled arms, seeking the safety and comfort of his touch. The last of her fragile doubts crumble as she relaxes into his embrace her head nestled under his chin against his chest, turning her face up to his. Gabriel responds by kissing her tenderly, his lips brushing against hers with a softness that makes her heart ache. The kiss, tender at first, soon deepens into something more passionate, more intense, teasing her mouth he catches her bottom lip between his teeth in sweet torment she responds with wanton need all pretence of indifference now forgotten. She runs her hand over his waist and broad back. It is as if all the years they have spent apart, all the unspoken words, are being conveyed through this single, searing connection.

When Gabriel finally draws back, Amelia is left dazed, her mind reeling from the intensity of the moment. Breathless she steadies herself by holding onto his arm, needing that physical connection to ground her. Gabriel's breathing is fast, his desire evident in the erotic tautness in his muscular body, coupled with the smouldering look he gives her as he gently runs his hand through her hair, cupping her head as he places a soft kiss under her chin along her collar bone, a gesture so tender it brings tears to her eyes, so incredibly sensual Amelia literally swoons as her legs go weak. Smiling softly, Gabriel takes Amelia by the hand, leading her out of the kitchen. Her mind is finally silent, in surrender to her body she follows him instinctively. They move through the house, a quiet unspoken agreement between them filled with an intimate understanding. Amelia points toward her bedroom, almost in a daze. Gabriel guides her across the living room towards the sanctuary of her bedroom, their steps quiet and deliberate.

As they cross the threshold into the privacy of her bedroom, Gabriel softly closes the door behind them, shutting the rest of the world away. The room is dimly lit, the soft glow of a bedside lamp casting a warm light over the bed. Gabriel turns to Amelia, his eyes never leaving hers, in that moment, everything else falls away, the past, the future, the fears, the uncertainties. Nothing matters apart from the two of them, here and now, in the present moment, two souls reunited once more after decades of distance. He steps closer, his hand still holding hers, Amelia feels the last of her doubts ebb from her mind. Gabriel leans in again, capturing her lips in another kiss, this one slower, deeper, filled with all the longing and love that has been building between them. That longing one of years spent worlds away from one another, not just this evening, their separation for so long had left a chasm in each other's hearts perhaps for the first time in forever they would come together to start to heal what was once torn apart.

Standing facing one another in the quiet of Amelia's bedroom, the rest of the world disappears into the background. All that exists is this moment, the connection between them, the unspoken promise of what is to come. In the soft light Gabriel quietly undresses Amelia remembering her graceful body, while honouring her scars that mark experiences, he is yet to discover. She has changed, then so has he. Amelia's body has a softness that comes with motherhood, a body that has celebrated the process of life forming within. Nothing about her mature body could in any way diminish her beauty nor dim her radiance, her sensual delight, her deeply passionate response to him and her complete surrender. Gabriel lifts her easily into the air eliciting a giggle as he lowers her to the bed, for a moment he stands over her allowing her image to once again imprint on his memory.

Gabriel savours every moment, he has anticipated their reunion for months now, but the reality is more than he could have anticipated. Touching her naked silhouette framed so perfectly in the soft light of her intimate room is a profound moment for Gabriel. Feeling the waves of her desire pulsate under his insistent fingers, lingering long enough to take her to heights of pleasure she had not touched before, brings an equally intense climax for Gabriel too. They lay for hours, spent emotionally and physically wrapped once more in one another's arms. Finding each other after so many years had proven something neither of them had expected, patience has its own reward and distance most certainly makes the heart grow stronger when passion is reignited.

Chapter 11

The early morning sunlight filters through the shutters in Amelia's bedroom. She stirs opening her eyes, the warmth of Gabriels body behind hers is a loving reminder of the passion spent merely hours before. He is still fast asleep his breathing slow and rhythmic. The smell of him is totally male arousing Amelia's desire instantly. Catching her breath she gently slides towards the side of the bed easing herself out of his embrace. Sitting on the edge of the bed Amelia turns to watch him, her mind starts to reel. What was she thinking. Had all sense left her? Stifling a nervous giggle Amelia silently tiptoed towards the bathroom grabbing clothes on the way.

The soft glow of the rising sun gradually warms the back garden, casting a delicate almost magical hue over the dew-covered grass and vibrant flowers. The tranquillity of the early morning is breathtaking, with only the gentle rustling of leaves breaking the silence. Opening the shutters quietly Amelia unlocks the patio doors leading from her bedroom. Once the doors are open it allows the fresh morning air and early sunshine to stream in, filling the room with golden warmth. She is wearing Gabriel's navy shirt and her pink pyjama bottoms, a relaxed and contented expression on her face. After taking a deep breath, savouring the peacefulness of the moment, she returns to the bed where Gabriel is still sleeping. Gently lying down facing him, Amelia tentatively runs her hand over Gabriel's arm, her smile faltering slightly as concern flickers in her eyes. Gabriel stirs, breathing deeply as he stretches, and then turns on his side to face her. He opens his eyes, his electric blue gaze softening as he sees her.

"Happy birthday, Amelia." Gabriel murmurs, reaching forward to stroke her hair tenderly. He leans in to kiss her, drawing back as Amelia hesitates. Gabriel, noticing the question in her eyes, pauses. "I think we need to talk..." He smiles gently. His words soft. "Will you make breakfast and coffee? I'll take a shower, then maybe we can sit outside and enjoy the morning together." Amelia nods, lowering her gaze as uncertainty clouds her face. Gabriel notices her hesitation softly adding... "Or perhaps you could join me in the shower if you like." Amelia laughs a sweet sexy sound, shaking her head.

"You shower; I'll do breakfast." Gabriel smiles, rolling off the bed he heads for the bathroom. Amelia watches him go, as if she can hardly believe he is real, a mix of emotions playing across her face. She catches her lip as the memory of last night's love making brings a warmth to her insides making her blush slightly. She and Gabriel had always shared a passionate relationship, last night had been entirely different. Her thoughts tease at the feelings he had once again awoken in her, weaving a web of emotions around her leaving Amelia lost in a delightful dream of passion, tenderness, and connection. Closing her eyes she instantly feels the longing in her body just from the thoughts of their love making. Gabriel had aroused sensations she had buried for far too long. He had always been a considerate lover but last night they had come together with a passion that was undeniable intense erotic yet achingly tender.

The sound of the shower brings her back into the present, Amelia sits up looking down at the crumpled bed sheets she strokes the impression on the bed left by Gabriel's sleeping body. She smiles indulgently, then in a burst of post love making energy jumps into action. In the kitchen, she busies herself making coffee, toasting bread, and feeding the cat who is more than a little put out at not sleeping with Amelia. She picks up Vivienne and cuddles her making the cat purr loudly. Putting her on her favourite seat by the window Amelia spies a pile of envelopes. Opening various birthday cards, she smiles at the heartwarming messages inside. Once the coffee is made and the toast buttered, she places everything on a tray then heads out to the garden.

The back garden is a delight for the senses filled with the freshness of the early morning energy. Bougainvillea and roses bloom in vibrant colours, creating a serene and beautiful atmosphere. Amelia sits outside on the patio, her eyes closed, soaking in the warmth of the sun. She looks relaxed and content, as if the weight of the world has momentarily lifted from her shoulders. Gabriel emerges from the house, wearing the same trousers from the day before and an LAPD t-shirt borrowed from Amelia's closet. His hair is damp from the shower; he has a towel draped around his shoulders. He walks straight over to Amelia without hesitation taking her face in his hands he kisses her deeply on the mouth. The smell of body wash and clean man envelop her a heady intoxicating mix given her recent thoughts.

"Good morning, beautiful." He says with a smile. "I hope you don't mind; I borrowed this from your closet. My shirt seems to have found a new home." Amelia's stomach flips she grins, her hand instinctively smoothing the shirt she is wearing. Gabriel does not sit down immediately. Instead, he picks up a cup of coffee and a piece of toast, taking a large bite, he wanders barefoot onto the lawn, enjoying the feel of the cool dew beneath his feet. Amelia watches him, he is so utterly at ease, her eyes soak in the beauty of his form drinking in every moment, watching him she realises what has been missing for all these years. Realisation is staring her in the face, everything she had denied for so long is now right here. Immediately her own negative thoughts cloud her mind, her expression shifting from contentment to uncertainty as doubts begin to creep into her head. After a moment of silence, she speaks quietly.

"So, Gabriel, what have you been doing with yourself for the past 20 years? Still dismantling companies?" Gabriel stops moving, he turns to face her, a vague smile playing on his lips. He lowers his gaze to the ground before responding.

"Not exactly." He pauses, as if considering his next words carefully. "Shall I start where you left, or do you want the short version?" Amelia winces, her body language immediately becoming defensive. She sits up straighter, bracing herself for what is to come. Gabriel, however, remains calm and composed, watching her intently. Amelia's voice trembles as she begins to speak.

"I am not proud of what I did, Gabriel. I didn't want to leave. I felt suffocated. I felt trapped, trying to be someone that I wasn't. You know, we were surrounded by people I didn't like or trust." She takes a deep breath trying to steady her strained voice. "I was so tired of second-guessing myself every time I met someone new. I kept thinking, did they know? Had that horrible lawyer you worked with told them about me...." Amelia barely pauses to take a breath, her mind races to find the right words to say. She gulps in air, her voice sounding strained. "I got so paranoid. The gossip around us was so cruel and destructive, I just couldn't think straight. I was constantly trying to justify who I was." Her words tumble from her trembling lips as she tries to keep her composure. She pauses, her eyes glistening with unshed tears. "Gabriel, you rescued me, for that I will always be grateful." She pauses talking to herself rather than him.

"How do I say this without sounding rude?" Taking a deep breath, she continues. "I felt like I had stepped into a prison. Don't get me wrong, I know it was not you; it was me. I had trapped myself in my past. It was with me all the time." She shifts uneasily. "Every time I looked at your friends, I felt like they judged me. It got so bad; I just couldn't shake it. I felt like you were always trying to defend me, always having to rescue me. I hated it." Hesitating she carries on. "I felt like a victim. There were times it was worse than being on the street. I couldn't deal with the knowing looks, people talking behind our backs. I know you felt it too, we argued about it often enough."

Amelia looks bereft as if the words that she has just released had in a way, been locked inside her chest keeping her hostage to her past decisions. Gabriel knew instinctively it was the release she needed but he is aware judging by her apparent anxiety there was still more she must let go of. Remaining silent Gabriel watches her, his expression unreadable as he listens to her. Amelia stands up, wringing her hands, her movements agitated and restless. She walks around the garden, looking at the flowers but not truly seeing them. Pain and regret almost etched on her face as she continued to speak.

"I am so sorry that I hurt you, Gabriel. I know I did. But I realized that if I had stayed..." She trails off, her voice breaking. "I could not have been truly happy with you like that. We were hurting each other so much, and I hated being like that. I had to become someone different, a better person." Turning to look at him her eyes implore his for compassion, Gabriel meets her gaze his expression neutral he steadily maintains eye contact with her, Amelia cannot keep his gaze, she looks away her words just audible. "I couldn't be the person you wanted me to be. I just knew that I would always be the prostitute you saved if I had stayed with you. I was so ashamed of what I had been." The truth in her own words makes Amelia wince, she reaches up and puts her hand to her forehead as if the very truth she has expressed is causing pain in her head.

"It was always there, lurking in the shadows, no matter how hard you tried to deny it. It came between us. You couldn't fight everyone, and I didn't want you to." She looks at Gabriel searching his face for understanding. Gabriel is silent his expression still unreadable. Amelia presses on, now she has started she has to make him understand. "I needed a clean start, somewhere no one knew me. I had to get over my own past, I just couldn't do that with you."

Gabriel flexes his shoulders as if shrugging off her truth, in his own way he too is processing what she has just said. The reality right now, was that this, these words, and emotions, were exactly what Amelia had needed to let go of. He had felt her pent-up tension all evening. Making love to her, he had known that even though she had experienced a deep physical release, she was still holding on to emotions that needed an emotional release. Amelia had needed to own her truth; she had to say it aloud, to let go of the pain that was holding her captive. He smiled ruefully to himself it had been harder to hear than he had anticipated but hopefully, after this morning, making love to her now would bring them closer than ever. Gabriel's body responds immediately as he too remembers the passion, they have so recently shared. He shifts trying to maintain his composure to allow her to continue. Gabriel watches her thoughtfully; his next words are more of a statement than a question.

"You didn't come back here straight away, though, did you?" Softly he continues. "I know, Amelia, I looked everywhere for you. You just disappeared. I had enough people searching for you. Where did you go?" Amelia meets his gaze, pausing she centres herself before she responds to him ready to finally answer the question that had haunted him for decades. For a moment, her voice wavered then clearing her throat she continued, her voice now steadier as she replies.

"I went to Seattle. I didn't know anyone there, so no one could tell you where I was...." Amelia lets the information register with Gabriel; she watches him actively trying to gauge his reaction. He is still hardly moving, he looks down at the coffee cup in his hand, considering her words. Amelia catches her lip between her teeth, her nerves beginning to get the better of her. Hesitantly she continues. "I changed my surname I.... I used your mentor's name. I knew you would never think to look for anyone with that name."
Gabriel looks up, his eyes meet hers directly for a moment, but it is him who looks away first, he smiles to himself, a bittersweet expression on his face as he looks away. Amelia cannot tell what he is thinking.

Gabriel walks over to the garden furniture sitting down, his posture appears relaxed, he is however, given his silence, clearly deep in thought. Amelia moves towards him, the distance between them suddenly unbearable after the closeness and intimacy they have shared. Amelia needs his reassurance that he is not going to reject her. She keeps her eyes fixed on a beautiful rose in full bloom next to where Gabriel is sitting. She gently touches one of the blooms, as if telling her story to the flower rather than facing Gabriel directly. As the morning sun continues to warm the garden, Amelia takes a deep breath, feeling the burden of the memories, she has just shared with Gabriel lift imperceptibly. The flowers around them, vibrant and full of life, contrast with the intensity of their conversation. She looks down at the coffee cup cradled in her hands, her fingers tracing the rim as if it could somehow anchor her in the present.

"I came back here when I thought you'd stop looking, by that time I had given birth to Maddy and completed my training at the academy..." Pausing once more for a moment Amelias eyes seem to cloud as she recalls the difficult memory, she continues, her voice soft but steady. "I needed to change my life, be someone I felt I could be proud of. Back in Seattle, I made the decision to become a police officer. I wanted to be different. That is why I chose to join the force." Amelia looks away lost momentarily in memories that hold their own degree of pain.

"Believe me, it was brutal at first. I was honest about who I had been. They accepted that in Seattle, and they took me on the training course." She sighs remembering what the early days in her training had brought in terms of emotional distress. "You can't begin to imagine what I had to deal with or how much fun they had with my history at the academy. I had to push through it, be honest, let people judge me based on what I could do, not what I had been." She stops abruptly, her words merely hinting at the resilience she had needed to develop just to survive the consequences of her past. Gabriel leans forward, his eyes softening as he taps the chair opposite him, silently inviting her to sit. Amelia hesitates for a moment before she takes the seat, still clutching her coffee cup. She sighs deeply, lifting the cup to her lips, then resting it back in her lap, seeking comfort in its warmth.

Gabriel reaches out, gently taking her cup from her hands and placing it on the table. His fingers lightly lift her chin, guiding her gaze to meet his. He offers her a small, understanding smile as his thumb brushes softly against her cheek. Sitting back in his chair, he continues to hold her gaze, his eyes filled with a quiet compassion. He could feel her body hesitantly relax; it was a deep subtle shift as if her soul had finally come to terms with her past. Silently he inwardly acknowledged with deep gratitude that God willing they had taken a huge step towards the future he had envisioned for them.

"Thank you." His voice was calm and reassuring. "I was not accusing you when I said you left, Amelia. I knew you needed to get this off your chest. I wanted to hear your version of the story, not the one I had created in my mind." Gabriel smiles at Amelia, his bright eyes clear and earnest. "Believe me, I made up a thousand different versions of why you left. But I needed to hear the actual truth from you." Amelia's face softens as she looks into Gabriel's eyes, his eyes so blue so intense and so undeniably gentle his forgiveness evident in the way he was speaking. Her expression softened as she began to feel a sense of ease, she hesitantly returned his smile, a small glimmer of hope shining through her uncertainty. Gabriel continued, his tone reflective and calm.

"Amelia, when you left, I knew that I was more to blame than you were." Hesitating he looks at her letting her absorb what he has just said. Quietly he continues. "That didn't stop me from being angry with you." He pauses, his emotions searingly honest, raw and sharp an expression she can't quite name in his eyes as they search her face for equal understanding. "I am glad you disappeared. With your shame and my anger, it was enough to kill any chance we had of being in love." He grins at her to reassure her. It had taken him years to get to the place where he held only a playful sentimentality towards thoughts of his past and the effect her disappearance had had on him. "I thought that if I married you, it would make everything all right. That it would stop people from making such a big deal out of it. But instead, it became this monster in our relationship...." Pausing it is Gabriels turn to look away, recalling memories of a time in his life he would most definitely rather forget.

"I knew it was destroying us both. I will always be grateful you left when you did. You set us both free." Gabriel's voice wavers slightly as he speaks, his vulnerability surfacing. "I'm not going to deny that it was incredibly hurtful, I was deeply damaged by it." His words burn with intensity as he continues. "I was consumed by my anger. It took over my life. I drank, I gambled, I womanised, I did everything I could to get you out of my head. I was like a man possessed." Gabriels's truth is straight, unflinchingly open and honest. His words are a statement of fact about his life; there is no blame attached to them. He sighs, his gaze drifting away from Amelia as he stares off into the distance, lost in thought.

"I managed to lose absolutely everything. I mean everything. It took me a hell of a long time and heartache to realise why you had gone. Now, I am just thankful you did." Considering his next words carefully he continues. "I had to find out who I was behind all the money, behind the facade we were trying to build...." He pauses staring at Amelia directly. "I lied to you, Amelia, but mostly, I had lied to myself about everything I was. What a fool I was. So proud, so certain. I am only sorry that you had to leave me so that I could realise the truth, to find it out who I really was. I know in my heart what you did was right."

Gabriel's voice trails off, the accountability of his confession settling between them. The garden, so full of life and beauty, felt like a peaceful haven in which these long-buried truths could finally be uncovered. Amelia watches him, her heart aching for the pain they both endured, yet also filled with a sense of relief that these words, so long unspoken, have finally been brought to light. Gabriel continues, his voice now softer but no less sincere.

"The last 20 years have been difficult, Amelia. At times, sheer hell. I have had to face serious demons from my past. When you lose everything, life forces you to take a long, hard look at who you are. When you see the truth about yourself, you have a choice: change, be better, or give up." He sighs the first evidence of the strain that this discussion is causing him. "I'm no quitter, Amelia." He looks at her with absolute sincerity. "Neither are you. I have survived. In fact, I am finally on the right road. I have made a success of my life, financially and otherwise. There are things I want to tell you, but it is not all happy stuff." He pauses, making the decision he has said enough. His tone shifts becoming more enthusiastic. Wanting to shift the conversation away from the heavy emphasis it has taken. Gabriel grins widely at her sending shivers down her spine as she looks at his radiant smile. "Today's your birthday, it's a celebration. We have found each other again. This is about looking forward. I want to celebrate that with you today."

Amelia feels torn as she watches him, hesitating, her emotions swirling inside her. Gabriel has been unflinchingly honest with her, now she must find the strength to do the same, no matter what the outcome. She knows that it is imperative that she must share the truth about Maddy with him, what she still doesn't know is just how far the ramifications of that truth will go. Making up her mind that no matter what may come she can't hide from this moment any longer Amelia has to tell him the secret that has been weighing on her heart for years. She opens her mouth, her voice wavering as she begins.

"Gabriel, there's something I need to tell you." Before she can continue, Gabriel deliberately interrupts, his tone full of bold emotion. Passionately he silences her confession.

"Amelia, I need you to know this. When you strutted into my life, sharp, sassy, and so damn sexy all those years ago, you were like a drug to me. I was totally out of control. I was so in love with you. I couldn't help how I felt. I was so jealous of everyone around you." His face is full of passion as he speaks. "I loved you so much it burned. Seeing you today, it is still there. I can feel it deep inside, but this isn't fire anymore. It's just true, deep love. Mia, I want to start again. I want to show you that I can be the man you wanted me to be." Gabriel leans forward, his gaze locking with Amelia's. "I could not see it before, Mia. I couldn't see this uncut diamond in front of me, my treasure. You were my treasure; I had no idea how to make you shine or how to love you the way you deserved." Pausing he pulls back to see her reaction.

"I promise you; I am different now. Let me show you. Let me show you that I can love you. I can be what you need." Gabriels's words are filled with so much emotion, such enthusiasm for life and such sincerity that tears spring to Amelia's eyes. She shakes her head, wiping at the tears as they fall. She stands up, unable to sit still any longer, her emotions too overwhelming.

"Gabriel, there is something I have to tell you." Her voice trembling with the magnitude of her confession. She takes his hands in hers, holding them tightly as she looks into his eyes, trying to find the courage to speak. Gabriel looks at her knowing what she is about to say to him. It is her secret to tell but he already believes with all his heart that Maddy is his daughter he just needs to hear her say the words. Amelia stares at his beautiful face a lifetime of experience etched so sensitively, he looks as if an artist has agonised over every line chiselling a profile that leaves her breathless. Amelia inhales deeply it is now or never this moment may take this man away from her forever and if that is the case then she will have only herself to blame.

Chapter 12

The admission lingers on her lips. Amelia takes a deep breath, straightens her shoulders as if summoning all her strength and composure from deep inside. She raises her gaze and looks Gabriel steadily in the eyes. Then just as she is about to utter the truth that she has kept hidden for so long, there is a loud bang inside the house as the front door bursts open with a loud crash, the sudden noise makes Viviene the cat leap up racing across the garden, disappearing under a bush for protection. The intimate atmosphere is shattered as a chorus of voices fills her bedroom, singing "Happy Birthday!" at the top of their lungs. Maddy, Joe, Liv, Georgia, and Albee all pile into the garden through the patio doors, a riot of balloons, streamers, party hats, and presents. The children are laughing and shouting, their excitement exuberant as they charge at Amelia with utter joy and delight. Only Joe appears to register the enormity of the scene his eyes flicking between Amelia and Gabriel with a hint of embarrassment. Joe quickly steps forward, offering an apologetic smile.

"Sorry, Auntie Mia. There was no way I could stop them. They have been up since dawn." Clearly embarrassed he explains, looking slightly sheepish. Gabriel returns Joe's look with a warm, understanding smile, though he is more than a bit taken aback by the sudden intrusion. Meanwhile, the rest of the group surrounds Amelia, hugging her and bombarding her with birthday wishes.

Amelia, though caught off guard, can't help but smile at the noisy, exuberant display of love from her family. She casts a glance at Gabriel her eyes full of tears and apologies, he smiles warmly back at her with an expression that speaks volumes, silently acknowledging that their conversation will have to wait. Liv, ever the observant one, notices the seismic change between Amelia and Gabriel. She grins suggestively at Amelia, her eyes sparkling with mischief.

"Hmm, I'm not sure who is more surprised, Mia; you or me!" Liv teases, her words bely her real understanding, she gives Amelia a playful nudge. "This lot's had me up since six. There was no way they were going to wait until 10. They have been planning this for months!" Liv hugs Amelia, genuinely relieved and delighted, looking up she catches Gabriel's eye over the top of Amelia's head. The two exchange a knowing look, and Gabriel subtly shakes his head, signalling that now is not the time for further revelations. It is the ever-observant Joe who witnesses their silent exchange, quickly checking to see if Maddy had noticed, a question forms in his mind, one he won't get the answer to until the following day in a way no-one could anticipate. Fortunately, Maddy is too preoccupied with her mother to pay attention. Maddy looks at Gabriel with a shy bright smile, which he returns with genuine affection. Placing his hand gently on the small of Amelia's back, Gabriel leans down to whisper in her ear.

"Mia, I am going to head back to the hotel. I have that meeting I mentioned. Can I borrow this?" He tugs playfully at the t-shirt he is wearing. "I'll give it back to you later." Amelia blushes deeply, aware of the eyes on them. Everyone has now noticed the LAPD t-shirt Gabriel is wearing and that Amelia has on his shirt. Maddy has a huge smile on her face as she watches her mom. The children, thankfully, remain blissfully unaware of the implications. Amelia nods blushing her eyes sparkle with an emotion Maddy has never seen in her mom, Amelia tries valiantly to maintain her composure.

"Yes, of course you can." She says shyly, her cheeks flush a deeper shade of pink, embarrassed she ushers Gabriel inside.

"Excuse me, guys, I'll be back in a minute." Amelia steps past Gabriel motioning for him to follow her inside. Once inside the privacy of her bedroom, Amelia turns to Gabriel, her face a mixture of emotions.

"Thank you, Gabriel. You have been so open with me this morning. There are things I need to tell you; I am sorry I can't do that now; not with everyone here." She hesitates, then adds. "Last night, you told Maddy you are free tonight. Are you?" Gabriel nods, a smile playing on his lips.

"Yes, I am." Amelia smiles, the relief evident on her face.

"Would you like to come to the dinner tonight that is at your hotel......as my date? We could, after the party, finish this conversation later." Gabriel's smile broadens into a grin.

"Nothing would make me happier." He steps closer, pulling her into a kiss, oblivious to the laughter and clapping coming from the garden. Amelia pulls back, grinning like a teenager, her heart racing with anticipation. "Does this suit me?" Gabriel asks playfully, gesturing to the LAPD t-shirt he's wearing. Amelia laughs.

"You can keep the t-shirt. Just give me a minute, I'll change out of your shirt." She turns to her closet, but Gabriel catches her hand.

"Keep it on. I like my shirt on you." He says with a playful wink. "It looks sexy. Besides, I like the idea of something of mine next to your skin." His words send a shiver down Amelia's spine. She turns back to him, blushing, then reaches into her closet to mischievously select an LAPD baseball cap. Placing it on Gabriel's head, she grins up at him.

"Does this mean I'm one of your guys now?" He asks with a chuckle.

"You've got potential." Amelia teases him back loving their easy banter. Gabriel leans down, placing a lingering kiss on her throat, right under her chin.

"I'd better go before I spoil the party by kicking everyone out so I can keep you to myself. I've waited far too long to have you back in my bed." His murmured words whisper against her warm skin, his voice thick with desire, Gabriel exposes her shoulder nipping her skin between his teeth, leaving Amelia reeling with desire once more. Amelia laughs, her laugh is full and free. She wants nothing more than to be alone with him again, the promise in his words sends a thrill through her. He raises his head and stares into her eyes in silent understanding, kissing her gently on the forehead. Gabriel breathes deeply inhaling the scent of her before he turns away heading for the garden once more. She watches as he heads for the patio doors, calling out to the others.

"I'll see you later, guys. Maddy, your mom says I can come to the party tonight, so I'll catch you there." Maddy beams at him, a faint blush colouring her cheeks as she waves goodbye. Amelia, feeling a pang of doubt, quickly shakes it off, reminding herself of the evening ahead. Gabriel turns back to Amelia, walking straight up to her he takes off the baseball cap with a grin. He leans in close, pressing his forehead to hers, his voice filled with emotion as he whispers.

"Thank God, I found you again." He kisses her hard on the mouth, his hands cradling her face as if she's the most precious thing in the world. When he finally pulls back, his ice-blue eyes are bright with happiness.

"Wear something sexy tonight." Gabriel's eyes sparkle with desire he turns away with a wink. "I'll meet you in the cocktail bar at seven." Amelia's face lights up at the thought of their evening together, a smile spreading across her lips. She watches him leave, then closes the door behind him, leaning against it for support as the emotions of the morning catch up with her. Liv rushes into the hallway, practically bouncing with excitement.

"I knew it! I knew it! He couldn't keep his hands off you!" Liv exclaims with delight, her eyes wide with glee. "Come on, I want to know all the details! No, wait, you can tell me in the car. We need to get you showered and dressed! This is so exciting..." Liv giggles, the sound making Amelia's face break into exuberant smiles too. "Come on Amelia. Let's get to the salon!" Amelia, still grinning like a teenager in love, nods and follows Liv back to her bedroom to get ready, her heart racing with the promise of what the evening will bring.

Chapter 13

Outside Amelia's pretty house Liv sits impatiently tapping the steering wheel of her bright yellow Porsche, searching through the music on her phone she selects the right playlist for their trip to the salon. Liv is itching to be away from the house so that she can find out exactly what Amelia and Gabriel discussed after they left dinner the night before. As soon as Amelia appears at the door, she starts the car revving the engine she grins at Amelia who acknowledges her impatient friend with a wave. There are kisses all round for Amelia as she skips down the path towards Liv, she shouts 'I love you all' to the family gathered to wave her off. Joe, Maddy, Georgia and Albee all sing exuberantly once more, a slightly off pitch and squeaky rendition of 'Happy Birthday' which makes Amelia laugh and Liv role her eyes

Liv looks so much like the rebellious teenager that Amelia remembered so well that it makes Amelia look twice at her, the excitement of the last 24 hours clearly rubbing off on all of them. Jumping into the car, Liv's huge smile shifts any lingering doubts from Amelia's mind, unconsciously she decides to leave her cares behind, well for the moment at least. With the roof down and the music playing Liv hits the accelerator as Rihana's 'Diamonds' blasts from the stereo, the morning sun casts a radiant hue over the streets as they speed away from the house, wind whipping through their hair. The upbeat rhythm matching the heightened emotions both women are filled with. Liv glances over at Amelia, a mischievous grin on her face as she presses harder on the gas pedal, the car roaring down the road. Amelia laughs, holding onto the edge of her seat, her hair flying wildly around her glowing face, she shouts.

"Liv, you're going to get us arrested before we even get to the salon!" Liv bursts out laughing, her exuberance showing as her eyes sparkle with genuine joy.

"Relax, Mia! You're the boss they wouldn't dare arrest you on your birthday. Enjoy babe this is going to be the best day ever!" Ever the voice of reason Amelia can't help herself when she places a hand on Liv's arm, squeezing it as Liv takes a corner a little too fast.

"Woah, Liv they might not arrest me, but they sure as hell will arrest you no matter who you're with." Liv concedes the obvious wisdom in Amelia's warning and slows to a more sensible pace; it needn't have mattered as they arrive at the salon shortly after. The car smells hot its breaks well tested by Liv, the thrill of the ride and the anticipation of the evening ahead filling the car with a sense of reckless abandonment, as they had zoomed through the streets of LA, the vibrant city passing by in a blur of colours and energy, almost as if the two women were reliving a different more care free time, a time when their greatest fear was not having the rent for the week.

After what feels like a thrillingly short drive they pull up to Liv's salon on Rodeo Drive. The building is modern and sleek, with large glass amber coloured windows that reflect the LA sunshine and the boulevard while protecting the privacy of the extremely high-end clientele inside. The salon's discreet sign in burnt copper italic letters hints at its purpose, 'More Than Just... A Pretty Woman'. Liv parks the Porsche with a flourish in her owners parking bay, turning off the engine as the music dies down, she turns in her seat, a giggle bubbling in her chest as she catches sight of her reflection in the rear-view mirror. Both are flushed and windswept, Liv looks over at Amelia, all thought of a sensible conversation left on the road behind them, her grin widens.

"Ready?" Amelia nods, her excitement palpable.

"Absolutely. Let's go." Positively buzzing the two friends, who look as if they have been through a wind tunnel, bounce arm in arm through the door of the salon. In complete contrast the salon is an oasis of calm, the ambience is a haven of luxury and tranquillity, with soft lighting, elegant décor, a subtle scent of lavender in the air. Liv suddenly remembers where she is, becoming a little self-conscious that she has gotten carried away with all the romance and drama. She needn't have worried as both Liv's staff and clients all adore her frank, funny and enthusiastic approach to life, she is after all the heart and soul of the business who has earned the right to her impressive success. From the moment they walk through the door Amelia and Liv are welcomed with genuine warmth, their entire day one of indulgence meticulously planned by Liv and her manager Sasha. Their first stop is the facial room, where they are pampered with a series of state-of-the-art treatments designed to make a women feel like a movie star. As the aesthetician gently massages Amelia's face, Liv chats animatedly about the plans for the rest of the day.

"After this, we're getting the full treatment, massages, waxing, the whole works. Then we'll grab some lunch and come back for hair, nails make-up and…" Liv can't help herself she is like a bottle of champagne waiting for the cork to pop. "Wait until you see the designer who is bringing in the dresses for us to chose from. Mia I am so, so excited. I've been following this guy for so long and he has finally offered to come over especially for you tonight. I did him a huge favour for his last fashion show, his hair and make-up team all got food poisoning, and he was really stuck. Nico is an absolute gem; you are going to love his designs…." Pausing to catch her breath Liv says in a quieter voice, "Mia you are going to look amazing tonight. I can't wait to see Gabriel's reaction when he sees you, I've been planning this for weeks."

The words are out of Liv's mouth before she can stop them, Liv presses her lips together holding her breath she stares at Amelia who is reclining in the beautician's chair, Liv is acutely aware she has said too much. She needn't have worried as Amelia is deeply relaxed enjoying the treatment too much to notice her friends face lose some of its brightness. With her eyes closed Amelia reaches out towards her best friend, opening and shutting her hand in an invitation for Liv to reach across and take her hand, when Liv takes Amelia's hand the friends grasp one another in an unspoken action of shared allegiance. Liv's whole body relaxes as Amelia sighs whispering.

"You always know how to spoil a girl, I could get used to this. Thank you in advance for a magical day darling, you are the best friend I could have ever wished for." Liv hearing those words smiles ruefully, thankful that Amelia's eyes are still closed, if they were open, they would have seen the tear that rolled down Liv's cheek. Thank goodness Amelia hadn't understood or suspected anything from what Liv had said. Checking herself for being stupid, Liv squeezed Amelia's hand one more time, getting up she briefly considered her reflection in the mirror before stepping into the corridor to speak to a member of her team. Amelia's eyes fluttered open registering Liv chatting and laughing with the staff member. Closing her eyes again she sighed deeply, having a best friend who owned an incredible beauty business had certainly had its perks over the years. Amelia allowed herself a gentle smile of satisfaction glancing at Liv she felt incredibly proud of all her friend had accomplished. Liv was utterly in her element smiling and laughing with her staff and clients, Amelia's heart swelled with love at what Liv's amazing hard work, determination and talent had achieved.

Liv had become a local celebrity in her own right, not only did she own the salon which was frequented by many of the rich and powerful ladies of LA, she has also been one of the first women to really embrace social media. Liv had a regular wellness podcast which she recorded from her small studio above the salon, she had a huge following of people from all walks of life. The reach of Liv's 'More than Just...' series had been amazing to watch. Liv was unashamed and used all her lived experiences to candidly help women struggling with their own self-esteem and confidence issues to embrace their power and fulfil their potential no matter what their age or circumstance. Liv had become an incredible role model who Amelia was blessed to call her best friend. Liv sensing her friend's eyes on her, turned, winking she grinned as if reading her thoughts.

Their shared history meant everything to both friends who had literally dragged themselves out of their own murky pasts to carve futures that held no evidence of their undeniable and at times brutal lived experience. Only Amelia and Jack knew of Liv's considerable contributions towards Amelia's charity and the shelter, her support of the women who found their way there showed the depth of Liv's compassion and kindness. Amelia knew there was no possible way she could have set the charity up without the amazing, consistent support that Liv and Jack had brought into her life. They had stood by Amelia in her darkest times. Their generosity, love and total kindness shone like a beacon in her life, the only family that Amelia had ever needed. Today wasn't just about Amelia it was about Liv too and Amelia was eternally grateful that her dearest friend who was more like a sister to her was right by her side to experience every moment. Amelia's memories of their time together would always hold a very special place in her heart. Today was shaping up to be another day that would be impossible to forget. Liv had thought of every treatment and pampering that a woman could need to make her feel like a million dollars.

A little while later Maddy arrived just in time for lunch, her eyes lighting up when she saw her mom looking so relaxed and happy. "You look so chilled Mom!" Amelia grinned her trademark wide smile taking years off her beautiful face, giving her daughter a quick hug.

"Thanks, sweet, I'm feeling pretty chilled too." Not far along the exclusive parade from Liv's salon was the fabulous bistro 'Rendezvous' that they headed to for lunch. The Maître De fussed effusively over his favourite client Liv, making a show of welcoming them by personally ushering them across the busy restaurant filled with LA's elite. The small party were seated at Liv's favourite cozy corner table with a great view of the boulevard and the other diners. The atmosphere in the chic restaurant was vibrant, with the chatter of other patrons filling the air, for the three women, it was a private intimate celebration. They ordered light salads and sparkling water, Liv insisting on a bottle of champagne to mark the occasion. Amelia hesitated when the glasses were poured, but under the encouraging smiles of Liv and Maddy she lifted her glass.

"Just a sip!" Amelia smiled indulgently, taking a small taste of the bubbly liquid, she silently allowed her mind to wander for a moment as she watched her two favourite women in the world chat and laugh at something on Maddy's phone. It took her breath away when she thought about how far they had come. Amelia's thoughts wandered back to the first day she gone shopping on the boulevard, in search of something to wear for dinner with Gabriel that day too, the memory brought a sharp pang of sadness which clouded her so far bright sunny day. Looking out of the window down the elegant street she recalled a memory that was so clearly marked in her mind. That day had been a day of contrasts where some of the women she had met had been callous and bitchy their snide comments and judgements affecting Amelia in ways they would never see or know. Their unkind remarks leaving indelible imprints on her fragile self-esteem, like tattoos on the soul. It had also been the day when Jack had really shown her what kindness from a stranger looks like. It was a day when Amelia had learned that light and dark were a balance, quite often alongside the best of days there were unsettling experiences which balanced the good with the bad. Life was not easy, it was complex and gritty interspersed with intense moments of joy, light and love. But with love there was also the possibility of heartbreak and loss.

Amelia placed her glass back on the crisp white tablecloth, smiling to herself she remembered how touched she had been by his gentle and nonjudgemental guidance. Jack had been the person who had shown Amelia what trust, respect and true friendship looked like with no agenda. That day had been one of the most memorable moments of her life and she would always love Jack for it. Ageing was a funny thing, taking a moment to look back over her life she could see how clearly all her decisions had shaped the events she had experienced, and one thing stood out above all else. The choices she had made whether consciously or unconsciously had dictated everything she had attracted into her life. Taking a moment to study what was happening to her today was making Amelia realise that no matter what happened with Gabriel she knew if she was truly honest with herself, that she had been the one who had been asking for change.

Over the past twelve months since Maddy had started college and learned how to drive, a distance had opened between them, one where she could see her daughter's independence showing itself clearly in the decision's she was making for herself. Amelia had raised Maddy to be independent and respectful. Maddy had known the loving, supported, safe childhood that Amelia had not experienced. Maddy was the number one priority in her life, over and above work and the shelter but that relationship was changing, and Amelia could feel the friction it was creating between them. Friction. That was a word and feeling that Amelia knew all too well. It was a constant in her working world, but she inwardly acknowledged it was also always there in her private life too, lurking inside her body, a friction, a knowing that she wasn't living the life she truly wanted, rather she was living the life she had designed to make herself feel better about the mistakes she had made. It was a life of repentance, and now she had to face the truth about herself and the repercussions of her own decisions.

Always sensitive to other's feelings Liv looked up at Amelia as if sensing her friend's introspection. Watching Amelia as she stared out of the window, she could see the doubt and deep musings that were making Amelia absentmindedly chew her bottom lip. Liv recognised that look, it was one of the reasons that she had agreed to Jack keeping the truth from Amelia. They had both seen the change in their friend over the last year. Amelia had become less, somehow, more absent, even a little down. Today wasn't a day when Liv was going to allow that mood, that doubt to ruin what was possibly going to be a turning point for Amelia. Reaching out to Maddy, Liv silently covered her phone with her hand making Maddy aware that they had been neglecting Amelia who had become a little withdrawn. Maddy immediately realised what Liv was doing taking the hint she put the phone on the table, looking at her mom she frowned slightly, concern clouding her bright eyes. Picking up her glass she coughed quietly to attract her mom's attention. Instantly Amelia refocused on her loved ones, a well-practised happy smile an immediate foil to cover her darker thoughts.

"I would like to propose a toast for you mom. It's your 40th Birthday today and I want to say Happy Birthday. You are the best mom ever and I'm so lucky to have you in my corner. Thank you for everything you do for me, for the times I forget and for the things you don't think that I notice. I do. I love you and I am so incredibly proud that you are my mom." Maddy lifts her glass to toast her mom, Liv follows suit, and Amelia too raises her glass her eyes shinning a little brighter after her daughter's loving words. Suddenly Maddy's phone starts to vibrate on the table. Her reaction one of pleasure as she picks it up to see who it is, she mouths to them with a grin as she excuses herself from the table.

"I've just got to take this. Be right back." Maddy slips away from the table laughing as she makes her way across the packed restaurant. Liv grins indulgently watching her God daughter go, a knowing smile on her face.

"Spencer, I'll bet." Amelia's words are flat. Liv turns to look at Amelia whose eyes betray her concern. Amelia smiles her expression softening. "Those two seem very into each other." Liv chuckles, sensing the disapproval in Amelia, she keeps it light.

"Young love, there's nothing quite like it. When you don't have anything to compare it to and you are so squeaky clean with no experience to make you cynical...." Liv sighs a little dramatically.

"I do worry about her judgement though Liv. She is very naïve, and she has had an easy, sheltered life, compared to most." Amelia's mood has shifted, and Liv does her best to lift her spirits.

"Come on Mia, she is a good girl. She knows what's right and what's not. I don't think anyone has it that easy now with social media. They are all living a life of comparison that we never had to.

Thank God. We were free to make our mistakes in private. Without and audience. Now people seem to feel they must share every detail, they are so over exposed, they aren't allowed to be sensitive and private." As Liv is talking the waiter comes over to clear away their finished plates. Amelia considers what Liv has just said. Liv was the closest person to an aunt that Maddy had in her life and Amelia would always be eternally grateful that they shared a very special bond, knowing that Maddy confided in Liv didn't bother her at all, unlike some women Amelia was not a jealous person. It was in fact far more important and a comfort to know that should anything happen to her at work, Maddy would have people who loved her close by. For a moment her thoughts wandered to the dangers of her job, her face clouding as she acknowledged her fears. Liv interrupted her train of thought as she leant across the table, lowering her voice conspiratorially.

"Speaking of being into someone, you've told me about the sex, but what's going on with Gabriel?" Liv leans on the crisp white linen with her elbows her face resting on her hands as she stares at Amelia. "And Mia, I need to know. Just who is the guy that he is with... Babaji? He seems sweet enough, but what's that all about? Are they business partners. Is he Yoda?" Liv giggles her face glowing, eager for a gossip, still the same old Liv. Amelia grinned back at her friend. You could take the girl off the street, but some of the street always stayed with the girl. Sighing Amelia looks down at her hands playing with the pretty amber ring she is wearing. She takes her time to answer not knowing what to say or really wanting to go into the detail of how she feels. It's all so new and sudden Amelia hasn't had a moment to process anything that has happened. Looking at Liv's shinning eyes she softens, her friend wants nothing more than her happiness Amelia is certain of that. What she can't be sure of at this point was how Gabriel would take the news that she had denied him a lifetime with his only child.

"I don't know Liv. I don't know who he is, we didn't talk about him. We didn't get chance.... It's complicated Liv you know that." Liv's eyebrows raise questioning her friend with a look.

"Complicated. Yes, I get that but come on. Mia it's your birthday; you're reunited with the love of your life. He's practically worshipping the ground you walk on. What's complicated about that?" Amelia leans back in her seat. She pauses before she carries on thinking about what she wants to admit to.

"There's so much history Liv. And... you know I haven't told him yet. I'm scared it will change everything." Liv reaches across the table, squeezing Amelia's hand.

"The truth is always hard at first. You'll figure it out Mia, you always do. He's coming tonight to celebrate with you so just enjoy it. You deserve this. You never know he may already suspect, and you never know it might not be such a big shock or surprise at all." Amelia's instantly looks up at Liv her eyes filled with concern she demands.

"Do you think he already knows?" Amelia's eyes are like saucers as she stares at Liv the reality of the question sinking in. Liv once more regrets what she has said when a quiet voice beside them interrupts making them both jump.

"Before He...? Knows what?" At that very moment Maddy arrives at the table. Both Liv and Amelia had been so preoccupied with their conversation that neither of them had noticed Maddy making her way back across the restaurant. Now neither of them can be sure what Maddy has heard. Amelia is lost for words but Liv, sharp and quick as always smoothly replies.

"Oh, Hi Maddy, we were just talking about Jack disapproving of your mom and Gabriel." Amelia blushes to her roots, the reply is brilliant but, even so, Liv has brought Amelia's uncharacteristic antics from last night up in front of her daughter.

"Oh... and Eww... I don't need to know about that. Mom if it's ok with you I'm going to get going." Maddy tries to make a hasty exit, but Liv shakes her head and makes her wait.

"Not so fast pumpkin. I need details!" Grinning at Maddy Liv knows they have avoided a catastrophe. Maddy returns Liv's smile her own smile wide and infectious.

"Sorry about that, just a friend from college wanted some advice. Are you guys ready shall we go?"

"Why are you always in a rush Maddy. Sit down I want to hear everything about this young man you are seeing. Spencer. When are you going to bring him over for me to inspect." Liv pats the seat next to her and Maddy sits down a little exasperated by Liv's delaying tactics.

"You can meet him later; he is coming with me tonight. He is bringing his camera too as I'd like him to meet Gabriel." Maddy shoots her mom a sideways glance checking to see if she is going to comment. At the mention of his name Amelia tenses. So far Maddy hasn't mentioned anything about him, Amelia doesn't feel ready to face that conversation yet. Liv is very aware that this entire conversation is making Amelia jumpy, trying to hide her friend's reaction, she squeezes Maddy's hand to get her attention Maddy turns to look at her. Liv smiles encouragingly.

"That's a great idea Maddy. Spencer can take some film of tonight it should be a fun evening and one we will all want to remember." She nods at Amelia a wide confident smile on her face, Liv has no intention of letting Amelia bring up the subject of Maddy's father yet, she knows that Amelia is nowhere near ready to broach that subject with her daughter. This was all proving to be far trickier to navigate than Liv had imagined as Amelia still didn't know the truth yet about the secret Jack and her were hiding. Inwardly Liv winced at the thought. How was she ever going to justify to her best friend how or why she had kept the plan that she, Jack and Gabriel had hatched to get them together again a secret. Now wasn't the time for any of this. Liv waved to the Maître De catching his eye he grinned. It was after all Amelia's birthday and cake was a great way to diffuse the tension between mother and daughter.

Much to Amelia's utter horror across the restaurant appeared a huge creation made of sugar, cream and strawberries, carried aloft by several members of the wait staff. The sheer number of candles made the top of the cake appear alight. Amelia couldn't help but laugh at Liv, who looked thrilled with the confectionary surprise. Amelia's face was now completely crimson as the entire restaurant serenaded her with a loud and raucous rendition of 'Happy Birthday' Liv's smile was simply beaming as Maddy filmed everything on her phone giving her the excuse to step away from the table and let her mom take centre stage. The birthday pantomime was exactly what was needed to free everyone from the conversation that no-one was ready to have. Liv made a show of sharing the cake with half the restaurant and the staff and the Champagne flowed as did the kisses and well wishes making Amelia once again temporarily forget the secret she had kept from the person she loved most in the world. Maddy seizing the opportunity to make her exit, kisses Liv, hugging her tightly.

"Thank you, Aunty Liv, for everything you do for mom and me. You mean the world to both of us." Her words make Liv pause, looking into Maddy's big beautiful blue eyes she felt her heart almost still in her chest. Maddy meant the world to Liv, and she deserved to know who her father was. Tears welled in Liv's eyes as she hugged her God daughter tightly.

"I love you so much darling. We are going to have so much fun tonight." Kissing her Aunty on the cheek Maddy released her, grinning into her smiling face.

"I love you too." Then turning away she bounced over to Amelia who was chatting and laughing with the couple at the next table. Maddy rested her chin on her mom's shoulder and whispered in her ear. "Is it ok if I head off now mom? I've got a few errands to run before the party and Spencer is picking me up, so I'll see you at the hotel, if that's ok?" Amelia half turned in her seat to look up at Maddy, half relieved that the conversation had been avoided.

"Yes of course it is sweet, I know Liv's got a full afternoon planned so you go ahead, and I'll see you later. Thank you for coming for lunch though..." Amelia pauses looking at her beautiful daughters face she is struck by the likeness to Gabriel. A pain crosses Amelia's chest, guilt grips her suddenly making her stand up abruptly. She turns around pulling Maddy into a tight hug.

Maddy is surprised by her mom's emotional embrace and the use of her childhood term of endearment 'sweet' but sensing the need to repair the distance between them she hugs her mom with equal emotion. Looking into her mom's eyes she see's tears spill onto her cheeks. A little taken aback by her out of character behaviour she asks.

"What's the matter mom? Has something happened? Are you Ok?" Amelia realises that Maddy has no idea why she is crying. Reaching up to wipe the tears away Amelia smiles to reassure her.

"I'm fine really, I am. It's just the birthday and the champagne. All of it. I'm just being silly. Really darling I'm all good. You go and get sorted and I will see you later... Thank you, Maddy..." Amelia pauses looking at Maddy she softly asks her. "You do know I love you Maddy, don't you?" Amelia hesitates then adds. "I'm sorry if you thought I was being hard on you. I just need you to be safe. You know that right?"

Maddy looks away from her mom not quite able to meet her eyes, it's as if her mother has a sixth sense about things that happen in Maddy's life. There is no possible way that Amelia can know what Maddy is about to do, but Maddy knows without a doubt it will cause trouble and is going to upset her mom. She is fully aware that they will have an argument because Maddy is about to do the one thing that Amelia has told her not to. Both women look at one another both holding a secret that the other doesn't know, both with secrets that will potentially change everyone's lives.

"I love you too mom. Happy Birthday. I'll see you later, you go and have fun this afternoon. I can't wait to see what Liv has picked out for you to wear this evening... Love you, Mom!" With that Maddy turns on her heal and heads out of the restaurant, she stops by the door and waves to the two most important women in her life before heading out into the bright afternoon sunshine, a look of determined defiance making her skip down the boulevard. Little does she realise that the risk she is about to take may mean this is the last time any of their lives will be the same again.

Watching Maddy go makes Amelia feel deeply uncomfortable. She had never lied to Maddy, in fact she made it a household rule to always tell the truth. The irony of that thought was utterly breathtaking for Amelia now. As she sits down once more at the table the truth won't allow her to see the joy in the evening ahead. That truth was stark and unforgiving. She was a fool; she had been lying to Maddy for her entire life and worse than that she had justified that lie by lying to herself too. How on earth was she ever going to make any of this right. The pain of her thoughts must have been written across her face as Liv watched her friend wrestle with the shadows that had kept her a prisoner in her own story.

Both Amelia and Liv shared so many parts of their lives that reflected their past, yet Liv held a much lighter, more glass half full kind of attitude to her past and her future, whereas Amelia was unbelievably hard on herself. Using her past mistakes as weapons to drive her forward in a kind of relentless crusade to make herself feel worthy. Liv knew better than anyone that Amelia's lack of self-worth was nothing to do with her life on the street, that had merely been the manifestation of her belief system. Mia's real story lay deep in her early past, her origin, with people who should have known better and in a story where cruelty was used as a weapon of control and manipulation. No wonder she had become a dreamer, it had shaped Amelia into a woman who was a survivor, a woman who was not prepared to stand by and watch others become victims without showing them another way.

Liv was so proud of her best friend, Amelia was one of the kindest most compassionate people she had ever met. Liv was under no illusion that without Amelia's help and unwavering belief in her, Liv's life could have been very different. Liv owed Amelia a huge debt for the compassion and love she had received from her. Amelia had believed in her before anyone else had, but the hard work, well that had been all Liv. She had grafted for years for everything she now enjoyed, and boy did she enjoy her life. Liv was thankful everyday for her husband, her children, her home and her business, she lived a blessed and happy life. She had the success and recognition that 20years ago she would never have imagined possible. Both of their lives had changed the night Amelia met Gabriel, and now Liv was determined that their story find its proper ending. Not the ending that had been created by a lawyer with a cruel vendetta. Taking a deep breath Liv paused pushing that thought aside. Now was certainly not the time to bring that forward, Riddick was part of their past and had no place in the future that Liv envisaged for her family.

"I think it's time we took this party back to the salon and work some more magic." Liv could see the doubt that clouded Amelia's face and she was having none of it, one way or another she would make this the best day of Amelia's life. Liv was up on her feet urging Amelia to do the same and within minutes they were once again being hugged and showered with kindness all the way across the restaurant. For once Amelia made the decision to leave the ghosts of her past exactly where they should be in the past. Shaking herself she put on her sunglasses as the two friends emerged into the afternoon sunshine, it's healing warmth a balm for both their nerves.

Within minutes they were back in the calm tranquil atmosphere of the salon and Liv whisked Amelia into one of the private booths to have her hair done. Liv taking charge, directing the stylists with a practiced eye.

"I want waves for Mia, nothing too tight, something that flows naturally, make sure to bring out that gorgeous chestnut in her hair." Amelia chuckled as she listened to Liv's instructions.

"You've got this all planned out, haven't you?" Winking at her through the mirror, Liv couldn't help feeling intensely relieved that everything was so far going to plan.

"Of course. Nothing but the best for you, my darling." Having her hair washed and head massaged allowed Amelia to release some of the tension her mind had created over lunch; Amelia was once again grateful for the many blessings in her life. The champagne toasts had made her feel a little drowsy, with her wet hair wrapped in a towel Amelia relaxed back into the luxurious big leather chair while she waited for the stylist to return, closing her eyes Amelia's last thought was that a short nap would be perfect, before the next stage of her transformation. Amelia's soft snoring made Liv peer around the booth door. Realising that she had fallen asleep Liv smiled, closing the door allowing her friend an afternoon siesta, they had plenty of time and Liv was after all the boss. She too decided that a quick forty winks were in order and curled up on the sofa in the staff room. Neither of them slept for long but it was a much-needed reboot for them both. The stylists worked their professional kind of creative magic, while Liv and Amelia kept the conversation intentionally easy about everything under the sun. Liv was determined to keep the atmosphere light and positive, the afternoon was filled with laughter, as they reminisced about old times, making plans for future adventures. Time seemed to fly, by late afternoon, their hair and make-up had been beautifully styled, their nails polished to perfection, now there was just the matter of the perfect dress. By the end of the day the final preparations for the evenings party were reaching a crescendo. Liv insisting that Amelia try on several dresses, each more glamorous than the last. Amelia eventually settling on a conservative long black dress; Liv however seemed far from convinced.

"I always wanted to be a fairy godmother!" With a clap of her hands Liv was on her feet. "Too safe." She emphatically declared, attempting to unzip the dress she deliberately messed with the zipper, so it sticks. Under her breath whispering in Amelia's ear so that the designer, Nico can't hear. "Oh no! Looks like you'll have to try on a few more." Amelia can't help but laugh, secretly pleased at the opportunity to try on more dresses. After several more outfits, she finally finds the perfect one, Liv's reaction says it all. "Wow, Mia. Now that really is more than just a dress... It's a statement! You look amazing!"

Amelia's face lights up with happiness as she looks at herself in the mirror. She feels beautiful, confident, for the first time in as long as she can remember, ready for the evening ahead. There is just the small nagging doubt that keeps pulling at her thoughts. How is she going to tell Gabriel, not only him, how was she going to tell Maddy too. Just as dark clouds can ruin a perfect sky, dark thoughts cloud her beautifully made-up smoky eyes, stifling a sob that threatens to ruin her makeup she excuses herself rushing to the bathroom to pull herself together. Once again Amelia finds herself staring at her own reflection in the salon's luxury bathroom mirror. Amelia takes a deep breath. In a firm voice she chides herself. Speaking out loud to an empty room.

"This was your choice not theirs. Now you, must make it right!" Standing to her full height she makes the decision that tonight is the night that will change all their lives. Silently she prayed for the future that Liv had talked about all afternoon, perhaps miracles really were possible. But a miracle like this needed more than just prayers it needed forgiveness from the two people who she was about to hurt. It maybe her birthday but this party was about so many other people than just Amelia, her future and that of her family rested on how she behaved now.

Chapter 14

The cocktail lounge at the Regent Beverly Hills Hotel is filling up with beautifully dressed guests. The elegant space filled with soft music and subtle lighting. There is an air of anticipation adding a buzz to the murmur of conversation as guests begin arriving. Several detectives, looking sharp in their tuxedos are already congregating in the swish hotel bar, chatting and laughing among themselves. Joe stands with a group of them, looking every bit the handsome gentleman in his tux, while Jack is at the bar, sharing a drink with Gabriel, who has his back to the room. The doors swing open; Liv and Amelia enter the lounge. As soon as they walk in, the room falls silent, all eyes turning to Amelia. She is radiant in her stunning gown, a floor-length, shimmering cream, halter neck, backless gown that accentuates her figure and makes her feel like a goddess. Amelia's beautiful hair cascades in waves down her back. Gabriel turns around; in an instant their eyes connect. As she confidently walks down the length of the cocktail bar, there's a chorus of wolf whistles from the detectives, who are genuinely shocked to see their boss looking so drop dead gorgeous.

The ladies pause to chat with Joe, who blushes as Liv kisses him fondly on the cheek, Joe being the gentleman offers Amelia and Liv his arms escorting them the rest of the way across the crowded room to his father and Gabriel. Jack's smile lights up proudly as he watches Olivia approach, he steps forward to take her arm from his son. As Amelia approaches Gabriel he stands a little taller his face flushing with admiration, his eyes widen with desire. Jack leans in to kiss Amelia's cheek, whispering something in her ear that makes her giggle before he steps aside. Gabriel's gaze travels over Amelia, his voice is filled with awe as he says admiringly.

"Mia... you look stunning." He pauses staring at her, his blue eyes positively sparkling with intensity. Stepping towards Amelia he leans in closely, whispering in her ear so only she can hear. "Do you realize every man in this room wants to be me right now? How lucky am I?" Gabriel's intention is to let the whole room know that she is his. Every fibre in his being intends to make sure that is the case. Amelia blushes, her heart fluttering.

"Thank you, Gabriel. You look as handsome as ever." Amelia murmurs, leaning in to kiss him on the cheek she can feel the tension in his frame as he brushes his body against hers, his hand goes to the small of her back as he pulls her towards him. The smell of his aftershave is exotic, sensual, making Amelia feel totally aware of him the moment he touches her. Gabriel's smile widens, he can tell immediately their connection is as strong as ever, their shared chemistry is evident for everyone to see, a playful glint appears in his eyes.

"I don't know though Amelia, I think there's something missing." He steps back, his gaze traveling over her with a teasing smile. Amelia looks momentarily taken aback, until she sees Gabriel reach into his pocket. From inside his jacket, he produces a long, narrow jewellery case. "Happy birthday, Amelia." His voice soft with affection. Amelia's eyes widen in surprise as she opens the box. Inside is a stunning, elegant diamond bracelet, a delicate chain of diamonds that sparkle with incredible clarity. Her breath catches as Gabriel takes the bracelet and gently fastens it around her wrist.

"It's so beautiful, Gabriel." She whispers, her voice tinged with awe. "Is it on loan?" Gabriel grins, shaking his head.

"No, Amelia. I made that mistake before. This one's a keeper." He holds her hand then leans in, pressing a tender kiss to her lips as if they're the only two people in the room. The world around them seems to fade as they share this quiet moment of connection. A little way from them, Jack and Liv watch the couple. Jack looks lovingly at Liv leading her away from the bar as they exit together, his arm around her waist, he bends down, his voice a soft whisper against her ear.

"Darling, our work here is done." Liv smiles up at him, her eyes sparkling with satisfaction as they leave the cocktail lounge behind, their hearts lightened by the successful reunion of their dear friends. Across the lobby of the luxurious hotel is the Michelin stared restaurant. Jack spots to of his oldest clients whose friendship goes back to the time when he managed the hotel. The beautiful couple seated at an intimate table wave Jack and Liv over.

"Edward... Mrs Lewis how lovely to see you both." Jack smiles broadly at the handsome couple.

"You both look wonderful. Join us for a glass of Champagne it's our anniversary." Edwards response is filled with sincerity. Immediately he stands up to shake Jacks hand, pulling out a chair for Liv so that she can sit next to the beautiful Mrs Lewis. Signalling to a nearby waitress he asks for two more champagne glasses. Once the glasses are filled the foursome toasts one another....

A little while later the evening has moved on. The festivities play-out inside the grand ballroom, fully decorated in all its splendour. Crystal chandeliers cast a warm glow over the elegantly set tables, each adorned with lavish centrepieces of fresh flowers. The soft hum of conversation fills the air, blending with the gentle strains of the band tuning their instruments on stage. Most of the guests are already seated at round tables, their eager anticipation creating a frisson of excitement in the ballroom as they await the evening's festivities. At the main table, positioned in the centre of the room, directly in front of the dance floor, sit Liv and Joe. Beside them is a distinguished-looking older man in a police dress uniform, this is Jerry, Amelia's boss, with his elegantly dressed wife. Next to them are Sylvia, the psychologist, and her husband, along with Gabriel, who looks every bit the charismatic gentleman in his tuxedo, and Babaji, whose serene presence adds a dignified calm to the table.

There are a few empty seats reserved for Maddy, Spencer, Amelia, and Jack.

As the band starts to play a lively tune, the doors to the ballroom open, and Amelia enters with Jack by her side. The moment they step inside, the entire room erupts into applause. Guests rise to their feet, clapping, cheering, their enthusiasm infectious. Spontaneously, Amelia's fellow officers break into a chorus of 'Happy Birthday,' quickly followed by a rousing rendition of 'For She's a Jolly Good Fellow.'

Amelia beams with joy, her smile radiant as she gracefully makes her way through the crowd, acknowledging the well-wishers with nods and waves. She looks stunning, her earlier nerves replaced by a genuine happiness that lights up the entire room. Gabriel watches her with a mixture of pride and admiration, his eyes never leaving her as she approaches the main table. Once Amelia reaches the table, the hotel Maître De steps forward, announcing.

"Dinner is served." The announcement prompts the guests to take their seats, the buzz of excitement still lingering in the air. Jack leans in close to Liv and Joe, his voice low with concern.

"Where's Maddy?" He asks, his eyes scanning the room. Joe, looking equally concerned, replies.

"I don't know, Dad. I thought she was coming with Spencer." Jack's brow furrows with worry.

"Have you tried her mobile phone son?" Joe nods, his expression uneasy.

"Yes, but it keeps going straight to her voicemail." Jack's worry deepens, his voice dropping to a near whisper.

"Try her again, Joseph. It's not like her. She knows how important this is." As Amelia takes her seat at the table, she immediately notices the empty chairs meant for Maddy and Spencer. Her face reflects her concern, but Jack catches her eye and offers a reassuring smile, mouthing the words.

"She's on her way." Amelia nods, relaxing slightly, though a trace of worry still lingers in her eyes. Under his breath, Jack leans toward Joe, urging him again.

"Try her again, please Joseph. I don't want her to miss this." Joe looks at his father, frustration evident in his voice.

"Okay, Dad, but what am I supposed to do? I'm not her boyfriend. She's made that clear enough, even for me." Jack places a hand on Joe's shoulder, giving him a reassuring squeeze.

"Don't worry, son. Just be patient. Your time will come. You'll see." With a resigned sigh, Joe rises from the table, his phone pressed to his ear. The ballroom is loud with chatter and music, so he moves to a quieter corner, muttering to himself as he dials Maddy's number once more.

"As long as I don't have to wait until I'm Gabriel's age, though." Obviously worried he grumbles under his breath.

Rewinding to a few hours earlier we are once again at Amelia's home, specifically Maddy's bedroom. The room is a whirlwind of activity as Maddy dances around, getting ready for the evening. Pixie Lott's 'Mamma Do' blares from her speakers, filling the room with an upbeat, rebellious energy. Maddy, clearly in high spirits, pulls out the same provocative outfit she wore on the strip the previous night, her hooker costume. She grins mischievously at her reflection in the mirror as she puts it on, her movements confident and defiant. Pulling a glamorous beaded short black dress off a hanger she grabs some heals to match and stuffs them into a bag. Suddenly, the doorbell rings, cutting through the music. Maddy hurries to answer it, still dancing to the beat. She swings open the door to reveal Spencer standing on the doorstep, looking dashing in his tuxedo. His expression, however, drops to one of shock as he takes in Maddy's appearance. Shaking his head in disbelief, Spencer hesitates at the threshold, clearly torn between disapproval and exasperation. Maddy, ever the charmer, pulls him inside with a playful grin.

"Come on, Spence." In her best flirty voice, she coaxes Spencer. "This is going to be so much fun." Spencer lets out a resigned sigh, allowing Maddy to work her persuasive magic on him. Despite his initial reluctance, he eventually gives in, and the two of them prepare to leave for the strip. Spencer looks at his watch he knows this is going to cause problems if Amelia finds out. The last thing he wants to do is upset a high-ranking police officer especially one he is trying to impress so she will let him date her daughter. He grimaces to himself, let's hope to God she doesn't find out. Lifting the camera back to his face he records Maddy once more. They are once again back on the strip, where Maddy is strutting confidently up and down the sidewalk, her defiant demeanour on full display. Spencer lingers some distance away, his camera rolling as he films her every move, capturing the raw intensity of her performance. Unbeknownst to them, the black pickup from the alleyway earlier looms in the distance on the other side of the road, a silent reminder of the danger that lurks nearby.

As dinner moves on in the grand ballroom, the concern for Maddy's absence begins to grow. Amelia, who had been enjoying the evening, starts to look increasingly anxious. She checks the time repeatedly, glancing at Gabriel and Jack, hoping for some reassurance. Her unease is mirrored by the others at the table, who exchange worried looks, the minutes tick by. With dinner now over, one of Amelia's younger detectives, Sam, decides to get the party started so heads over to the DJ asking for some dance music to be played. The DJ obliges; the dance track 'Evacuate the Dance Floor' floods the ballroom with its upbeat rhythm. The dance floor quickly fills with happy couples, eager to let loose and enjoy the night.

Sam, ever the cheeky spirited one, makes his way back to the main table. With a playful grin, he takes Amelia by the hand, with Gabriel's amused nod of approval, pulls her to her feet. Amelia can't help but grin back, feeling a bit of the tension melt away as she's dragged onto the dance floor. The two of them are surrounded by an energetic mass of happy friends, Amelia's laughter echoing through the room. Gabriel watches them indulgently from the sidelines, his eyes twinkling with affection as he sees her so full of life. After a short time, Joe, who has been quietly observing, asks Liv to dance. They join the crowd on the dance floor, moving in sync with the lively beat. Gabriel, deciding that it's time to intervene, makes his way over to Amelia and Sam. With a charming smile, he steps in, thanking Sam and guiding Amelia into his arms. Together, they continue to dance, sharing genuine laughter their chemistry a connection evident to anyone watching. As the song comes to an end, Gabriel and Amelia move to the side of the dance floor, needing to raise their voices to be heard over the next track. Amelia, still smiling, turns to Gabriel.

"This is such an amazing evening." Amelia smiles at him, though her eyes betray a lingering worry. "I just wish Maddy would hurry up. I don't know what's keeping her. She's a good girl; she's not normally late." Gabriel pulls her to him his arm around her waist he gives a reassuring look.

"Don't worry, Amelia. I'm sure she's fine." Amelia, unable to shake her concern, continues.

"Gabriel, I've been meaning to ask you, just who is this Babaji? I know you've got this whole James Bond thing going on, but isn't he a bit old to be a manservant?" She smiles, trying to inject some lightness into the conversation. However, Gabriel's face changes, becoming suddenly serious. He leans in close, his voice a whisper in her ear. Amelia's expression shifts from curiosity to shock as she processes his words. Just as she begins to comprehend what he's telling her, the music in the ballroom drops to a lull, amplifying the impact of her response.

"What!" Amelias voice rings out, louder than she intended. "You mean to tell me you're married?"

Chapter 15

Amelia's words hang in the air, drawing the attention of several couples on the dance floor. They pause in their steps, intrigued by the unfolding drama. Her face flushes with disbelief and anger. She turns abruptly, storming off the dance floor. Gabriel, realizing the gravity of the misunderstanding, quickly follows her, grabbing her arm, he attempts to stop her.

"Amelia, wait!" Urgently Gabriel calls after her. "Calm down. You don't understand what I just said. I said that Babaji was my brother-in-law, not my servant. I didn't say that I was married." Amelia throws him a fierce look, shaking her arm free. She continues towards the table, her anger boiling over. Gabriel catches up to her again, refusing to let her walk away without explaining. They stop just behind Babaji, who sits as silent and composed as ever. "Amelia, will you please listen to me. You've got this all wrong!" Gabriel pleads; his voice laced with frustration. Amelia, her voice sharp and cutting retorts.

"You're damn right I got it wrong Gabriel! You walk back into my life, steamroll me so I can't think straight. You sweet-talk me, tell me you love me, then you sleep with me...." She pauses glaring at him. "Now. Here, you have the audacity at my birthday to tell me that you're married. Not just that.... you've even brought your brother-in-law to my party. How dare you?" Gabriel looks at her, trying to keep his composure, he smiles wryly looking down he shakes his head.

"Amelia, why are you so quick to judge me? Are you done...." He defiantly stares back at her passion flashes in his eyes. "If you'd give me a chance to finish what I started to say, you'd understand. I was married, Amelia. My wife, Babaji's sister, Samara, died ten years ago. She drowned." Silence falls over the table as the impact of Gabriel's words sinks in. Amelia's face drains of colour, the realization hitting her in the solar plexus. Just as the tension reaches its peak, Joe approaches, looking confused by the scene he's walked into. Gabriel, keeping his gaze on Amelia, continues.

"Amelia, I swore that if I saw you again, I'd be truthful, no matter how difficult it was. When you asked me who Babaji was just now, I couldn't lie to you. Amelia, this...." Gabriel gestures between them. "You and me? It's been so unexpected. No one could have planned this. You caught me off guard, that's all." Amelia now utterly devastated is overwhelmed with emotion, she looks at Gabriel, her eyes filling with tears. The room around her seems to blur as she struggles to process everything. She glances at Babaji, feeling a pang of guilt for her earlier outburst. Covering her mouth with her hand, she shakes her head, unable to speak. Gabriel steps closer, his voice soft and comforting. "It's all right, Amelia. Come and sit down." He gently guides her to her seat.

"I'm so sorry, Gabriel." Amelia whispers, her voice trembling. "When you said this morning... Oh, Gabriel, I never imagined you'd been married." Amelia's nerves have completely gotten the better of her. The full realization that Gabriel has led a life she knows nothing about suddenly dawns on her, she looks at him as if seeing him for the first time. Gabriel smiles at her gently, leaning forward to kiss her lightly on the cheek.

"Relax, Amelia. Darling, this is your night. We'll talk about this tomorrow." His tenderness brings fresh tears to Amelia's eyes. She looks at him, mouthing.

"I'm so sorry." Gabriel brushes away her tears with his thumb, his expression one of understanding and compassion. Sensing the need to lighten the mood, Jack reaches for the champagne bottle, standing to make a toast.

"Champagne, anyone?" Jack smiles encouragingly at Amelia his voice a touch louder than necessary to break the tension. He looks at Amelia with such warmth in his expression.

"Amelia, tonight I think we can make an exception to the rule." He hands her a glass of the newly opened champagne. Amelia, still shaken, downs it in one go, surprising everyone at the table. Jack raises an eyebrow, then chuckles as he refills her glass. Amelia, her emotions still raw, looks across the table at Babaji. Despite the turmoil of the last few minutes, Babaji meets her gaze with a warm, forgiving smile. His eyes, soft and gentle, seem to convey a deep understanding. For the first time that evening, Amelia feels a genuine connection with him, one that transcends words. Jack stands up, raising his glass high, his voice carrying warmth and humour.

"I would like to propose a toast to my most lovely, dear friend Amelia, who has the most generous, loving, forgiving heart of anyone I know." The words in his toast hold a touch of irony, his tone teasing, earns a few chuckles from the crowd. "Amelia, my darling, we love you. Happy birthday." Everyone within earshot raises their glasses, echoing Jack's sentiments with a resounding.... "To Amelia!" The clinking of glasses fills the room, and Amelia, despite the emotional rollercoaster she's been on, can't help but smile warmly at her friends and colleagues. She joins in the toast drinking rather more champagne than she intended. Amelia turns towards Gabriel apprehension making her frame tense. Gabriel places his hand on her bare back making her jump slightly as his touch sparks desire once more in her oversensitive system. His powerful presence beside her calms her nerves. Slowly Gabriel traces tiny circles on her soft skin, an intimate touch that does little to settle her erratic pulse, rather she feels excitement begin to ignite the desire in the pit of her stomach and heat rising in her body. Gabriel leans in close, his words barely a whisper.

"How long do we have to stay at this party? I want to take you upstairs and show you how much I've missed you." Gabriel sits forward reaching for his water with his other hand as the one behind

Amelia slips slightly lower his fingers graze dip in her lower back. She jumps nearly spilling her Champagne. Gabriel leans across her steadying her hand he takes the glass from her placing it back on the table.

"Perhaps that's not such a great idea given that you haven't drunk in a while" Gabriel leans in a little closer and murmurs. "I want you to remember everything about tonight." His words seem to hold a promise that makes Amelia's stomach flutter with anticipation. Sensing her response Gabriel moves his hand and lets it rest on her thigh under the table. Amelia's entire system is in high alert, she is surrounded by so many people who want her attention yet all she wants to do is let Gabriel lead her out of the ballroom and up to his suite. As if he can read her mind his fingers tighten imperceptibly on her thigh applying a pressure that makes her hold her breath. It's Amelia's boss Jerry who is the person who unexpectedly interrupts her private moment with Gabriel, he rises from his seat. With a determined stride, he makes his way to the stage, taking the microphone from the maître d'. He taps on a small table to get everyone's attention, his voice booming over the microphone as the DJ lowers the music.

"Ladies and gentlemen, quiet please. Thank you." Jerry's voice commands the room. "I'm sure that you all know why we're here tonight. And no, Bill...." Shaking his head he quips, nodding towards a colleague. "It's not just for the free bar." A raucous group of young officers all cheer meaning Jerry must wave them to be quiet again. "We are here to celebrate with one of our own, a very, very special member of our team." The crowd quiets, all eyes on Jerry as he continues. "I've never met anyone like Amelia Cartwright. She is truly one of a kind. Amelia is the kind of person you can call on day or night, someone who'll stand by your side when others won't even stand up. She is a real lady, a very rare, very special person."

Amelia feels her cheeks flush with a mixture of pride and embarrassment as the room turns its attention to her. Jerry's words, though sincere, are almost too much for her to take in. Especially given that Gabriel has yet to remove his hand she feels suddenly very exposed. Silently she removes his hand making Gabriel chuckle as he sits back in his chair.

"It's been an absolute pleasure to work alongside her and to call her my friend." Jerry says, his voice filled with genuine emotion. "I am tremendously proud that we're here to honour such an important person from our department on her birthday. Amelia, you've been a model officer for your entire career. This award isn't just from the department. In fact, I don't remember any other officer receiving it, especially one so young." Amelia's heart races as she realizes what Jerry is leading up to. The room is silent, everyone hanging on his every word.

"Amelia." Jerry continues. "It is with real pleasure that I announce you're going to receive the Commendation of Integrity for your outstanding contribution and service to the people of LA. Your efforts and commitment, especially through your charitable foundation, have made a tremendous impact on the lives of women who are disregarded, forgotten, and abandoned." Everyone in the ballroom stands up and cheers, the team who Amelia works with can't contain their delight in her success, they are jubilant, it takes several minutes for Jerry to regain control of the audience some of whom are already a little worse for wear. Amelia is nearly beetroot from blushing; it was all a little too much for her introverted sensitive nature to be the centre of this kind of attention. Jerry is getting a little annoyed at the raucous response and bangs the microphone on a nearby table, instantly the noise dies down Allowing him to continue.

"This award is the cities way of showing our deep appreciation and thanks to you Amelia." The room erupts in applause once more, and Amelia can hardly believe what she's hearing. She looks around, stunned, as her colleagues and friends cheer for her. Jerry waits for the noise to die down before he speaks again. "Now." He says with a smile, waving to the crowd to quieten them all once more. "The mayor is out of town this week so he can't be here to give you this award, he had asked Jack to stand in. I'm sure everybody knows that

Jack is the Chief Executive of the Sinclair Cartwright Foundation." Jack nods modestly from his seat, the attention momentarily shifting to him.

"However." Jerry continues, his tone turning slightly more serious. "Jack has asked me this evening if he could pass this honour to someone else. He wants someone very special to present this award to Amelia tonight. So, it is with great pleasure that I'd like to ask Mr. Gabriel Sinclair to come up and present Amelia with her award." There is a collective gasp followed by clapping and cheering as Gabriel, composed and dashing as ever, stands up. He straightens his jacket, offering Amelia a reassuring smile before he makes his way to the stage. Amelia sits frozen in her seat, utterly dumbstruck. Her mind races as she watches Gabriel ascend the stage, the room spinning slightly as reality sinks in, she reaches for her glass again taking another slug of the fizzy bubbly she drains the glass.

Gabriel reaches the microphone, taking it from Jerry with a nod of thanks. The room quiets once more, all eyes on him as he prepares to speak. Amelia can only stare, the emotions swirling in her stomach ricochet between pride, confusion, and something deeper that she can't quite name, she swallows hard realising its dread. The stage is set for a moment she knows she will never forget. Gabriel takes the microphone, his voice steady and filled with emotion.

"Thank you very much, Chief Superintendent Wilson." Gabriels smooth velvety voice deep and rich flows over the microphone as if he has been presenting all his life, there is not a hint of nerves in his demeanour as he begins, his eyes locking onto Amelia's. The room falls into silence.

"Twelve months ago, I never dreamed that this night would take place. In fact, I never imagined I'd see Amelia again." He pauses addressing his speech to Amelia as if she were the only person in the room.

"You see, I lost Amelia a very long time ago. I was very careless with valuable things in those days. I was totally blind to the treasure that was right in front of my eyes." Gabriel's rich deep voice seems to lull the entire ballroom under his charismatic spell. The room falls into a hushed silence, every ear attuned to Gabriel's words. "However, thanks to the powers that be. 'Kismet.' Some of you may call it. I returned to L.A. about nine months ago for the first time in nearly 19 years. And no...." Gabriel pauses for affect then he adds with a chuckle.

"I was not in a correctional facility during that time." The audience erupts in light-hearted laughter, easing the tension. Amelia's breath catches in her throat as she stares at Gabriel his words starting to fan her nerves. Gabriel continues. Amelia holds her breath, gripping the table she seems to sense what's coming. "It was in this city that a certain young woman stole my heart. So, for old time's sake, I came back to this very hotel where we first met. It was during that stay that I also met Jack St John, so imagine my surprise when I ran into my old friend again. As many of you know, Jack used to run this place, until Amelia convinced him that his talents were better suited to a group of very colourful ladies of the night. I was utterly fascinated when Jack explained to me that Amelia had persuaded him to become the Chief Executive of her incredible foundation." A ripple of laughter spreads through the audience. Gabriel remains focused, his gaze never leaving Amelia, whose expression seems frozen as Gabriel's words register.

"Well, as luck would have it, Jack took pity on me, and we had dinner. He told me how Amelia had returned to L.A. then shared all about her incredible work here when she joined the police force." He pauses staring at Amelia, as his eyes catch the reflection from the overhead lights, they seem more intense than ever. "When Jack told me the name of the charity, I was astounded. When I heard that name, I dared to hope that maybe, just maybe, there was a chance for Amelia and me to reunite once again. You see, Sinclair is my surname and Cartwright you all obviously know is Amelia's name, but what you might not know is it's the name she took, Cartwright is the name of my mentor, a man who meant the world to me, and only Amelia truly knew that." Gabriel pauses, his voice growing more solemn.

"I'm sure some of you are wondering what this tale has to do with tonight. If you will indulge me, I'll explain." Gabriel pauses taking a deep breath he continues. "The first time I came back to L.A., I couldn't stay. I had business commitments in India. But over the past nine months, I've been in regular contact with Jack through the charity. My own organization is now a firm supporter of this amazing foundation. This week, I'm pleased to announce that we've just opened the very first Cartwright Sinclair Foundation shelter in the city of Mumbai for women who are vulnerable, displaced and lost." The room is filled with a burst of applause. Gabriel waves his hand for quiet so he can continue. His eyes have never left Amelia's face as he needs to see the impact his words are having on her.

"Amelia, I can't wait to take you to see this shelter and the work that it's starting to do." Amelia's gaze has dropped to her lap but at the mention of her name her head snaps up her expression unreadable. Once again Gabriel's eyes search Amelia's face for signs of her reaction. He continues.

"Amelia Cartwright is one of the bravest most incredible women I've ever known, but I must say, I'm glad tonight she's not armed." Grinning broadly, he laughs. "Jack assures me she left her gun at home because, looking at her face right now, I think she may possibly shoot me and you too, Jack." A wave of laughter washes over the crowd, but Amelia is barely holding it together. Gabriel looks at her, his expression softening.

"Amelia darling, you are the love of my life. Once you get over the shock of turning 40 and arresting me this weekend, I'm sure we'll look back on this and laugh. But for now, it gives me the greatest pleasure to ask you to come up on stage and receive this wonderful award. Ladies and gentlemen, I give you the incredible Amelia Alice Cartwright." The applause is thunderous as everyone gets to their feet, Amelia, no longer able to avoid the inevitable, stands up. Starring at Gabriel defiantly she downs another glass of champagne, trying to steel herself for what comes next. A manic smile is plastered on her face as she makes her way to the stage, her steps measured and deliberate. As she passes Jack, she leans down slightly, muttering through gritted teeth.

"He's right. I'm going to hunt you down, old man, then I'm going to kill you." Jack grins, unperturbed.

"No problem." Laughing he quips. "Just remember, you'll get a longer sentence for assaulting a senior citizen." As she stands straight, she catches a glimpse of Liv's face looking worried, Amelia's eyes flash an angry look in her direction, Liv unable to hold her gaze looks down, red faced. Amelia steps towards the inevitable 'coup de gras' the finale nail in the end of their promising reunion. Crossing the dance floor her march to the stage, seems to take an excruciating length of time due to her high heels, or possibly the several glasses of bubbly Amelia has already consumed, due in the most part to the many confessions Gabriel has conceded during the past hour. With her back bolt upright, a strained smile still etched on her face, she climbs the stairs finally reaching Gabriel. Suddenly, the oh so charming, man of her dreams no longer looks quite so certain of his fool proof plan to win her back. As he stands with the award in his hand, a slightly goofy smile apologetically softens his expression, Amelia leans in as if to kiss him, instead she hisses under her breath.

"You son of a bitch. You planned this whole thing. I can't believe I fell for it. I hate you." Gabriel chuckles softly, leaning in closer.

"Not as much as I love you." Amelia forces another smile, turning to face the crowd as laughter bubbles up, this time less manic however still tinged with disbelief. Taking a deep breath, she addresses the room.

"It's rare, my team will testify to this on my behalf, that I'm ever left speechless. Today, I can quite honestly say there are simply no words to express the depth of emotion that I feel right now. Simply none." Her eyes flick to Jack and Gabriel, both of whom return her gaze with expressions that hint at their own private amusement and satisfaction. She continues. "To be honoured by your friends and colleagues is one thing, but to receive this recognition from the people of this city is something else entirely. For that, I am deeply touched and incredibly humbled. Thank you." Pausing to gather her thoughts, Amelia looks out at the sea of faces, many of whom she has worked with for years.

"I'm not going to stand here and list all the people I need to thank, because there are far too many to name. So, I'll just say this, to all of you: Your support, kindness, love and encouragement have helped me to push through and reach for dreams that, in the past, I never imagined I'd achieve. The love I've received has kept me safe and protected. I love you all from the bottom of my heart, and I just can't thank you enough." Through barely concealed tears she glances back at Gabriel, who is watching her with an expression that could melt even the hardest of hearts.

Chapter 16

Amelia stands on stage, the applause ringing in her ears, her heart is pounding sadly for a very different reason. A single tear escapes her skilfully made-up eyes, rolling down her cheek as she looks at Gabriel. Her emotions are in turmoil; she forces herself to smile through it. For a moment, their eyes lock, Amelia takes a deep breath trying desperately to steady herself, a cascade of tears threatening to ruin her makeup. Biting her lip, she manages to hold them back though the salt, stings her eyes making them redden. Gabriel sees instantly her conflicted emotions stepping towards her he escorts her off the stage. Amelia accepts his help as she has no other choice. Her body is taught she is almost rigid with high emotions she cannot allow anyone else to see. Slowly, she descends the stage steps to another loud chorus of 'For She's a Jolly Good Fellow' her back stiff, every step heavy with the weight of her anger and confusion.

As she crosses the dance floor, she's met by a throng of happy faces, Amelia is showered with hugs and kisses from her friends and colleagues, all the while her mind is elsewhere. The smile remains plastered on her face, sadly it's frozen, not reaching her eyes. When she finally arrives at her seat, she looks directly at Liv, her best friend. Amelia's voice is sharp and filled with betrayal.

"Did you know about this, Liv? Were you in on it too?" Liv hesitates, her face a mixture of guilt and concern. She nods slowly, reaching out to Amelia.

"Amelia, please, let me explain!" Amelia pulls away, her voice trembling with hurt.

"Don't touch me, Liv. You're supposed to be my best friend. How could you?" Liv withdraws, looking down, ashamed. She opens her mouth to speak, but Amelia cuts her off with a glare. Grabbing a glass of champagne from the table, Amelia downs it in one swift motion, her eyes blazing with anger as she glares at Liv and Jack.

"Don't say another word, either of you. There's nothing you can say right now that could make this better. How could you do this to me? How could you go behind my back like this, Jack?" Gabriel steps in, his voice calm but firm.

"Because I asked them to, Amelia. Until I knew I was free to stay here, I didn't want Jack to tell you he'd seen me." Amelia turns on him, her eyes filled with unshed tears, her voice quivering with barely contained feelings.

"You... you. I can't even look at you right now. Just leave me alone, Gabriel." Her composure cracks as she quickly stands up almost knocking her chair over, she pauses gathering herself. Wiping the tears that have spilled down her flushed cheeks Amelia steadies herself, taking a deep breath, she squares her shoulders.

"Mia please. Wait!" Liv's desperate plea falls on deaf ears. Turning away from her loved ones, Amelia heads across the dance floor out of the ballroom. The enormity of the evening finally crashing down on her. For a moment, the table is silent, everyone exchanging looks of concern as they watch Amelia make her way through the well-wishers. No-one says anything although the mood has gone from jovial to subdued. Each of them knowing that they could not have anticipated Amelia's reaction, but each wishing it had gone better. What mattered most now was making sure they limited the collateral damage. Then, almost as one, Gabriel, Joe, Jack and Liv rise and follow her.

The stunning grand reception lobby of the Regent Hotel is uncharacteristically quiet. The restaurant opposite now closed. The party in the ballroom is in full swing the strains of dance music filter through its sumptuous luxury changing the usually restrained atmosphere of the lobby to one of frivolity. As Amelia's loved ones spill out of the ballroom the noise momentarily increases as the doors swing wide, the merriment of the party guests shouts and laughter carrying across the elegant ambience. On the other side of the reception, they spot Amelia, she is standing facing Spencer her hands gripping his arms. Spencer spots Joe pointing towards him he says Joes name to Amelia. She spins round to look at him her complexion is ashen the shock in her expression making her face a mask of horror. Spencer, dressed in a tuxedo and holding his camera, stands next to her, looking desperately towards Joe and the group as he tries to comfort her. Amelia's knees buckle, she clutches her stomach, doubling over as if in pain. She reaches out for the reception desk to steady herself, her wide eyes locking onto Gabriel as her vision blurs. Before she can collapse, Gabriel is there, sprinting across the lobby to catch her just as she begins to faint.

In one smooth motion, he lifts her into his arms, his eyes scanning the room for a place to lay her down. Amelia's eyelids flutter as she begins to come around. Gabriel gently lowers her onto a nearby sofa, his expression a mixture of concern and urgency. Spencer, pale and shaken, stammers barely able to get the words out.

"It's Maddy... I don't know how to tell you this... she's been kidnapped." Joe's voice erupts, filled with panic and disbelief.

"What? What the hell do you mean? How do you know?" Amelia, still disoriented, hears Spencer's words making her eyes snap open, the reality hitting her like a sledgehammer. She sits bolt upright, her voice frantic as she demands answers.

"Spencer, tell me right now. What happened? What do you know?" Spencer is still visibly trembling; he struggles to find the right words.

"I didn't just see it happen...I, I filmed it. It's all on here." His voice falters, holding up his camera as if it's a lifeline. Amelia's face pales as she looks at Jack, her voice barely a whisper.

"Jack, find me somewhere I can watch this now." Jack is already in motion, signalling to the reception desk for a key. "Spencer, what exactly did you see?" Amelia's voice is laced with fear and impatience. Gabriel steps in, his voice steady but urgent.

"Amelia, we need to do this somewhere private." Amelia barely acknowledges him, as she stands up her body shakes with fear, Gabriel grabs her to steady her, she is barely aware he is holding her, her entire focus is on Spencer, Jack returns to lead them to a nearby conference suite. Amelia sways slightly, Gabriel tightens his grip around her waist, guiding her across the lobby. Inside the conference suite, the atmosphere is tense with anxiety and fear. Spencer quickly sets up the video while Amelia, Gabriel, Jack, Liv, and Joe gather around the screen, their faces taut with worry. Before pressing play, Spencer turns to Amelia, his face lined with guilt.

"There's something you need to know before I show you this." Now Spencer looks genuinely terrified, his voice shaking.

"What is it, Spencer? Is she hurt?" Amelia demands, her voice rising in pitch.

"No, no, it's not that." Spencer stammers. "When I got to your house tonight, Maddy opened the door, and she was... she was dressed in that hooker costume again. She called me earlier and asked me to bring the camera. I thought she wanted me to film the event here. But then she insisted that we go back to the strip. She said she needed to impress some guy in the film industry... I told her it was a bad idea, but she wouldn't let it go. She said it would only be for an hour and then she'd change in the car, and you'd never know." Spencer's words tumble from his pale face. Joe explodes with anger.

"And you let her?" He lunges at Spencer, pinning him against the wall. Joe's rage is uncontrollable, Jack and Gabriel have no choice but to step in to restrain him. Amelia, leaning heavily against the table, shouts, her voice commanding.

"Joseph, this isn't helping! Save it. We're wasting time." She turns to Spencer, her eyes blazing. "Spencer, tell me now, where is Maddy?" The room falls silent as the tension reaches its peak. The video screen flickers to life, and everyone holds their breath, bracing for what they are about to see. Spencer voice quivers with emotion he is obviously in shock.

"Everything was going well. I'd been filming Maddy for about 40 minutes. She'd spoken to maybe one or two guys, nothing major. It seemed slow, I made her promise not to get in any cars or to make any deals with anyone. She agreed, she said she wouldn't take any risks." He pauses, then points at the screen, his fingers trembling slightly. "There, look." Urgently he points at a white transit van. "Can you see? Maddy goes to the window to speak to the guy. Look she is even laughing with him. She points towards me, she obviously telling him we are filming. Then this other guy opens the side door of the van. There, see through the windscreen. Can you see him?" Even though they can all clearly see what is happening on the screen Spencer narrates, his voice stressed and rushed. Amelia, Gabriel and the others watch intently, leaning in closer to the screen as the drama unfolds in front of them.

"She's even smiling at him." Spencer continues his voice dropping. "Then he just grabs her. No warning, he just pulls her in... She fights him. Look you can see her struggling." There is stunned silence in the room as the reality of what they have just watched begins to register. Amelia's face goes even paler; she looks like she may even be sick. Liv starts to cry, burying her face in Jack's shoulder, he holds onto her tightly, the strain and disbelief making his face look older suddenly. Gabriel mutters under his breath.

"Dear God.... Did you follow them?" Spencer is beginning to shake as shock starts to set in as he relives his recent trauma. He stares at Gabriel his face white.

"Yes. Yes, I did." His voice breaks starting to tremble with emotion. "I put my camera on the dash so I could keep filming. There, look. I'm right behind them." Once again, the group stares intently at the screen, their eyes glued to the events being played out in the raw disturbing footage. The film shows the transit van pulling away from the curb, with Spencer's car following close behind, as the camera is on the dash the screen vibrates making the picture more difficult and less focused.

"We're getting out of the city." He narrates as the scene continues, his voice wavering. "But the van starts to pull away. My car's old. I couldn't keep up. I'm trying to get closer, then this truck comes out of nowhere and hits me."

As he speaks there is a tremendous crash on the screen, the picture tumbles, the camera flipping and spinning before it lands in the footwell of the passenger side of the car. The only picture remaining momentarily is a shot of Maddy's black high heels, the ones she had intended to change into for the party. The shop is also accompanied by Spencer's frantic voice as he swears and yells. The sound falls eerily quiet in the aftermath of the crash as the car becomes motionless. There is a screeching of tyres and the sound of Spencer muttering as he tries to grasp what has just happened. The picture changes again as he grabs the camera checking it is still recording then he points it at the windscreen which shows two vehicles accelerating away. The first the white van, the second the black pickup that had just rammed Spencer off the road. Then the continuing footage shows Spence struggle with the door, trying to get out of the car as he attempts valiantly to get a close-up on the vehicles as they speed away. There is panic in his voice as he exclaims "What the fuck just happened!"

As he pans the camera around the empty street there is no-one there to witness the crime, Spencer turns the camera on his car which shows the extent of the damage inflicted by the much larger pick-up. He nearly drops the camera as he tries the pull his phone from his pocket. We hear him trying to make a call to Amelia, but the call goes to her answer machine. The picture goes black as Spencer stops the film. His voice shakes as he explains.

"Whoever was in that pick-up hit me hard. They must have known I was following the van. They just ran me off the road." Joe who had been tight lipped and silent during the film speaks up.

"If there were two cars, then this was professional hit." Amelia, deep in thought, suddenly snaps to attention.

"Liv. Go and get my bag from the ballroom. I need it. Go now, Liv. It's got my phone in it. But Liv. Don't say a word to anyone about this. Do you understand me Liv? Not a word. Not even to Jerry." Liv looks white and shocked that Amelia has asked her to do this, she looks to Jack for support. He nods so she wipes her tears with the back of her hand and silently nods once at Amelia. As she turns towards the door Jack follows her putting a comforting hand on her back. Opening the door for her he kisses her forehead. Summoning all her courage Liv straightens her shoulders and heads across the lobby. Amelia meanwhile turns her attention to Joe. Her voice now steady, more controlled as her training starts to kick in.

"Joseph. I need you to go to the station for me. Get my badge, and get my guns, they are both in the safe in my office. There is a change of clothes in there too, bring my boots they are next to my desk. Don't say a word to anyone about this, I'll text you the safe number…. Someone knew I'd be here tonight and knows about this." Joe looks at her with concern.

"But how would they know that Maddy was on the street tonight? None of us knew that doesn't make sense." Amelia registers what the young detective is saying his words a keen observation. Amelia agrees with a nod of her head. She turns looking at Spencer a question forming in her mind.

"Spencer. Who knew that the two of you were going out there tonight? Who did you talk to? Was it someone at my office or a friend? Think Spencer this is important." Spencer looks taken aback he stammers as he rushes to answer Amelia's questions.

"I… I swear I haven't spoken to anyone tonight. Just Maddy and you guys. I didn't even know until I got to your house tonight what she wanted to do. I thought we were coming straight here." Amelia bites her lip, clearly struggling to piece everything together.

"Then it must have been Maddy, someone she had spoken to… but who would she talk to about this?" Amelia moves about her space deep in thought she is not asking anyone else, she just needs to gather her own thoughts and try to work out who or what Maddy had done since she last saw her at lunch.

"Wait! She took a call at lunch, she said it was some guy on your course Spencer. She said his name…. Damn it I can't remember I wasn't really paying attention." Amelia looks annoyed at herself as she starts to pace, she blurts out, talking fast. "When she got up from the table..." Amelia is talking aloud but it is obvious she isn't speaking to anyone but herself. "Liv was kidding with her about it when she came back, teasing her that it was you. She said it wasn't, and Liv asked her if she was trying to make you jealous.... Why can't I remember his name." Amelia paces, wracking her memory as Liv rushes back in with her bag. Amelia snatches her phone out of the bag, quickly unlocking it. She glances at Liv, who looks pale but determined, she demands.

"Liv, who was that guy that Maddy was talking to on the phone at lunch? Think, Olivia, it's important. What did she say his name was?" Liv hesitates, looking a little bewildered, she stares at Amelia blankly.

"Think Liv!" Amelia demands starring at her friend. The abruptness of her tone shakes Liv out of her reverie; she closes her eyes trying to remember. Blurting out she recalls.
"Uh, Mick...No, Mac, I think... Why?"

"Do you know him?" Amelia turns sharply to Spencer, her tone demanding an answer. "Do you know him?" Spencer nods, a look of realization dawning on his face.

"Yeah, but he's a real loser. He's on our course. Why would he have anything to do with this?"

"God knows." Amelia mutters. "We need to start somewhere. Have you got his number?" Spencer nods again, already pulling out his phone. "Right." Amelia continues, her voice gaining strength. "Joe, go to the station. Take Spencer with you. Tell Dave I need him on this. Get the numbers off those vans. I want to know who they belong to. No one else, Joe. Not yet. I trust Dave get him with you on this; he can find out off Maddy's cell number who she spoke to. I'll work out what to say to Jerry." She pauses looking at Spencer. "We can trace her cell phone!... Get Dave on this Joe!" For a moment Amelia takes a breath feeling a sense of control she has a way to track Maddy. It's short lived as Spencer shakes his head.

"Her phones in my car with her bag and clothes for the party that she brought to change into. Sorry" Spencer's shoulders slump, guilt written all over his expression. Amelia stares blankly at him for a moment then her mind shifts again.

"Spencer, give Joe her phone he can find out who she spoke to today. Get hold of this guy, Mac. Find him. See if Maddy told him anything." Joe nods, determination in his eyes as he heads toward the door. Amelia calls after him. "Spencer, take your camera, help Dave and Joseph get the numbers off those vans. I want to know who they belong to. See if you can find them on any CCTV cameras. Joe, send Spencer back with my stuff. Make damn sure the safeties are on those guns, though." As Joe and Spencer are about to leave, Amelia's phone beeps. It's a message. The phone vibrates on the table where she has just put it. Joe, noticing her sudden panic, comes back towards her. Amelia's face is unreadable her blood runs cold as she hands him the phone, Joe notices her hand is icy as he takes it off her. Joe reads the message aloud to everyone:

"We have your daughter. We want the 10 million in the police vault. You have until 3 a.m. to get it. Then you will get your instructions. Do not involve anyone else or she dies. We know where you are. We know who you're with. Don't mess this up or she dies. Fail to get the money and she dies. 3 a.m." Gabriel and Jack both looked shocked as Joe reads the message. Gabriel looks like the wind has been knocked out of him, he leans on the table on his fists his knuckles turning white, he looks up at Amelia as Jack speaks.

"Amelia." Jack says softly, trying to keep his voice steady. Amelia is totally focused on Joe barely hearing Jack.

"Joseph, go now and stay in contact, keep a low profile. It could be someone in the ballroom who's involved. Dave is at the station I'll call him, so he knows you are on the way, the two of you go now. Spencer, get my things and get back here with those guns." Amelia's voice is firm almost mechanical her words sound hollow. Joe nods, looking back at Amelia with a mixture of fear and determination. He looks at his mentor, the woman he most admires in the world, straight in the eyes.

"I won't let you down Amelia." She nods returning his look, Joe is the one person who truly understands what is happening, Amelia trusts him unequivocally.

"Take her phone too, her password is her birthday, see if Dave can trace that message.... Joe! Watch your back. If you need me. Call. Let me know the minute there is anything I need to know." Once the young men have left Amelia begins pacing again, her mind racing. She looks at Jack, her voice steely.

"I need some coffee, strong and black. Then I need all of you to go back into the ballroom. You must act like everything is fine. If anyone asks where I am, just say that I'm not feeling to well so I'm getting some air...." She pauses straightening her shoulders her face set in an expression none of them recognise pure steely determination. Holding up her hand to them all she silences any argument.

"Don't argue with me. Just listen." The others start to talk but she cuts them off. "Listen, all of you. I've no idea what this is about, it must be someone on the inside. That money's been in the safe for way too long for this not to be an inside job. I know I'm asking a lot, but you must do this for me. There is a whole room full of cops in there, someone knows what's happening. Please.... Please!... Just do as I ask."

Jack gets up, going to hug Amelia, putting her hand up once more she stops him, pulling back, she shakes her head, obviously trying to keep it together. She holds Jack's forearms, looking into his eyes for reassurance. He nods, instead he squeezes her forearms looking her in the eye for a few moments before he lets her go, turning away he walks across the conference room in a calm manner, Jack realises that what Amelia needs right now is for everyone to listen and follow what she says. Collecting Liv on the way to the door, he puts his arm around her as she begins to shake, tears spilling down her face. Gabriel starts to speak. Amelia cuts him off with a look. He hesitates, then follows the others out of the room. Amelia only turns around as the door closes, her shoulders slumping. She sinks into a nearby chair, releasing an agonizing sob, the guttural sound echoing around the empty room. Outside the conference room door, Gabriel pauses, listening to the heartbreaking sound. He leans his back against the door closing his eyes he shakes his head in frustration, worry written across his face. Jack moves towards the door to go back in, Gabriel stops him, shaking his head. Stepping back Jack eyes Gabriel silently conceding that Amelia is no longer his sole concern he turns hugging Liv they continue back to the ballroom, Liv first visits the bathroom to pull herself together and check her makeup.

It takes Liv a monumental effort to pull herself together. Forcing fake smiles as they return to their table, each of them bracing for what they are about to do next. Jack is grateful that the party is in full swing with many people far too immersed in the revelry or simply too drunk to notice the quiet drama unfolding. Following the others back to the ballroom Gabriel's pace quickens he strides purposefully towards their dinner table his only thought to get Babaji safely upstairs so he can somehow help Amelia even if she doesn't want him to. He acknowledges Jack with a nod a look of grim determination on his face he quietly tells Jack what he intends on doing next. To anyone looking on Gabriel is his calm charming self, smiling and laughing with one or two of Amelia's colleagues he explains that she has over done it with the Champagne but will be back soon. Collecting the elderly gentleman Gabriel then carefully escorts Babaji out of the party. Jack and Liv make a valiant effort of pretending everything is normal as the party is in full swing. The DJ is hammering out dance tunes keeping the partygoers happy. No one appears to notice that the VIP, along with nearly everyone from the main table is missing. Jack discreetly speaks to Sylvia who tries to keep her reaction as neutral as possible, she grips Jacks arm for reassurance. He pats her hand and excuses himself going to rescue Liv who is struggling to keep it together at the table.

As Jack stands next to the main table, he spots Jerry at the bar talking to several of the department's detectives. He makes an executive decision and approaches Jerry tactfully asking for his assistance with a message for the mayor, he extracts Amelia's boss and brings him back to the table where he explains the real reason for Amelia's absence. Jerry is a consummate professional and barely even flinches as Jack explains what is happening across the hotel lobby. He makes a show of patting Jack on the arm as if sharing a joke with him. The two men sit at the table with Liv and Slyvia tactically deciding what happens next. Jerry is busy taking mental notes of who is still in the ballroom. He takes his phone out and makes a call to an old friend who he knows he can trust, then another to Joe.

Chapter 17

In the outskirts of LA, it's late, the darkness is eerie, there is a distinctly creepy vibe, tinged with an undercurrent of menace. This is not an area you would visit during the day and certainly not under the veil of darkness. At the end of a deserted road are various rundown shops, one such dilapidated business covers a large corner plot, it is a seemingly empty, disused and very rough. Once a garage, now there are many old wrecks of cars abandoned, littering the large forecourt. To one side of the reception is a rusty shuttered bay its roller shutter is halfway up, weak electric light filters through from somewhere beyond the decaying facade. Inside the garage it's dark and dirty, with parts of old cars scattered around. A beaten-up car sits on a mechanic's ramp above a pit, left behind as if waiting for a ghostly technician to show up and offer some care. Below it, in the shadows, is a lonely figure curled up against the wall, Maddy.

Her hands are tied behind her back. Her feet are bound with some sort of plastic flex. Suddenly, Maddy moves violently, shaking, trying desperately to free herself. She stops abruptly as she hears raised voices coming through the doorway. The two gangsters Magpie and Stretch saunter in, followed by the two students. One of them has a camera balanced on his shoulder, filming the entire scene. The younger men's faces are obscured by masks. Magpie, the leader of the group, looks down at Maddy with a cruel smirk.

"Don't worry, sweet thing, we sent mommy a message. She's a smart cookie, your mom. We'll get our money, so you'll be on your way home soon enough. Isn't that right, Stretch?" Stretch, his hulking accomplice, grins wickedly. "But if she's not, little girl, we're going to be having some real fun with you." Magpie sneers menacingly at Maddy making her recoil even more as he jumps down into the bay. "I think we'll start by sending bits at a time. What do you think, boys? What should we send first?" Stretch rubs his jaw, where faint scratch marks are visible.

"Dunno, Mags. She scratched me up. Real bad. How about you let me knock her teeth out?" Magpie stands over Maddy, looking down at her with predatory eyes.

"Hmm... Interesting. How about we have a bit of fun before she starts bleeding." Maddy starts to thrash and kick out, pure terror in her eyes. "Oooh..., Stretch." Magpie taunts. "Looks like we've got us a feisty one here. Grab hold of her for me." There is a loud coughing from one of the two men filming. Mac and Hugo begin to realise they are in way over their heads. They fidget nervously with the camera, making it clear they are uncomfortable. The situation is spiralling out of control, it's clear this wasn't part of their plan. They cough ridiculously trying to disguise their voices. Mac, tries to sound authoritative, shouting dramatically.

"That's not part of the agreement! No-one's supposed to get hurt!" Magpie turns to them with a sneer.

"Yeah, well things change kid. Don't they Stretch." Magpie pulls himself up out of the pit motioning to Stretch with a cock of his head, the two men lunge for the boys. "Grab 'em." Magpie's harsh command takes the younger men by complete surprise. Stretch dives towards Hugo knocking the camera out of his hands. It crashes to the floor, the image on the screen spinning before it goes black and pieces of broken plastic burst across the dirty tiles. The youngsters put up no defence against the much larger men who restrain them with ease. Magpie pulls the balaclavas off their heads allowing Maddy to see exactly who has been behind the 'prank'. The boys look horrified at the sudden exposure and very young. Hugo, his voice shaky, sniffs loudly trying to keep it together.

"You sure aren't getting anymore money now!" Hugo eyes Magpie warily with a mix of fear and defiance in his eyes. Neither of the youths can look at Maddy. Magpie bursts out laughing, a harsh sound that echoes through the grimy space.

"I don't want your money, you dumb kid. I want my money. You just gave me the perfect way to get it back. Thanks for that, lads. Guess what, boys. You'll be going down for a whole lot more than kidnapping your mate for a poxy film assignment." Mac and Hugo exchange panicked glances, as the two older men share the punchline of their cruel manipulative joke. The reality of their stupidity and the situation the boys find them in starts to dawn on them. Magpie leans in, his grin widening.

"So, you were jealous of little Miss Goody two-shoes, huh? Did it piss you off that she was better than you? That she's always teacher's pet." Magpie mocks the youngsters, the boys try to protest, he cuts them off with an angry snarl. "Shut it and listen. Maybe I won't kill you both. Actually-lads, I quite lie you. Wish I'd had the balls to think of doing something like this when I was your age. You've got balls alright; I'll give you that. We might even make criminals out of the pair of you yet." The threat beneath his words is unmistakable, unknowingly the two youngsters have made a pack with a particularly nasty gangster, and he wasn't going to let them go without expecting his pound of flesh. The boys hang their heads in shame, unable to look at Maddy the consequences of their clever plan suddenly coming into sharp focus. They now know how recklessly arrogant they have been. Hugo pleads.

"Look, just please don't hurt her. She's our friend, sort of. We just got sick of her always coming up with the best ideas. Her and that idiot Spencer. We just wanted to get the shot of you snatching her. Please, can you. Can you let her go?" A look of real fear replaces any cockiness that had been there before, Mac interrupts.

"You were supposed to let her go like we agreed. Maddy's always good for a laugh. She'd have got it. We talked at lunchtime, she was cool. She's been boasting about what she was going to do for weeks now. When she said about the party it made sense. That's why it had to be today." Mac, his voice barely a whisper adds. "We've been so stupid. Listen, I've got more money I can get for you. What do you say if I can get you another three grand, can we forget the whole thing?" For a moment Magpie and Stretch exchange looks, almost as if they are considering the offer. Then they both simultaneously burst out laughing, a cruel mocking sound. Magpie wipes a tear from his eye.

"You guys! You just crack me up... We're after a bit more than that, Mac, my boy. Your little girlfriend in there? Well, her mommy is going to get us our 10 million that's sat in the police vault. All we've got to do is wait for her to go an' fetch it." The boy's face's register what Magpie is saying. Fear, then shock making them look white and terrified as they realize just how badly their 'brilliant scheme' has gone wrong. Hugo stammers.

"Yeah, but...but they're not just going to hand it over to you. How do you know it's even there? They could have moved it." Magpie leans in closer, his expression darkening.

"Don't you worry your pretty little head about that." He viciously rubs Hugo's head with his knuckles. "We know exactly where that money is. We've got ourselves a very special friend in that department who's been waiting for a chance to clear his tab with us for a very long time. He doesn't like your girlfriend's mommy at all. Not one bit. If you think we're bad, you should meet this guy. He's a real asshole." Magpie arrogantly curls his lip with a look of complete contempt.

"Come on Stretch it's nearly time." Unceremoniously the thugs proceed to drag the two young men off into another room. Shouts of anger and struggle can be heard as the door slams shut, leaving Maddy alone again. The camera lies abandoned on the floor, the screen flickering in the dim light. Maddy, has heard every word of the exchange between the boys and her captures, now driven by pure desperation, she begins to struggle anew, as if her life depends on it.

Back in the Conference Room, Amelia has pulled herself together. She's downed gallons of coffee, urgently she is talking on her phone while scribbling notes furiously. A tray with a pot of steaming coffee sits nearby. Gabriel quietly opens the door, stepping inside he softly closes the conference room door behind him. He's removed his bow tie and jacket, replacing them with a simple black jumper. Amelia glances at him as she hangs up the phone. Addressing him in a cold tone.

"I thought I asked you to stay in the ballroom, Gabriel." Gabriel meets her gaze evenly.

"Yes, I know what you asked me to do. Babaji was tired, so I took him upstairs. Like it or not, Amelia, I'm staying right here." Amelia stares at him for a long moment deciding not to argue the point as she has far more pressing matters to contend with. She looks back down at her notes, her mind racing. Gabriel speaks quietly his tone firm. "You're going to have to tell someone, Amelia. Can you get into the vault yourself? I thought those things were protected against stuff like this." Amelia looks up at him, confused.

"What...? Oh no, I don't need to get into the vault, Gabriel." Gabriel's brow furrows.

"Yes, you do, Amelia. You've got to get the money. You must pay them. Mia, this is Maddy." Amelia's eyes flash with anger as she snaps.

"Yes, Gabriel, I know it's Maddy! And if I pay them, they're going to kill her." Gabriel's voice rises in desperation.

"Amelia, she's, our daughter!" He stares at her, the words hanging in the air. Amelia freezes, then slowly turns to face him. "Don't try to deny it." Gabriel continues, his voice breaking slightly. "I know she's my daughter, Amelia. That's what you wanted to tell me this morning isn't? Please don't try and deny it. Besides she looks just like my mom." Amelia's gaze drops to the floor, her heart pounding. She knows what Gabriel is saying is the truth, but she's not ready to admit it. Not now especially after this evening. Instead, she says the words she knows will hurt him the most.

"You're wrong, Gabriel. So very wrong. Maddy is my daughter. She's mine." Her voice is cold, distant. "Her father was a cadet at the academy where I started training in Seattle. He left the moment he found out I was pregnant." She pauses watching to see if the words have had the effect she intended. "What's the matter,

Gabriel? You're not the only one with a past, you know." Gabriel's face falls, the hurt evident in his eyes.

"I was so sure." He whispers, more to himself than to her. "So sure, she was mine." Amelia watches as the life drains from his expression leaving him looking grey and drawn. She's dealt him a cruel hard blow, and she knows it. Turning away, her hand begins to shake as she picks up her coffee, staring out at the night sky through the conference room window she feels ashamed of herself for lying to his face. Closing her eyes she frowns. Revenge tastes bitter. Gabriel studies her back in silence, trying to process what he's just heard. The door opens again. Spencer comes in with Amelia's things. She turns to acknowledge the younger man, grateful for the interruption she strides purposefully over to him inspecting her fresh clothes in the hold-all he carries. Spencer starts to speak to her. Gabriel remains where he is, listening intently, trying to come to terms with what she has just said to him. While he updates her, Spencer hands Amelia several files, along with her guns, badge, and boots.

"I left the recording with Dave, he's got Maddy's phone too. It was Mac who she spoke to at lunchtime. I didn't even know they were friends. Maddy's never mentioned him." Spencer looks at Amelia's strained expression guilt makes him look away. The events of the evening have taken a toll on him. Not one for drama Spencer is a creative at heart a quality that Maddy is fascinated by a large part of the attraction he held for her.

"Thank you for bringing these Spencer." Amelia considers what he has just told her for a moment. "Do you know anything more about him? Who he hangs out with. What he's into?" Spencer shrugs.

"To be honest I've never paid much attention to him. There's a few of them that hang out in a group. I think one of his mates is called Hugo he is in my psychology class. I don't like him though he is a rich kid whose daddy pays for...." Spencer stops mid-sentence suddenly he remembers something. Looking at Amelia he stares at her his eyes wide. "Shit! I just remembered he's got a brand-new black pickup truck. I saw him taking a bunch of kids out in it last week." He opens his mouth again shocked that he'd overlooked something so obvious. "I'm so sorry I didn't even think until you said about Mac's friends." Amelia walks towards him seeing for the first time how rough he looks.

"Thanks Spencer that's the first piece of real information we can use. I'll call Joe now and get Dave on this. You go home and take a shower. I'll let you know what happens." Spencer smiles weakly.

"I don't think I can go home yet. I need to help. Shall I go back to the station then I can tell Dave what I remembered?" He pauses waiting for her approval. "I'd like to help; I need to help."

Amelia can see the emotion in Spencer's face the guilt underlaying his feeling of responsibility, clouded by fear for Maddy. She nods.

"I'll call Joe and tell him you are coming back. When you're done get some food then go home. Go now Spencer." Amelia steps towards him touching his arm. "I know how Maddy can be. She is tough to say no to. This is on me Spencer I should have never let her take this risk in the first place." Spencer looks at Amelia's face, he straightens his shoulders, standing tall her forgiveness gives him some relief. He smiles a shy smile then awkwardly backs towards the door. Nodding in Gabriel's direction he heads out of the conference room. Amelia grabs a nearby phone off the table dialling Joes number she brings him up to speed on her conversation with Spencer. At the same time, she swiftly changes into jeans, a shirt, and boots without a second glance at Gabriel.

"Go easy on him Joe, Spencer didn't have anything to do with this he just got caught in the crossfire." Before she finishes the call, she adds. "Let Dave know he's on the way back. Follow it up then find out where this Hugo kid lives…. I don't know what the hell's going on, or how these kids are mixed up in this…. Yep, I know, that's what I'm thinking too, it's drug money in the vault, it came from Hectors gang when we busted them. Yeh, I know Joe, but we still don't know who's behind it all." Amelia stops suddenly. "Joe, I need you to go and speak to Connor he's in the cells, stick him in one of the interview rooms see if he knows what's going on.... Yeah, I know but this is way too much of a coincidence for it all not to be connected." She pauses listening to Joe while finishing getting changed, Amelia sits to pull on her black healed leather boots the phone is tucked between her chin and shoulder all the while listening to Joe. She stands up straight as if to emphasis a point to Joe. Amelia is totally focused on what Joe is saying to her, she stands starring out into the dark night.

"I hear what you're saying Joe, I agree. No, I didn't see that.... Yes. Yes, I agree I think Jerry needs to hear all of this... He's still in the ballroom. Yes. I do. Tell Dave to trace that number.... I know we don't... Joe right now it doesn't matter, this is on me. I'll square it with Jerry. He is probably the only one I know for sure doesn't have anything to do with this.... Why? Because Hector killed his partner 10 years ago. Jerrys never had enough proof though.... Yep, that's it. Let me know how it goes with Conor. We don't have much time. Yes, the bags are in the lock up. Ok yep." Amelia ends the call. Her face is clouded with concern; she sits grabbing some case notes that Spencer brought with him she scours the pages looking for something. Gabriel watches her, the weight of their earlier conversation weighs heavily on his mind. Finally, he turns away, looking out of the window, lost in his own thoughts.

Chapter 18

Amelia is pacing up and down, a bundle of nerves and tension. She's on the phone with Joe again, her voice low and urgent.

"I know. Yes, I understand, Joe.... Okay.... Yes, just put it in the bag. I'll let you know when.... Yes, meet me in the garage here.... Good. Yeah. Okay. Ring me when you're here." She hangs up, taking another mouthful of the now tepid coffee. Gabriel, who has been standing quietly by the door, finally speaks.

"Amelia, I heard what you said about the vault money. Please, Amelia, will you listen to me? Just stand still and listen. Let me help. I've got money, Amelia. If you can get me a little bit more time, I spoke to my lawyer. I can get you that money." Amelia turns on him, her eyes flashing with anger. The frustration has been building inside her all evening, she needs someone to lash out at, without thinking she rips into Gabriel.

"You haven't changed a bit, Gabriel. Not one bit. All I've seen this evening is that you're just as much of a control freak as you ever were." She pauses, biting her lip her own gaze is guarded. "Somehow, you dragged Jack and my friends into your lies. Gabriel, sometimes money won't solve everything. I can't buy Maddy back. The minute I give them what they want, she's dead." The reality of her words is finally given air for the first time. Her worst fear, that the outcome of this whole evening may be catastrophic, ending in tragedy is very real. Saying the words out loud somehow makes the savagery of the situation more real.

"This is the real world. My work Gabriel, it's not the movies. This is reality. Something you seem to know nothing about." Turning away she leans on a table. She looks wound so tightly she could snap. Her eyes flash with an emotion Gabriel has never seen before. He realises that beneath it all Amelia is terrified. "You just think you can throw money at people, dazzle them with your charm. But you've no idea. You don't know me, Gabriel. You don't even come close to understanding me. You never did. We come from different worlds." Her words cut deep. Gabriel stands his ground, though the hurt in his eyes is undeniable.

"You're so certain that you have all the facts, aren't you, Amelia? Well, I hate to disappoint you. You're the one who's wrong." Gabriel stands to his full height facing her, his own eyes determined. "You, my darling, have no idea what's happened to me in the last 20 years. You've judged me purely on what you think you know. You have absolutely no idea what's happened to me since you walked out on me without looking back...." Pausing Gabriel stares at Amelia an unfathomable look in his eyes, there is tension in his jaw, a deep furrow above his eyes betrays the pain his words carry.

"Yes, Amelia, it was you. You disappeared, not me. I tried to find you, but you didn't want to be found. That much is obvious. The more I looked, the angrier I got." Gabriel's voice cracks the raw emotion evident as he sits down, leaning forward his shoulders drop seemingly defeated. Amelia, however, remains standing, staring out of the window at the night, her heart a whirlwind of conflicting emotions, she is determined not to give him an inch. Gabriel sits forward in his chair, anxiety written in every nerve in his body, his head buried in his hands. He feels the gravity of everything that has happened this evening mixed with everything he's lost and everything he thought they could become. He looks up at Amelia's back. She's standing rigid, every muscle in her body tense, her anger barely contained. Gabriel feels the gulf between them, a chasm that seems impossible to cross. He stares at her, trying to find the words that could bridge the gap. Frustrated he stands walking down the conference room he puts some space between them; he moves towards the window going to look out at the scene below. He gazes into the distance through the mirrored glass to the images of downtown L.A., his mind is far away, lost in memories of his past in India. As he peers into the distance his eyes glaze and soften as he sees the life he had with Samara superimpose on the scene. A simple, peaceful existence, a life of quiet contentment and deep connection. He recalls her kindness, her courage, and the warmth she brought into his broken world. The memories of India and Samara are starkly different from the present he's experiencing now, in this cold reality in L.A.

It was in India that Gabriel began to change, where he started to awaken spiritually, discovering a new purpose, a new way of being. Suddenly a noise outside the door brings his awareness into the room as he's brought back to the present, to the bleak reality of the conference suite. He can't stand the silence between them any longer. He knows he must break through it, to reach her somehow, even if she won't listen.

"When I couldn't find you...." Gabriel begins to speak, his voice low. "I started to drink. I gambled big. Like I told you this morning, I never do anything small. So, I lost it all. I knew I was going down, so did James." He pauses turning to lean against the window he studies Amelia's back as he speaks to her hoping the mention of his much-loved mentor will penetrate her closed demeanour. "I gave him back his company before I destroyed everything. Then James had a heart attack, and he was gone too. Riddick, our friend, the lawyer, you know who I'm talking about. He took great delight in dismantling everything I'd built." Gabriel glances out of the window smiling riley to himself, he stands tall straightening his shoulders as if he needs to shake the emotion of the words from his frame.

"After all, I'd taught him how to do it. So, he got his revenge. I just stood by and watched him take it all. I didn't care. I'd lost the only people I loved. I didn't want any of it. Not the life and certainly not the people. I was done." He pauses, searching for some reaction from Amelia, she remains silent, seemingly unmoved. Gabriel knows she can hear him that she is listening, he could tell that every word was going in as she was completely still, her body registering every sound.

"So, you see, Amelia." He continues, a sigh leaving his chest in one long breath. "I know loss. It's been a companion of mine for a very long time." Amelia doesn't flinch she seems to be holding her breath; her body is so still. She doesn't speak. The tension between them is electric. Gabriel knows he needs to continue. "I left America." Gabriel continues, his voice growing softer, more reflective. "I took a backpack, my passport, and I just... left. I needed to find something real, something outside of private jets and limousines. I found it. I found what it's like to live with nothing. I found real people. I started to feel again. I was traveling, somehow, I ended up in India. That's where I met Samara." At the mention of his first wife's name Gabriel watches for any sign that his words are reaching her, there is a slight shift in her stance, Amelia remains still, her back firmly turned towards him.

"Samara was different from anyone I'd ever known." Gabriel carries on, his voice tinged with fondness and sorrow. "She was older than me, a widow. She'd lost her husband, sadly she was estranged from her only son." Gabriel turns away from Amelia and leans on the window frame his head against the cold pane of glass as if the sharpness may ease his painful memories. He continues, his voice quieter, these memories were far more intimate, he was sharing private thoughts as much to himself as to Amelia. She watches him out of the corner of her eye, scanning his body for emotion.

"I helped her find her son, then with Babaji's help, they healed. Samara was lonely, so was I. We loved each other, but it was different. It wasn't intense like it was with you. My life with her was quiet and safe, she helped me heal. She was my friend." Gabriel stands up straight once more his gaze drops to the floor, the depth of his memories stirring feelings of love once more within his heart. Still, Amelia doesn't respond, there is the smallest of change in her stance, he can sense her listening, even if she won't show it.

"We spent five years together." Gabriel says quietly, his eyes distant as he remembers. "In that time, I became a different man. I learned to appreciate the simple things, to find joy in a life that wasn't driven by ambition." He pauses looking into the dark distant night sky. Turning around again he faces Amelia studying her across the distance between them.

"There was always a part of me that needed to succeed, to build something. Samara's son had a small film company. I helped him with it. Working again reignited that fire in me. For some reason this time, it was different. This time, literally everything I touched turned to gold, I'm certain it's only because I stopped chasing it. Success just... flowed. I started an internet business because it was easy, something I could do from anywhere. It made millions, far more than I'd ever made before." Gabriel's voice falters, as he looks at her, one of the most painful memories from the past comes to the surface. "Then one day, I was in Delhi on business, and I got a call. Samara had gone out in our small boat on the reservoir by our home. She slipped." He pauses the pain in the admission acute.

"She fell in. No one could save her." Gabriel falls silent, the pain of that loss still raw, still haunting. He waits, hoping for some reaction, some acknowledgment from Amelia. She remains still, her silence heavy and impenetrable. He knows that Amelia's mind is totally preoccupied with thoughts of Maddy but for some reason he feels he wants to tell her his truth now. While they are together alone before the madness begins. Amelia's back remains turned, her silence unbroken, Gabriel notices the slight shift in her posture. He knows she's heard every word, even if she didn't want to. Slowly, Amelia turns around. Gabriel's sighs deeply as he meets her gaze. There's a flicker of compassion in her eyes, but she remains guarded. Her arms are still crossed, her face expressionless. Gabriel can see the battle raging within her, the pull of the past, the weight of the present.

"Babaji saved me." Meeting her gaze with an unwavering look Gabriel continues, his voice thick with emotion. "Samara saved me first then when she died.... If it weren't for Babaji, I would have fallen into an abyss I'd never come back from. I owe him everything."

The silence between them seems like a chasm it stretches, vast with unspoken words. Then suddenly, Amelia's phone beeps loudly. The sound cuts through the tension like a knife. She glances at the screen, and her face instantly becomes taut as she reads the message. Her hands tremble slightly as she hands the phone to Gabriel. He takes the phone and reads the message: 'You have until 4:00a.m. Bring the money to Munro Airstrip in a holdall. Come alone. If we see anyone, she dies. If you don't bring the money, she dies. Mess up, she dies.' Amelia's face is devoid of colour, the pain evident in her eyes, her expression taught with anxiety. Instinctively reaching for her guns, she checks them with practiced precision, her movements sharp and efficient.

"I need your car." This is the first time she has spoken to Gabriel; her voice is steady but laced with tension. Gabriel looks at her, holding her gaze.

"There's not a chance in hell you're going without me, Amelia. Besides, you've been drinking. I'll drive. You can drop me close by, but I'm coming with you." Amelia hesitates, then nods, knowing he's right. She's been drinking, and though she's tried to sober up, it's not enough. She needs him, even if she doesn't want to admit it.

"Fine." She agrees, her voice clipped. "But you do exactly as I say. She's my daughter, Gabriel. I'm responsible for her. Do you understand?" Gabriel's eyes soften as he looks at her, his expression determined.

"I understand, Amelia." As Amelia lifts the phone to her ear she catches Gabriel's eye for the first time. There is a softening in her eyes the recognition that she has heard him, lifts Gabriel's heart. Amelia turns away, as Joe answers the call. There is a knock on the conference room door. The door opens and Jack steps back in the room looking grim. He quickly assesses the atmosphere in the room but doesn't comment on it. After a few minutes Amelia comes off the phone.

"I've just spoken to Joe; Dave's got a lead." Jack listens interrupting her.

"Amelia, I know you don't want anyone's help. I think you should talk to Jerry he is sober. He knows me well enough to know that something is going on." Amelia nods.

"I was going to ask you to get him for me Jack. I agree he is one of the people I am completely certain of. There are some guys around him though who I don't trust. So, keep it low key please Jack. Joe is on his way I'll bring Jerry up to speed on the way to the garage." Jack nods, heading to leave, as he reaches the door, he turns the handle opening it then almost as an afterthought he asks.

"What else did Joe say?" Amelia's voice is strained the tension evident in her words.

"Spencer's footage gave them a partial plate on the van. Dave is running it now. And we've found out more about this 'Mac' kid. He's got a record, nothing major, just cannabis but he's the one who spoke to Maddy earlier." Amelia's expression tightens. The strain is evident in every fibre of her being. "Dave is pulling in every resource we've got without making anyone suspicious." Jack looks at her, compassion and love in his eyes he is desperate to reach her.

"Amelia, you must be careful. If these guys know that the money is in the vault, they've got connections in the Department..." Amelia cuts him off.

"I know, Jack, I will be careful. Listen Jack, I know Joe hasn't told you about this. Jack, he has been training for this kind of situation he wants to become a specialist. Trust him, I do. We haven't got much time now. Where's Jerry now?" Jack looks taken aback. He has always known Joe had much bigger ambitions, but this was news he hadn't expected to hear tonight.

"Jerry is in the lobby. I asked him to wait there." Amelia raises her eyebrows as she looks at him. All around her people were surprising her in ways she least expected, none of which were to her pleasure.

"Thats fine Jack. Jerry should know you're right. I trust him." Jack opens the door calling to Jerry he stands aside as Amelia's boss strides through the door. Jerry pauses taking in her appearance combined with the half empty coffee pot and her discarded evening gown he frowns. Jack closes the door.

"Ok Mia, I know Jacks told me the basics now I need you to level with me." As Jerry strides into the room Gabriel is left in no doubt as to the consummate professionalism of Amelia's boss. Jerry immediately grasps the severity of the nightmare scenario that his friend and long-standing colleague is facing, a very real and appalling situation that no police officer of Amelia's outstanding career should ever find herself dealing with. There is no time for platitudes, and he makes no attempt to console Amelia knowing full well that she is valiantly holding herself together for the sake of her daughter.

Addressing her directly he looks her straight in the eyes standing opposite her, Amelia stands straight to her full height as she regards her boss. Something in the normality of the respect between them brings a kind of stoic confidence back into her stance, his appearance just what she needed to bring clarity to her mind as she answers his direct questions with equally direct answers. She delivers all the information without sentimentality or emotion giving Jerry the confirmation that she is more than able to carry herself in this most difficult of circumstances.

Only once he has all the information that he needs to hear and see, does he reach forward to give her shoulders a reassuring squeeze. She is after all one of the finest officers he has ever worked with and there was no way he was about to risk her or her daughter's life over drug money, whatever she needed he was prepared to consider. Amelia as ever didn't let him down. He listened carefully to everything that she and Joe had so far done in their decision-making process and Jerry had complete faith in her ability to see the plan through. Ultimately this was her daughter they were talking about, and Jerry knew that she had to be the one to take the decisive action, if not she would never recover from the outcome, whatever that was to be.

Jack and Gabriel can only observe at this point. Gabriel silently marvels at Amelia's ability to remain composed even in the height of the tension in the situation. Gathering all her equipment, bomber jacket, phone and guns she prepares herself to leave.

"We need to move fast. They've given us until 4.00a.m to get to the airstrip so that doesn't give us much time. Joe is meeting me downstairs in the garage. Gabriel is driving me there. We will swop over at the entrance to the airstrip, so that Gabriel can find cover." Shaking his head Jerry holds up his hand, he stops Amelia in her tracks as she is heading towards the conference room door, about to leave.

"Wait there Mia!" Jerry's tone is firm. He is the one person who commands her deepest respect, his words stop her in her immediately. "I've already called in back-up from outside the department. Jackson is waiting for my call for the details. He thinks just like I do that this goes way back. I trust him completely. He will pick me up on the way." He holds his hand up to stop any protest that Amelia may have. "Save it Mia. There is no way I am not going to be there for you and Maddy. We will keep our distance, but Joe already knows, and he will be in contact with me, so you don't have to wear a wire. They won't see anyone apart from you." Amelia stands still for a moment taking stock of the men standing in the room with her, three amazing men, all focused on hers and Maddy's wellbeing, how could she refuse any of the help and support that they offered.

"Of course, Jerry, that's the right call." For the first time for several hours Amelia smiled at them all, a slight smile but one that let them all know she was grateful. Jerry returned her smile with one that meant business.

"You make damn sure you were a vest, Joe too. No question." He paused coming to stand beside her, putting a reassuring hand on her shoulder he squeezed it, then in an uncharacteristic show of affection he pulled her into a tight bear hug, stepping back his tone final as he added. "You stay safe. No hero stuff, you hear me. Shoot the bastards if you have to. Just bring our girl home."

Both Jack and Gabriel have silently been listening to the exchange between Amelia and Jerry for the past 10 minutes. Both men left in no doubt about the gravity of the situation and the extent to which Amelia's life as a high-ranking police officer is a complete revelation to them. A little in awe of her Gabriel stands waiting for instructions. Amelia's expression gives little away. She watches as Jerry leaves. He shakes Jack's hand, acknowledging Gabriel across the room with a half-smile and a nod. Gathering herself Amelia shrugs on her LAPD jacket over her crisp white shirt. Checking her guns into her holster she puts them in the duffle bag that Spencer had brought them in earlier. With a determined look she heads to the door. Gabriel follows silently behind holding the door for Jack. Jack's only option is to follow them out of the conference room through the hotel down to the parking garage. Amelia, Gabriel and Jack move quickly and silently through the hotel deliberately avoiding any inebriated guests on the way, they move through the quiet hallways of the hotel, keeping well out of sight as they make their way towards the parking garage. The tension is palpable, each of them fully aware of the graveness of the moment. As they approach the garage, they spot Joe's car idling while he waits for them next to Gabriels Aston Martin. The large 4x4 dwarfing the sports car, its engine rumbling as it stands waiting for them to arrive. Joe immediately jumps out, hurrying to the trunk as they draw near. He opens it with swift efficiency, revealing two large hold-all's an impressive rifle, and several handguns next to a couple of bullet proof vests.

    Amelia goes to inspect the items with Joe her eyes scanning the contents as she and Joe quietly discuss tactics, their conversation clipped and intense. Jack stands back, listening silently, his face set in grim resignation. Joe places the bags into the trunk of Gabriel's car, his movements precise, that of a trained professional. Joe passes Amelia her vest first making sure it's secure and tight before putting on his own. Jack observes his son with a degree of pride as he has never seen Joe so in command of himself. A profound respect fills his heart easing some of the worry that conflicts his thoughts. Stepping forward he pulls Joe into a tight embrace, holding his son's face between his hands, searching his eyes as if memorizing every detail.

"Be careful, Son." Jack says quietly, his voice heavy with emotion. Joe nods, hugging his dad to reassure him Joe's expression is resolute. As he climbs back into his car, he exchanges a look with his father, then with Amelia. Without another word, Joe slams the car into gear and tears out of the garage, the tyres screeching as he speeds away into the night. Gabriel, watching the scene unfold, silently climbs into the driver's seat of his own car, starting the engine. The low throaty rumble fills the garage with sound and vibrations, breaking the tense silence. Jack walks over to Amelia, his gaze filled with concern. He pulls her into a hug, whispering something in her ear that only she can hear. Amelia pulls back, her eyes are focused her expression resolute and determined.

In the car Gabriel watches reading her lips as she looks into her friend's eyes. She quietly says, "I know." She returns Jack's embrace with fierce intensity as she hugs him tightly, before turning away, her mind consumed with the mission in front of them. With a last look at her friend, Amelia strides towards the passenger side of Gabriel's car, opening the door with purpose. She slides into the seat, her expression set. Gabriel glances at her, then shifts the car into gear. As they pull out of the parking garage the tyres squeal against the concrete, the car surging forward into the pre-dawn darkness. Jack stands alone in the garage, he is completely still as he watches the taillights fade into the distance, the cold silence of the early morning wrapping around him like a shroud.

Chapter 19

Across the city in the dark, grimy depths of the disused garage, Maddy is still lying in the pit. The dim light reveals her determined expression, it's clear that she's managed to free her hands from the bindings that had held her captive. She is bruised, exhausted, but defiant. Suddenly, the door to the side room creaks open, the two older men, Magpie and Stretch, saunter out, their footsteps echoing ominously through the garage. Magpie, smirking, jumps down into the pit, moving to untie Maddy's feet.

Maddy has been waiting for this moment. As soon as Magpie's hands free the ropes, she springs into action. With a swift, brutal movement, she launches herself at him, her fists and feet a blur of motion. Despite her small stature, Maddy fights like a trained warrior, years of martial arts classes finally paying off, every strike driven by desperation and fury. The fight is vicious, brutal, and relentless. Maddy lands a solid punch to Magpie's jaw, sending him staggering back. She uses the moment to scramble out of the pit, her breath ragged as she makes a desperate bid for freedom. Just as she reaches the edge of the garage, a dark shadow looms behind her. Stretch, unseen and silent, swings a piece of wood, hitting Maddy hard across the back of her head. The impact is sickening. Maddy crumples to the ground knocked unconscious. Magpie, recovering from the beating, spits blood from his mouth as he climbs out of the pit, fury etched into his features.

"Little bitch!" He growls, wiping his face with the back of his hand. He glares at Stretch, who stands over Maddy's limp form.

"You better not have killed her, Stretch. We need her alive." His voice is full of venom, barely masking his anger. Stretch, slightly panicked, bends down and checks Maddy's pulse.

"She's breathing, Mags." He mutters, relieved.

"Good." Magpie snaps. "Tie her up properly this time, dumbass. Put her in the car. If I didn't need her, I'd shoot her right now." He spits blood on the ground in disgust. "Make sure those two morons are locked up in the office. I've got to let Riddick know we're leaving." Magpie pulls out a burner phone, already dialling as he stalks out of the garage. "Yeah, it's me...." His voice is tense as he looks up and down the deserted road in front of the garage. "We're moving now. Tell Riddick everything's on track." His tone is hard, cold and calculating, as he disappears into the shadows. Stretch, meanwhile, drags Maddy's limp body across the dirty floor, throwing her into the back seat of the only decent car in the garage. Magpies pride and joy a big Lincoln Continental. Stretch grabs a length of rope and ties her hands in front of her, this time making sure the knots are tight.

Meanwhile across the city Gabriel's car, sleek and gleaming white powers through the night reflecting the glow of the streetlights off its pearlescent bodywork as it races down the highway. Once more Gabriel's hands grip the steering wheel tightly, his square jaw set with grim determination. The car's headlights pierce the darkness ahead, illuminating the empty road. Amelia sits beside him, her face tense, her eyes vaguely aware of the scenery streaming past them she returns her focus to the road ahead. The only sound in the car is the satnav's sporadic velvety female voice cutting through the silence between them politely affirming directions.

I little way ahead of them Joe's car speeds along a parallel route, his music blaring loudly through the speakers the irony of the song that's playing not lost on Joe. Daniel Beddingfield's anthem 'Gotta-get through this' belts out it's chorus as his phone rings, the screen lighting up with Jerry's name. Silencing the music Joe answers, keeping his eyes fixed on the road as he discusses the strategy they've planned. His voice is calm, but there's a steely edge to it, a resolve that's unshakable. As they talk, Joe spots the airstrip looming towards him. He takes the next exit, peeling off from the main road he heads to the far end of the tarmac looking for a place to hide his car. Some way behind him Gabriel continues straight, each of them following their designated paths. Joe's plan is to loop around and approach the abandoned airfield from behind, where he'll have a better vantage point. Jerry has assured him back up isn't far away. Meanwhile, Gabriel pushes forward, driving Amelia straight to the main entrance of the airstrip, every second counting as they close in on the designated exchange spot.

Back at the garage the scene is tense as Hugo and Mac, both panicked and guilt-ridden, realise the potentially dire fall out from their actions. They struggle with their poorly tied ropes, listening as the kidnapper's car screeches away. Hugo, with a fierce urgency, turns to Mac.

"We've got to get out of here, Mac. They're going to kill her. We're going to get done for murder, both of us." The fear in Hugo's voice sparks a reaction in Mac, but he's already sinking into despair, staring blankly at the door.

"It's no good, Hugo. That door's solid. We're stuck, and they've got Maddy. My mom's going to kill me." Hugo, disgusted by Mac's defeatist attitude, snaps.

"Don't be such a fuckin' loser! Get up and help me!" He kicks at Mac to jolt him into action. It has its desired effect as Mac pulls himself off the floor, together, they renew their efforts, slamming into the door with all their might. Kicking it repeatedly the old frame finally gives way, splintering as the door bursts open. They exchange a brief look of shock before Hugo shouts.

"Grab the camera! It's the only thing we've got to prove this wasn't meant to happen." Mac picks up the camera off the floor, they race out of the garage toward the waiting pickup. Their faces pale with fear, knowing that time is running out for Maddy.

Munro airstrip, the first light of dawn creeps over the horizon, casting long shadows across the tarmac. The place has an otherworldly feel about it, with old planes, rusting machinery, and empty hangars scattered about. The atmosphere inside Gabriel's car is strained neither wanting to talk. Gabriel pulls up a safe distance from the meeting point. The silence lingers between Amelia and Gabriel. Both are on edge, the pressure of the impending exchange pressing down on them. Amelia speaks first, her voice firm with the practised control of her profession fighting hard to keep a lid on her parental fear.

"Gabriel, I need you to promise me you will stay out of sight." Amelia insists, her voice wavering. She points to a patch of undergrowth far from the airstrip. "Look there. You can't be seen..." She points towards a grove of trees. Seeming to need to justify her command she says forcefully. "This is my job. I know what I'm doing. Stay well hidden. They can't know anyone's with me." Gabriel opens his mouth to argue, the look in her eyes stops him cold. He nods, swallowing his objections.

"Just...Please be careful." Gabriel's tone is steady although his words are laced with concern. Amelia's resolve doesn't waver.

"I will. But you can't interfere, trust me Gabriel I know what I'm doing. Go, now." Gabriel opens his mouth to argue, Amelia cuts him off, her voice steely.

"Please, Gabriel, you promised. This is what I do. I'm trained for this. You don't know these kinds of people. I can't afford to worry about you and Maddy." Gabriel studies her for a moment, his jaw clenched.

"Amelia nobody is trained for this, not even you!" He nods. Without another word, he exits the car looking back at her one last time. Amelia's eyes are locked on him, a mix of determination and fear. She manages a smile, her face white and taught, her nerves stretched, her eyes wide, adrenaline coursing through her body. Gabriel starts to say something, his words catch in his throat. Instead, he gives her a small, reassuring smile before turning and sprinting towards the cover of the undergrowth. He moves quickly, making sure he's out of sight where she has asked him to hide.

Amelia climbs into the driver's seat catching sight of her own face in the mirror the strain is evident. Today she looks every one of her 40 years. Amelia's knuckles whiten as she now grips the steering wheel, her mind racing through the plan. She knows the risks, she's not leaving without daughter, no matter what she will protect Maddy. Amelia moves the car out of sight driving towards the runway. Once his car is out of sight Gabriel breaks cover heading towards the back of one the hangers much closer than Amelia had envisioned. Totally unaware of his new location as she drives onto the airstrip. Amelia navigates Gabriel's car carefully between the hangars, finally parking in an open space on the tarmac. The air is still, the pre-dawn light altering the scene as the sky's colour begins to change. It's colder than she thought, her mind scans the scene taking in every facet of the view from the car, a shiver runs down her spine, dismissing it purely as a sure sign the seasons are merging, she shakes herself like a fighter preparing for the ring.

Getting out of the car she goes to the trunk to place her guns in the best place to conceal them, before closing the lid she takes the safeties off the guns. Amelia checks the large holdalls that Joe had put there. Inside the bags are stacks of old newspapers, certainly not the cash that the kidnappers were expecting, Amelia is under no illusion their reaction to her deceit would necessitate deadly force. Steeling herself she walks around the car. Standing by the front she rests her hip against the hood the only sign of her nerves is from her mouth, her lip twitches as she chews the inside of her cheek.

The engine of the car is still running it hums softly behind her, a reminder that there's no turning back now. She's ready, or as ready as she'll ever be. This confrontation could determine her daughter's fate not to mention her own, leaving the car running would mean that getting Maddy away from here would be as easy as she could possibly make it. Straightening Amelia hears another engine. The dawn air is cool against her skin, now she barely notices. Every nerve in her body is on high alert. Her eyes squint as the engine is too loud to be a car. Within seconds a small Lear jet lands on the nearby runway taxing steadily across towards the hangers, it stops its engines idling noisily. Sensing danger she stands tall knowing she is being watched. Amelia tenses they hadn't planned for this. Across the tarmac the headlights of a large American car snake towards her position. Amelia tenses. Across the airstrip, Joe positions himself on the ground, dressed head to toe in black. His rifle is equipped with a long-range scope, giving him a clear view of Amelia and the surroundings. As he scans the area, he spots movement near the hangars. His heart skips a beat when he recognizes Gabriel sneaking between the buildings. Joe's jaw clenches.

"Gabriel, you idiot. What the fuck are you doing?" Muttering under his breath, Joe adjusts his scope to keep an eye on both Gabriel and the unfolding situation. The sound of the jet forcing him to lie completely flat trying to conceal his position. In the back seat of the kidnappers' car, Maddy stirs, groaning as she regains consciousness. Her head throbs, she moans as the rope biting into her skin, her wrists burn from the tightness of the knots. She blinks against the light, trying to piece together where she is. Through the blur she sees Magpie talking on his phone, his voice sharp and sinister.

"Yeah. We're here. I see her car. She's alone. It's time."

Chapter 20

Amelia stands motionless, completely still she resembles an ethereal statue in the early dawn light. Her eyes locked on the approaching car. The kidnappers' car comes to a halt a few yards away. The passenger door opens and Magpie steps out, a cocky smirk on his face.

"You got my money Cartwright?" Magpie sneers, waving his gun casually. "Show me your hands. Take your jacket off Cartwright. TURN AROUND. SLOWLY!"

Amelia complies, slowly easing off the bomber jacket throwing it on the floor, she raises her hands very deliberately turning to show she is unarmed. The white fitted shirt she's wearing is tucked neatly into her jeans; the bullet proof vest covers her torso. The cuffs of her shirt are folded showing off her brown slim forearms her only jewellery the stunning diamond bracelet that Gabriel gave her as a birthday gift still wrapped around her wrist. Sparkling brilliantly in the early morning light it seems oddly out of place in the scene, a vivid contrast to the stark darkness of the situation. Her bullet proof vest the only visible evidence she is a cop. Standing tall she withstands the appraisal of the criminal in front of her. Her expression is cold, calculating this man has her daughter.

"Where's Maddy? I want to see my daughter." Magpie chuckles darkly.

"You don't get to make demands, Cartwright. Money first, then the girl." Her patience is razor-thin, her anger barely contained.

"Show me my daughter. Now." Magpie's grin widens.

"Easy now. Wouldn't want to do anything rash, would we?" He nods toward the car tapping the hood with his gun. "Stretch, bring her out." Stretch drags Maddy from the back seat, shoving her forward. She's bruised and filthy, but alive. The sight of her daughter, beaten and battered, sends a surge of fury through Amelia. The breath in her chest seems to freeze as Amelia fights her own reaction. Her hands tremble, as she forces herself to stay composed. She can't afford to lose control now. From a distance, Gabriel and Joe both react, their hearts lurching at the sight of Maddy. Gabriel, from his hidden vantage point, takes a sharp breath, whispering to himself.

"Jesus Christ." The reality of the situation strikes him hard as he sees his daughter for the first time since her abduction, battered and terrified. He moves forward changing his position once more. While across the airstrip Joe tightens his grip on the rifle, the crosshairs trained on Stretch's head. He's ready to pull the trigger, suddenly Maddy moves, making him freeze as her head comes into his sightline. Swinging the rifle away he curses as rage swirls in the pit of his stomach. He can't risk hitting her, clenching his jaw he refocuses. Suddenly, the roar of the Lear jet engine fills the air as the small plane taxis down the runway, coming to a stop between the hangers. Its door opens, revealing a shadowy figure inside, the pilot standing at the door motions to Magpie. The jet blocks Joe's line of sight, forcing him to reposition. Amelia's face remains a mask of control, inside, she's a maelstrom of emotion. Her eyes flicker with rage as she locks onto Magpie.

"Money now Cartwright or I'll put a bullet in her head." Magpie's dark eyes show zero compassion. His tone is stone cold. Amelia turns walking to the back of her car, opening the trunk she retrieves her guns, deftly putting them behind her in the belt of her jeans. Standing up straight she drags the heavy bags towards the front of the car dropping them some feet from Magpie. She straightens looking Maddy directly in the eye she smiles love radiating towards her daughter. As she blinks, she refocuses on Magpie her expression hardens immediately.

"There you go! You've got what you want. Let her go." Magpie just laughs.

"Step back." Amelia does as she's told, stepping away she watches Magpie carefully assessing when to strike. Magpie bends to open one of the bags he snatches the one closest to him, his eyes eager, greedy and stupid. Tearing open the zip the bag reveals bundles of newspaper. He stares at it, disbelief morphing into rage.

"You, stupid bitch!" he roars. "Kill her!" Anticipating his reaction in a flash, Amelia is already drawing her gun, without hesitation firing a single shot into Magpie's leg. He screams, collapsing to the ground. Stretch panics, wildly aiming his gun at Amelia, shielding himself behind Maddy. His shot goes wide. Amelia barely flinches her eyes never leaving Maddy kicking Magpie's weapon out of reach. She lunges towards stretch her gun aimed at his head. Maddy takes the initiative and stamps on the kidnapper's foot with her heal, as he yelps in surprise, she yanks herself free diving away from him as Stretch panics. At the same time Joe races across the airstrip running at full pelt he stops once he has the kidnapper in his sight his rifle aimed first at Stretch then at the aircraft now heading towards the runway, he fires several shots at the plane catching the windshield the plane glides slowly to a halt.

Amid the chaos Stretch turns to flee. Suddenly a long-range shot rings out it grazes his arm he screams, turning once more towards Maddy his arms flailing, blood pours from the flesh wound. His gun still in his hand a literal loose cannon. While the commotion unfolds out of nowhere, Gabriel has sprinted across the tarmac coming behind Magpies car he lunges at Stretch pushing him out of the way desperately trying to protect Maddy, he reaches her in the split second that another shot is fired. He throws himself in front of her. The deadly second shot, intended for Stretch, strikes Gabriel instead, causing his body to lose momentum mid-air, clutching his chest the impact sends him crashing to the ground.

Amelia sees everything in a heartbeat. Her world narrows to the sight of Gabriel and Maddy falling to the ground. The scene registers as if it plays out in slow motion in front of her. Unable to reach Maddy she cries out, racing towards them. In the distance, the black pickup barrels onto the tarmac its tyres screeching. Police sirens wail as backup arrives, cornering the jet whose pilot has obviously been injured the police surround the plane before its occupants can escape. Maddy sobs as Amelia reaches her, pulling her into a protective embrace. Gabriel lies motionless nearby, blood seeping from his chest. The scene is utter chaos, shattered lives hanging in the balance as the police cars descend sirens blaring bringing the promised reinforcements. Sadly, they are too late.

The sound of approaching police sirens the backup promised by Jerry fills the air as law enforcement swarms the airstrip. Stretch, trying to flee in the car, is quickly apprehended, unable to escape the tightening net. Amelia lies on the dirt-covered ground, feeling the cold seep into her bones. Every nerve in her body is screaming as she rolls over to Gabriel. He lies motionless, barely breathing. Blood seeps from the wound in his chest, staining the ground beneath him. Amelia's hands shake as she frantically tries to stem the flow, her fingers slipping on the wet, sticky warmth. She presses harder, desperation clawing at her insides.

"Gabriel, stay with me." Agonizingly she pleads, her voice cracking with hysteria. "Look at me, Gabriel. Stay with me. I love you. Please, stay with me!" His eyes flutter open, just for a moment, catching sight of Amelia's tear-streaked face. He tries to focus, but the pain is too much. Slowly, his eyelids begin to close, his strength fading. Amelia's heart shatters as she watches the life drain from him.

"No, no, no! Gabriel, don't you dare close your eyes! Stay with me!" In the distance, the wail of sirens grows louder, the sound mingling with the distant hum of a helicopter cutting through the morning air. The airstrip is now flooded with police, and emergency vehicles racing toward them. Amelia barely notices the commotion. Her entire world has narrowed to the man lying in her arms, the man she's losing with every second that passes.

Joseph sprints towards them, phone in hand, yelling into it as he frantically calls for help. His eyes widen in horror as he sees the scene before him, Amelia, covered in blood, screaming Gabriel's name as he slips further away. Joseph drops to his knees beside them, trying to help, but the sight of Gabriel's blood on his hands makes him recoil. He stares at Maddy as she too faints, scooping her into his arms he cradles her cold body against his own, huge tears flowing down his dusty face.

A helicopter's blades whir in the distance, growing louder as it approaches. The medics are quick, their hands steady and efficient as they work to stabilize Gabriel. Amelia seems numb, she watches, as they load him onto a stretcher. Her shirt, once white, is now a grim tapestry of blood and dirt. She looks down at her hands, trembling as they're stained with the life that's slipping away. Maddy has regained consciousness and is stretchered off with Joe to an ambulance. Magpie too bleeding and cursing he screams in pain as he is transferred to an ambulance accompanied by an officer. The helicopter readies to lift off, to transport Gabriel toward the hospital, once Amelia knows Joe is with Maddy, she climbs in after him. Her eyes never leave his face, willing him to hold on. The ride feels both endless and too short as they speed toward the only hope Gabriel has left. When they land at the hospital, the world becomes a blur of movement and noise. Gabriel is rushed inside, doctors and nurses swarming around him. Amelia stands there, frozen, covered in his blood, unable to process the whirlwind around her.

Stuck in what feels to Amelia like a weird time warp she stands alone in the waiting room, Amelia's mind races, trapped in a loop of fear and regret. Her hands, now shaking uncontrollably, press against her blood-stained clothes, as if she can somehow hold herself together. Shock sets in as the doors swing open, and a wave of familiar faces rush towards her. The room swims the floor coming to meet her.

Coming to, Amelia tries to focus, around her bed are faces she loves. Jack, Olivia, and Jerry. Their voices merge into one as the sound suddenly returns with her vision. Amelia's head throbs, the ache in her body makes her wince, she reaches up realising there is a drip attached to her hand. Confusion makes her head spin as she sits up trying to swing her legs off the bed.

"Whoa there Mia." Jacks soft firm voice is right beside her. His gentle hands pull her shoulders back towards the bed. Suddenly remembering the scene at the airstrip reality crashes back into the room making Amelia groan and push to sit back up.

"Maddy! Jack! Where's Maddy?" Feeling him squeeze her shoulders she looks up at his reassuring smile

"She safe Mia. She is down the corridor with Joe" The relief is only momentary though. Once again Amelia pushes to sit up.

"Gabriel!" She cries. "Jack where is he? Jack, tell me, what's happened to Gabriel?" Jack once again squeezes her gently.

"Lie back Mia you are in shock." Amelia's eyes fly open Jack hasn't told her where he is. She grips Jacks hand not letting him look away.

"Jack where is he?" She demands.

"Mia you must listen to me. He is here at the hospital. Mia they are doing everything they can to save him." Amelia hears his words but can't process them.

"No.... No, No Jack what are you saying where is he? I need to see him, Jack. Tell me now where he is." Jack nods taking her in his arms he whispers to her.

"He is in surgery Mia. It's going to be a while." Amelia's eyes are wide pools of agony in her pale face. Her hair is still matted from Gabriel's blood, her face is dirty, and blood stained. Her clothes smell of his blood too, as she looks down, she gasps in utter horror her mind reeling at the tragic turn of events. Tears fill her devastated eyes, unchecked they start to stream down Amelia's face creating clean channels through the dirt and blood. Liv steps towards her devastated friend she ushers the men out of the room preparing to clean Amelia up. A nurse brings in a fresh hospital gown. Helping Liv they gently change Amelia out of her ruined clothes. Liv calls to Jack from the doorway of Amelia's room.

"Jack call Slyvia please, ask her to pick Mia up some fresh clothes will you. I'm not sure how long we can keep her in this bed. She can't go wandering around the hospital in a gown." Jack nods knowing full well that Amelia will be back on her feet in a matter of minutes as soon as she has had fluids and some food. She is in deep shock, but he knows that Amelia is the most resilient person he has ever met which means that her recovery will be fast. He quickly dials Sylvia's number. Following his wife's instructions Amelia has fresh clothes delivered to the hospital within an hour.

Amelia's eyes are glassy, her expression dazed as she tries to make sense of what's being said. Now dressed, she asks the nurse to remove the empty drip. A surgeon steps into the room, his face solemn.

"Ms Cartwright." He addresses her, his tone serious. "Gabriel's still in surgery. It's critical. He's lost a massive amount of blood. I'm sorry it's not better news. This could take time. I need to ask, are any of you blood relatives? He needs all the help he can get his blood type is incredibly rare." Amelia's voice cracks as she responds.

"I... I know Doctor. No, we aren't. But... my daughter, Maddy... she's the same blood type. Gabriel's her father." The words tumble out, raw and unfiltered. "Please Doctor.... She doesn't know. She doesn't know that Gabriel's her dad. They have only just met one another, and I haven't told either of them yet." The doctor nods, understanding the difficulty of the delicate situation.

"We'll do everything we can. If you want him to have the best chance, then I'm sorry but someone needs to tell her, or she isn't ever going to see her father again. You must decide but just make it quick. I'll keep you updated." Amelia's legs feel weak, the judgement in the doctor's tone making her feel even worse. As she stands up, she begins to sway, unsteadily. Even though she has only just got out of the hospital bed she has to see her daughter. She follows the doctor, wanting to be with Maddy, needing to tell her the truth she's kept hidden for so long. She signals to Jack to come with her, seeking his support for what's about to come.

In Maddy's hospital room, the atmosphere is clinical. Maddy lies in the bed, looking small and fragile, surrounded by police, doctors, and nurses. Her face is bruised, her eyes red from crying. The room feels stiflingly serious as the officers finish their questions, finally giving her a moment of peace. As Amelia enters, the room falls silent. Everyone instinctively steps back, giving mother and daughter the space they need. Joe smiles at Amelia glad to see her on her feet again. His own clothes still filthy from earlier the exhaustion showing in his clouded eyes he can't quite meet her gaze. Joe gets up, immediately making room for Amellia.

"Stay Joe. I think Maddy needs you here." Joe nods stepping aside so that Amelia can sit on the edge of Maddy's bed, her hand trembling as she strokes her daughter's battered face. Maddy looks up at her, tears welling in her eyes.

"I'm so sorry, Mom." She whispers, her voice trembling. "I should never have gone out again. I didn't know... I didn't know this would happen." Maddy dissolves into floods of tears. Amelia's heart breaks at the sight of her daughter's guilt-ridden face. She knows she must tell her the truth now, a truth that will change everything.

"Maddy, sweetheart." Amelia begins, her voice barely above a whisper. "Maddy it's ok. I'm just so relieved you are here. You are ok, aren't you? Did they.... Did they hurt you sweetheart?" Amelia must ask Maddy the question but it's the answer that frightens her more. Maddy silently shakes her head.

"Only cuts and bruises Mom. I'll be ok honestly." Amelia takes a deep breath, silently thanking God they hadn't touched her daughter. Softly she reaches out to stroke Maddy's face grateful that her daughter is back safe from harm's way. The reality of what she now has to say makes Amelia's heart sink.

"There is something I need to tell you. And I am so, so sorry that it can't wait, you must hear this now." Maddy's tear-filled eyes search her mother's face, sensing the importance of what's coming. Amelia takes a deep breath, forcing herself to speak.

"Maddy. Gabriel... Gabriel is your father." The words once said can never be taken back. They strike the air like a bell that is rung signifying a sliding doors moment. Maddy blinks, confusion and shock clouding her expression.

"What... what are you talking about?" Maddy stammers, her voice rising in panic. "No. No, that's not true!" Maddy starts to climb off the bed trying to put distance between herself and the words that Amelia is saying, her mother reaches across the bed to try and stop her. The room spins as the revelation hits Maddy like a freight train. She pushes Amelia away, her mind unable to grasp the truth. "Why didn't you ever tell me Mom. Get out!" She screams, her voice raw with anguish. "Get out!"

Amelia stumbles back, the pain of her daughter's rejection cutting deep. She stands at the foot of the bed, her heart breaking, knowing she's lost Maddy's trust in the worst possible way. Joe steps forward, wrapping Maddy in his arms, trying to calm her down.

"It's okay, Maddy. I've got you. It's going to be okay." Joe whispers, his voice filled with pain as he looks at Amelia the truth of his pain different to hers.

She silently watches two of the most beloved people in her life reel from yet another blow, their hearts ripped wide open at three small words 'Gabriel's your father'. They cling to one another. Joes embrace that of a man fiercely protective of the woman he loves. Maddy's pain more obvious than Joe's. He had done what Amelia asked of him. Joe had been the man she chose to wield the gun. He had been the one to pull the trigger and now he was the one who had to hold the truth that he may just have killed the father of the woman he loves.

Amelia couldn't ever imagine a worse thing than breaking someone's heart. Standing looking at the shattered expressions in front of her she realised she had broken four hearts in her life. Maddy's, Joe's, Gabriel's and her own. A cold desolate feeling settles in her chest. Her next words could only cause more pain, but she has to say them. Amelia watches, tears streaming down her face, feeling more helpless than she ever has.

"Maddy... Gabriel needs blood." Her words shake as her voice breaks. "He needs your blood; you are the same rare blood group. You are both Rhnull blood type. You know it's called Golden blood

Maddy it's so rare." The devastating effect of Amelia's words causes Maddy to have a panic attack. She sobs, clinging to Joe, unable to catch her breath or to process the nightmare her life has become. A nurse comes in to give Maddy oxygen as her heart rate monitor is beeping loudly, Joe steps aside still holding her hand tight, his heart breaking for her, for all of them. The truth about Gabriel being Maddy's father is too much for her to deal with, especially after everything that's happened.

The enormity of the day's events crushes Amelia, she turns, her steps unsteady as she leaves the room, Maddy can't stand her to be anywhere near, so she leaves to make way for the team who come to take her blood. Amelia stands outside the room, just outside the doorway, she watches as Maddy tries to regain her breath, her eyes meet her mother's, she turns away asking Joe to send her mother away. Joe turns towards the doorway his face ashen the hurt in his eyes almost too much for Amelia to bare. She backs away turning to run down the corridor. Amelia is unaware of the time as she wanders the hospital corridors, lost in a haze of pain and exhaustion. The world around her is a blur of activity, families reuniting, children crying, doctors rushing by. Life continues, indifferent to her agony.

Amelia drifts through the hospital, her mind numb, until she finds herself outside the ICU. A nurse meets her a worried look on her face. Amelia listens to the words that spill from the young woman's mouth barely able to register as she is led towards an ICU bay. Through the window, she sees Gabriel, wired up to monitors, fighting for his life. She leans against the glass, pressing her forehead against it, her breath fogging the pane. The enormity of everything seems surreal, rocking the fabric of her reality. The lies, the secrets, the love she never allowed herself to fully feel.

She reaches up to push hair out of her eyes, feeling at once the matted sticky mess she presses her hand to her mouth as she inhales, she smells Gabriel's blood on her fingertips, the blood that was safely inside his body only hours ago. Her body slumps against the window drained of all strength. The only thing keeping her standing is the hope, however faint, that Gabriel will pull through and this nightmare will be over.

Chapter 21

Standing out the ICU Amelia seems frozen, she is motionless, her eyes locked on Gabriel through the glass. The doctor's voice drifts over her like a distant echo.

"Amelia, you really should go home. You look exhausted. There's nothing you can do for him now. He's heavily sedated, and we need him to stay that way for at least 24 hours to give his heart a chance." The Doctor places his hand on Amelia's shoulder squeezing it to bring her awareness back, he can see she is still dealing with the aftermath of the trauma of the day. Once she gives him eye contact, he starts to give her the facts.

"The bullet missed his heart by fractions of a millimetre. Any closer, and we'd have lost him." Amelia barely registers the words. Her gaze now fixed on Gabriel's still form. She's a ghost of herself, drained of all energy, her mind and body battered by the whirlwind of the past few days.

"But I should be here if he needs me." She whispers, more to herself than to the doctor. "I should be here if he wakes up." The doctor's expression softens.

"Amelia, he's not going to wake up tonight. In fact, we may induce a coma. You should go home. I'll call you as soon as I know any more. If we're going to wake him, then we'll let you know." The concerned medic stands in front of her forcing her to look at him he clasps her arms making her focus on his words.

"He's going to need you, Amelia. He's going to need you to be there for him. But you are going to have to be strong, and you're not strong right now. You're exhausted."

He hands her a prescription for a sleeping pill, Amelia only nods absently, her mind elsewhere. She takes the slip of paper without looking at it and walks away in a daze. As she reaches the lift, she stops, staring blankly at the buttons, then lets the prescription slip from her fingers into the trash can. Behind her she hears a familiar voice, as she turns, she feels Jack catch her as once again she slips into a faint. Sometime later Jack takes Amelia home. His eyes filled with pain and worry as he watches her. Helping her up the path she feels fragile, never in all the years he has known her has he seen Amelia in such a state. Opening her front door with his keys he helps her through the door into her quiet home.

Inside her house, the silence is deafening. The echoes of the morning spent with Gabriel linger in every corner. The coffee cups from their breakfast still sit on the table outside, untouched. Her birthday balloons and cards lie scattered around the living room, reminders of a celebration that feels like a lifetime ago. Amelia visibly winces when she sees the evidence. Wordlessly she nods at Jack dragging herself to the bedroom, her heart heavy with the memory of the last time she was there, with Gabriel.

Her bed is still unmade; the sheets tangled from their lovemaking. The scent of Gabriel's aftershave clings faintly to the linens, and the sight of it breaks her. Sobbing, she collapses onto the bed, kicking off her shoes and pulling the covers over her. She buries her face in the pillow, trying to find some comfort in the remnants of his presence. Jack listens to his friends' heartbroken sobs, resolutely he sets about tidying up the house. When he has cleared the evidence of everything that could hurt his dear friend, he collects a blanket and pillow from the laundry cupboard and taking off his shoes makes a bed of the sofa. Before he turns off the light, he calls Olivia listening to his lovely wife as she sobs down the phone.

Night follows day, and Amelia is jolted awake by the shrill ring of her phone. For a moment, she panics, fumbling for the device, her heart pounding. She listens intently, then a smile breaks across her face. Hope surges through her as she leaps out of bed, grabbing fresh clothes and heading to the bathroom. She turns on the shower, her exhaustion momentarily forgotten. Jack is waiting for her in the kitchen, breakfast made and freshly brewed coffee filling the kitchen with a rich aroma. Amelia is in a hurry to leave but Jack forces her to sit down and have a piece of toast and some hot sweet coffee. He can see that even though she has slept the evidence of the toll the previous day has taken on her is still present in the haunted look in her beautiful eyes. Barely able to sit still Amelia hugs Jack tightly she heads for the door, he can't stop her leaving but insists the compromise is a travel mug of coffee and the toast with honey in a napkin. Back at the hospital, Amelia stands with the doctor outside the ICU.

"He's still sedated. There's a long way to go still but he has been conscious which is a good sign." The doctor who had sent her home is still on duty, although he is obviously finishing his long shift handing over to the early team. He greets Amelia reassuring her gently. "We're monitoring him carefully. He's sleeping right now, but you can go in. Just sit quietly. No excitement, okay?" Amelia hugs him tightly thanking him and the nurses profusely her grin stretches from ear to ear, her heart lifting with relief. She quietly enters the room, her eyes never leaving Gabriel's face. She pulls a chair close to his bed, leaning in to smooth the hair away from his forehead. Her fingers tremble as she touches him, her tears falling softly onto the sheets. For a few moments she simply sits staring at his face deeply grateful that he has made it through the night.

"I love you, Gabriel." She whispers, her voice thick with emotion. Taking his hand, she kisses it, pressing her cheek against it to feel the warmth of his life force. Even though Gabriel is sleeping Amelia starts to pour her heart out needing to say the words she hasn't been able to until now. "I do I love you.... So much. I'm so sorry I was awful to you at the party. I was just so shocked. And then Maddy... what happened with Maddy... I wasn't thinking straight. But you were there. You tried to save her. You didn't care if she was your daughter. You are a beautiful, courageous, stupid man."

She lets out a small, tearful laugh. "I nearly lost you. I don't think I'd ever get over losing you again, Gabriel. I love you so, so much." She pauses, her breath hitching. "You were right... She's yours. Maddy is your daughter. I'm so sorry I let you think that she wasn't. When I left you all those years ago, I didn't know I was pregnant.... But then I found out, and I was just too afraid. Afraid that if I came back, you wouldn't want me. Or you'd take her. Or I'd lose you both. I was such a fool." Amelia's voice breaks, as she sobs quietly into the bed. Amelia feels his hand weakly squeeze hers. As she looks up Gabriel's eyes flutter open, he looks at her. His lips curl into a faint smile as he tightens his hold of her hand.

"You could never lie, Amelia." Gabriel murmurs, his voice weak but full of warmth. "I knew Maddy was mine the moment I saw her. She's gorgeous like you... but she's stubborn like me." Amelia's breath catches in her throat, her eyes wide with shock.

"Gabriel..." She whispers, unable to believe he's awake. Jumping to her feet she stares down at him. Before she can say more, Gabriel turns his head slightly, looking toward the back of the room. There, sitting quietly in the corner, is Babaji, who has been present the whole time. Amelia hadn't even noticed him.

"Babaji." Gabriel says softly, "Do you have that box?" Amelia is taken aback, watching as Babaji rises slowly from his chair. He approaches her with a gentle smile, holding out a small ring box. Amelia's hands tremble as she takes it, her eyes widening as she opens it to reveal the engagement ring, she had left behind all those years ago.

"Your mom's ring." Amelia is visibly shocked she inhales, her voice barely audible. Gabriel's smile deepens.

"It's your ring, Mia. I gave it to you. When I married Samara, I gave her a different ring. This one was always yours. When we were in India, Babaji suggested I bring it with me, just in case." He pauses wincing in pain. "I...I planned to see you the night of your birthday. Jack and I... we planned it all. He was so sure that you still cared for me. Jack was certain I could charm you." His breath catches in pain, his voice growing weaker. "I love you, Mia. I always have. Will you...

will you wear my ring again?" Babaji reaches across the bed, touching Amelia's hand gently. In perfect English, he continues for Gabriel.

"My sister loved Gabriel very much. But she always knew that you were the true love of his life. She made her son and me promise that if anything happened to her, we would make him come and find you." Amelia's eyes widen in shock.

"You speak English!" To say she is stunned is an understatement, how could that vital piece of information slipped past her, her words are laced with embarrassment. Amelia's face burns with colour as she remembers her earlier behaviour. "I'm so…. So very sorry…. I, I was so rude to you." Babaji smiles warmly.

"These last few days have been difficult for you. I thought you were charming." His words are kind, but Amelia feels bereft her cheeks flush bright red at the memory of the evening before. Babaji reaches across and squeezes her hand in a surprising act of compassion, Amelia feels her tension ease as she gazes down at the ring. With trembling hands, she slides the beautiful huge solitaire onto her finger, it fits exactly as it once had, a little taken aback Amelia stares at the ring that is once again on her hand, 20years after Gabriel had first put it there. Like a lost heirloom that has found it's way home, Amelia is mesmerised by its brightness, the moment feels a little surreal, as if she is dreaming.

As she looks up her smile starts to fade as to her utter dismay Gabriel's eyes close again. The heart monitor next to him flatlines, sending a piercing alarm through the room. As if in slow motion they witness the frantic response of the crash team. The ICU room erupts into controlled chaos. Doctors and nurses flood in, their voices sharp and urgent as they rush to Gabriel's side. Amelia is pulled back, ushered out of the room, once more she stands on the other side of the glass, a spectator witnessing the drama. She sobs quietly her hands pressed against the glass window as she watches in horror, the impressive diamond dazzles as it catches the overhead electric lights sparkling brilliantly Amelia brings it to her lips and kisses it as if somehow by touching it the ring may in some way grant her wish for the man who has just given it back to her. Amelia's heart feels like it's being torn apart as she stares helplessly at the valiant efforts to revive him.

Babaji steps up beside her, covering her hand with his own, as if sensing the need for Gabriel's presence he squeezes her cold fingers, warming them with his soft, gentle touch. He begins to pray softly, his voice steady and calm, the foreign words oddly comforting, his voice steady and calm despite the turmoil around them. Amelia's breath hitches as she watches the medical team working, her fear and desperation mirrored in the reflection of the glass just inches from her face. After what feels like an eternity, there's a flicker on the monitor. A faint heartbeat registers, the resuscitation team quickly stabilizes Gabriel, before making the decision to take him back to theatre. Amelia's shoulders slump in relief, tears of gratitude stream down her face as she clutches Babaji's hand. She turns to the older man feeling once more bereft and deeply grateful in the same moment, shaking she sobs into his shoulder, very gently he pats her back his eyes never leaving Gabriel's face. Amelia regains a little of her composure, but it is short lived as one of the Doctors comes out to take them to a side ward to explain the next stage in Gabriel's battle.

Just down the corridor standing quietly is Maddy and Joe. They had been on their way for an update on Gabriel's condition before the hospital discharged Maddy. She stands with her back pressed against the wall Joe by her side. Maddy's eyes are like saucers as she watches her mom fall apart in front of her. Turning to Joe she buries her head in his chest wanting to erase the sight of her mom's desperation. Joe pulls her into him wrapping his arms around her he gently kisses the top of her head. They stay motionless waiting for a sign that the immediate crisis has been dealt with. Only when Joe has seen the Doctor come out to Amelia and Babaji does he guide Maddy away. He had watched the relief wash over Amelia as she was very briefly allowed back into Gabriel's room. Now was not the time for Maddy to visit her father, he would bring her back later when he had spoken with Jack and Liv and asked them to come and distract Amelia.

Gabriel's fight for his life is far from over, his condition still critical, the complications not easily resolved. As the team continues their work, Amelia stays close by, praying silently for the man she loves, hoping against hope that this time, she won't lose him. By the end of the day everyone has received the shocking news that Gabriel has come through a second surgery, but he is in a coma that is not medically induced. The doctors try their best to reassure Amelia that it's probably a temporary setback however there is concern that due to Gabriel's significant loss of blood there could well have been some degree of brain damage.

Over the following days' time seems to slip past in a blur. Maddy, still too emotional refuses to see Amelia, the two women who have spent a lifetime together now barely able to come within feet of one another. Maddy carries a heart smashed to pieces by a lie that she considers unforgivable. Joe is left in no man's land, dealing with his own trauma at shooting Gabriel while coming to terms with Maddy's rejection of Amelia, his boss, mentor and a woman who has earned his deepest love and respect due to her integrity. Now Joe must find a way to negotiate his own disappointment that Amelia is flawed, deeply damaged by a past that has finally caught up with her.

Over the next few weeks, Amelia's life becomes an endless loop of hospital visits, work, and sleepless nights. Gabriel remains in a coma, his condition stable but unchanged. Every day, Amelia visits him, her exhaustion etched deeply into her face. She speaks with the doctors regularly, their updates offering little comfort. The strain of holding on to hope while confronting the harsh reality is taking its toll. Maddy was discharged the day after the incident. However, much to Amelia's distress, she had decided to move out of their home. Putting Liv in an almost impossible position, Maddy had begged to be allowed to move into their home for the time being, seeking distance and space to process the turmoil of emotions she was grappling with. Liv, ever the peacemaker, was doing her best to care for Maddy while keeping the lines of communication open between mother and daughter. Maddy's struggle to come to terms with her father's identity and his critical condition becoming more than she could deal with alone Maddy had sort the constant reassurance of Joe.

Each day, Amelia was a constant by Gabriel's side, watching over him, talking to him, reading to him, hoping for any sign of improvement. Gabriel remained locked in his silent battle. Babaji too was there daily, always at Gabriel's bedside, praying softly, reading passages aloud, or simply sitting in quiet contemplation. Amelia and Babaji had grown closer during these visits. She found comfort in his calm quiet presence and the unwavering faith he had in Gabriel's recovery.

Amelia soon has no choice other than to throw herself back into her work, determined to find justice for Maddy and bring down those responsible for the kidnapping. She interviewed Hugo and Mac, the two students who played a role in instigating the plot. Both are charged, though their sentences are lenient given their age and level of involvement. However, Magpie and Stretch, the real criminals, are not so lucky. Magpie, now hobbling on crutches, is transferred to a prison hospital, awaiting his sentence. Both men face severe sentences for their crime, kidnapping and extortion. Magpie desperate for leniency informs on Riddick and the syndicate that had been behind some of the most nefarious crimes in LA going back over two decades.

In one particularly intense moment, Amelia leads a raid on the upscale office of Riddick, now out on bail, he is the man behind the entire scheme. The scene is tense as Amelia, determined and resolute, points her gun at Riddick, who sits arrogantly behind his desk. His bravado falters as he's dragged away by officers, spewing curses at her. Amelia doesn't flinch. Her eyes burn with the fire of justice as she watches him being taken away. It was Riddick who had tried his best to destroy hers and Gabriel's life from the very start. An utterly poisonous individual with zero conscience, his actions were always about creating the maximum damage he simply revelled in hurting people.

Chapter 22

Amelia spends all her time divided between the hospital and work. It is one morning while she gets ready for work that life once again shifts on its axis throwing everything she knows into a state of disbelief.

Wrapped in a towel, Amelia stands staring in disbelief at the pregnancy test she holds in her trembling hand. The results show positive, her face goes pale, as the test kit slips from her fingers, clattering to the floor. Despite her apparent outward strength, Amelia's world is shaken to its core by the discovery she is once again pregnant with Gabriel's baby. As she clutches the basin, trying to steady herself the enormity of the situation washes over her. The news leaves her in shock, unable to comprehend how to handle another life-changing event when Gabriel's fate is still so uncertain. The day passes with Amelia on autopilot barely able to register the other officers and detectives in her department. She has become a cause for concern for Jerry as she has dropped weight and looks as if sleep is hard to come by. Jerry calls both Jack and Joe into his office.

"Jack, I know that things have been tense between Liv and Amelia since Maddy moved in with you guys, is there anyway Liv can try to get through to her. She looks like a ghost; I don't suppose she's eating." Jerry sighs he watches as Amelia switches off her office light completely oblivious to the meeting happening just feet away in her boss's office.

"See what I mean? I don't think she even realises you're here Jack!" Frustrated he stands up, coming round his desk he leans back against it folding his arms he stares at Joe. "Son, can you help me sort this. Get Maddy to speak to her mom. Mia needs her and I'm damn sure Maddy needs her mom too." He unfolds his arms gripping the desk he leans forward staring at Joe.

"It's not a request it's an order Joe! I need Mia back." Joe wordlessly nods standing up he catches his dad's eye before opening Jerry's door and heading back to his desk. Jerry eyes Jack silently waiting for his friend's response. Jack sighs looking jaded the stress of the last few weeks showing in the tension around his mouth.

"I don't think it's as simple as that Jerry. Joes still struggling himself too. Shooting Gabriel has really taken him to a dark place he is going to need support with this. Have you spoken to Sylvia about him?" Jerry nods his head.

"Yes, absolutely it's mandatory with everything that's happened, but I will have a meeting with her later. Has he opened to you about it? He adores Amelia they are very close, but he doesn't seem to want to talk to her now. Is there any news on Gabriel yet? Any improvement?" Silently Jack shakes his head. Jack takes on Jerry's barrage of questions answering the only one that he can at that moment.

"I know Joe feels so guilty about the shooting, this is so personal. It's so close he can't separate the job from his feelings for Maddy or Amelia. If Gabriel doesn't get through this, I don't know what's going to happen to any of them." Both men are now leaning side by side against Jerry's desk looking at the department which is subdued the spark seemingly almost gone.

"Damn it!" Jerry stands rubbing his face with his hands in frustration as if trying to clear his mind, he shakes himself seeming annoyed. "This isn't his fault Jack, he did what was asked of him he is a bloody good detective, Jack he is going to be one of the best." Jerry turns away from his friend walking across his office he opens the door forcefully. "Bill, can you get me an update on what's happening with the wiretap on Hector Ramirez's lawyer. We need it asap if we are going to move on the information we got from Conor."

He turns going back to sit next to Jack. "The information Conor and Magpie gave us goes so much further than what happened with Maddy. If we are going to get all of them sent down, then I want to make damn sure Hector goes down too this time." Jerry stands his hands on his hips. His forehead creased with furrowed lines of determination.

"Will Connor's testimony be enough do you think? Amelia said he's turned state's evidence." Jack crosses his arms as he listens to Jerry. His face tense with concern. The last thing Amelia needed right now was any one from the gangs being out on the streets again, the stress of the last few weeks was taking its toll on everyone most especially her.

"I hope so, but this groups so damn corrupt I'm not sure who is on the pay roll. I mean let's face it if they can manipulate a good young cop like Sam whose father has been in the police his whole career then who else is taking bribes." Jerry stops pacing choosing to sit back down next to his friend. The two old friends sit side by side contemplating the complications of the situation. Sylvia makes her way across the department heading towards Jerry's office. Jack stands to greet her smiling warmly they hug one another. Jack excuses himself leaving the colleagues to discuss the very sensitive subject of his son's mental wellbeing.

Later, at the hospital, Amelia sits by Gabriel's bed, the pregnancy test now placed beside him on the nightstand. She tries to find the words to tell him, instead they come out as choked sobs.

"Gabriel, she whispers through her tears instead they come out as choked sobs. "I'm pregnant... We're going to have a baby." Her voice cracks with emotion. "Please Darling, please wake up. This is your chance to have a baby, I need you to meet our child, what am I saying our children. I want you and Maddy to have a chance. She is such a beautiful soul Gabriel, I know you will love her so much.... Can you please, please wake up. Come home, be here with us."

Overwhelmed by emotion, Amelia kisses Gabriel tenderly, her tears mingling with the hope she clings to. Unable to bear the intensity of her feelings, she hurriedly leaves the room, rushing down the hospital corridor toward the bathrooms. Unbeknownst to Amelia, Maddy stands a little way off, having just arrived. She watches her mother flee. Confusion and concern etched on her face. Once Amelia is gone, Maddy walks into Gabriel's room, her steps hesitant. She sits by his bed, her eyes drawn to the pregnancy test lying beside him. Slowly, she picks it up, staring at the positive result. The realization hits her hard: her mother is pregnant. She's going to have a sibling; a wish she's had her entire life. How cruel that the joy of this news is obliterated by the sorrow of seeing her father, a man she's only just begun to know lying motionless in a hospital bed, possibly never to meet his unborn child or truly be a part of her life.

The pressure of it all is too much for Maddy. The tears come quickly, and she crumples into sobs, leaning on her forearms on Gabriel's bed her shoulders shaking with the force of her grief. Babaji enters the room quietly, seeing her distress, he comes to sit beside her. He doesn't speak at first, just rests a comforting hand on her shoulder. After a moment, he begins to tell her stories, they are stories of Gabriel's life, about her father's time in India, his marriage to Samara, and how deeply he loved both women who he shared his life with. Maddy listens, finding solace in Babaji's words. His wonderful stories so full of love and warmth, she listens to his tales laughing through her tears, she starts to understand piece by piece the man her father is, beyond the stranger she's only just met. Babaji's calm kindness provides a sense of peace that Maddy desperately needs. As they talk, she feels the anger and confusion inside her slowly ease, replaced by a growing sense of compassion and acceptance. Despite everything, Maddy knows that her family, broken and fragile as it is, needs to find a way to heal, just as she does. Knowing though it may take time, she begins to believe that they might just be able to do it, together if Gabriel survives this nightmare. What she fears the most is what will happen to her beloved mom if Gabriel deteriorates. Shuddering at the thought Maddy pushes it to the back of her mind.

Meanwhile down the corridor in the toilets Amelia takes her time in the hospital bathroom, her emotions all over the place. Sighing she looks in the mirror wiping the smudged mascara from beneath her eyes. At least she can now blame her emotional rollercoaster on her hormones. She silently chides herself knowing she is just making up excuses, blaming her hormones is far too easy a lie even for her to accept, she screws up her tissue throwing it in the bin. Looking in the mirror she sighs disappointed with her own appearance. Amelia is aware that she looks rough, the strain is all too evident in the huge dark circles beneath her eyes. The once tailored jacket she is wearing is now a little too baggy, pulling the lapels together she tries to smooth out unseen creases. With a weary sigh she heads out of the bathroom towards the elevators. Pressing the button Amelia stands back waiting for the doors to open.

When they do, she is met by Liv and Joe who have both just arrived to visit Gabriel. As soon as Amelia sees Liv, she can't hold it together a moment longer bursting into tears she falls into Liv's open arms utterly distraught. Joe steps out of the lift pressing the button for Liv he catches her eye knowingly. His heart heavy, Joe heads down the corridor to Gabriel's room. He stands outside the door for a little while watching Maddy and Babaji talk, the older man seems to bring some comfort to Maddy, holding his breath he hears her laugh for the first time in weeks, the sound goes through his body lifting his spirits it's a sound he has missed more than he realised.

Babaji catches sight of Joe, patting Maddy's arm he excuses himself allowing Joe to come into the room. Maddy turns to look at him her eyes slightly pink still sparkle with tears. Maddy reaches over to the nightstand and picks up the pregnancy test she hands it to Joe. Joe looks confused.

"Maddy." He says softly, trying to approach the situation delicately. "I saw your mom just now. She seemed really upset." Maddy sighs, not taking her eyes off Gabriel.

"Yeah, I know," she murmurs. "It's so strange, isn't it? He never knew me, and now he might never know this baby either. Life is just so unfair." Joe's heart sinks as he assumes Maddy is talking about her own pregnancy. He steps closer, his voice full of concern.

"Maddy... I. I'm so sorry. You don't have to go through this alone. I know Spencer isn't good for you. I've always felt that way. And honestly... I love you. I always have. I want to be there for you, for this baby. I want to protect you. Maddy, I'd marry you tomorrow if you'd let me." Maddy finally looks up at Joe, her expression a mixture of confusion and surprise.

"Joe... what are you talking about?" Joe gestures toward the pregnancy test in her hand.

"I'm talking about this. You don't have to go through this pregnancy or whatever you decide to do, on your own. Let me be there for you." Realization dawns on Maddy's face as she understands Joe's mistake. A small, bittersweet smile tugs at her lips.

"Joe, no... it's not what you think. This isn't my baby. It's my mom's. She's the one who's pregnant, with Gabriel's baby." Joe's eyes widen in shock, his mouth opening slightly as he processes the truth.

"Your mom...? Oh... Maddy, I'm so sorry. I didn't realize. I just saw how upset you were, and I thought..." Maddy chuckles softly, the tension in the room easing slightly.

"Thank you for the offer, Joe. Perhaps before we get engaged, maybe we should try going on a date first?" Joe lets out a relieved laugh, shaking his head at his own misunderstanding.

"Yeah, that might be a good idea." Maddy reaches up wrapping her arms around Joe's neck, pulling him down for a tender kiss. At first, Joe is too surprised to respond, then almost instantly he wraps his arms around her tightly, holding her close as he kisses her back with all the feelings he's kept hidden for so long. A nurse enters the room to check on Gabriel's monitors, the two of them pull apart, slightly embarrassed but smiling. Joe looks at Maddy with a renewed sense of determination.

"I know things are intense for you right now, Maddy. But you've got to talk to your mom." His words gentle but firm. "She needs you, and you need her. You've always been so close. Don't let this come between you two." Maddy's smile fades as she thinks about the distance that's grown between her and her mother.

"I know. I've been so angry with her for keeping him away from me. You're right. I need to hear her side of the story." Joe nods, squeezing her hands reassuringly.

"You'll never understand why she did it unless you talk to her. And whatever her reasons were, I'm sure it's because she loves you." Something changes in Maddy's expression. Standing she takes hold of Joes hand leading him over to the window. Looking into his eyes Maddy sees the depth of the love he has for her; she has seen how what happened to Gabriel has been so unbelievably hard for Joe to come to terms with. Sensing his need for her forgiveness she leans in and kisses him, softly this time, as if finally able to accept it's time for her to return his love, her games have caused enough damage. Maddy accepts that she is as much to blame for Gabriel lying in the hospital as anyone else. Letting go of blame is the only way any of them can recover now. Joe is a little taken aback by Maddy's kiss. He pulls back to look at her knowing he is in danger of losing himself to her if they continue. Maddy smiles lovingly up at him.

"It's ok Joe, I love you too. I always have I just wasn't ready before, but I am now." Joe doesn't need asking twice he kisses her passionately drinking in her love as she surrenders her mouth too him for the first time, he truly feels her return his desire, within seconds the heat between them intensifies. The nurse comes back into the room disturbing the passionate embrace once more, there are blushes all around as the young lovers make way for Gabriel's team to come and do their rounds. Joe leads Maddy out of the room but not before Maddy has stopped and pressed a soft kiss on Gabriel's forehead.

"Sleep well Dad… just come back to me soon," she whispers against his warm skin.

Chapter 23

As the elevator doors close, Amelia attempts to regain her composure, stepping back from Liv her face is crest fallen, embarrassed that her emotions have got the better of her once more. They stand silently in the small space, neither one of them certain how to take the first step. Liv watches her friend, noticing the exhaustion etched deeply on Amelia's face, her tear-stained cheeks, and the tension in her body. When the elevator reaches the ground floor, Amelia and Liv step out. Both women sense the need to clear the air between them, Liv gently guides Amelia towards the hospital's quiet café. They find a secluded table by an open window, the breeze offering a small reprieve from the clinical atmosphere of the hospital. They sit in silence for a moment, both women lost in their thoughts. Amelia's hands tremble slightly as she stares down at the untouched cup of coffee in front of her. She breaks the silence blurting out.

"I'm pregnant, Liv." Liv stares at her for a moment, shock at Mia's sudden outburst registering, she takes a breath her voice soft but steady.

"When did you find out Mia?" Amelia swallows hard, her voice barely above a whisper.

"This morning. I've been feeling off for a few days, queasy... I just didn't want to believe it. But I knew, deep down, something was different." Liv's eyes widen slightly, and she reaches out to take Amelia's hand.

"Oh, Mia... I don't even know what to say. I'm so sorry." Her eyes flash to her friends with deep concern registering in them, realising her words may have hurt Amelia she quickly continues.

"Mia, not about the baby! I'm sorry about everything. I never wanted things to happen this way. I never wanted you to find out about Gabriel like that. Jack and I... we never meant to hurt you." Amelia looks up, her eyes filled with pain.

"But you did, Liv. Both of you did. You and Jack... you went behind my back. You decided what was best for me, without even asking how I felt. Do you have any idea how betrayed I felt? How blindsided?" Liv nods, guilt heavy in her eyes.

"I know, Mia. I know. I didn't even find out that Jack had been in touch with Gabriel until a couple of weeks ago." She takes a breath studying Mia's face. "When I found out, I was furious. Jack and I had the biggest fight we've ever had. I didn't speak to him for days. But Mia, Jack only did what he thought was right. He thought Gabriel deserved a chance to make things right with you." Amelia shakes her head, her voice trembling with emotion.

"It wasn't Jack's decision to make, Liv. It was mine. I've spent my life trying to protect Maddy, to protect myself. Then suddenly Gabriel's back, and everything's turned upside down. I didn't need that. I didn't need the past coming back to derail me." Liv's reaches across the table taking her friends hand, she needs the physical touch to somehow reconnect with Amelia. As she talks her grip on Amelia's hand tightens.

"You weren't protecting yourself, Mia. You were punishing yourself. You've been alone for so long, and it's not because you wanted to be. You've been shutting people out, pushing them away. You can't keep doing that. You deserve to be happy; Jack saw that before you did. He wanted to help you find that happiness, even if it meant stepping on a few toes." Amelia's eyes fill with fresh tears as she finally looks up at Liv.

"Why didn't you tell me, Liv? You and Jack both knew. You didn't tell me. You let me walk into that party, completely blindsided. How could you do that to me? Why didn't you just talk to me? Why did you both have to go behind my back?" Liv sighs deeply, her expression softening. Momentarily she sits back releasing her grip on Amelia.

"Because, Mia, you're stubborn as hell. You've always been so focused on everyone else that you forget about yourself. Jack and I, we saw how unhappy you were. I've always known you still loved Gabriel, even if you didn't want to admit it. We were just trying to give you a chance to see that for yourself." Liv pauses looking Amelia directly in the eyes. "Be honest Mia if I had told you that Gabriel was coming to see you. What would you have done?... You know, you would have wanted to run. I just thought this way he would get the chance to talk to you." Amelia looks away, the tears finally spilling over. Liv reaches for her friends' hands again clasping them tightly across the table.

"I just wanted you to have a second chance Mia. Now that everything is different. You, me all of it.... And Maddy.... She is a big girl now. No one can take her away from you." Mia looks at Liv, wide eyed tears begin to stream down her face. She can't argue with Liv. Deep down she knows that if she had been warned that Gabriel was coming to see her, it was more than likely true that she would have found a way to escape again.

As Liv tries to comfort Amelia, she remembers clearly the last time they had found themselves in the same situation all those years ago. Looking at Amelia's tearstained face she reminds Liv of the same beautiful young woman who had made one of the hardest decisions of her life. Amelia had kept her baby a secret from the man she loved and done it alone. Forged a life of meaning and purpose out of the ashes of her past.

"And now I'm pregnant, again.... Gabriel might never wake up to know this baby. Just like he never knew Maddy." Amelia's words bring Liv's focus back into the present her heart aches for her friend, she reaches out to wipe away Amelia's tears.

"Mia, you're not alone in this. We're all here for you. Jack and I, we've always been here for you, even if it didn't feel like it. Gabriel...

he's a fighter. He'll pull through.... He must." Amelia sniffles, trying to regain her composure.

"I don't know, Liv. I don't know if I can do this." Liv smiles gently. Her eyes filled with determination.

"You can, Mia. You're one of the strongest people I know. You've survived so much, and you'll survive this too. When Gabriel wakes up, because he will, you'll have a chance to start over. A chance to be happy again." Amelia looks at her friend, her expression softening.

"I'm so sorry, Liv. I never meant to be so angry with you and Jack. I just... I've been so scared." Liv squeezes her hand again reassuringly.

"I know, Mia. You don't have to be alone anymore. Jack and I knew you were scared it's why we have both been so worried about you." Amelia's expression clouds as her eyebrows draw together a deep frown creases her forehead. For some reason Amelia just can't let it go, she feels emotion rise in her chest, her words tumble from her lips in reaction. Liv is just a scapegoat for her to shout at.

"Worried about me? Why? I was fine, Liv. I didn't need this. I didn't need Gabriel coming back and turning my life upside down." Liv releases Amelia's hands, sitting back in her seat she patiently studies Amelia.

"You weren't fine, Mia. You were alone, and you've been alone for so long. You may have broken Gabriel's heart.... You know you broke your own too. No matter how many people you help, no matter how many lives you save, you can't fill that hole inside you with work." It's Amelia's turn to sit back now, frustration and pain mixing in her eyes.

"What hole, Liv? I've had relationships. I've been with other men. Why does everyone think they know what's best for me? I'm not one of your podcast guests you can therapize Liv!" Liv gives her a sad smile not allowing herself to be drawn into an argument when she knows that Amelia is venting her pain.

"I wouldn't ever do that to you Mia. I have far too much respect for you." Liv pauses allowing Mia to hear her sincere words. She waits until she can see that her friends' emotions are shifting, she can feel the waves of pain echoing through her friends' heart and mind, Mia's whole system is trying to cope with the trauma she has experienced while coming to terms with an enormous, life changing situation.

"It's because we love you, so much Mia. It's not about you being with other men. It's about helping you find real happiness again, the kind you had with Gabriel. Jack and I only wanted to give you a chance to see that for yourself." Amelia's voice softens. There's still a trace of sadness in her words.

"I just wish you hadn't gone behind my back, Liv. I feel like everyone decided what was best for me without even asking how I felt." Liv sighs deeply, her tone growing more serious.

"Amelia, you're wrong about Gabriel. And you're wrong about yourself. You and I... we're damaged goods, Mia. You know our history. You know what we've been through. It takes a very special man to accept us, flaws and all. Jack is that man for me, and I believe Gabriel is that man for you." Liv looks Amelia directly in the eyes once again not flinching from the words she believes Mia needs to hear. "What have you always said to me Mia. You have always told me that I'm, More Than just….my past. More than just the crap that happened. You are the one who told me I deserved so much more than what I was settling for."

Pausing so her words can sink in. "You Amelia are the reason I changed everything, the reason I started to believe that I could be, more than all the past pain. Amelia you are the reason the salon is called 'More than just….' You know you are." Amelia looks at Liv's earnest face, tears welling up in her eyes again she smiles weakly at her friends' passionate words.

"Liv, I don't know if I can go through this. What if Gabriel doesn't make it? What if I lose him all over again?" Liv tightens her grip on Amelia's hand.

"Then you'll face it, one day at a time, just like you always have. But you can't keep pushing him away, Mia. You can't keep punishing yourself for the past. Gabriel loves you, and he always has. You deserve to be loved, Mia. Truly loved. You must find a way to forgive yourself, just let him in." Amelia's tears spill over, and she nods, finally understanding what Liv is saying.

"I just don't know how to do that. I'm so scared Gabriel is going to die." Liv smiles gently, brushing another tear from Amelia's cheek.

"It's okay to be scared. You are stronger than you think. And you don't have to do this alone. You've got Jack, and you've got me. And if you let him, you'll have Gabriel too." Amelia takes a deep breath, trying to absorb Liv's words.

"I do still love him, Liv. But I'm terrified. What if he doesn't make it? What if he never wakes up?" Liv meets her gaze with quiet intensity she doesn't need to say any more, she grips Mia's hands tightly her eyes full of love. Amelia looks at her friend, the weight of the world still pressing down on her, but a small glimmer of hope starts to break through.

"Thank you, Liv. I don't know what I'd do without you." Liv looks down at their hands, then hesitates before speaking again.

"You know, Mia, Jack likes to think that you played fairy godmother in our relationship. He's convinced that you were the one who brought us together, like some benevolent force. But that's not true, is it?" Amelia looks at Liv, slightly puzzled, distracted from her own overwhelming thoughts. Liv's words make her look up.

"What do you mean?" Liv lets out a small laugh, shaking her head.

"I never told Jack, but you didn't exactly approve of us at first. In fact, you made it pretty, damn clear that you didn't think we were right for each other. You even tried to talk me out of it." Amelia's eyes widen.

"Liv, that was a long time ago. Look at you two now. You're the picture of happiness. I was wrong, clearly." Liv nods, a soft smile playing on her lips.

"Exactly, Mia. You were wrong about us, just like you are wrong about Gabriel too. Jack and I worked because we fought for it, because we believed in it. Gabriel... he's always loved you, more than you realize. You've been through so much, Mia, now it's time you let yourself be loved. Truly loved." Amelia's eyes fill with tears once more, this time, they are tears of realisation, of understanding.

"I guess... I guess I was just afraid of getting hurt again. But you're right, Liv. It's time to let go of the past." Liv smiles, brushing away Amelia's tears once more.

"You've got this, Mia. No matter what happens, you've got people who love you. We're all in this together." Amelia nods, a faint smile tugging at the corners of her lips.

"Thank you, Liv. I don't know what my life would be without you all." Liv grins, her usual playful demeanour returning.

"Hey, that's what best friends are for, right? Now, let's finish this coffee and figure out what's next. We've got a baby on the way, a daughter who needs her mom, and a man who's fighting to come back to you. You've got a lot to live for, Mia."

Chapter 24

The maternity ward is quiet, the sterile scent of antiseptic lingering in the air. Amelia stretches out on the examination table, her hands resting protectively over her growing belly. The radiologist's gentle voice fills the room, explaining the scan results, it isn't until she said the word 'twins' that Amelia's world once more feels completely upended.

"Twins?" Amelia's voice is quiet as it echoes the radiologist words, the sound barely above a whisper. The word dances in the air like a fragile promise, something almost too delicate to grasp.
"Yes." The radiologist replies, her tone practical and cheerful, to her she was delivering good news of healthy babies, there was no way she could possibly understand the current drama that was unfolding in Amelia's life. "Two healthy heartbeats, two babies."

Amelia gasps at the confirmation, her hand covering the sound as it escapes her shocked lips, her eyes fill with tears as she nods, her mind struggling to process this new information. The image on the screen begins to blur as the tears well her eyes sparkling with their unshed moisture. She manages a smile, although it is shaky, even uncertain at best, this is news that she was in no way ready to receive. Her own heart skips a beat her breathing becoming shallow. Amelia struggles to sit up needing to regain some control she wipes her exposed belly with the napkin to remove the gel from the ultrasound. The nurse seemingly unaware of the degree of shock that her patient is currently trying to process, carries on talking about dates and how important regular scans are for geriatric mothers especially considering a multiple birth.

Leaving the ward, Amelia's steps falter feeling heavier, laden with the burden of this revelation. The hospitals vastness stretching out before her, the sterile walls closing in as she made her way across the labyrinth of corridors to Gabriel's room. The nurses greeted her with the same soft smiles they had worn for weeks now, familiar with her daily visits. But today, everything felt different. Inside Gabriel's room, the rhythmic beeping of machines the only sound. Gabriel lay still, as he had for months, suspended between life and something else. A nurse was there adjusting his IV, her movements precise, routine. Amelia watches, her gaze lingering on the man she once knew so well, now a figure of silent endurance. Moving to his bedside, her fingers brush over his hand. It was warm, solid, Amelia took great comfort every day in the simple fact that he was still there, still fighting. Leaning down, she press's a kiss to his forehead, then lifting his hand to rest on her stomach.

"Gabriel." Whispering, her voice thick with emotion. "We're having twins." The words are filled with emotion both heavy and light, filled with joy and an undercurrent of sorrow. Forcing a smile, Amelia desperately tries to make it real, as if her happiness alone can wake him, somehow bring him back to her. The door behind her softly opens, allowing Maddy to enter the room, followed closely by Joe. Maddy's eyes catching sight of the scan picture in Amelia's hand, the reality of what it represents crashing over her like a wave. Without warning, she dashes into her mother's arms, tears spilling down her cheeks. Amelia holds her daughter close, the two of them clinging to each other as if the world might shatter if they let go.

Joe stands in the doorway, watching with quiet intensity. His eyes catching Amelia's. A moment of clarity and understanding passes between them, a silent acknowledgment of all that has gone before, and all that is still to come. Amelia mouths thank you to him, Joe responds with a silent nod the simple gesture saying more than words ever could. The gulf that had grown between Amelia and Maddy over the long months that had passed was now perhaps ready to begin to close. There was a tentative healing in their embrace, a recognition of shared pain, of mutual loss. The distance between them had been wide, but now, holding her daughter, Amelia felt that perhaps they could find their way back to each other. Joe stepped further into the room his presence steady and grounding. He placed a hand on Maddy's shoulder, his touch offering silent support. He stared at Amelia his gaze steady.

"Are you ok?" Joes' kind voice steady, calm, and assured. Amelia smiled at Joe, though her expression is tinged with weariness. Stepping back from Maddy she hands her daughter the scan picture. Taking the picture tentatively, Maddy stares at it not quite able to decipher the images clearly, she looks at her mom her eyes questioning.

"It's twins." Amelia's words are simple; their effect however is profound. The news instantly registers with both Maddy and Joe as they are equally shocked by the news. Maddy gasps then squeals in delight throwing her arms around her mom's neck nearly knocking her off her feet.

"I can't believe it mom. Are you ok? How are you?" Amelia nods knowing that the question holds many layers and the answer if far from simple. They stand together by Gabriel's bed, united by the history of love they have for one another and now by the fragile love they each hold for him, for the life, his life that hangs in the balance. As the room settles into quiet, Amelia finds herself reflecting on the long, painful journey that has brought them here. The months of waiting, the nights spent in silent vigil, the countless moments of doubt and fear. It has been a trial of endurance, of faith, and now, with the news of the twins, it feels as though life is testing her once more.

"Maddy." Amelia speaks softly, looking into blue eyes so familiar it's as if she is looking into Gabriel's. Chiding herself silently this is the first time she has allowed herself permission to compare father and daughter, now looking at them together their likeness is undeniable. "Are you ready to talk to me? I know you have questions. You deserve the answers. I'll do my best to tell you

Everything you want to know." For a moment Maddy looks taken aback, almost afraid to hear details from her mom that may make the uneasy truce too difficult to maintain.

"I'm not sure Mom. I don't want to be upset with you again. You are dealing with a lot. I think perhaps you need to rest and not get upset or stressed about all this now. To be honest I'm worried about you. I love you. I need to know you are ok."

Amelia hadn't considered that Maddy would be worrying about her or the pregnancy. Suddenly looking at her, Maddy seemed very young and vulnerable Amelia realised that Maddy was coping with potentially losing one parent while also dealing with the possible complications of her mother's pregnancy at the age of 40. There were real concerns that a geriatric pregnancy, Amelia found herself wincing at the implications of the word, but there were real health concerns that a complicated pregnancy could bring and suddenly the realisations of the implications for Maddy became clear for Amelia. What Maddy needed now was reassurance not more drama or trauma.

"I understand Maddy. Would it be ok if I wrote you a letter then we can share how we feel without arguing or getting stressed at one another. I want you, to tell me, how you feel about all this once you've heard what I have to say. Please believe me when I say I do not expect you to be ok with me keeping Gabriel away from you. Maddy it's the biggest mistake I have ever made. I should have found a way to let you both be in one another's lives." Amelia sighs looking down at her baby bump. "There is no way I can ever make up for that time for you, I was young, frightened and foolish. Not to mention stubborn and determined." Amelia's hazel eyes meet Maddy's bright blue ones, beyond anything else there is still a strong bond of love that united them. "The only thing I can do Maddy is ask for you to forgive me. As I will have to do with your dad when he wakes up." Amelia's words trail away as she tenderly looks at Gabriel gently lifting his hand, she squeezes it cradling it to her bump. For the first time ever, Amelia willingly refers to Gabriel as

Maddy's dad. The word holds such a powerful meaning to both women, such a simple word with so many layers to it.

"I can only pray that I get the chance to make amends for the pain I've caused you both." Unshed tears brim in Amelia's eyes. Tears filled with foolish regret. Maddy's heart swells in her chest as she sees the pain evident in her mom's expression. Knowing now what it feels like to fall in love with a man, Maddy cannot even begin to imagine how painful it must have been to walk away from someone who her mom so evidently loved so much.

"Don't cry mom." Maddy's words hold so much loving compassion that Amelia looks up. "If it helps you to write a letter then yes go ahead, but I think now I've talked to Auntie Liv about it, why you did it, and how hard it was for you." She sighs, continuing. "I forgive you mom; I love you so how could I not forgive you especially when I know what an amazing life you have given me considering what you gave up for me."

Maddy's words bring fresh tears once more, now the tears that had been welling in Amelia's eyes come tumbling down her cheeks unchecked. Her daughter's love like her own was unconditional, that didn't mean that boundaries hadn't been crossed, it meant that above all else love would conquer over any trial. Amelia for the first time in her adult life felt a weight in her heart shift, the burden of her secret had finally been taken away, she was free of the heaviness that had become a permanent resident in her heart keeping her from believing she had the right to be happy. Taking a deep breath, her whole body shook as if finally shaking off the shackles of her own judgement. Without knowing Amelia had burdened her soul allowing herself to become a slave to her own cruel self-judgement that had punished her relentlessly. It would be over the coming months that healing from that prison would open Amelia's heart in ways she could never have imagined allowing her to view life with an entirely new perspective, one which began with self-forgiveness and ended in grace and gratitude.

Looking at her daughter's beautiful face, love shining from her innocent eyes Amelia's heart melted. Maddy's willingness to live free of guilt, fear or judgement allowed Amelia to unlock the prison in which she kept her own heart. Maddy's simple choice was love over pain. Forgiveness over blame. Freedom over guilt. Compassion over judgement. Maddy didn't need her mom to justify what had happened she just stepped past it with a wisdom that flowed as easily as the rain on a spring day washing away the winter blues and bringing new life to spring.

Amelia realised that no matter what happened this time, she wasn't alone. Maddy's presence by her side was a gentle balm, a reminder of the strength they both possessed. And Joe, with his quiet resolve, his unwavering support, was the anchor they both needed. Pulling Maddy towards her once more, she wrapped her daughter in an embrace that held an ocean of love in it. Maddy's shoulders dropped as she absorbed the love she had always known, for the first time in months Maddy could let go of her fear and tension that had settled between them. Now forgiveness bridged the gap between their hearts allowing the healing balm of true love to flow. Later in the stillness of the Gabriels room, Amelia leant down to kiss his hand, resting it once more on her belly.

"We're right here, Gabriel," she whispered. "We are all right where we are supposed to be."

Chapter 25

Amelia waited in the arrival's terminal, her eyes scanning the crowd as passengers from an international flight began to emerge. Her posture expectant, Amelia looked relaxed, a softness in her expression as she waited, a quiet hope had taken up residence in her mind, bringing more ease to her heart. Then she spotted him, Babaji, moving gracefully through the throng of travellers, his traditional robes flowing around him as he walked. His serene presence a stark contrast to the bustling airport. When their eyes met, Amelia's face brightened, Babaji's gentle smile mirrored hers. As he approached, Amelia stepped forward to greet him, they embraced warmly, a gesture that spoke of the deep bond they had formed over the past months. Babaji's touch immediately reassuring, his embrace filled with a quiet strength that Amelia had come to rely on.

"Thank you for coming back." Amelia smiled radiantly. "It's so good to see you again." Amelia reached to take his luggage from him. Immediately Babaji stopped her, squeezing her hand to remind her he was a gentleman. Placing his bag carefully onto the airport trolley he carefully navigated through the crowd. Babaji smiled as he followed Amelia through the airport arrivals, there was a new lightness in her voice despite the weight of worry she carried in her heart about Gabriel. "I hope everything went well during your visit." Babaji nodded, his eyes twinkling with affection.

"Yes, it was necessary to return home, but my heart remained here with you and Gabriel. How is he?" His question gentle, the concern as ever evident in his tone. Amelia's smile faltered slightly, her eyes reflecting the sadness that had once again settled in her over the long weeks since Babaji had left.

"There's no change yet." She admitted quietly. "I pray every day, hoping he'll wake up. Babaji…" Her voice catches as she glances down at her growing belly. "We're having twins." The older man's face immediately lit up with a joy that seemed to transcend the moment. He reached out, placing a hand over Amelia's, his touch warm and full of reassurance.

"That is the most beautiful news I've heard for a long time." He replied softly. "With God's grace Gabriel will wake up to see his children. I believe that with all my heart." Together, they walk arm in arm through the terminal, an unlikely pair in the eyes of the onlookers. Amelia's figure beginning to show the undeniable signs of pregnancy, her body subtly transformed by the lives growing within her. Beside her, Babaji's traditional attire marked him as a man from another world, yet the connection between them was undeniable, a bond forged in shared hope and faith.

As they left the airport and headed toward L.A. in Amelia's car, the cityscape unfolded before them. The skyline familiar, yet today it felt different somehow, as if the journey they'd undertaken had changed the way Amelia saw everything. The trip back to the hospital was filled with easy conversation as Amelia navigated the traffic Babaji's presence reassured her, renewing her sense of hope, making the drive feel lighter.

At the hospital, Babaji insisted on spending time alone with Gabriel, as he always did when he was in L.A. He moved through the sterile corridors with the calm authority of a man who has seen much of life's suffering and joy. When they reached Gabriel's room, Babaji's demeanour shifted slightly, becoming almost reverential. He sat by Gabriel's side, his hand resting on Gabriel's, beginning to pray softly, his voice a soothing murmur in the quiet room. Amelia lingered for a moment in the doorway, watching the scene with a mixture of hope and heartache. This had become their routine, she and Babaji, caring for Gabriel in their own ways, united by the belief that he was going wake up. Leaving Babaji to his vigil, Amelia quietly stepped away giving the two brothers their privacy, returning home she prepared the evening meal.

Back at her house, Amelia prepared the guest room for Babaji. The familiarity of the task bringing her a small measure of comfort. When he returned later that evening with Jack, the three of them shared the simple meal she had prepared, talking softly about their day, their hopes for Gabriel, and the future. The conversation always easy, marked by the mutual respect and affection that had grown strongly between them. As Amelia showed Babaji to his room, she smiled at him, feeling a deep sense of gratitude for his presence in her life. He had become more than a friend, he was a guide, a steadying force as she navigated the uncertainty of the days ahead. She had discovered so much about herself, her life and her beliefs. What she understood now so clearly was that this journey was a journey of faith, of waiting, of patience, of believing in the impossible, above all, surrender when control is taken out of your hands. Amelia had learned the only way to survive was to surrender to a power far greater than she could ever begin to comprehend. She just knew that she had found a quiet strength she hadn't known existed. As they said goodnight, Amelia paused, her hand resting on the doorframe.

"Thank you, Babaji. For everything." He looked at her, his eyes filled with a quiet wisdom.

"We are on this path together, Amelia. And we will see it through." She nodded, feeling the truth of his words settle deep within her. Despite the darkness, despite the waiting, there was light ahead. There was hope, with Babaji by her side, she knew she won't have to face it alone.

The morning light filtered softly through the curtains as Amelia woke. She lay still for a moment, gathering her thoughts, before quietly getting out of bed. Last night she had dreamt of Gabriel as she did many nights. On the nights when her anxiety got the better of her, she dreamt of the night Maddy was taken, the night when Gabriel nearly died. In those dreams he was always just out of reach she could never quite touch him, never protect him, never change what happened. Then there were the dreams like last night. Those were the dreams she loved the most. Dreams of days spent in sunshine revelling in the love they shared for one another, making love as they had the last night, they were together. It was these dreams that stayed with Amelia the longest, before she even opened her eyes it was as if she could smell Gabriel's skin, feel the warmth of his touch and bask in his absolute love.

Pulling on a light robe, she padded to the window looking out into the garden. There, in a quiet corner among the roses, sat Babaji, cross legged on the grass, his prayer beads moving rhythmically through his fingers, Vivienne her cat nestled on his lap more than likely purring loudly. She smiled softly the serenity of the scene touching her, she knew full well that the intentions behind his prayers were for Gabriel, herself and most importantly for their children, this beautiful kind man offered a moment of calm amidst the turmoil that had dominated her life.

Amelia moved to the kitchen and began to prepare breakfast; her actions deliberate and careful. She filled a pot with water, setting it to boil, and arranged a simple meal on a tray. The routine comforting, grounding her as she tried to push away the thoughts that had plagued her every waking moment. Her gaze drifted toward the garden, where just a few months ago, she and Gabriel had shared breakfast, talking and laughing, wrapped in the glow of making love, coming back to one another and discovering their love once again.

Frowning as her hand hesitated over the coffee pot, if only she had told him then about Maddy. Shaking her head how would that have changed anything the day, everything would still have happened the way it did. Gabriel acted because he had already believed Maddy was his. Her hand began to shake, and tears filled her eyes. Gabriel. He once again occupied so much of the space in her mind now. Smiling ruefully to herself she silently acknowledged, let's face it, he always had. With the tray in hand, Amelia made her way outside. The garden alive with the gentle hum of morning, birds chirping, the soft rustle of leaves in the breeze, and the faint, sweet scent of roses in full bloom. Babaji noticed her approach rising to join her, his presence as calming as the garden itself. Sitting beside her on the bench, for a moment, they simply share the silence, the connection between them needing no words. Suddenly, the emotion Amelia has been holding back erupted. Tears spilled down her cheeks as she tried to speak, the words catching in her throat. Babaji reached out, patting her face with a tender hand, his touch gentle and reassuring. She looked at him through her tears, her expression a mix of sorrow and gratitude. Without saying anything, allowing her the space to cry, to release the tension that had been building for so long. Amelia wiped her tears away, turning her face toward the sun. She closed her eyes, drawing in a deep breath as the warmth washed over her. For a moment, feeling something close to peace, a fleeting sense of surrender to the present, to the garden, to the life that continued around her, and growing within her. Babaji's voice gentle when he spoke.

"Amelia, when you look at this beautiful garden, how do you feel?" Amelia opening her eyes, turned to him.

"It's quiet." She replied, her voice steady but soft. "Calm. The roses smell beautiful. It reminds me of Gabriel. I feel peaceful here." Babaji studied her, his gaze searching for something deeper.

"And when you look at Gabriel lying in the hospital bed, how do you feel then?" The question causes an immediate shift in Amelia's demeanour. The peace that had briefly touched her face fading, replaced by a deep sadness.

"I feel sad." She admits, her voice trembling slightly. "I want him to wake up, to come back to me. I feel so helpless, Babaji. Every time I see him; it's like I'm losing him all over again." Babaji reaches out and squeezes her hand, his grip warm and reassuring.

"Next time you're with him, try to remember this garden, this feeling of peace." He says gently. "Allow yourself to surrender, to let go, as you do when you're here. Open your heart and let him feel your love, not your pain. Remember, Amelia, the man you love is not the shell you see in that hospital bed. He's not the house, as I once heard it said. He's the one who lives inside." Amelia looked down at their joined hands, the compassion of his words settling over her.

"But what if he dies?" Her voice trembles as she speaks, barely above a whisper. "What if I lose him forever?" Babaji's eyes are full of understanding as he meets her gaze.

"Amelia, right now, I know you feel that all your choices have been taken away, that you are powerless against what may happen. Yes, there is a possibility that Gabriel may die. But you must decide how you will love him in this moment. You can choose to let him feel the depth of your love, not the weight of your sorrow. Let him feel the warmth that comes from your heart, not the sadness that overwhelms you."

A tear slips down Amelia's cheek, this time, she doesn't wipe it away. Instead, she nods slowly, absorbing the wisdom in Babaji's words. The heaviness in her chest lightening just a little, for the first time in weeks, she felt as though she could breathe more freely. Together, they sit in companiable silence enjoying the garden, the sun climbing higher in the sky, bathing them in light. The future remaining uncertain, but in that moment, Amelia understood that while she couldn't control what lay ahead, she could control how she chose to love. And in that choice, she found a strength she thought she had lost.

Weeks later in Gabriel's hospital room, the quiet hum of machines is the only sound, the sterile atmosphere, clinical, a constant reminder of the potential for healing or loss a strange equilibrium between hope and despair. The room a reflection of Amelia's love and persistence, filled with personal touches, photos pinned above the bed, ultrasound images taped nearby, and a few of Gabriel's favourite books stacked on the bedside table. Though he lay motionless, his mind was far from still.

Inside Gabriel's dream state, memories played like an old film reel. Faces flash, Amelia's smile, Maddy's laughter, the gentle sway of trees from the garden where he and Amelia once had breakfast. The images blur and dissolve into another scene, one from long ago in India. Gabriel is sitting in a sacred space, meditating quietly. The air is fragrant with incense; the walls echo with ancient chants. Babaji sits nearby, serene, his presence a calming anchor. Across from them, on a large, ornate wooden chair, sits an elderly man with an overwhelming spiritual presence. Though the man's face is indistinct, his aura radiates wisdom and peace.

The wise elderly master, his movements slow with age, reaches out and places a trembling hand on Gabriel's head. The simple act is profound, and Gabriel is overwhelmed. Tears stream down his face as if a dam has broken within him. The weight of his past, his regrets, his fears, all of it dissolves under the master's touch. In the background, an ethereal figure lingers, Samara, Gabriel's first wife. Her presence is both comforting and sorrowful, a bittersweet reminder of the life he once knew.

The scene shifts, and Gabriel finds himself in a modest sanctuary, surrounded by a diverse group of people, all dressed simply, singing gentle, soulful songs. The music is soothing, and the atmosphere is one of deep communal peace. Samara appears again. Her presence radiant. She approaches Gabriel with a soft smile. Her eyes filled with understanding and love. She takes his hands, guiding him to Babaji, who stands nearby. There is a quiet moment of exchange, a wordless farewell. Samara gently places Gabriel's hands into Amelia's, symbolically passing him from the life he had to the life he's destined to have. The scene fades into darkness, the warmth of Samara's touch lingering as the final image of Gabriel's dream.

Back in the hospital, the scene is vividly different. The room is filled with life and love, it's Gabriel's birthday, and his family are gathered in celebration. Colourful banners and balloons brighten the space, and the air is filled with laughter. Maddy and Joe are there, Liv and Jack too, all of them eager to honour Gabriel despite his condition. Amelia, now six and a half months pregnant, stands by Gabriel's side, her face glowing with happiness. Her joy is palpable, the babies within her kicking with enthusiasm as if sensing the celebration. Amelia places Gabriel's hand on her rounded belly, laughing as she feels the twins' energetic movements. She bends down to kiss his face, her voice light and filled with affection as she speaks to him, as she always does, as if he can hear every word. But then, something changes. She freezes, feeling his hand twitch on her stomach. For a moment, she thinks she must be imagining it, suddenly it happens again, his fingers contracting slightly, then releasing. Her breath catches in her throat, eyes wide with shock and hope.

Amelia's heart pounds as she stares at Gabriel's face, searching for any sign that this is real. His eyelids flutter, then slowly, miraculously, they open. His gaze is unfocused, but it's there, he's there. The room falls into stunned silence, all eyes turning toward him as the impossible happens. Amelia's smile trembles with emotion, her tears flowing freely as she sobs in relief and joy.

"Gabriel?" Joe, quick to act, dives through the door to get the doctor, his voice ringing with urgency. The others stand frozen, unable to believe what they're witnessing. Gabriel, after all these months, is regaining consciousness. Amelia holds his hand tightly, pressing it to her belly where the babies kick in response, as if welcoming their father back to the world. Gabriel's eyes lock onto hers, and though his strength is not yet there, the connection between them is undeniable. A tear slips down his cheek as he takes in the sight of her, the love that has carried him through, the love that has waited for him to return.

The doctor rushes in disbelief clouding his expression he realises Gabriel has defied the odds by regaining consciousness. What follows is hours of tests but for a moment, all that exists is Amelia and Gabriel, their hands entwined, their future suddenly, beautifully, within reach again.

Gabriel's hospital room is quieter now, the initial rush of activity and emotions having settled into a softer, more intimate atmosphere. The afternoon light filters through the window, casting a warm glow over the room. Gabriel lies back against the pillows, his voice still slightly hoarse from disuse. He gazes at Amelia with a mixture of awe and gratitude.

"I can't believe it's been nearly seven months." Gabriel's voice cracks slightly. "Look at you. I've missed it all. I'm so sorry, Amelia. This must have been so hard for you. Thank goodness you've had Jack and Liv." Amelia stares at him, unable to fully process the miracle of his steady recovery of consciousness. She still can't believe that he's awake, talking, and here with her.

"And Maddy and Joe." She adds, her voice trembling with emotion. "And especially Babaji. He's been my rock. The stories he's told me about you, Mr. Sinclair... My, my, you've had a colourful life. It appears I hardly know you at all." Gabriel smiles, the muscles in his face slowly remembering how to move again. Each small action is a struggle, yet he savours every moment, every sensation.

"What about Maddy?" Gabriel's voice is filled with genuine concern. "How's she taken it?" Amelia's expression softens.

"Maddy took a while. She was very angry with me. She's okay now, but that's down to Joe, really. She finally realised how much he loved her, how important that is and that it was right in front of her. Maddy's not about to make the same mistake as me." She pauses watching him intently. "Joe took it really hard at first, especially when I had to break the news to Maddy that you were her dad as he'd nearly killed you." Gabriel grimaces, the irony not lost on him. His telltale humour returning, just the thought bringing a smile to his eyes. Every mention of Maddy brings a warmth to his face that tugs at Amelia's heart.

"Yeah, I bet that was a tough conversation. Not the best way to win a girl's heart, shoot her dad." They both laugh, the moment quickly turns serious. Amelia's eyes fill with tears.

"Gabriel, I am so, so sorry I lied to you about Maddy. I don't... I don't think..." Gabriel gently interrupts her.

"Let's not do this now, Mia. We both made mistakes. Our future starts today, here. We can't keep going over the past. We have our future and the future of our children in front of us now. It's time to leave what's happened in the past." Amelia looks at him a little in awe of his ability to let go of the past with no hint of bitterness. He sees her questions cloud her eyes and reaches for her hand letting his fingers gentle weave between hers. Bringing her hand to his mouth his eyes lock on hers and he whispers softly.

"I lost the last 7 months because I was trying so hard to prove I could protect our daughter. I don't want to have to keep proving to you that I love you and our children. I need you to believe me when I say, I love you and if it's in my power I will always stand beside you and them in this life I promise." Gabriel pauses letting his words sink in. Amelia sensing his caution goes a little pale, she stares at him her eyes widening in concern.

"What do you mean if it's in your power in this life Gabriel?" He sighs squeezing hold of her hand he pauses bringing her fingers once again to his lips, he gently kisses her hand looking into her troubled eyes he reassures her.

"Amelia none of us are promised tomorrow. After all of this we must be grateful for every moment we get to share together. Each new day we have now, really, truly is a gift. I don't think I will ever take another minute for granted...." Gabriel pauses looking at Amelia his eyes filled with love. "I also can't promise that any of us; me, you, Maddy, Joe or these babies will all live until we are old and grey. That's not how life is. People are taken from us, sometimes without any warning.... Every day we get to spend together truly is a gift it's our most precious 'present'." Gabriel leans forward to stroke her face tenderly. "I will always treasure what I have to share with you now my darling."

Amelia takes a deep shaky breath nodding. An enormous smile erupts across her face and taking his face in her hands she stretches to kiss him. Not quite able to reach because of her ample belly she bursts into laughter as she tries to stand. Once on her feet she attempts to sit next to him and give Gabriel a cuddle all of which cause the pair of them much hilarity as trying to fit a now very round, very pregnant, Amelia and Gabriel into one hospital bed while Gabriel is still hooked up to various monitors proves a little impossible.

She settles for a kiss and tries valiantly to stand up but in the process knocks out one of the monitors for Gabriels's heart registering a flatline on the monitor and setting off all the resuscitation alarms. The room floods with medics all instantly ready to respond to the emergency only to find Amelia red faced and flailing in her moment of relief.

The team are unequivocally relieved as both Gabriel and Amelia have become like family to many members of the hospitals extraordinary staff. From the doctors, nurses, cleaners and the kitchen staff everyone has heard of their story and Gabriel coming out of his coma has been a cause for much celebration, the story has even made the local news.

Chapter 26

During the weeks that follow Gabriel makes a steady recovery though it is slower than he had hoped. Gabriel is a regular patient at the hospital attending various appointments from physio, heart specialist, through to plastic surgeons, Gabriel is not in the least bit interested in how ascetically pleasing his large scar is, if anything he sees it as evidence of his attempted heroism or stupidity as he regularly reminds himself.

Not one to argue with his doctors he recognises how incredibly blessed he is to still be alive and is eternally grateful for the dedication of the staff who have all focused on supporting his amazing journey back to health. Gabriel made a silent promise to himself that God willing he would once again be strong enough to raise money for the hospital to support the staff who have cared for him. Without their unflinching compassion and professionalism Gabriel believed, heart and soul, that he wouldn't have lived. Though he has yet to decide how, he is determined that this experience would create a new purpose in his life, one that would help to shape a new way of supporting medical professionals and carers the world over.

Several weeks after his birthday he is on one of his regular visits to the hospital as an outpatient, taking time between appointments to visit the hospital garden, the sun filters through the trees, casting a warm glow over Gabriel as he sits in a wheelchair, laughing with Joe and Maddy. The three of them are deep in conversation, the atmosphere light and filled with joy. Gabriel's strength is slowly returning, and though he's still recovering, the progress he's made is evident in the way he engages with his daughter and Joe, his voice stronger, his laughter more frequent.

Suddenly, an enormous commotion announces the arrival of Jack and Liv. Amelia, nearly eight and a half months pregnant, waddles beside them, looking both tired and incredibly fed up. She groans as she lowers herself onto the bench beside Gabriel, rolling her eyes at her own discomfort. Gabriel smirks, teasing her with a playful comment about how he's starting to think she might be carrying triplets instead of twins.

"Oh, shut up." Amelia retorts, laughing as she smacks him playfully on the arm. As she bends down to kiss him, her expression changes, she gasps letting out a shocked squeal, her movements freezing in place. Everyone stares at her, the garden suddenly silent. Then, with wide eyes, Amelia looks down at her feet as clear fluid runs down her legs pooling at her feet.

"My waters just broke!" Her exclamation filled with a mix of surprise and panic. Grasping her stomach she doubles over panting. "Help. Ouch for the love of God that hurts, damn it. Gabriel what am I supposed to do. I'm supposed to be having my pre-op check for the section."

Chaos erupts immediately. Joe springs into action, dashing off to valiantly find another wheelchair. Jack and Liv hover around Amelia, trying to help but only adding to the confusion as Amelia's contractions start to kick in immediately, she yelps in pain, her knees starting to give as she tries valiantly to stay upright. Maddy seeing her mother in real agony suddenly freezes unable to process or know how to help she looks pleading at her father who is just as surprised as she is, they catch one another's eye, unspoken reassurance passing between them. Maddy is torn between laughter, fear and concern as she watches the scene unfold, grateful that she is surrounded by the people she loves most in the world, she is truly relieved this has happened at the hospital and not back at the house, Maddy knows that her mom is in the best possible place. Grabbing her dad's hand, she squeezes it for comfort making Gabriel's heart swell with love. Gabriel stands helping Amelia to sit in the wheelchair he had been using, holding her hand he looks her in the eyes.

"Everything is going to be alright Mia. We are here in the best place and the staff will know what to do." Gabriel smiles stroking her face with his free hand. Amelia squeezes his other hand tightly as another contraction kicks in. The agony of the contraction ricocheting through her body she lets out a cry nearly deafening Gabriel as his face was very close to hers.

Within moments, Joe returns, a wheelchair clattering in front of him. With a sense of urgency mixed with hilarity, both Gabriel and Amelia are wheeled side by side through the hospital corridors at breakneck speed, accompanied by laughter, nervous excitement, and a few wide-eyed glances from staff and patients. The maternity ward receives them wrapping them in warm certainty the staff immediately taking control of the situation. Within a matter of moments, a decision is made, and Amelia is taken for an emergency Caesarean section to keep both mother and babies safe.

Later that day, the relative calm of the maternity ward has returned, where the chaos has given way to a peaceful, serene atmosphere. Amelia's hospital room is filled with the soft scent of flowers and the gentle hum of voices. Pink balloons float above the bed, and bouquets of roses and lilies are scattered around the room. The lighting is warm, casting a gentle glow over everything. Amelia lies propped up in bed, looking radiantly happy. Her exhaustion has melted away, replaced by the deep contentment of new motherhood, the euphoria of the birth and a mixture of pain relief taking the edge off and making her feel a little high. In her arms, she cradles a tiny baby girl, swaddled in a soft pink blanket. Beside her, Gabriel holds their other daughter, gazing down at her with awe and wonder. His eyes are filled with tears, but his smile is wide and full of joy. The room is quiet, except for the soft coos of the newborns. Jack and Liv stand at the foot of the bed, beaming with pride, while Joe and Maddy linger near the doorway, their eyes bright with emotion. Amelia meets Gabriel's gaze, and they share a look of pure new parental love and gratitude.

"Have you decided on names yet?" Liv's face creases into smiles as Amelia hands her one of the girls.

"We have, actually, Babaji blessed the girls as soon as they were born." Amelia smiles indulgently at her friend. "You are holding Lillian Alice Samara, Lilly for short she is named after Gabriel's mom, my grandma and for Baba's sister of course. Maddy wanted to name her other sister Charlotte, Olivia, Grace. I think you said Lottie or was it Charlie you liked Maddy?"

Jack's face flushes with emotion as he looks at Maddy, tears brim in his eyes, he is totally surprised that Amelia would name her baby girl after his beloved first wife. Jack is a little overcome with emotion as he looks up into Amelias' smiling face, she looks radiant though very tired. Liv is equally moved by the names she fans her face desperately trying to hold onto her emotions. Jacks voice breaks as he speaks.

"Thank you, Mia that means the world to me. I'm sure you are ready for some rest now we should let you sleep. These young ladies are going to be demanding your attention soon enough, I'm sure."

Only Maddy hears Joe's sharp intake of breath at the mention of his mum's name. She catches her mom's eye and mouths 'Thank you'. Maddy threads her arm through Joe's hugging him tightly. She has shared so much more with Joe over the last 9 months. Seeing his eyes mist with tears makes her heart swell with love for him. Maddy knows that he wants to ask her to marry him, she also knows that she won't hesitate in accepting his proposal. Looking at the joy on her parents faces Maddy realised that it probably won't be long before they too tried for a baby,

Jack chuckled softly a sound so filled with love and affection a tear escapes Liv's eye as she watches the man, she adores coo over the newborns. Liv hands Jack baby Charlotte then goes to help Amelia rearrange the bed and get ready to feed the babies. For the first time it would be Gabriel leaving Amelia in hospital for the night.

"Maddy I've asked if it's ok for you to stay tonight with your mom to help her, I'm still more of a liability than help. Is that, ok? We've got the new nanny starting tomorrow, I thought you'd like the chance to be together tonight?" Gabriel smiles lovingly at his daughter who responds with equal delight.

"Thanks Dad. I'd love that." The sound of the word Dad seems to linger in the air, a precious word that means so much to every single person in the room most especially Maddy and Gabriel neither of them would ever tire of saying or hearing it. Very soon the baby girls are safely in their mom's arms, everyone leaves the room to give the new parents some space to get accustomed to the new routine.

"Wow!" Gabriel sits back in his chair as he studies his girls. "What have I done in this world to have been given this. All of you? A second chance, with all my girls." His voice trails off as he watches the babies suckle mesmerised by Amelia's immediate connection.

"Does it feel strange to have babies after such a big gap between Maddy?" It's a fair and honest question which takes Amelia by surprise, she hadn't had time to think about how she would feel about becoming a mom again. So much had happened during her pregnancy that she hadn't even considered her own feelings about motherhood again.

"It feels very right actually. If anything I feel much calmer this time, less fraught about being the perfect parent. That may change though there are two of them this time." Pausing Amelia looks out of the window remembering the first few days with Maddy.

"Maddy wasn't very well in the hospital when I gave birth. It wasn't an easy birth and then she got jaundice. I was very stressed and such a perfectionist. I, I felt very alone." She pauses trying to gauge Gabriel's reaction. "I know you said that we should leave the past where it is." She pauses watching him stare at the babies. "I'd like you to know about Maddy when she was little. I'm just not sure how to talk to you about it I feel so guilty." Gabriel stands slowly covering the distance between them. He leans down to kiss all his girls on the top of their heads. Hovering over Amelia, he tips her face up to his and covers her mouth in deep tender kiss.

"You can tell me every detail. I can't wait to hear. It is different this time Amelia we are all here with you. We are a family now, everyone is going to help, these little girls are going to be so loved." Kissing the tip of her nose he returns to his seat. "I'll be so glad when this fatigue starts to lift, then I can be of more use to you, my darling." Gabriel's term of affection makes Amelia's heart swell with love for him every time he uses it. For one moment a shadow crossed her mind as she watches him. Sensing her change in energy he smiles at her.

"I can hear them, Mia" he smiles at her a teasing expression in his eyes as the creases form the laughter lines that are now so familiar to Amelia. "I can literally hear the cogs turning in your mind. What's bothering you darling?" He never ceased to surprise her these days it was sometimes as if he could literally read her like a book. Taking a deep breath Amelia sighed.

"It's just a thought that keeps bothering me and I need to know if it's bothering you too." She looks at him waiting to see if his mood shifted. As always Gabriel remained calm and relaxed with no hint of negativity to change his thoughts. Chiding herself Amelia silently acknowledged that she had enough negativity to share for them both, a long career in the police making her turn more frequently to a belief in the glass being not just half empty but bone dry.

"Come on woman, don't keep me in suspense. What's got that brow of yours all knotted up again?" Gabriel was teasing her, he took great pleasure in trying to iron out the wrinkles in her mind, so much so that she had nicknamed him 'Chi' Gabriel thought it was because of his love of chi lattes but much to Amelia's secret amusement it was after her steam iron. Amelia smiles at him not wanting to spoil their wonderful moment but still a nagging thought wouldn't leave her, so she just had to ask him.

"Gabriel, I know you have told me that we can't keep going over the past.... It's just I need to know. Do you ever feel angry at me for denying you the chance to spend all those years with Maddy?" As she said the words she could feel the slight change in atmosphere in the room, almost as if someone had opened a window and there was an unwelcome draft.

"Hmmm.... I should have known it would be a pretty big one if it was going to come up today." Taking his time to answer was common for Gabriel so it didn't surprise Amelia when he closed his eyes momentarily. What did surprise her was when he started to snore. For a moment Amelia thought he was joking, he wasn't he had fallen fast asleep. She managed to last half an hour silently wishing she could get out of bed and prod him. The nerve of the man. She chided herself for being so mean it had after all been a full-on day. The twins had been delivered by an emergency Caesarean section all of which had been very dramatic, and she had to admit, quite traumatic not to mention worrying, for both Gabriel and Maddy both of whom had been allowed into the theatre to be with her when they had given her the epidural. Maddy had been the first to hold one of the babies as Gabriel was watching from the back of the theatre in his wheelchair.

Maddy had passed her sister, his daughter to him once she had been cleaned up and as he held her, she simply starred at her dad the two of them instantly bonded. Her twin sister on the other hand made her presence felt from the moment she was released from Amelia's body. Her little frame vibrating with cries at the indignity of being both brought into the world so suddenly and at the same time separated from her twin even if only momentarily while she was checked over by the team of midwives. Both babies were strong, healthy and a good weight for twins. Amelia got chance to kiss them both and welcome them into the world and once she had come out of the theatre, she was given the babies to nurse.

The babies were beginning to stir so Amelia reached across to call for one of the nurses to come and help her. As the nurse entered, she giggled at the sight of Gabriel fast asleep in the chair. Amelia smiled back.

"He's had a long day." The irony is not lost on the nurse; she offered to get them both a cup of tea and some sandwiches once the twins were latched on and feeding. Gabriel must have sensed he was the focus of some amusement as he stretched, waking from his nap. Looking at him it was outrageous that he could still look so ridiculously handsome with crumpled clothes and bed hair. Grinning at her he innocently asked.

"Where were we?" Amelia's arms were well and truly full, so there wasn't a hope in her finding something to throw at her impossibly infuriating fiancé. Once the girls had been fed Gabriel took Lilly first, gently following the nurse's instructions on the best way to wind a newborn. Gabriel took to it like a proverbial duck to water, grinning from ear to ear as he gently cradled the little girls in his hands, they seemed so tiny, and he was completely enraptured. Once the girls were tucked up together sleeping peacefully Gabriel turned his attention towards Amelia. She looked tired and though the conversation could have waited for another day he wanted to clear all her doubts once and for all.

"Amelia have you ever considered that you were actually right." Gabriel reached across the babies to hold Amelia's hand, softly stroking the inside of her wrist. She looked at him through sleepy eyes.

"What do you mean?" As his words registered with Amelia she opened her eyes, Gabriel leant forward so that she could see his eyes clearly and know that he meant every word he was about to say.

"I mean, you were right when you ran away and didn't tell me about Maddy." Now Amelia was wide awake, he had her full attention. "When you left, I told you that I was angry." Gabriel studies Amelia's expression, her eyes, wide and fully focused on his words. He continued, "if you had stayed and we had got married, that anger was inside me, it hadn't found a way out, one way or another it would have come to the surface. You leaving just precipitated what was already there. It was inside me, from my childhood. If you had stayed, we probably wouldn't have made it. You were right I would have taken Maddy and gone for full custody."

Gabriel lets his confession sink in. Amelia leans back on the bed the realisation that she had made the right decision for all of them occurring to her for the very first time. Gabriel smiles a deep, loving smile, one that touches her heart.

"You followed your instincts. You just didn't realise it at the time. You didn't know that that is what you were doing. Your heart spoke to you, and you listened.... I thank God every day that you did. You were brave when I was not thinking straight and we now have the future and the family that both of us dreamt about all those years ago, we just had to live separately to find our way back to one another. Amelia stares at him questions forming in her mind.

"But what if we hadn't ever met one another again. How can you be so sure that it was right." Gabriel smiles at her again. Just then Maddy arrives back coming to relieve Gabriel, Joe has come with her to give him a lift back to Amelia's house. Gabriel smiles at his older daughter always happy to see her, this time though he knows he must finish the conversation that is open between him and Amelia.

"Maddy can you just give your mom and me a couple of minutes she has just asked me one her very important questions and if I don't answer her, she won't sleep tonight." Grinning at Gabriel Maddy puts her bag by the bed and kissing the babies asks.

"I'll go and get some hot chocolate does anyone else want some?" With an order for 4 hot chocolates Maddy and Joe discreetly leave Gabriel to answer Amelia's burning questions. Once the door closes Gabriel turns to her again.

"How am I so sure about all this, is that what you asked....? I'm sure Amelia because I believe that what is meant for you will not pass you by. I believe that I was meant to be Maddy's father, just as much as I was meant to be a father to these two beautiful little ones. But I had to learn how to be the father that they all needed me to be. That wouldn't have happened if we had stayed together all those years ago. I had so much to learn, so much ego to let go of and so much love to find in my soul...." He pauses, an easy smile rest on his soft lips. "I'm just grateful that I didn't have to do it at the expense of you all, because I know for me to be the man I am today, to be the husband you deserve I had to lose everything and be literally left with just my sandals and my soul." Gabriel sits back in his chair and allows what he has said to find it's place in Amelia's heart.

When it does, when the truth resonates deep inside her heart she smiles softly at the man sitting opposite her, on the outside an older version of the man she had fallen for, but this man the Gabriel she could now see more clearly than ever before, this was her true love, her soul mate. The man she had waited most of her life for and the love they now shared was truly what love was all about.

She had always loved him, they were meant for one another, this time around the Gabriel she now had was the one she had longed for. He had always been confident and charismatic able to charm the birds from the trees, the man sitting across from her now showed a tenderness and compassion that ran deeply through everything he touched. Watching him talk to the hospital staff was a pleasure, he had time for everyone, and everyone seemed to matter to him. What he said he meant, not in a superficial way but with every fibre of his being. He loved with his whole heart and was as good as his words on the first day he regained consciousness.

Gabriel truly treated every day as a blessing. Maddy had positively blossomed in the love of her father, his interest in her thoughts, beliefs and dreams made her face light up and her soul glow. It was also wonderful to watch Gabriel with Joe. Jack had always been an amazing father to Joe, he was an upright, good young man who was becoming everything she had hoped he would, Joe was destined for a top position if he continued to follow the guidance of the mentors, he was lucky enough to have around him. In Gabriel he had found an unlikely friend and the two of them bonded over a love of the outdoors, in particular fishing which had at first surprised Amelia until she realised it was a place where Gabriel liked to go to just spend time in nature.

Watching her family heal was perhaps for Amelia one of the most humbling experiences of her life. Looking at Gabriel she realised she was ready to make the decision that she had been thinking about for some time.

"Gabriel?" The question in her tone brought his sparkling blue eyes instantly up to meet hers. "I've made a decision." Now she had his full attention. "I'm going to resign from the police." She paused watching his reaction. He went completely still for a moment, holding his breath as he looked into her eyes, searching for a sign that she was perhaps uncertain or deciding something that she didn't totally believe was right. Amelia returned his look with openness, smiling softly. Gabriel's expression had remained steady until he saw the smile form on her face at which point the corners of his eyes creased into the deep laughter lines and a huge beaming smile erupted across his beautiful face. His brilliant blue eyes sparkled a little brighter as tears welled in them. Gathering her into his arms he kissed her deeply.

"I didn't think this day could get any better darling. Are you sure? I know how hard you have worked; Jerry is going to be a very unhappy man! But…. Thank God." His grin bursts across his face instantly pulling her to him to hug Amelia so tightly the babies start to cry.

"Shush, shush little ones." He gently strokes their faces trying to settle them again while kissing their mommy repeatedly. Amelia's chuckle is a soft sound that makes him stand and stare at the girls cradled together on the bed.

"Like I said so, so lucky…Thank you my darling. It's something I have wanted to ask of you, but I didn't feel it was fair. Now I'll sleep better." They had come so far, and now, with their family complete, they were finally where they were always meant to be, together, surrounded by love, and ready to embrace the future. It wasn't long before Maddy and Joe returned with the warm drinks, Amelia was getting very tired, so the two men gave Amelia and Maddy the room to get settled for the evening. Gabriel softly kissed Amelia as she settled down the bed her eyelids already heavy. The babies next to her bed together in their cot. Gabriel lingered for a moment over them kissing them tenderly he whispered a pray softly, one that only Amelia could hear.

"Sleep well my love." He whispered.

As he passed Maddy he kissed her forehead, her sweet green perfume instantly recognisable as his daughter's special fragrance he hadn't realised just how deep a father's love for his daughters could be and now there were three of them, more than enough love to last one man many lifetimes.

Chapter 27

One year later to the day the scene is very different. A long way from LA in another continent, the scenery is spectacular. A breathtaking Indian villa perched near the top of a hill. Its whitewashed walls draped in vibrant pink bougainvillea that cascaded down over its expansive balconies toward the lush gardens below, beyond the ocean sparkling magically. The sky a brilliant blue, the sun shining brightly, casting a warm, luminescent hue over everything. The villa spectacularly adorned with colourful decorations in preparation for an elegant wedding, Gabriel and Amelia's wedding day.

The guests were beginning to arrive, dressed in exquisite wedding attire. The colours of their outfits rich and varied, with saris in deep reds, golds and vibrant blues, blending beautifully with the flowers and twinkling lights that surround the villa. There is an air of joy and celebration as friends, family, officers, and doctors gather to witness this special day. Gabriel stands near the altar, with Joe his best man by his side, looking fit, tanned and handsome, a picture of health after his full recovery. His smile is broad, his eyes shining with happiness as he greets guests who are shown to their seats in the garden.

Seated at the front, Liv and Sylvia can be seen holding the twins, now 12 months old. The twin girls are dressed in the most beautiful soft pink outfits each with tiny sparkles which catch the sunlight, they gurgle happily in the arms of their doting godmothers. The scene is filled with laughter and anticipation, a gentle hum of conversation as the guests settle into their seats. Soft strains of romantic classical music float from beyond the garden as a small band of musicians prepare for the day's entertainment.

Inside the villa, the hallway is grand, with a sweeping staircase that curves elegantly down to the entrance. Jack stands at the bottom of the staircase, his eyes bright with emotion. The soft sound of footsteps echoes as Maddy appears, she is stunning in her bridesmaid dress, she curtsies at the top for his approval then descends the stairs. She stops to kiss Jack on the cheek, her smile radiant. Jack pulls Maddy into a gentle hug, kissing the top of his now daughter in law to be, head. As Maddy has her bouquet in one hand she hugs him tightly with other hand, her beautiful engagement ring sparkling in the light. Stepping back, she smiles up at Jack her face luminous with joy she is radiant now she has got over her morning sickness. Her hand instinctively goes to her stomach as butterflies make her feel a little nervous. Other than Joe her mom is the only person who knows she is pregnant, reaching up she motions to Jack that she wants to whisper something to him.

"You are going to be a Grandad." Maddy's words have the desired effect on Jack. His lip trembles as he looks at her, his eyes filling with tears. She kisses him on the cheek then turning away she heads to the wedding party.

Following her daughter down the grand staircase, Amelia appears hesitating for maximum effect she beams at Jack before gracefully descending the staircase. Amelia's elegant wedding gown is stunning, in a soft almost latte colour the gown is covered in tiny diamanté's, it's delicate folds flow softly around her. Her beauty pure understated glamour, Amelia glows with the joy of the day. Jack's pride and emotion are evident as she reaches him. He takes her hands, kissing her gently on the forehead. Handing her the bouquet of white orchids which he holds he pauses to look at her.

"My darling girl." Jacks' words catch in his throat, his voice thick with emotion. "You look radiant." Amelia smiles, her eyes shining with happiness.

"I feel so happy, Jack. Congratulations Grandpa." She replies softly. They share a tender moment. Jack's eyes filled with love and pride. He then tucks Amelia's hand through his arm, together they walk out into the sunshine, where Gabriel waits, next to Joe his best man. As Maddy appears making her way slowly over to the assembled congregation Joe leans over and whispers in Gabriel's ear.

"We wanted you to know that our wedding present to you and Mia is a baby. You are going to be a grandad!" The look of sheer surprised delight on Gabriel's face is captured beautifully by the wedding photographer whom Joe had warned just before walking down the aisle. Gabriel is thrilled and can't wait to hug Maddy as she too arrives shortly behind him. As Gabriel pulls her into a huge hug, she laughs out loud and whispers in his ear.

"Guess what, this one's a boy." Gabriel literally shouts for joy, making everyone laugh as he promptly bursts into tears. He is only just pulling himself together when Jack arrives with his beautiful bride. Gabriel can't help but hug Jack and when he tells his friend that it's a boy, both begin leaping about like a couple of kids much to the amusement of everyone else. If Joe and Maddy had wanted to keep the news quiet, there was not a chance of that happening as by the time Gabriel and Jack had stopped crying and kissed Amelia and Liv everyone now knew about the baby. It takes several minutes for everyone's excitement to settle long enough for the happy couple to exchange their vows.

The garden was a vision of magic, a perfect blend of natural beauty and elegant design. The ceremony had been intended to be both intimate, yet enchanting, a mix of traditional and contemporary elements but as with the best laid plans it had taken on an air of celebration and jubilation. Babaji standing before them, beaming with delight performed the wedding rites. Gabriel and Amelia exchanging vows, grinning at one another, their love clear for all to see. As Babaji announced them husband and wife, a huge cheer went up from the guests, Gabriel pulled Amelia into a deep, loving kiss their union at last complete.

The day unfolds with a whirlwind of celebration. Indian dancers' whirl and twirl, their costumes a blur of colour, while the guests enjoy a splendid banquet filled with traditional dishes. Laughter fills the air, the clink of glasses and the rhythm of drums echoing through the villa. It is a day of pure joy, of love fully realized. As the sun begins to set, casting long shadows across the garden, the guests start to leave, their faces flushed with happiness. Joe and Maddy help Jack and Liv gather the twins, allowing the newlyweds some privacy. The goodbyes are heartfelt, and as the last guests depart, the villa grows quiet, leaving Amelia and Gabriel to their new life together.

In their bedroom, the night air is exotic warm and sweet, the aroma of jasmine flowers and incense gently wafts through the open windows, the night sky an inky backdrop for its diamond carpet of stars that twinkle brightly. Gabriel sits upright in bed, a book resting on his chest, spectacles perched on the end of his nose, he has fallen asleep while Amelia showers. His brown chest is bare, the scar that runs the length of his torso, a reminder of what they've endured, it has faded but remains noticeable. The room is charming, a mix of comfort and elegance, the newlyweds' suitcases are packed and ready for their honeymoon.

Amelia stands in the doorway of the ensuite, watching Gabriel with a soft smile on her face. She is dressed in a beautiful, white, delicate floor length negligee, her hair falling loosely around her shoulders. The light in the bathroom silhouettes her slender frame giving her skin a soft golden glow Amelia clicks off the light leaving only the bedside light to cast its subtle warmth upon her sleeping husband, she moves quietly toward the bed.

"He sleeps." Amelia gently sits beside him on the bed watching him. The words whisper from her lips with a gentle laugh as she reaches to remove Gabriel's glasses. As she takes them off, Gabriel's eyes flutter open. He gazes at her, his expression one of deep love and contentment. As he leans forward, she stops him his face inches from hers.

"You know Gabriel, this.... Everything that has happened to us to bring us to this moment today.... This is so much, more than just happiness, it's a dream come true." Smiling Gabriel doesn't need to answer her she knows he feels it too. He reaches forward, cupping her face in his hands, pulling her down toward him. Their lips meet in a passionate kiss. A kiss filled with the promise of forever. They hold each other close, the worries and trials of the past fading into nothingness, love and passion consume them as together they begin the journey into married life. The night stretches on, and under the starry skies of the Indian subcontinent, they find peace in each other's arms. Drifting into blissful sleep their lives would become the happily ever after that Amelia had once long ago dreamed, they could be.

The End

With love to those who hearts ache to feel the magic of connection and true love. I hope you find what your heart is searching for.

Printed in Dunstable, United Kingdom